FIRE FROM HEAVEN

FIRE
FROM
HEAVEN

MARY RENAULT

PANTHEON BOOKS

A Division of Random House, New York

When Perdikkas asked him at what times he wished to have divine honors paid him, he answered that he wished it done when they themselves were happy. These were the last words of the King.

Quintus Curtius

FIRE FROM HEAVEN

1

The child was wakened by the knotting of the snake's coils about his waist. For a moment he was frightened; it had squeezed his breathing, and given him a bad dream. But as soon as he was awake, he knew what it was, and pushed his two hands inside the coil. It shifted; the strong band under his back bunched tightly, then grew thin. The head slid up his shoulder along his neck, and he felt close to his ear the flickering tongue.

The old-fashioned nursery lamp, painted with boys bowling hoops and watching cockfights, burned low on its stand. The dusk had died in which he had fallen asleep; only a cold sharp moonlight struck down through the tall window, patching the yellow marble floor with blue. He pushed down his blanket to see the snake, and make sure it was the right one. His mother had told him that the patterned ones, with backs like woven border-work, must always be let alone. But all was well; it was the pale brown one with the grey belly, smooth as polished enamel.

When he turned four, nearly a year ago, he had been given a boy's bed five feet long; but the legs were short in case he fell, and the snake had not had far to climb. Everyone else in the room was fast asleep; his sister Kleopatra in her cradle beside the Spartan nurse; nearer, in a better bed of carved pearwood, his own nurse

Hellanike. It must be the middle of the night; but he could still hear the men in Hall, singing together. The sound was loud and discordant, slurring the ends of the lines. He had learned already to understand the cause.

The snake was a secret, his alone in the night. Even Lanike, so near by, had not discerned their silent greetings. She was safely snoring. He had been slapped for likening the sound to a mason's saw. Lanike was not a common nurse, but a lady of the royal kindred, who reminded him twice a day that she would not be doing this for anyone less than his father's son.

The snores, the distant singing, were sounds of solitude. The only waking presences were himself and the snake, and the sentry pacing the passage, the click of his armor buckles just heard as he passed the door.

The child turned on his side, stroking the snake, feeling its polished strength slide through his fingers over his naked skin. It had laid its flat head upon his heart, as if to listen. It had been cold at first, which had helped to wake him. Now it was taking warmth from him, and growing lazy. It was going to sleep, and might stay till morning. What would Lanike say when she found it? He stifled his laughter, lest it should be shaken and go away. He had never known it stray so far from his mother's room.

He listened to hear if she had sent her women out in search of it. Its name was Glaukos. But he could only hear two men shouting at each other in Hall; then the voice of his father, the loudest, shouting them both down.

He pictured her, in the white wool robe with yellow borders she wore after the bath, her hair loose on it, the lamp glowing red through her shielding hand, softly calling "Glaukos-s!" or perhaps playing snake-music on her tiny bone flute. The women would be looking everywhere, among the stands for the combs and paintpots, inside the bronze-bound clothes chests smelling of cassia; he had seen such a search for a lost earring. They would get scared and clumsy, and she would be angry. Hearing the noise from Hall again, he remembered his father did not like Glaukos, and would be glad that he was lost.

It was then he resolved to bring him back to her now, himself.

[2]

This must be done, then. The child stood in the blue moonlight on the yellow floor, the snake wound round him, supported in his arms. It must not be disturbed by dressing; but he took his shoulder-cloak from the stool, and wrapped it around both of them, to keep it warm.

He paused for thought. He had two soldiers to pass. Even if both turned out to be friends, at this hour they would stop him. He listened to the one outside. The passage had a bend in it, and a strongroom was round the corner. The sentry looked after both doors.

The footfalls were receding. He got the door unlatched, and looked out to plan his way. A bronze Apollo stood in the angle of the wall, on a plinth of green marble. He was still small enough to squeeze behind it. When the sentry had passed the other way, he ran. The rest was easy, till he got to the small court from which rose the stair to the royal bedchamber.

The steps went up between walls painted with trees and birds. There was a little landing at the top, and the polished door with its great ring handle in a lion's mouth. The marble treads were still scarcely worn. There had been nothing but a small harbor town on the lagoon at Pella, before King Archelaos' day. Now it was a city, with temples and big houses; on a gentle rise, Archelaos had built his famous palace, a wonder to all Greece. It was too famous ever to have been changed; everything was splendid, in a fashion fifty years old. Zeuxis had spent years painting the walls.

At the stair-foot stood the second sentry, the royal bodyguard. Tonight it was Agis. He was standing easy, leaning on his spear. The child, peeping from the dark side-passage, drew back, watching and waiting.

Agis was about twenty, a lord's son of the royal demesne. He had on his parade armor, to wait upon the King. His helmet had a crest of red and white horsehair, and its hinged cheek-flaps were embossed with lions. His shield was elegantly painted with a striding boar; it hung upon his shoulder, not to be put down till the King was safe in bed, and then not out of arm-reach. In his right hand was a seven-foot spear.

The child gazed with delight, feeling within his cloak the snake softly stir and twine. He knew the young man well; he would have

liked to jump out with a whoop, making him throw up his shield
and point his spear; to be tossed up on his shoulder, in reach of the
tall crest. But Agis was on duty. It would be he who would scratch
upon the door, and hand Glaukos to a waiting-woman; for himself
there would be Lanike and bed. He had tried before to get in at
night, though never so late as this; they always told him nobody
could enter except the King.

The floor of the passage was made of pebble mosaic, checkered
black and white. His feet grew sore from standing, and the night
chill came on. Agis had been posted to watch the stairs, and only
that. It was a different matter from the other guard.

For a moment he considered coming out, having a talk with Agis,
and going back. But the slither of the snake against his breast reminded him he had set out to see his mother. That, therefore, was
what he was going to do.

If one kept one's mind upon what one wanted, the chance appeared. Glaukos, too, was magical. He stroked the snake's thinned
neck, saying voicelessly, "Agathodaimon, Sabazeus-Zagreus, send
him away, come, come." He added a spell he had heard his mother
use. Though he did not know what it was for, it was worth a trial.

Agis turned from the stairs into the passage opposite. There was
a statue a little way along, of a lion sitting up. Agis leaned his shield
and spear on it, and went round behind. Though stone sober by
local reckoning, he had drunk before going on duty too much to
hold till the next watch. All the guards went behind the lion. Before
morning, the slaves would wipe it up.

The moment he started walking, before he put down his weapons,
the child knew what it meant and started to run. He flew up the
cold smooth stairs on silent feet. It always amazed him, when with
children of his own age, how easily they could be outrun or caught.
It seemed impossible they could really be trying.

Agis behind the lion had not forgotten his duty. When a watchdog barked, his head went up at once. But the sound came from the
other way. It ceased, he straightened his clothes and picked up his
arms. The stairs were empty.

The child, having pushed to behind him, silently, the heavy door,
reached up to fasten the latch. It was well polished and oiled; he
coaxed it home without a sound. This done, he turned into the room.

A single lamp was burning, on a tall standard of bright bronze, twined with a gilded vine and resting on gilded deer's-feet. The room was warm, and breathing all over with secret life. The deep curtains of blue wool with embroidered edges, the people painted on the walls, all stirred with it; the flame of the lamp breathed too. The men's voices, shut off by the heavy door, were no more than murmurs here.

There were close scents of bath-oil, incense and musk, of resined pine-ash from the bronze hearth-basket; of his mother's paints and oils and the phial from Athens; of something acrid she burned for magic; of her body and her hair. In the bed whose legs were inlaid with ivory and tortoiseshell and ended in lions' paws, she lay sleeping, her hair falling across the worked linen pillow. He had never seen her in such deep sleep before.

It seemed she had never missed Glaukos, to sleep so soundly. He paused, to enjoy his stealthy undisturbed possession. On her tiring-table of olive-wood, the pots and bottles were clean and closed. A gilded nymph upheld the moon of her silver mirror. The saffron night-robe was folded on a stool. From the room beyond where her women slept came a faint distant snore. His eyes strayed to the loose stone by the hearth, under which lived forbidden things; he had often wished to try working his own magic. But Glaukos might slip away. She must have him now.

He stepped softly up, the unseen guard and lord of her sleep. Gently the cover of marten skins, edged with scarlet and fringed with bullion, rose and fell above her. Her brows were drawn clearly above the thin smooth lids which seemed to show through them the smoke-grey eyes beneath. Her lashes were darkened; her mouth was firmly closed, the color of watered wine. Her nose was white and straight, and whispered faintly as she breathed. She was twenty-one years old.

The cover had fallen back a little from her breast, where, till lately, Kleopatra's head had too often lain. She had gone to the Spartan nurse now, and his kingdom was his own again.

A strand of her hair spilled down towards him, dark red, strong, and shining in the moving lamplight with streaks of fire. He pulled forward some of his own, and set them together; his was like rough-wrought gold, gleaming and heavy; Lanike grumbled on

[5]

feast-days that it never held a curl. Hers had a springy wave. The Spartan woman said Kleopatra's would be the same, though now it was like feathers. He would hate her, if she grew more like their mother than he was. But perhaps she would die; babies often did.

In the shadows, the hair looked dark and different. He looked round at the great mural on the inner wall: the Sack of Troy, done by Zeuxis for Archelaos. The figures were life-sized. The Wooden Horse towered in the background; in front, Greeks plunged swords into Trojans, rushed at them with spears, or carried on their shoulders women with screaming mouths. In the foreground, old Priam and the child Astyanax weltered in their blood. That was the color. Satisfied of this he turned away. He had been born in this room; the picture held nothing new for him.

Round his waist, under his cloak, Glaukos was wriggling, no doubt glad to be home. The child looked again into his mother's face; then let fall his single garment, lifted delicately the blanket's edge, and still twined with the snake slid in beside her.

Her arms came round him. She purred softly, and sank her nose and mouth into his hair; her breathing deepened. He pushed down his head under her chin; her yielding breasts enclosed him, he could feel his bare skin cling to hers, all the length of his body. The snake, too tightly pressed between them, squirmed strongly and slid aside.

He felt her wake; her grey eyes with their inner smoke-rings were open when he looked up. She kissed and stroked him, and said, "Who let you in?"

While she still half-slept and he lay wrapped in bliss, he had been ready for this question. Agis had not kept proper lookout. Soldiers were punished for it. Half a year had gone by since he had seen from the window a guard put to death on the drill-field by the other guards. After so long an age, he had forgotten the offense, if he had ever known it; but he remembered the small distant body bound to the post, the men standing round with javelins poised at the shoulder; the shrill taut command followed by a single cry; then, when they had all crowded in to jerk out the bristling shafts, the head lolling, and the great spill of red.

"I told the man you wanted me." No need for names. For a child fond of talking, he had learned early how to hold his tongue.

Her cheek moved in a smile against his head. He had hardly ever heard her speak to his father, without being aware she was lying about one or another thing. He thought of it as a skill she had, like the snake-music on the bone flute.

"Mother, when will you marry me? When I'm older, when I'm six?"

She kissed the nape of his neck, and ran her finger along his backbone. "When you are six, ask me again. Four is too young to get handfast."

"I'm five in Lion Month. I love you." She kissed him saying nothing. "Do you love me best?"

"I love you altogether. Perhaps I shall eat you up."

"But best? Do you love me best?"

"When you are good."

"*No!*" He rode her waist with his knees, pummeling her shoulders. "Really best. Better than anyone. Than Kleopatra." She made a soft sound, less reproof than caress. "You do! You do! You love me more than the King."

He seldom said "Father" if he could help it, and knew it did not displease her. Through her flesh he felt her silent laughter. She said, "Perhaps."

Victorious and exulting, he slipped down beside her. "If you promise you love me best, I'll give you something."

"Oh, tyrant. What can it be?"

"Look, I've found Glaukos. He came into my bed."

Folding the blanket back he displayed the snake. It had coiled round his waist again, having found this pleasant.

She looked at the burnished head, which lifted from its resting-place on the child's white breast, and softly hissed at her.

"Why," she said, "where did you find this? This is not Glaukos. The same kind, yes. But this one is much bigger."

They gazed together at the coiled snake; the child's mind filled with pride and mystery. He stroked the reared neck, as he had been taught, and the head sank down again.

The lips of Olympias parted, and the blacks of her eyes grew wide, invading the grey irises; he saw them like soft silk, pleating together. Her arms slackened about him; he was held in the grasp of her eyes.

[7]

Mary Renault

"He knows you," she whispered. "Tonight, when he came, be sure it was not for the first time. He must have come often, while you slept. See how he clings to you. He knows you well. He comes from the god. He is your daimon, Alexander."

The lamp flickered. The end of a pine-brand slipped into the embers, and threw up blue flame. The snake squeezed him swiftly, as if to share a secret; its scales trickled like water.

"I shall call him Tyche," he said presently. "He shall have his milk in my gold cup. Will he talk to me?"

"Who knows? He is your daimon. Listen, I will tell you—"

The muted noises from the Hall broke out loud as its doors were opened. Men shouted to each other good-nights, jokes or drunken taunts. The noise flowed in on them through their closed defenses. Olympias broke off, gathered him close into her side, and said softly, "Never mind, he won't come here." But he felt her taut with listening. There was a sound of heavy feet, a stumble and a curse; then the rap of Agis' spear-butt on the floor, and the slap of his soles as he presented arms.

The feet came scuffing and tramping up the stairs. The door flew open. King Philip crashed it behind him, and without a glance at the bed started taking off his clothes.

Olympias had pulled up the covers. The child, eyes round with alarm, had for a moment been glad to lie hidden. Then, cowered in the womb of soft wool and scented flesh, he began to feel horror of the danger he could not confront or see. He worked down a fold to make a peephole; it was better to know than to guess.

The King stood naked, one foot up on the cushioned stool of the toilet-table, loosing his sandal strap. His black-bearded face was cocked sideways to see what he was doing; his blind eye was towards the bed.

For a year or more, the child had run in and out of the wrestling-ground, when anyone dependable would take him off the women's hands. Bare bodies or clothed, it was all one, except for being able to see men's war-scars. Yet his father's nakedness, seldom seen, always disgusted him. Now, since one eye had been blinded at the siege of Methone, he had become frightful. At first he had kept it covered with a bandage, from which blood-tinged tears had stained a track down into his beard. Then these had dried, and the bandage

[8]

had come off. The lid, which the arrow had pierced on its way in, was puckered and streaked with red; the lashes were gummed with yellow matter. They were black, like his good eye and his beard, and the mats of hair on his shins and forearms and chest; a track of black hair led down his belly to the bush, like a second beard, between his loins. His arms and neck and legs were seamed with thick scars, white, red or purple. He belched, filling the air with the smell of stale wine, and showing the gap in his teeth. The child, glued to his peephole, knew suddenly what his father looked like. It was the ogre, one-eyed Polyphemos, who had picked up Odysseus' sailors and crunched them raw.

His mother had risen on one elbow, with the clothes pulled up to her chin. "No, Philip. Not tonight. It is not the time."

The King took a stride towards the bed. "Not the time?" he said loudly. He was still panting from the stairs on a full stomach. "You said that half a month ago. Do you think I can't count, you Molossian bitch?"

The child felt his mother's hand, which had been curved around his body, clench into a fist. When she spoke again it was in her fighting voice. "Count, you wineskin? You're not fit to know summer from winter. Go to your minion. Any day of the month is the same to *him.*"

The child's knowledge of such things was still imperfect; yet he had a feeling of what was meant. He disliked his father's new young man, who put on airs; he loathed the secrets he sensed between them. His mother's body had tightened and hardened all over. He held his breath.

"You cat-a-mountain!" said the King. The child saw him rush upon them, like Polyphemos on his prey. He seemed to bristle all over; even the rod that hung in his black bushy crotch had risen by itself and was thrusting forward, a sight of mysterious horror. He pulled back the bedclothes.

The child lay in his mother's arm, his fingers dug into her side. His father started back, cursing and pointing. But it was not at them; the blind eye was still turned that way. The child perceived why his mother had not been surprised to feel his new snake beside her. Glaukos had been there already. He must have been asleep.

"How dare you?" panted Philip hoarsely. He had had a sickening

[9]

shock. "How dare you, when I forbade it, bring your filthy vermin in my bed? Sorceress, barbarian witch . . ."

His voice stopped. Drawn by the hatred in his wife's two eyes, his one eye had moved that way, and he had seen the child. The two faces confronted one another: the man's empurpled, with the wine, and with anger heightened now by shame; the child's as brilliant as a jewel set in gold, the blue-grey eyes fixed and wide, the skin transparent, the delicate flesh, taut with uncomprehended agony, molded close to the fine bones.

Muttering something, Philip reached by instinct for his robe to cover his nakedness; but there was no more need. He had been wronged, insulted, exposed, betrayed. If his sword had been at hand, he might well have killed her.

Disturbed by all this, the child's living girdle writhed, and lifted its head. Till now, Philip had not seen it.

"What's that?" His pointing finger shook. "What's that upon the boy? That thing of yours? Are you teaching *him* now? Are you making *him* into a back-country, snake-dancing, howling mystagogue? I tell you, I'll not endure it; take heed of what I say, before you suffer; for by Zeus I mean it, as you will feel. My son is a Greek, not one of your barbarous cattle-lifting hillmen . . ."

"Barbarous!" Her voice rose ringing, then sank to a deadly undertone, like Glaukos' when angered. "My father, you peasant, sprang from Achilles, and my mother from the royal house of Troy. My forebears were ruling men, when yours were hired farm-hands in Argos. Have you looked in a mirror? One can see the Thracian in you. If my son is Greek, it is from me. In Epiros, our blood runs true."

Philip gritted his teeth. It squared his chin and broadened his cheekbones, which were wide already. Even under these mortal insults, he remembered the child was there. "I scorn to answer you. If you are Greek, then show a Greek woman's manners. Let us see some modesty." He felt the lack of clothes. Two pairs of grey eyes, smokily rimmed, stared from the bed. "Greek schooling, reason, civility, I mean the boy to have them as I have had. Make up your mind to that."

"Oh, *Thebes!*" She threw out the word like a ritual curse. "Is it Thebes again, now? I know enough of Thebes. In Thebes they made you a Greek, in Thebes you learned civility! In Thebes! Have you heard an Athenian speak of Thebes? The byword of Greece for boorishness. Don't make such a fool of yourself."

"Athens, that talking-shop. Their great days are done there. They should keep quiet about Thebes for shame."

"It is you should do that. What were *you* in Thebes?"

"A hostage, a pledge of policy. Did I make my brother's treaty? Do you throw that in my face? I was sixteen. I found more courtesy there than you ever showed me. And they taught me war. What was Macedon, when Perdikkas died? He had fallen to the Illyrians with four thousand men. The valleys lay fallow; our people were afraid to come down out of the hill-forts. All they had were the sheep whose skins they wore, and those they could hardly keep. Soon the Illyrians would have taken everything; Bardelys was making ready. Now you know what we are and where our frontiers stand. Through Thebes, and the men who made me a soldier there, I came to you a king. Your kindred were glad enough of it."

The child, pressed to her side, felt her breath drawn in and in. Blindly he waited for the unknown storm to break from the lowering sky. His fingers clenched on the blanket. He knew himself forgotten now, and alone.

The storm broke. "A soldier, was it, they made you there? And what else? What else?" He could feel her ribs convulsed with rage. "You went south at sixteen, and by then already the country all around was full of your by-blows, don't you think I know who they are? That whore Arsinoe, Lagos' wife, old enough to be your mother . . . Then the great Pelopidas taught you all the learning Thebes is famous for. Battle and boys!"

"Be silent!" roared Philip, loud enough for a battlefield. "Have you no decency before the child? What does he see in this room? What does he hear? I tell you, my son shall be brought up civilized, if I have to . . ."

His voice was drowned by her laughter. She drew back her hand from the child, to thrust her body forward. With her arms and open palms propping her weight, her red hair falling forward over her naked breasts and the child's open mouth and eyes, she laughed till the high room echoed. "*Your* son?" she cried. "*Your* son!"

King Philip breathed as if he had just run the long-race. He strode forward and raised his hand.

Starting out of a perfect stillness, in one flash of movement the child threw off the curtain of his mother's hair, and stood upright on the bed. His eyes, dilated, looked almost black; his mouth had whitened. He struck at the lifted arm of his father, who from mere astonishment withdrew it. "Go away!" screamed the child, glittering and fierce as a forest wildcat. "Go away! She hates you! Go away! She will marry me!"

For three long breaths, Philip stood rooted, mouth and eyes gaping, like a man clubbed on the head. Then diving forward, he seized the child by both shoulders, swung him through the air, let go with one hand while he wrenched the great door open, and tossed him outside. Taken unawares, rigid with shock and fury, he did nothing to help himself. His sliding body reached the head of the stairs and began to tumble down them.

With a great clattering din, young Agis let fall his spear, dragged his arm out of his shield-straps, and taking the stairs in threes and fours leaped forward to catch the child. At the third stair down he reached him, and picked him up. His head seemed not to have been struck, and his eyes were open. Up above, King Philip had paused with the door in his hand. He did not slam it till he had seen that all was well; but of this the child knew nothing.

Caught up along with him, startled and bruised, the snake whipped free of him as he began to fall, poured itself down the stairs, and was gone into the dark.

Agis, after his first start, had seen what it was. The child was enough to think about. He carried him downstairs, and sitting at their foot took him on his knees, looking him over by the light of the torch in its wall-sconce. He felt stiff as a board, and his eyes were turned up to show the whites.

In the name of all gods below, thought the young man, what shall I do? If I leave my post, the Captain will have my blood. If his son dies on my hands, the King will. One night last year, before the new favorite's reign began, Philip had looked his way, and he had pretended to be dense. Now he had seen too much; his fortunes, he thought, would sell dear at a sack of beans. The child was looking blue about the lips. In a far corner was Agis' thick wool nightcloak, ready for the cold small hours. He picked it up, wadded a fold between the child and his own hard corselet, and wrapped him round. "Come," he said anxiously. "Come, look, all's well."

He seemed not to be breathing. What do do? Slap him, like a woman in a laughing-fit? It might kill him instead. His eyes were moving, and focusing. He drew in a crowing breath, and gave a violent scream.

Deeply relieved, Agis loosed the cloak round the struggling limbs. He clucked and muttered as if to a frightened horse, not holding him in too hard but letting him feel firm hands. In the room above, his parents were calling down curses on one another. After time Agis did not reckon—he had most of the night before him—these sounds died down, and the child began to weep, but not for long. Having come thus far to himself, soon he fell quiet. He lay biting his lower lip, swallowing, and gazing up at Agis, who tried suddenly to remember how old he was.

"That's my young captain," he said gently, moved by the almost manlike struggle on the childish face. He dried it with the cloak, and kissed it, trying as he did so to picture what this golden boy would look like when he was old enough for love. "Come, sweetheart, you and I will stand guard together. We'll look after one another, eh?"

He enfolded the child and stroked him. After a time, the quiet, the warmth, the unconscious sensuality of the young man's caresses, a vague awareness of being more admired than pitied, began to heal the enormous wound which had seemed his whole and only self. It began to close, sealing in all within it.

Presently he put out his head from the cloak and looked about. "Where is my Tyche?"

What did the strange child mean, calling upon his fortune? Seeing Agis' face look blank, he added, "My snake, my daimon. Where did he go?"

"Ah, your lucky snake." Agis thought the Queen's pets entirely loathsome. "He's hiding awhile, he'll soon be back." He wrapped more cloak round the child; he had begun to shiver. "Don't take it to heart, your father didn't mean it. It was only the wine in him. Many a clip on the head I've had from mine."

"When I'm big . . ." He paused to count on his fingers, up to ten. "When I'm big, I'll kill him."

[13]

Agis sucked in his breath through his lower teeth. "Ss-ss! Don't say such a thing. It's god-cursed to kill a father, it sets the Furies after a man." He began to describe them, but broke off as the child's eyes widened; he had had more than enough. "All these knocks we get when we're young, that's how we learn to bear our wounds, when we go to war. Look. Move over. Look what I got, the first time I fought the Illyrians."

He pulled back the kilt of scarlet wool from his thigh, and showed the long ridged scar, with a pit where the spearhead had plowed through almost to the bone. The boy gazed with respect, and felt it with his finger.

"Well," said Agis, covering it again, "that hurt, you can guess. And what kept me from yelling out, and being shamed before the Companions? My father's clips on the ear. The fellow who gave me that never lived to boast of it. My first man, he was. When I showed my father his head, he gave me my sword belt, offered up my boy's girdle-cord, and feasted all our kindred." He looked along the passage. Would no one ever come by, and take the child to his bed?

"Can you see my Tyche?" he was asking.

"He'll not be far. He's a house-snake. They don't wander. He'll come for his milk, you'll see. It's not every boy can tame a house-snake. That's the blood of Herakles in you, I daresay."

"What was *his* snake called?"

"When he was a newborn babe, two snakes crept into his cradle—"

"Two?" His fine brows drew together, frowning.

"Ah, but these were bad ones. Zeus' wife Hera sent them, to choke him dead. But he grabbed them by their necks, one in each hand . . ." Agis paused, silently cursing himself. Either it would give the child nightmares, or, and maybe likelier, he would go off and try to throttle a viper. "No, this only happened, you see, to Herakles because he was the son of a god. He passed as King Amphitryon's son, but Zeus had begot him on Amphitryon's Queen. So Hera was jealous."

The child listened alertly. "And he had to work. Why did he work so hard?"

"Eurystheus, the next King, was envious of him, because he was the better man, a hero, and half divine. Eurystheus was only a mortal, you understand, and Herakles had been meant to have the kingdom. But Hera caused Eurystheus to be born first. That's why Herakles had to do his Labors."

The child nodded, like one to whom all has been made clear. "He had to do them, to show he was the best."

Agis missed these words. He had heard at last, along the passage, the captain of the night guard, going his rounds.

"No one's been by, sir," he explained. "I can't think what the nurse can have been about. The child was blue with cold, running about the Palace mother-naked. He says he's looking for his snake."

"Lazy bitch of a woman. I'll shake up some slave-girl to go in and rouse her. It's too late to disturb the Queen."

He strode rattling off. Agis hoisted the child across his shoulder, patting his buttocks. "Bed for you, Herakles, and not before time."

The child wriggled down, to clasp both arms round his neck. Agis had sheltered his wounds and not betrayed them. Nothing was too good for such a friend. He shared his secret, since it was all he had to give.

"If my Tyche comes back, tell him where I've gone. He knows my name."

Ptolemy, known as the son of Lagos, cantered his new chestnut towards the lake of Pella; there was good riding-land along the shore. The horse was a gift from Lagos, who had grown fonder of him with the years, though his childhood had been less happy. He was eighteen, a dark big-boned youth whose strong profile would grow craggy in later life. He had speared his boar, and could sit at table with the men; had killed his man in a border skirmish, and changed his boy's waist-cord for a red leather sword belt with a horn-handled dagger in its slot. It was agreed he brought Lagos credit. In the end they had done pretty well by one another; and the King had done well by both.

Between the pine woods and the lake, he saw Alexander waving to him, and rode that way. He was fond of the boy, who seemed to belong nowhere: too bright for the seven-year-olds, though not yet seven; too small for the older boys. He came running through the marshland, hard-caked with summer around its scrubby reeds; his huge dog rooted after voles, coming back to push its dirty nose in his ear, which it could do with both forepaws on the ground.

"Hup!" said the youth, and hoisted him in front on the cloth saddle-square. They trotted along in search of a stretch to gallop. "Is that dog of yours still growing?"

"Yes. He's not big enough for his paws."

"You were right; he's Molossian both sides sure enough. He's growing his mane."

"It was just about here, where we are now, the man was going to drown him."

"When you don't know the sire, they don't always pay for rearing."

"He said he was rubbish; he had a stone tied round him."

"Someone got bitten in the end, or so I heard. I shouldn't like a bite from that dog."

"He was too little to bite. I did it. Look, we can go."

The dog, glad to stretch its great legs, raced by them along the broad lagoon which linked Pella with the sea. As they galloped full-out along its verge, mallards and gulls, dangle-foot herons and cranes, came beating and honking from the sedges, startled by their thunder. The boy in his high clear voice sang loudly the paean of the Companion Cavalry, a fierce crescendo tuned to the rhythm of the charge. His face was flushed, his fair hair fluttered from the peak upon his brow, his grey eyes looked blue, he shone.

Ptolemy slowed to breathe the horse, and extolled its virtues. Alexander replied in terms as expert as a groom's. Ptolemy, who sometimes felt responsible, said, "Does your father know you spend so much time with the soldiers?"

"Oh, yes. He said Silanos could teach me throwing at the mark, and Menestas could take me hunting. I only go with my friends."

Least said, then, soonest mended. Ptolemy had heard before that the King preferred even rough company for the boy, to leaving him all day with his mother. He flicked the horse to a canter, till a stone lodged in its frog and he had to dismount and see to it. The voice of the boy above him said, "Ptolemy. Is it true you're really my brother?"

"What?" His start freed the horse; it began to trot away. The boy, who had at once got hold of the reins, pulled it firmly up again. But the young man, disconcerted, walked at its head without mounting.

Perceiving something amiss, the boy said soberly, "They were saying it in the guardroom."

They paced on in silence. The boy, sensing consternation more than anger, waited gravely.

Ptolemy said at length, "They may; but they don't say it to me. Nor must you. I'd have to kill a man if he said it."

"Why?"

"Well, one must, that's all."

There was no answer. Ptolemy saw with dismay that the boy was bitterly wounded. It was something he had not thought of.

"Come," he said awkwardly, "a big growing boy like you, if you don't know why . . . Of course I'd gladly be your brother, that's nothing to do with it, that's not it. But my mother's married to Father. It would mean I was a bastard. You know what that is."

"Yes," said Alexander, who knew it was a deadly insult.

Sensing confusion if not ignorance, Ptolemy did a brother's duty. His blunt questions got blunt answers; the boy had used his ears among his guardroom friends. It seemed, though, that he thought the birth of offspring called for some further magic. The young man, having dealt sensibly with the matter, was surprised by the long intent silence at the end.

"What is it? It's the way we are all born, nothing wrong with it, the gods made us so. But women must only do it with their husbands, or the child's a bastard. That's why the man wanted to drown your dog: for fear he'd not run true to strain."

"Yes," said the boy, and returned to his thoughts.

Ptolemy felt distressed. In his childhood, when Philip had been only a younger son and a hostage too, he had been made to suffer; later he had ceased to be ashamed. If his mother had been unmarried he could have been acknowledged, and would not have been sorry. It was a matter of the decencies; he felt he had treated the boy meanly, not to have made this clear.

Alexander was looking straight ahead. His dirty childish hands kept a managing grip on the reins, minding their own business, making no demand on his thought. Their capacity, so far beyond their growth, approached the freakish; it gave an uneasy feeling. Through his face's puppy roundness, a gem-clear profile already

[17]

began to show. Ptolemy thought, The image of his mother, nothing of Philip at all.

A thought struck him like a thunderflash. Ever since he had been eating with the men, he had been hearing tales about Queen Olympias. Strange, turbulent, uncanny, wild as a Thracian maenad, able if she was crossed to put the Eye on you: fittingly the King had met her in a cave by torchlight, at the Mysteries of Samothrace; had been mad for her at first sight, even before he knew what house she came of; and had brought her, with a useful treaty of alliance, in triumph home. In Epiros, it was said, until quite lately women had ruled without men. Sometimes the drums and cymbals sounded all night in her pine grove, and strange piping came from her room. It was said she coupled with serpents; old women's tales, but what happened in the grove? Did the boy, so long her shadow, know more than he should? Had it only now come home to him?

As if he had turned a stone from a cave-mouth of the Underworld, letting loose a swarm of bat-squeaking shades, there passed through Ptolemy's mind a score of bloody tales going back for centuries, of struggles for the throne of Macedon: tribes fighting for High Kingship, kindred killing kindred to be High King; wars, massacres, poisonings; treacherous spears in the hunting-field, knives in the back, in the dark, in the bed of love. He was not without ambition; but the thought of plunging in that stream made his marrow cold. Dangerous guesswork, and what proof could there ever be? Here was the boy in trouble. Forget the rest.

"Listen," he said. "Can you keep a secret?"

Alexander lifted his hand and pronounced with care an oath enforced with deadly curses. "It's the strongest," he finished. "Silanos taught it me."

"That's too strong. I absolve you of it. You must be careful of oaths like that. Now the truth is, your father did get me on my mother; but he was no more than a boy, fifteen. It was before he went to Thebes."

"Oh, Thebes." His voice echoed another.

"He was old for his age that way, well known for it. Well, never mind that, a man can't wait till he's wedded, nor have I done if you want the truth. But my mother was married to Father already, so it dishonors them to talk of it. It's one of the things a man must have blood for. Never mind if you see why or not; that's how it is."

"I won't talk." His eyes, already deeper set than other children's, were fixed upon the distance.

Ptolemy fiddled with the horse's cheekstrap, thinking unhappily, Well, what could I say? Someone else would have told him. The boy still in him rescued the defeated man. He halted the horse.

"Now, if we were sworn blood-brothers, we could tell everyone that." He added, cunningly, "But you know what we have to do?"

"Of course I know!" He gathered the reins in his left hand, and held out the right, clenched fist turned upward, a blue vein showing at the wrist. "Come on; here, do it now."

Ptolemy drew from his red belt the new sharp dagger, seeing the boy focused by pride and resolution to a single gleam. "Now wait, Alexander. It's a solemn thing we're doing. Your enemies will be mine and mine yours, until we die. We will never take up arms against each other, even if our own kin are at war. If I die in a strange land you will give me my rites, and so I will do for you. It means all that."

"I promise. You can do it here."

"We don't need so much blood." He avoided the offered vein, lightly nicking the white skin. The boy looked down smiling. Having pricked his own wrist, Ptolemy pressed the cuts together. "It's done," he said. And well done, he thought; some good daimon prompted me. Now they can't come to me saying, "He is only the Queen's bastard and you're the King's, so claim your rights."

"Come on, brother," said the boy. "Get up, he's got his wind now. Let's really go."

The royal stables were built in a broad square of stuccoed brick, with stone pilasters. They were half empty; the King was holding maneuvers, as he did whenever a new thought about tactics came to him.

Alexander, on his way to watch, had stopped to see a mare which had just foaled. As he had hoped, no one was about to say she was dangerous at such a time. He slipped in with her, coaxed her, and

Mary Renault

stroked the foal while her warm nostrils stirred his hair. Presently she nudged him, to say that was enough, and he let them be.

In the trodden yard, with its smells of horse-piss and straw, leather and wax and liniment, three strange horses had just come in. They were being rubbed down by foreign grooms in trousers. Their head-stalls, which a stable slave was cleaning, were oddly bedizened; glittering with gold plates, topped with red plumes, and with winged bulls worked on the bit-pieces. They were fine tall horses, powerfully built, not overridden; a spare string was being led through.

The household officer on duty remarked to the horse-master that the barbarians would have a good wait ahead of them, before the King came back.

"Brison's phalanx," said the boy, "are all ways still with their sarissas. It takes a long time to learn." He was able, so far, to lift up one end of these giant spears. "Where are those horses from?"

"All the way from Persia. Envoys from the Great King, to fetch back Artabazos and Menapis."

These satraps, after an ill-judged revolt, had fled to Macedon for refuge. King Philip had found them useful; the boy had found them interesting. "But they're guest-friends," he said. "Father won't let the Great King have them back to kill them. Tell the men not to wait."

"No, it's a pardon, I understand. They can go home free. In any case, envoys are entertained whatever message they carry. It's the proper thing."

"Father won't be back before noon. I think later, because of the Foot Companions. They can't do close-and-open order yet. Shall I fetch Menapis and Artabazos?"

"No, no, the envoys must have an audience first. Let these barbarians see we know how to do things. Attos, stable all those horses by themselves, it's always the foreigners bring sickness in."

The boy had a good look at the horses and their harness, then stood in thought. Presently he washed his feet at the conduit, looked at his chiton, went in and put on a clean one. He had listened often when people questioned the satraps about the splendors of Persepolis: the throne room with its gold vine and tree, the stairway up which a cavalcade could ride, the curious rites of homage.

Persians, it was clear, were ceremonious. As far as he was able without help, and at the cost of some pain, he combed his hair.

In the Perseus Room, one of Zeuxis' showpieces where guests of rank were received, a chamberlain was watching two blue-tattooed Thracian slaves set small tables with cakes and wine. The envoys had been seated in chairs of honor. On the wall above them, Perseus was rescuing Andromeda from the sea-dragon. He was one of the ancestors, and was said to have founded Persia too. It seemed that his breed had changed. He was naked, except for his winged sandals; the envoys wore the full Median dress which the exiles during their stay had laid aside. Every inch of these men but their hands and faces was covered up with clothes; every inch of the clothes with embroidery. Their round black hats were stitched with spangles; even their beards, trimmed into little round curls like snail shells, seemed embroidered too. Their fringed tunics had sleeves; their legs were cased in trousers, notorious sign of a barbarian.

Three chairs had been placed; only two bearded men were sitting. The youth with them, an aide, stood behind the senior envoy's chair. He had long silky blue-black hair, a skin of ivory, a face both haughty and delicate, and dark brilliant eyes. His elders being in talk, he was the first to see the boy standing in the doorway, and flashed at him a charming smile.

"May you live," he said walking in. "I am Alexander son of Philip."

Both bearded heads came round. After a moment both men rose, and invoked the sun to shine on him. The chamberlain, retaining his self-command, pronounced their names.

"Please sit down. Refresh yourselves, you must be tired after your journey." He had often heard this stock phrase. He became aware they were waiting for him to sit first, the first time this had happened to him. He clambered into a chair which had been put ready for the King. His sandal-tips did not reach the floor; the chamberlain beckoned a slave to get a footstool.

"I have come to entertain you, because my father is out reviewing the army. We expect him back about noon. It depends on the Foot Companions, whether they get close-and-open order right.

Mary Renault

They may be better today. They have been working very hard at it."

The envoys, chosen for their fluent Greek, leaned forward. Both were somewhat unsure with the broad patois of Macedon, its Doric vowels and blunt consonants; but the child's voice was very clear. "Is this your son?" he asked.

The senior envoy answered, demurely, that he was the son of a friend, and presented him. The youth, with a deep bow, declined again to sit, but smiled. For a moment they lit up at one another. The envoys exchanged delighted glances. It was all charming; the pretty grey-eyed prince, the little kingdom, the provincial naivety. The King drilled the troops himself! It was as if the child had boasted that the King cooked his own dinner.

"You don't eat your cakes. I will have one too." He took a small bite; he did not want his mouth full. What he knew of etiquette did not stretch to small talk during meals. He came straight to business.

"Menapis and Artabazos will be glad they're pardoned. They often talk about home. I don't think they'll ever rebel again. You can tell King Ochos."

The senior envoy had followed most of this in spite of the un-couth tongue. He smiled into his black mustaches, and said he would not fail to do so.

"And what about General Memnon? Is he pardoned too? We thought he might be, after his brother Mentor won the war in Egypt."

The envoy's eyes blinked a moment. Mentor the Rhodian, he said presently, was a worthy mercenary, and no doubt the Great King was grateful.

"He's married to Artabazos' sister. Do you know how many children they have now? Twenty-one! All alive! They keep having twins. Eleven boys and ten girls. I only have one sister. But I think that is enough."

Both envoys bowed. They were informed of the King's domestic discords.

"Memnon speaks Macedonian. He told me how he lost his battle."

"My prince," smiled the elder envoy, "you should study war from victors."

[22]

Alexander looked at him thoughtfully. His father always took trouble to find out where losers had gone wrong. Memnon had cheated a friend of his over a horse-deal; he would not have minded telling how he lost his battle; but he smelled patronage. If the youth had asked, it would have been different.

The chamberlain sent off the slaves, lingering himself for the rescue which would surely soon be needed. The boy bit sparingly at his cake, going over in his mind his most important questions; there might not be time for all. "How many men has the Great King in his army?"

Both envoys heard this aright; both smiled. The truth could do only good; he could be trusted, no doubt, to remember most of it. "Beyond number," said the elder. "Like the sands of the sea, or the stars on a moonless night." They told him of the Median and the Persian bowmen, the cavalry on the great horses of Nisaia; and the troops of the outer empire, Kissians and Hyrkanians, Assyrians with plaited bronze helmets and iron-spiked maces, Parthians with bow and scimitar; Ethiopians in leopard and lion skins who painted their faces red and white for battle and shot arrows tipped with stone; the Arab camel corps; the Bactrians; and so on as far as India. He listened round-eyed, like any child hearing marvels, till the tale was over.

"And they all have to fight when the Great King sends for them?"

"Every one, upon pain of death."

"How long does it take them to come?"

There was a sudden pause. It was over a century since Xerxes' expedition; they themselves did not know the answer. They said the King ruled over vast dominions and men of many tongues. From India, say, to the coast it might be a year's journey. But there were troops wherever he might need them.

"Do have some more wine. Is there a road all the way to India?"

It took time to dispose of this. In the doorway people were elbowing to listen, the news having spread.

"What's King Ochos like in battle? Is he brave?"

"Like a lion," said the envoys both together.

"Which wing of the cavalry does he lead?"

The mere awe of him . . . The envoys became evasive. The boy took a larger bite of cake. He knew one must not be rude to guests, so he changed the subject. "If the soldiers come from Arabia and India and Hyrkania, and can't speak Persian, how does he talk to them?"

"Talk to them? The King?" It was touching, the little strategist a child again. "Why, the satraps of their provinces choose officers who speak their tongues."

Alexander tilted his head a little, and creased his brows. "Soldiers like to be talked to before a battle. They like you to know their names."

"I am sure," said the second envoy charmingly, "they like *you* to know them." The Great King, he added, conversed only with his friends.

"My father converses with those at supper."

The envoys murmured something, not daring to catch each other's eyes. The barbarity of the Macedonian court was famous. The royal symposiums, it was said, were more like the feasts of mountain bandits snowed up with their spoils, than the banquets of a ruler. A Milesian Greek, who swore to having witnessed it, had told them King Philip thought nothing of stepping down from his couch to lead the line of dancers. Once, during an argument carried on in shouts across the room, he had shied a pomegranate at a general's head. The Greek, with the effrontery of that race of liars, had gone on to claim that the general had replied with a hunk of bread, and was still alive, in fact still a general. But if one believed no more than half, the least said the best.

Alexander for his part had been wrestling with a problem. A tale he disbelieved, and wished to check, had been told by Menapis. An exile might want to make the Great King look foolish. But these people would inform on him, and he would be crucified when he got home. It was wicked to betray a guest-friend.

"A boy here told me," he therefore said, "that when people greet the Great King they have to lie flat down on the ground. But I told him he was silly."

"The exiles could have told you, my prince, the wisdom of that homage. Our master rules not only many peoples, but many kings. Though we call them satraps, some are kings by blood, whose forebears once ruled for themselves, till they were brought into the empire. So he must be raised as far above other kings as they above their subjects. Under-kings must feel no more shame to fall down before him than before the gods. If he seemed less than this, his rule would soon pass away."

The boy had listened and understood. He answered courteously, "Well, here we don't fall down before the gods. So you need not do it to my father. He's not used to it; he won't mind."

The envoys clutched at their gravity. The thought of prostrating themselves before this barbaric chief, whose ancestor had been Xerxes' vassal (and a treacherous one at that) was too grotesque to offend.

The chamberlain, seeing it was high time, came forward; bowed to the child, who he thought deserved it, and invented a summons which could be explained away outside. Sliding down from the throne, Alexander bade goodbye to each, remembering all their names. "I am sorry I can't come back here. I have to go to the maneuvers. Some of the Foot Companions are friends of mine. The sarissa is a very good weapon in a solid front, my father says; the thing is to make it mobile. So he'll go on till they get it right. I hope you won't have long to wait. Please ask for anything you want."

Turning beyond the doorway, he saw the beautiful eyes of the youth still fixed on him, and paused to wave goodbye. The envoys, chattering together in excited Persian, were too busy to see their exchange of smiles.

Later that day, he was in the Palace garden teaching his dog to fetch things, among the carved urns from Ephesos whose rare flowers died in the bitter winters of Macedon unless they were brought indoors. From the painted stoa above, his father walked down towards him.

He called the dog to heel. Side by side they waited, prick-eared and wary. His father sat down on a marble bench, and beckoned towards the side of his seeing eye. The blind eye had healed now; only a white patch on the iris showed where the arrow had gone in. It had been a spent one, to which he owed his life.

"Come here, come here," he said, grinning and showing strong white teeth with a gap in them. "Come tell me what they said to you. You set them some hard questions, I hear. Tell me the answers. How many troops has Ochos, if he's put to it?"

He spoke in Macedonian. As a rule he spoke Greek to his son, for the good of his education. His tongue freed by this, the boy began to talk: of the Ten Thousand Immortals, of archers and javelineers and axmen; how cavalry chargers would bolt from the smell of camels; and how kings in India rode on black hairless beasts, so huge they could carry towers upon their backs. Here he cocked his eye at his father, not wanting to seem gullible. Philip nodded. "Yes, elephants. They are vouched for by men I have found honest in other ways. Go on; all this is very useful."

"They say people who greet the Great King have to lie down on their faces. I told them they need not do it to you. I was afraid someone might laugh at them."

His father's head went back. He gave a great belly-laugh and slapped his knee.

"They didn't do it?" asked the boy.

"No, but they had your leave. Always make virtue of necessity and see you're thanked for it. Well, they were lucky to get off better from you than Xerxes' envoys did from your namesake, in the hall at Aigai." He settled himself at ease. The boy stirred restlessly, disturbing the dog, which had its nose on his instep.

"When Xerxes bridged the Hellespont and brought his hosts to eat up Greece, he sent envoys first to all the peoples, demanding earth and water. A handful of earth for the land, a flask of water for the rivers; it was the homage of surrender. Our land stood clear in his way southward; we should be at his back when he went on; he wanted to make sure of us. So he sent us seven envoys. It was when the first Amyntas was King."

Alexander would have liked to ask if this Amyntas was his great-grandfather or what; but nobody would tell one straight about the ancestors, any later than the heroes and the gods. Perdikkas, his father's elder brother, had been killed in battle, leaving a baby son. But the Macedonians had wanted someone who could fight off the Illyrians and rule the kingdom; so they had asked his father to be King instead. Further back than this, he was always told he would know when he was older.

"In those days, there was no Palace here at Pella; only the castle up at Aigai. We held on then with our teeth and nails. The western chiefs, the Orestids and Lynkestids, thought themselves kings; Illyrians, Paionians, Thracians crossed the border every month to take slaves and drive off cattle. But all those were children beside the Persians. Amyntas had prepared no defenses, as far as I could learn. By the time the envoys came, the Paionians, who might have been sought as allies, had been overrun. So he gave up, and did homage for his own land. You know what a satrap is?"

The dog started erect and looked about it fiercely. The boy patted it down.

"Amyntas' son was called Alexandros. He would be about fourteen or fifteen; he had his own Guard already. Amyntas feasted the envoys in the hall at Aigai, and he was there."

"Then he had killed his boar?"

"How do I know? It was a state banquet, so he was there."

The boy knew Aigai almost as well as Pella. All the old shrines of the gods, where the great festivals were held, were up at Aigai; and the royal tombs of the ancestors, the ancient grave-mounds kept clear of trees, with their cavelike doorways, their massive doors of worked bronze and marble. It was said that when a King of Macedon was buried away from Aigai, the line would die. When the summer grew hot at Pella, they would go up there for the cool. The streams never dried there, coming down from their ferny mountain glens, cold from the upper snows; tumbling down all over the bluff, by the houses, through the castle court, till they joined together and plunged sheer down in the great fall which curtained the sacred cave. The castle was old, thick and strong, not like the fine columned Palace; the great hall had a round hearth, and a hole in the roof to let out the smoke. When men shouted there at the feasts, the sound would echo. He pictured Persians with curled beards and spangled hats, picking their way over the rough floor.

"There was drinking. Maybe the envoys were used to weaker wine; maybe they felt free to do as they liked, having got what they came for without trouble. One of them asked where the royal ladies were, saying it was the custom in Persia for them to attend the feasts."

"Do Persian ladies stay on for the drinking?"

"It was a barefaced lie, not even meant to deceive; pure insolence. Persian ladies are closer kept than ours."

"Did our men fight?"

"No, Amyntas sent for the women. Those of Paionia were already slaves in Asia, because their men had defied Xerxes. In justice to him, I don't think he could have done better than they. He had no army, as we would understand it. The Companions from his own demesne; and the tribal levies, whom their lords would train if and how they chose, and would not bring at all if they did not choose. He had not taken Mount Pangaios with the gold mines. I did that. Gold, my boy, gold is the mother of armies. I pay my men round the year, war or no war, and they fight for *me*, under my officers. Down south, they turn them off in the slack times, and the hired men find work where they can. So they fight only for their own strolling generals, who are often good in their way, but still just hirelings themselves. In Macedon, *I* am the general. And that, my son, is why the Great King's envoys don't come asking for earth and water now."

The boy nodded thoughtfully. The bearded envoys had been civil because they must, though the youth was different. "And did the ladies really come?"

"They came, affronted as you can guess, not deigning to dress their hair or put on a necklace. They expected to appear a moment, and then retire."

Alexander pictured his mother getting such a summons. He doubted she would show herself, even to keep the people of the land from slavery. If she did, she would dress her hair and put on every jewel she had.

"When they learned they were to stay," Philip went on, "they went over, as decent women would, to the far seats by the wall."

"Where the pages sit?"

"Yes, there. An old man who had it from his grandfather showed me the place. The boys got up for them. They drew their veils and sat silent. The envoys called out compliments, urging them to unveil; for which, if their own women had done so before strange men, they would have cut off their noses; oh yes, and worse, believe me. In this indignity, young Alexandros saw his mother and his sisters and the rest of the royal kin. He was enraged, and reproached his father. But if the Persians saw, they thought nothing of it. Who cares if the whelp barks, when the dog is quiet? One said to the

King, 'My Macedonian friend, better these ladies had not come at all, than sit there a mere torment to our eyes. Pray observe our custom; our ladies converse with guests. Remember, you gave our King earth and water.'

"It was the sight of the naked sword. One may suppose a silence. Then the King went over to his womenfolk, and led them to sit on the ends of the Persians' supper couches, as the flute-girls and the dancing-girls sit in the southern cities. The young prince saw the men lay hands on them, and his friends hardly held him back. Then suddenly he grew quiet. He beckoned the young men of his guard, and chose seven who were still beardless. These he spoke to in private and sent out. Going up to his father, who no doubt looked sick if any shame was in him, he said, 'Sir, you are tired. Don't sit out the drinking, leave the guests to me. They shall lack nothing that befits them, I give my word.'

"Well, it was a way for the man to save his face. He warned his son to do nothing rash, and then excused himself. The envoys, of course, supposed that nothing was now forbidden. The prince showed no anger. He came up all smiles, and did a round of the couches. 'Dear guests, you honor our mothers and our sisters. But they came in so much haste, eager to do you courtesy, they feel hardly fit to be seen. Let us send them along to the bath, to dress and put on their ornaments. When they return, you will be able to say that here in Macedon, you were treated as you deserve.'"

Alexander sat upright with shining eyes. He had guessed the prince's plan.

"The Persians had wine, and the night before them. They did not complain. Presently in came seven veiled ladies in splendid clothes. One walked to each envoy's couch. Even then, though they had forfeited by their insolence the rights of guest-friends, he waited to see if they would behave themselves. When the truth was plain, he gave a signal. The young men in the women's robes whipped out their daggers. The bodies rolled down on the platters and fruit-stands and spilled wine, almost without a cry."

"Oh good!" said the boy. "It served them right."

"They had of course their retinue somewhere in the hall. The doors had been made fast; none could be let out alive to bring word to Sardis. It could never be proved they had not been waylaid by

bandits as they went through Thrace. When all was done, the bodies
were buried in the forest. As the old man told me, the young Alexandros said, 'You came for earth and water. Be content with earth.'"

The father paused, to enjoy the applause of a glowing silence.
The boy, who had been hearing tales of vengeance since he could
follow human speech—no old house or peasant tribe in Macedon was
without one—thought it as good as the theater.

"So when King Xerxes came, Alexandros fought him?"

Philip shook his head. "He was King by then. He knew he could
do nothing. He had to lead his men in Xerxes' train with the other
satraps. But before the great battle at Plataia, he rode over himself,
by night, to tell the Greeks the Persian dispositions. He probably
saved the day."

The boy's face had fallen. He frowned with distaste. Presently he
said, "Well, he was clever. But I'd rather have fought a battle."

"Would you so?" said Philip grinning. "So would I. If we live, who
knows?" He rose from the bench, brushing down his well-whitened
robe with its purple edge. "In my grandfather's time, the Spartans,
to secure their power over the south, made treaty of alliance with
the Great King. His price was the Greek cities of Asia, which till
then were free. No one has yet lifted that black shame from the face
of Hellas. None of the states would stand up to Artaxerxes and the
Spartans both together. And I tell you this: the cities will not be
freed, till the Greeks are ready to follow a single war-leader. Dionysios of Syracuse might have been the man; but he had enough
with the Carthaginians, and his son is a fool who has lost everything.
But the man will come. Well, if we live we shall see." He nodded,
smiling. "Is that great ugly brute the best you can find for a dog?
I will see the huntsman, and find you something with good blood
in it."

Leaping before the dog, whose hackles had risen bristling, the
boy cried out "I love him!" in a voice not of tenderness but challenge
to the death.

Cross with disappointment, Philip said, "Very well, very well. You
need not shout at me. The beast is yours, who is going to harm it?
I was offering you a gift."

There was a pause. At length the boy said stiffly, "Thank you,

Father. But I think he'd be jealous, and kill the other one. He's very strong."

The dog pushed its nose into his armpit. They stood side by side, a solid alliance. Philip shrugged and went indoors.

Alexander and the dog started wrestling on the ground. The dog knocked him about, holding back as it would with a growing pup. Presently, their limbs involved together, they lay drowsing in the sun. He pictured the hall at Aigai, littered with cups and plates and cushions and Persians sprawling in gore, like the Trojans on his mother's wall. At the far end, where the attendants were being killed, the youth who had come with the envoys was fighting on, the last one left, standing his ground against a score. "Stop!" cried the Prince. "Don't dare kill him, he's my friend." When the dog woke him by scratching itself, they had been riding off on horses with plumed headstalls, to see Persepolis.

The mild summer day declined to evening. On the salt lake of Pella fell the shadow of its island fort, where the treasury and the dungeons were. Lamps glimmered in windows up and down the town; a household slave came out with a resined torch, to kindle the great cressets upheld by seated lions at the foot of the Palace steps. The lowing of homebound cattle sounded on the plain; in the mountains, which turned towards Pella their shadowed eastern faces, far-distant watch-fires sparked the grey.

The boy sat on the Palace roof, looking down at the town, the lagoon, and the little fisher-boats making for their moorings. It was his bedtime, and he was keeping out of his nurse's way till he had seen his mother, who might give him leave to stay up. Men mending the roof had gone home, without removing their ladders. It was a chance not to be wasted.

He sat on the tiles of Pentelic marble, shipped in by King Archelaos; the gutter under his thighs, between his knees an antefix in the shape of a gorgon's head, the paint faded by weather. Grasping the snaky hair, he was outstaring the long drop, defying its earth-daimons. Going back he would have to look down; they must be settled with beforehand.

Soon they gave in, as such creatures did when challenged. He ate the stale bread he had stolen instead of supper. It should have been hot posset, flavored with honey and wine; the smell had been tempting, but at supper one was caught for bed. Nothing could be had for nothing.

A bleat sounded from below. They had brought the black goat, it must be nearly time. Better now not to ask beforehand. Once he was there, she would not send him away.

He picked his way down the long spaces of the ladder-rungs made for men. The beaten earth-daimons kept their distance; he sang himself a song of victory. From the lower roof to the ground; no one was there but a few tired slaves going off duty. Indoors Hellanike would be searching; he must go around outside. He was getting too much for her; he had heard his mother say so.

The Hall was lit; inside, kitchen slaves were talking Thracian and shifting tables. Just ahead was a sentry, pacing his round; Menestas with his red bushy beard. The boy smiled and saluted.

"Alexander! Alexander!"

It was Lanike, behind the corner he had only just turned. She had come out after him herself. She would see him in a moment. He started running and thinking together. Here was Menestas. "Quick!" he whispered. "Hide me in your shield." Not waiting to be lifted, he clambered up the man and wrapped arms and legs around him. The wiry beard tickled his head. "Little monkey!" muttered Menestas, clapping the hollow shield across him just in time, and backing up to the wall. Hellanike passed, calling angrily, but too well-bred to talk to soldiers. "Where are you off to? I've no business . . ." But the boy had hugged his neck, dropped away and gone.

He threaded byways, avoiding the middens, for one could not come dirty to serve a god; and reached safely the garden-close by his mother's postern. Outside on the steps a few women were waiting already with their unlit torches. He kept out of their way beyond the myrtle hedge; he did not mean to be seen till they were in the grove. He knew where to go meantime.

Not far away was the shrine of Herakles, his paternal ancestor. Inside his little portico, the blue wall was dusky in evening shade, but the bronze statue stood out clearly, and its eyes of inlaid agate caught the last of the light. King Philip had dedicated it soon after his accession; he had been twenty-four, and the sculptor, who knew how to treat a patron, had done Herakles about that age, but beard-less in the southern style, with his hair and his lion-skin gilded. The fanged mask of the lion was put on like a hood above his brow, the rest formed a cloak on his shoulders. The head had been copied for Philip's coinage.

No one was watching; Alexander went up to the shrine, and rubbed the right toe of the hero above the edge of the plinth. Just now on the roof he had called upon him in their secret words, and he had come at once to tame the daimons. It was time to thank him. His toe was brighter than the rest of his foot, from many such rub-bings.

From beyond the hedge he heard a sistrum tinkle, and the mutter of a finger-drum lightly brushed. A torch threw its glow on the painted doorway, turning dusk to night. He crept up to the hedge. Most of the women had come. They had on bright thin dresses; they were only going to dance before the god. At the Dionysia, when they went up from Aigai into the mountain forests, they would wear the real maenad dress, and carry the reed thyrsos with its pine-cone top and wreath of ivy. Their dappled robes and fawnskins would not be seen again, but be thrown away with their bloody stains. The little skins they wore now were softly dressed and buckled with wrought gold; their wands were delicate scepters, gilded and trimmed with jewelers' work. The priest of Dionysos had just arrived, and a boy leading the goat. They were only waiting for his mother to come out.

She came, laughing in the doorway with Hyrmina from Epiros; dressed in a saffron robe, and gilt sandals with garnet clasps. The ivy-wreath in her hair was gold, its fine sprays trembled glittering in the torchlight whenever she moved her head. Her thyrsos was twined with a little enamel snake. One of the women carried the basket with Glaukos in it. He always came to the dance.

The girl with the torch carried it round to all the others; their flames leaped up, making eyes shine, and the red, green, blue, yellow of the dresses deepen like jewels. Standing from the shadows, there hung like a mask the sad, wise, wicked face of the goat, its topaz eyes and its gilded horns. A wreath of young green vine-clusters hung round its neck. With the priest and his serving-boy, it led the way to the grove; the women followed talking quietly. The sistra

[33]

gave soft jangles as their bearers walked. Frogs croaked in the stream
that fed the fountains.

They went up on the open hill above the garden; this was all
royal land. The path threaded winding, between myrtles and tamar-
isk and wild-olive bushes. Behind them all, out of sight, led by the
torches, the boy stepped lightly.

The tall dark of the pine wood loomed ahead. He left the path,
and slipped cautiously along through the brush. It was too soon to
be seen.

Lying flat on the springy pine-needles, he looked out from a
sheltering hollow at the grove. They had stuck their torches into
sconces speared into the ground. The dancing-place had been prepared, the altar garlanded, the rustic trestle set with the wine cups
and the mixing-bowl and the sacred fans. On his plinth, cared for as
always, cleansed from bird-droppings, washed and polished so that
his brown-tinted marble limbs had the sheen of youthful flesh, stood
Dionysos.

Olympias had had him brought here from Corinth, where he had
been carved to her commands. He was nearly life-sized, a youth of
about fifteen, fair-haired, with the slim muscles of a dancer. He wore
ornate red boots, and a leopard-skin on one shoulder. A long-shafted
thyrsos was grasped in his right hand; the left held out a gilt cup in
welcome. His smile was not Apollo's, which says, "Man, know yourself; that is enough for your little life." This was a beckoning smile;
its secret was for sharing.

They stood in a ring with joined hands, and sang an invocation,
before the goat was sacrificed. It had rained since the last blood
was shed there; he came up without fear, and only when the knife
went in gave one wild lonely cry. His blood was caught in a shallow
cup and mixed with wine for the god. The boy watched quietly, his
chin propped on his hands. He had seen countless sacrifices, in the
public sanctuaries and in this grove, where in infancy he had been
carried to the dancing, and slept on pine-mast to the blood-pulse of
the drums.

The music had started. The girls with the finger-drums and sistra,
the girl with the double flute, began softly swaying to their own
time. Glaukos' head in his opened basket was swaying too. Pace and
sound built up; arms linked behind waists, the women beat the

ground with their feet, their bodies arching forward and back, their hair falling loose and swinging. They drank neat wine, for the dances of Dionysos; after the sacrifice, they had drunk along with the god.

He could come out soon; he would never be sent back now.

The girl with the cymbals brought them together high over her head in a throbbing clang. He crept forward till he was almost in the torchlight; no one saw him. Turning slowly at first, to leave breath for singing, they were hymning the Triumph of the God.

He could hear most of the words, but he knew the hymn from memory. He had often heard it here. After each verse the cymbals clanged, and they sang each time louder the chorus, "Euoi, Bakchos! Euoi! Euoi!"

His mother began the hymn, hailing the god as son of Semele, born of fire. Her eyes and cheeks and hair were bright, her gold garland shimmered, her yellow dress threw back the torchlight, as if she herself were alight.

Hyrmina from Epiros, shaking her black hair, sang how the infant god had been hidden in Naxos to save him from jealous Hera, and guarded by singing nymphs. The boy crawled nearer. Above his head was the wine table; he peered over its edge. The cups and the mixer were old, with pictures painted on them. He reached down a cup to look; there was some wine still in it. He tipped out a drop or two, in libation to the god, for he was well trained in such matters; then he drank the rest. The strong unwatered taste was sweet enough to please him. The god seemed glad to have been honored; for the torches were brighter, the music became magical. He knew that soon he would dance.

They sang how Zeus' child was brought to the woodland lair of old Silenos, who taught him wisdom till, outstripping his teacher, he found the power in the purple grape. Then all the satyrs worshipped him, for the joys and furies in his hand. The song had a twirling lilt, the dance spun round like a wheel round a well-greased axle. By himself among the trees, the boy began to step out the time and clap his hands.

The god grew to a youth, fair-faced and graceful as a girl, but burning with the levin-fire that had been his mother's midwife. He went out to mankind, showering all good gifts on those who perceived his godhead, but dreadful to unbelievers as a ravening lion.

[35]

His fame increased, he grew too bright to be hidden. Jealous Hera could be deceived no longer. By his shining and his power she knew him, and sent him mad.

The music spiraled, quicker and higher, the music skirled like the death-shriek of small prey in a midnight wood, the cymbals dinned. The boy, hungry already and thirsty now from the dance, stretched tiptoe to reach another cup. This time it did not catch his breath. It was like the fire from heaven in the hymn.

The wild god wandered, through Thrace and across Hellespont, over the Phrygian heights and south to Karia. His worshippers who had shared his joy did not forsake him, but stayed to share his madness. It brought them ecstasy, for even his madness was divine. He followed the Asian coast to Egypt, whose wise race welcomed him; he rested there to learn their wisdom and teach them his. Then filled with madness and divinity, he set out over the unmeasured leagues of Asia, traveling east. On he danced, gathering worshippers as fire kindles fire; he crossed the Euphrates on a bridge of ivy, the Tigris on a tiger's back. Still he danced on, over plains and rivers and mountains high as Caucasus, till he came to the land of India at the outer edge of the world. Beyond was nothing but the encircling Stream of Ocean. The curse of Hera was spent. The Indians worshipped him; wild lions and panthers came meekly to draw his chariot. Thus he came back in glory to the Hellene lands; the Great Mother cleansed him of all the blood he had shed when he was mad; and he gave gladness to the hearts of men.

They raised the chorus; the boy's voice shrilled with the flute. He had thrown off his chiton, hot with the dance, the torch-flames and the wine. The gold wheels of the lion-drawn chariot turned beneath him, the paeans sounded, rivers drew back for him, the peoples of India and Asia danced to his song. The maenads were invoking him; he leaped from his chariot to dance among them. They broke their whirling ring, laughing and crying aloud to him, and closed the ring again, so that he could circle his own altar. As they sang, he danced around it, trampling the dew, making his magic, till the grove spun round him and he did not know earth from sky. But there before him was the Great Mother, with a wreath of light in her hair; she caught him in her arms, and kissed him over; and he saw on her golden gown the red prints from his bloodstained feet, where he had trodden in the place of sacrifice. His feet were as red as the boots of the painted statue.

He was wrapped in a cloak, and laid on a deep pine-mat, and kissed again, and told softly that even the gods, when they are young, must sleep. He must stay there and be good, and in a little while they would all go home. It was warm on the pine-smelling needles, in the crimson wool; the heave of sickness had passed and the torches had stopped turning. They burned lower in their sconces, but still friendly and bright. Looking out from the folded cloak, he saw the women go off into the pine grove, hand in hand or with arms entwined. In other years, he would try to remember if he had heard deeper voices, answering theirs down in the wood; but the memories were deceitful, and each time they were invoked spoke with a different voice. At all events, he was not afraid, nor lonely; there was whispering and laughter not far away. A dancing flame was the last thing he saw before his closing eyes.

2

He was seven years old, the age at which boys left the care of women. It was time to make a Greek of him.

King Philip was at war again on the northeast Chalkidian coast, securing his boundaries, which meant stretching them. His marriage grew no easier; rather than a wife, it seemed to him, he had wedded a great and dangerous noble who could not be reduced by war, and whose spies knew everything. From a girl she had grown into a woman of striking beauty; but, girl or youth, it was the young who roused desire in him. For a while young men had contented him; then, after his fathers' custom, he had taken a wellborn young concubine with the status of a minor wife. Olympias' outraged pride had shaken the Palace like an earthquake. She had been seen at night, near Aigai, going with a torch to the royal tombs; it was ancient witchcraft, to write a curse on lead and leave it for the ghosts to work on. It was said a child had been with her. He had looked at his son when next they met; the smoke-grey eyes had met his, unflinching, haunted, mute. As he went away he felt the eyes in his back.

The war in Chalkidike could not wait; nor should the boy. Though not big for his years, he was forward in everything else. Hellanike had taught him his letters and his scale (his high voice was true and

[38]

its pitch was perfect); the soldiers of the Guard, and even of the barracks, to whom he escaped every second day, had taught him their peasant dialect, and what else one could only guess. As for what he had learned from his mother, that was best not thought of.

When Kings of Macedon went to war, it was second nature to guard their backs. To the west, the Illyrians had been subdued in the first years of his reign. The east he was about to deal with. There remained the old dangers of tribal kingdoms: conspiracies at home, and feuds. If before he marched he had taken the boy from Olympias, and appointed some man of his own as governor, both these evils were certain.

Philip took some pride in seeing where a pass could be turned without a battle. He slept on the problem, and woke remembering Leonidas.

He was Olympias' uncle; but more Hellenized than Philip himself. As a young man, in love with the idea rather than the ideas of Greece, he had traveled south, making first for Athens. Here he had acquired a pure Attic speech, studied oratory and composition; and sampled the philosophic schools just long enough to decide they could only undermine sound tradition and the findings of common sense. As was natural to a man of his birth, he made friends among the aristocracy, hereditary oligarchs who looked to the good old days, deplored the times, and, like their forebears back to the Great War, admired the customs of Sparta. In due course Leonidas went to see it.

Used by now to the high diversions of Athens, drama festivals, music contests, sacred processions put on like great performances, supper clubs with their verse-capping and well-read wit, he had found Lakedaimon stiflingly provincial. To a feudal lord of Epiros, with deep roots in his demesne, the racial rule of Spartiate over Helot was foreign and uneasy; the blunt-spoken familiarity of Spartiate with Spartiate, and with himself, struck him as boorish. And here too, as in Athens, the great days were over. Like an old dog thrashed by a younger one, which will show its teeth but keep its distance, Sparta had not been the same since the Thebans had marched up to the walls. Barter had gone out, money had come in and was prized here as elsewhere; the rich had amassed great lands,

[39]

the poor could no longer pay their shot at the citizens' public mess-tables, and had sunk to mere "by-dwellers" whose gallantry had bled out of them with their pride. But in one respect he had found them equal to their past. They could still rear disciplined boys, hardy, uncoddled and respectful, who did what they were told at once without asking why, stood up when their elders entered, and never spoke till spoken to. Attic culture and Spartan manners, he had thought as he sailed homeward; combine them in the pliant mind of youth and they would give you the perfect man.

He returned to Epiros, the consequence of his rank increased by his travels. Long after his knowledge was out of date it had been universally deferred to. King Philip, who had agents in all the Greek cities, knew better than this; nonetheless, when he talked with Leonidas he became aware that his own Greek was rather Boeotian. Along with the Attic speech went the Hellene maxims: "Nothing in excess"; "Well begun, half done"; and "It is a woman's glory not to be spoken of, either for praise or blame."

Here was the perfect compromise. Olympias' kin was honored. Leonidas, who had a passion for correctness, would allot her the dues of a highborn lady, himself the dues of a man. She would find him harder than even Philip to meddle with. Through his southern guest-friends he could engage all the proper tutors the King had not time to find, and ensure they were sound in politics and morals. Letters were exchanged. Philip rode off, his mind at rest, leaving orders that Leonidas be given a state welcome.

On the day he was expected, Hellanike laid out Alexander's best clothes, and had her slave fill him a bath. Kleopatra came in while they were scouring him. She was a podgy child, with Olympias' red hair and the square build of Philip. She ate too much because she was often unhappy, knowing their mother loved Alexander more, and differently.

"You're a schoolboy now," she said. "You can't come in the women's rooms."

When he found her in trouble he would often console her, amuse her or give her things. When she threatened him with her womanhood, he hated her. "I shall come in when I like. Who do you think will stop me?"

"Your teacher will." She began chanting it, jumping up and down. He leaped out, soaking the floor, and threw her in with all her clothes on. Hellanike laid him wet across her knee and beat him with her sandal. Kleopatra mocked him, was beaten in turn, and thrust out screaming, to be dried by the maid.

Alexander did not weep. He had understood the whole business of the appointment. No one had needed to tell him that if he did not obey this man, it would lose his mother a battle in her war; nor that the next one would then be fought over himself. He was scarred within by such battles. When another threatened, the scars throbbed like old wounds before the rain.

Hellanike combed his tangled hair, making him clench his teeth. He cried easily at old war-songs where sworn comrades died together, at a falling cadence of the flute. He had cried half a day, when his dog fell sick and died. Already he knew what it was to mourn the fallen; for Agis he had wept his heart out. But to cry for his own wounds would make Herakles forsake him. This had long been a part of their secret compact.

Bathed, combed and dressed, he was summoned to the Perseus Room, where Olympias and the guest sat in chairs of honor. The boy had expected an aged scholar; he saw a spruce upright man in the forties, his dark beard scarcely grizzled, looking about like a general who, though off duty, will remember it all tomorrow. The boy knew a good deal about officers, mostly from below. His friends kept his secrets, and he kept theirs.

Leonidas was genial, kissed him on both cheeks, set firm hands on his shoulders, was sure he would be a credit to his ancestors. Alexander submitted civilly; his sense of the realities made him stand through it all like a soldier on parade. Leonidas had not hoped to see the Spartan training so well begun. The boy, though too beautiful for safety, looked healthy and alert; no doubt he would prove teachable. "You have reared a fine child, Olympias. These pretty babyclothes show your care. Now we must find him something for a boy."

His eyes moved to his mother, who had embroidered herself his tunic of soft combed wool. Sitting straight in her chair, she gave him a little nod, and looked away.

Leonidas moved into his Palace quarters. To negotiate for suitable teachers would take time. Those eminent enough would have schools to leave; some must be looked into, for dangerous thoughts. His own work must begin at once; he saw it could not be too soon.

The drilled look had been illusion. The boy had done as he liked; got up at cocklight or had his sleep out; run about with boys or men. Though grossly spoiled, one must own him not a milksop; but his speech was dreadful. Not only was he nearly Greekless; but where had he learned his Macedonian? One might suppose he had been begotten against a barrack wall.

Clearly, school hours were insufficient. His life must be taken in hand from dawn till dusk.

Every morning before sunup he was at exercise; twice round the running-track, swinging the hand-weights, leaping and hurling. When breakfast came at last, it was never quite enough. If he said he was still hungry, he was told to say it in proper Greek; to be answered, in proper Greek, that spare breakfasts were good for the health.

His clothes had been changed for homespun, harsh to the skin and unadorned. It was good enough for the kings' sons of Sparta. Autumn came on; in colder and colder weather, he was hardened off by going cloakless. Running about to keep warm made him much hungrier, but he did not get much more food.

Leonidas found himself obeyed; doggedly, without complaint, with steady unconcealed resentment. It was all too clear that he and his regime were simply a detested ordeal, which the boy endured for his mother's sake, sustained by pride.

He was uneasy, but could not breach the wall. He was one of those men in whom the role of father, once achieved, blots out all memories of childhood. His own sons could have told him so, had they ever told him anything. He would do his duty by the boy, and knew of no one who could do it better.

Greek lessons began. It soon appeared that Alexander was in fact quite fluent. He simply disliked it; a disgrace, as his tutor told him, when his father spoke it so well. He repeated it briskly; soon learned to write it; and expected, as soon as he left the schoolroom, to lapse into broad Macedonian and the argot of the phalanx.

When he understood he had to speak Greek all day, he could scarcely credit it. Even slaves could use their home tongue to one another.

He had respites. To Olympias, the tongue of the north was the heroes' unspoiled heritage, Greek a degenerate patois. She spoke it to Greeks as a courtesy to inferiors, and to them alone. Leonidas had social duties, during which his captive could escape. If he could get to the barracks at mess-time, there was always porridge to spare.

Riding he still enjoyed; but he soon lost his favorite escort, a young officer of the Companions, to whom he offered an accustomed kiss as the man lifted him down. Leonidas saw from the stable yard. Ordered out of hearing, and seeing his friend flush scarlet, the boy thought a limit had been passed. He walked back, and stood between.

"I kissed him first. And he has never tried to have me." He used the barrack term, knowing no other.

After a speechless pause, he was marched away in silence. In the schoolroom, still without a word, Leonidas beat him.

He had given far worse to his own sons. Rank and Olympias had their claims. But it was a boy's beating, not a child's. Leonidas did not own to himself that he had been waiting for the chance, to see how his charge would take it.

He heard no sound but the blows. He had meant at the end to bid the boy turn and face him; but was forestalled. He had looked only for a Spartan fortitude, or self-pity. He confronted dry wide eyes, their irises stretched to a pale rim round the black; hard-shut white lips and dilated nostrils; a blazing rage, condensed by silence like the core of a furnace. For a moment, he had a sense of actual menace.

Alone among those at Pella, he had seen Olympias' childhood. But *she* would have flown in straight away with her nails; her nurse's face had been scored with them. This containment was another thing. One even dreaded lest it break.

His first instinct was to take the boy by his scruff, and thrash the defiance out of him. But though a narrow man he was by his lights a just one, with an exacting self-esteem. Moreover, he had been brought here to rear a fighting King of Macedon, not to break in a slave. The boy had at least controlled himself.

[43]

"The silence of a soldier. I approve a man who can bear his wounds. No further work today."

He received in exchange the look which accords grudging respect to a mortal enemy. As the boy went out, Leonidas saw a bloodstain on the back of his homespun chiton. It would have been nothing in Sparta; yet he found himself wishing he had not hit quite so hard.

The boy said nothing to his mother; but she found the weals. In the room where they had shared many secrets, she clasped him weeping, and presently they wept together. He stopped first; went to the loose stone under the hearth, pulled out a wax mammet he had seen there, and urged her to bewitch Leonidas. She took it quickly away, saying he must not touch, and besides it was not for that. It had a long thorn stuck through its phallos, but had failed to work on Philip, though often tried. She had not known the child was watching.

For him, the comfort of tears had been brief and false. He felt betrayed, when he met Herakles in the garden. He had not cried for the pain, but for his lost happiness; he could have held back if she had not softened him. Next time she must not know.

They shared a plot, however. She had never been reconciled to the Spartan clothes; she had loved to dress him. Reared in a house where ladies sat in Hall like the queens of Homer, to hear the ancestral heroes sung by bards, she was contemptuous of Spartans, a race of faceless obedient infantry, and unwashed women half soldier, half brood mare. That her son should be forced into the likeness of this grey and plebeian race would have enraged her, had she thought it could be done. Resenting even the attempt, she brought him a new chiton worked in blue and scarlet, saying, as she tucked it into his clothes chest, that there was no harm in his looking like a gentleman when his uncle was away. Later she added Corinthian sandals, a chlamys of Milesian wool, and a gold brooch for its shoulder.

Good clothes made him feel himself again. Discreet at first, he grew careless with success. Leonidas, knowing where to lay the blame, said nothing. He merely went to the chest and took the new clothes away, along with an extra blanket he found hidden there.

He had challenged the gods at last, thought Alexander; this must be the end of him. But she only smiled ruefully, and asked how he could have let himself be found out. Leonidas must not be defied; he might be offended and go home. "And then, my darling, we might find our troubles only starting."

Toys were toys, power was power. Nothing to be had for nothing. Later she smuggled him other gifts. He was more wary, but Leonidas was more vigilant, and took to searching the chest every so often, as a matter of course.

More manly gifts, he was allowed to keep. A friend had made him a quiver, a perfect miniature with a shoulder sling. Finding it hung too low on him, he sat in the Palace forecourt to undo the buckle. The tongue was awkward, the leather stiff. He was about to go in and find an awl to prize it, when a bigger child walked up and stood in the light. He was handsome and sturdy, with bronze-gold hair and dark grey eyes. Holding out his hand he said, "I'll try, let me." He spoke with confidence, in a Greek which had got beyond the schoolroom.

"It's new, that's why it's stiff." He had had his day's work of Greek, and answered in Macedonian.

The stranger squatted beside him. "It's like a real one, like a man's. Did your father make it?"

"Of course not. Doreios the Cretan did. He can't make me a Cretan bow, those are horn, only men can pull them. Koragos will make a bow for me."

"Why do you want to undo it?"

"It's too long."

"It looks right to me. No, but you're smaller. Here, I'll do it."

"I've measured it. It wants taking in two holes."

"You can let it out when you're bigger. It's stiff, but I'll do it. My father's seeing the King."

"What does he want?"

"I don't know, he said to wait for him."

"Does he make you speak Greek all day?"

"It's what we all speak at home. My father's a guest-friend of the King. When I'm older, I'll have to go to court."

"Don't you want to come?"

[45]

"Not much; I like it at home. Look, up on that hill; no, not the first one, the second; all that land's ours. Can't you speak Greek at all?"

"Yes, I can if I want. I stop when I get sick of it."

"Why, you speak it nearly as well as I do. Why did you talk like that, then? People will think you're a farm boy."

"My tutor makes me wear these clothes to be like the Spartans. I do have good ones; I wear them at the feasts."

"They beat all the boys in Sparta."

"Oh, he drew blood on me once. But I didn't cry."

"He's no right to beat you, he should only tell your father. How much did he cost?"

"He's my mother's uncle."

"Mm, I see. My father bought my pedagogue, just for me."

"Well, it teaches you to bear your wounds when you go to war."

"*War?* But you're only six."

"Of course not, I'm eight next Lion Month. You can see that."

"So am I. But *you* don't look it, you look six."

"Oh, let me do that, you're too slow."

He snatched away the sling-strap. The leather slipped back into the buckle. The stranger grabbed it angrily. "Silly fool, I'd nearly done it."

Alexander swore at him in barrack Macedonian. The other boy opened his mouth and eyes, and listened riveted. Alexander, who could keep it up for some time, became aware of respect and did so. With the quiver between them, they crouched in the pose of their forgotten strife.

"Hephaistion!" came a roar from the columned stoa. The boys sat like scuffling dogs over whom a bucket has been emptied.

The lord Amyntor, his audience over, had seen with concern that his son had left the porch where he had been told to wait, invaded the Prince's playground and snatched his toy. At that age they were not safe a moment out of one's sight. Amyntor blamed his own vanity; he liked to show the boy off, but to have brought him here was stupid. Angry with himself, he strode over, grabbed him by the back of his clothes, and gave him a clout on the ear.

Alexander jumped to his feet. He had already forgotten why he had been angry. "Don't hit him. I don't mind him. He came to help me."

"You are good to say so, Alexander. But he disobeyed."

For a moment the boys exchanged looks, confusedly sharing their sense of human mutability, as the culprit was dragged away.

It was six years before they met again.

"He lacks application and discipline," said Timanthes the grammarian.

Most of the teachers Leonidas had engaged found the drinking in Hall too much for them, and would escape, with excuses which amused the Macedonians, to bed, or to talk in each other's rooms.

"Maybe," said the music-master, Epikrates. "But one values the horse above the bridle."

"He applies when it suits him," said Naukles the mathematician. "At first he could not have enough. He can work out the height of the Palace from its noon shadow, and if you ask him how many men in fifteen phalanxes, he hardly has to pause. But I have never brought him to perceive the beauty of numbers. Have you, Epikrates?"

The musician, a thin dark Ephesian Greek, shook his head smiling. "With you he makes them serve the use; with me, the feeling. Still, as we know, music is ethical; and I've a king to train, not a concert artist."

"He will get no further with me," said the mathematician. "I would say I don't know why I stay, if I thought I should be believed."

A roar of bawdy laughter sounded from the hall, where someone with talent was improving a traditional skolion. For the seventh time they bawled the chorus.

"Yes, we are well paid," said Epikrates. "But I could earn as much in Ephesos, between teaching and concert work; and earn it as a musician. Here I am a conjurer, I call up dreams. It's not what I came to do. Yet it holds me. Does it never hold you, Timanthes?"

Timanthes sniffed. He thought Epikrates' compositions too modern and emotional. He himself was an Athenian, pre-eminent

[47]

for the purity of his style; he had in fact been the teacher of Leonidas. He had closed his school to come, finding at his age the work grow burdensome, and glad to provide for his last years. He had read everything worth reading, and when young had once known what the poets meant.

"It appears to me," he said, "that here in Macedon they have enough of the passions. One heard a great deal about the culture of Archelaos, in my student days. With the late wars of succession, it seems chaos returned. I will not say the court is without refinements; but on the whole, we are in the wilds. Do you know youths come of age here when they have killed a boar and a man? One might suppose oneself in the age of Troy."

"That should lighten your task," said Epikrates, "when you proceed to Homer."

"System and application are what we need for that. The boy has a good memory, when he cares to use it. At first he learned his lists quite well. But he cannot keep his mind on system. One explains the construction; one quotes the proper example. But apply it? No. It is 'Why did they chain Prometheus to the rock?' or, 'Who was Hekabe mourning for?'"

"Did you tell him? Kings should learn to pity Hekabe."

"Kings should learn self-discipline. This morning he brought the lesson to a stop, because, purely for syntax, I gave him some lines from *Seven against Thebes*. Why, if you please, were there seven generals; which led the cavalry, the phalanx, the light-armed skirmishers? 'It is not to the purpose,' I said, 'not to the purpose; attend to syntax.' He had the insolence to answer in Macedonian. I had to put my thong across his palm."

The singing in Hall was broken by quarrelsome drunken shouts. Crockery crashed. The King's voice roared out; the noise subsided; a different song began.

"Discipline," said Timanthes meaningly. "Moderation, restraint, respect for law. If we do not ground him in them, who will? His mother?"

There was a pause while Naukles, whose room it was, nervously opened the door and looked outside. Epikrates said, "If you want to compete with *her,* Timanthes, you had best sweeten your medicine, as I do mine."

"He must make the effort to apply. It is the root of all education."

"I don't know what you are all talking about," said Derkylos, the gymnastic trainer, suddenly. The others had thought he was asleep. He was reclining on Naukles' bed; he thought effort should alternate with relaxation. He was in his mid-thirties, with the oval head and short curls admired by sculptors, and a fine body kept painstakingly in shape; as an example to pupils, he used to say, but, thought the envious schoolmasters, no doubt from vanity. He had a list of crowned victors to his credit, and no pretensions to intellect.

"We were wishing," said Timanthes with patronage, "that the boy would make more effort."

"I heard you." The athlete raised himself on one elbow, looking aggressively statuesque. "You have spoken words of ill omen. Spit for luck."

The grammarian shrugged. Naukles said tartly, "Will you tell us, Derkylos, *you* don't know why you stay?"

"It seems I'm the one with the best reason. To keep him, if I can, from killing himself too young. He has no safety-stop. Surely you've seen that?"

"I fear," said Timanthes, "that the terms of the palaestra are to me arcane."

"I've seen it," said Epikrates, "if you mean what I suppose."

"I don't know all your life histories," said Derkylos. "But if any of you has seen red in battle, or been frightened out of his skin, you may remember putting out strength you had never known was in you. At exercise, even in a contest, you could not find it. There is a lock on it, put there by nature or the gods' wisdom. It is the reserve against extremity."

"I remember," said Naukles presently, "in the earthquake, when the house fell on our mother, I lifted the beams. Yet later I could not move them."

"Nature wrung it out of you. Few men are born whose own will can do it. This boy will be one."

Epikrates said, "Yes, you may well be right."

"And I reckon it something off a man's life each time. I have to watch him already. He told me once that Achilles chose between glory and length of days."

"What?" said Timanthes, startled. "But we've scarcely begun Book One."

Derkylos gazed at him in silence, then said mildly, "You forget his maternal ancestry."

Timanthes clicked his tongue, and bade them good night. Naukles fidgeted; he wanted to get to bed. The musician and the athlete strolled off through the park.

"It's useless talking to *him*," said Derkylos. "But I doubt the boy gets enough to eat."

"You must be joking. Here?"

"It's the regime of that stiff-necked old fool Leonidas. I check his height each month; he's not growing fast enough. Of course you can't call him starved; but he burns it all up, he could take as much again. He's very quick-thinking, and his body has to keep pace, he won't take a no from it. Do you know he can hit the mark with a javelin while he's running?"

"You let him handle edged weapons? At his age?"

"I wish grown men were all as neat with them. It keeps him quiet . . . What is it drives him like this?"

Epikrates looked round. They were in the open, no one near. "His mother has made a good many enemies. She's a foreigner from Epiros; she has the name of a witch. Have you never heard whispers about his birth?"

"I remember once— But who'd dare let *him* hear word of it?"

"He seems to me to have a burden of proof upon him. Well, he enjoys his music for itself, he finds release in it. I have studied that side of the art a little."

"I must speak to Leonidas again about his diet. Last time, I was told that in Sparta it would be one spare meal a day, and find the rest off the land. Don't tell it abroad, but I feed him myself sometimes. I used to do it now and then at Argos, for some good boy from a poor home . . . These tales—do you believe them?"

"Not with my reason. He has Philip's capacity, if not his face or his soul. No, no, I don't believe them . . . Do you know that old song about Orpheus, how he played his lyre on the mountainside, and found a lion had crouched at his feet to listen? I'm no Orpheus, I know; but sometimes I see the lion's eyes. Where did it go, after the music, what became of it? The story doesn't say."

"Today," said Timanthes, "you have made better progress. For the next lesson, you may memorize eight lines. Here they are. Copy them on the wax, on the right side of the diptych. On the left, list the archaic word-forms. See you have them correctly; I shall expect you to repeat those first." He handed over the tablet, and put away the roll, his stiff blue-veined hands shaking as he worked it into its leather case. "Yes, that is all. You may go."

"Please, may I borrow the book?"

Timanthes looked up, amazed and outraged.

"The *book?* Most certainly you may not, it is a valuable recension. What do you want with the book?"

"I want to see what happened. I'll keep it in my casket, and wash my hands each time."

"We should all like, no doubt, to run before we can walk. Learn your passage, and pay attention to the Ionic forms. Your accent is still too Doric. This, Alexander, is not some suppertime diversion. This is Homer. Master his language, then you may talk of reading him." He tied the strings of the case.

The lines were those in which vengeful Apollo comes striding down the peaks of Olympos with his arrows rattling at his back. Worked over in the schoolroom, hammered out piecemeal like some store-list being inventoried by kitchen slaves, once the boy was alone they came together: a great landscape of clanging gloom lit by funereal fires. He knew Olympos. He pictured the dead light of an eclipse; the tall striding darkness, and round it a faint rim of fire, such as they said the hidden sun had, able to strike men blind. *He came down like the fall of night.*

He walked in the grove above Pella, hearing the deep shuddering note of the bowstring, the hiss of the shafts, and thinking it into Macedonian. It found its way, next day, into his repetition. Timanthes rebuked at length his idleness, inattention, and lack of interest in his work, and set him at once to copy the passage twenty times, with the mistakes again by themselves.

[51]

He dug away at the wax, the vision dispersed and faded. Timanthes, whom something had caused to look up, found the grey eyes considering him with a cold distant stare.

"Do not daydream, Alexander. What are you thinking of?"

"Nothing." He bent again over his writing-stick. He had been wondering if there was any way of getting Timanthes killed. He supposed not; it would be unfair to ask his friends, who might be punished, and would feel it a disgrace to kill such an ancient man. It would make trouble, too, for his mother.

He went missing next day.

After huntsmen had been out after him with dogs, he was brought back at evening by a woodcutter on his lean old donkey; bruised black, covered with bloody grazes from a tumble down some rocks, and with a swollen foot which would not bear him. He had been trying, said the man, to get along on hands and knees; at night the forest was full of wolves, no place for the young lord alone.

He opened his mouth long enough to thank this man; to demand that he be fed, because he was hungry, and given a younger ass, which he had promised him on the way. These things attended to he became mute. The doctor could scarcely get from him more than yes or no, and a wince when the foot was moved. The compress and splint were put on; his mother came to his bedside. He turned his face away.

She put aside her anger, which belonged elsewhere; brought him a supper of all the treats Leonidas had banned; propped him against her breast while she fed him with sweet mulled wine. When he had told her all the trouble, as far as himself he understood it, she kissed him, tucked him in, and went off in a towering rage to quarrel with Leonidas.

The tempest shook the Palace, like a clash of gods above the Trojan plain. But many weapons which had served her against Philip were here denied her. Leonidas was very correct, very Athenian. He offered to leave, and tell the boy's father why. When she emerged from his study (she had been too angry to wait and have him sent for) everyone hid who saw her coming; but the truth was, she was in tears.

Old Lysimachos, who had lain in wait for her since, starting out, she had swept by him unseeing, greeted her as she returned, and said with no more fuss than if she had been a farmer's wife in his native Akarnania, "How is the boy?"

No one paid attention to Lysimachos. He was always about, a Palace guest-friend since early in Philip's reign. He had backed his accession when support was urgent; had proved good company at supper, and been rewarded with the hand of an heiress in royal wardship. On the estate it brought him, he farmed and hunted. But the gods had denied him children; not only by her, but by all women he had ever lain with. This reproach being ready to any man's hand who chose to throw it, he thought hubris would ill become him, and was an unpretentious man. His one distinction was to have the run of the royal library; Philip had added to Archelaos' fine collection, and was careful whom he let loose inside. From the depths of his reading-cell, Lysimachos' voice could be heard murmuring by the hour over the scrolls, tasting words and cadences; but nothing had come of it, no treatise, history or tragedy. His mind, it seemed, was as infertile as his loins.

Olympias, at the sight of his square blunt face, his grey-blond hair and beard and faded blue eyes, felt a homely comfort, and asked him into her private guest-room. Once bidden to sit, he sat while she paced about, and offered harmless murmurs whenever she paused for breath, till she had run herself to a stop. Then he said, "My dear madam, now the boy has outgrown his nurse's care, don't you think he may need a pedagogue?"

She wheeled round so sharply that her jewels clattered. "Never! I will not have it, the King knows that. What do they want to make of him, a clerk, a merchant, a steward? *He* feels what he is. All day these lowbred pedants are working to break his spirit. He has scarcely an hour, from his rising to his lying down, when his soul has space to breathe. Now is he to live like some captive thief, marched about in charge of a slave? Let no one speak of it in my hearing. And if the King sent you word to do it, tell him, Lysimachos, that before my son shall suffer that I will have blood for it, yes, by the Three-fold Hekate, I will have blood!"

He waited till he thought that she would hear him, then said, "I should be sorry too to see it. Rather than that, I myself would be his pedagogue. In fact, madam, that is what I came to ask for."

Mary Renault

She sat down in her tall chair. He waited patiently, knowing she had paused, not to ask herself why a gentleman should offer for a servant's work, but whether he would do.

Presently he said, "It has often seemed to me that Achilles has come again in him. If so, he needs a Phoinix. '. . . *You, godlike Achilles, were the son I chose for my own, That someday you would keep the hard times from me.*'"

"Did he do so? When Phoinix spoke those words, he had been rooted up in his age from Phthia, and brought to Troy. And what he was asking, Achilles did not grant."

"If he had, it would have saved him sorrow. Maybe his soul has remembered. As we know, the ashes of Achilles and Patroklos were mingled in one urn. Not even a god could sift the one from the other. Achilles has come back with his fierceness and his pride, and with Patroklos' feeling. Each of them suffered for what he was; this boy will suffer for both."

"There is more," she said, "as men will find."

"I do not question it. Just now, this is enough. Let me try with him; if he cannot do with me, I will let him be."

She got up again, and took a turn about the room.

"Yes, try," she said. "If you can stand between him and those fools, I shall be your debtor."

Alexander was feverish at night, and slept most of next day. Lysimachos, looking in next morning, found him sitting up in the window, his good foot dangling outside, and shouting down in his high clear voice; two Companion Cavalry officers had come in from Thrace on the King's business, and he wanted news of the war. This they gave; but refused to take him riding, when they learned they were to catch him as he jumped down from the upper floor. Laughing and waving they clattered off. As the boy turned away with a sigh, Lysimachos reached up and carried him back to bed.

He submitted easily, having known the man all his life. As early as he had been able to run about, he had sat on his knee to hear his stories. Timanthes indeed had said of him to Leonidas that he was, rather than a scholar, a learned schoolboy. The boy at least was glad to see him, and confided to him the whole tale of his day in the woods, not without bragging.

"Did you walk on that foot just now?"

[54]

"I can't, I hopped." He frowned at it with displeasure; it was hurting him. Lysimachos eased the pillow under.

"Look after it. The ankle was Achilles' weakness. His mother held him by it, when she dipped him in the Styx, and forgot to wet it after."

"Is that in the book, how Achilles died?"

"No. But he knows he will, because he has fulfilled his death-fate."

"Didn't the diviners warn him?"

"Yes, he was warned that his death would follow Hektor's, but still he killed him. He was avenging Patroklos, his friend, whom Hektor had killed."

The boy considered this intently. "He was his best friend of all?"

"Yes, from when they were boys together."

"Why didn't Achilles save him first, then?"

"He had taken his men out of the battle, because the High King had insulted him. The Greeks were getting the worst of it without him; that was as he'd been promised by the god. But Patroklos, who had a feeling heart, when he saw old comrades falling came to Achilles weeping for pity. 'Lend me only your armor,' he said, 'and let me show myself in the field. They will think you are back; it will be enough to scare them off.' So Achilles gave him leave, and he did great deeds, but . . ." He was stopped by the boy's shocked stare.

"He couldn't do that! He was a general! And he sent a junior officer, when he wouldn't go! It was his *fault* Patroklos died."

"Oh, yes, he knew. He had sacrificed him to his pride. That was why he fulfilled his death-fate."

"How did the King insult him? How did it start?"

Lysimachos settled himself on the stool of dyed sheepskin by the bed.

As the tale unfolded, Alexander found to his surprise that it could all have happened, any day, in Macedon.

The harebrained younger son, stealing the wife of his powerful host; bringing her and the feud to his father's hold—the old houses of Macedon and Epiros could tell such tales by the score. The High King had called up his levies and his under-chiefs. King Peleus, being over-age, had sent his one son, Achilles, born of a goddess

[55]

queen. When at sixteen he came to the plain of Troy, he was already the best of the warriors.

The war itself was just like some tribal skirmish in the hills: warriors whooping each other on into single combats without asking leave; the infantry, it seemed, scrambling about in rabbles behind the lords. He had heard of a dozen such wars in the lifetime of men who told the story, breaking out from old feuds, or flaring up over blood shed in a drinking-brawl, the moving of a boundary stone, an unpaid bride-price, a cuckold mocked at a feast.

Lysimachos told it as he had pictured it in his youth. He had read the speculations of Anaxagoras, the maxims of Herakleitos, the history of Thukydides, the philosophy of Plato, Euripides' melodramas and Agathon's romantic plays; but Homer returned him to his childhood, when he had sat on his father's knee to hear the bard, and watched his tall brothers walk clanking sword at hip, as men still did in the streets of Pella.

The boy, who had always thought less of Achilles for making all this trouble only about a girl, now learned that she was a prize for valor, which the King had taken away to humble him. Now he well understood Achilles' anger. He pictured Agamemnon as a stocky man, with a strong black beard.

So, then, Achilles was sitting in his war-hut, self-exiled from his glory, playing his lyre to Patroklos, the only one who understood his mind, when the King's envoys came to him. The Greeks were in extremity; the King had had to eat dirt. Achilles should have his girl returned. Also, he could marry Agamemnon's own daughter with a huge dowry of lands and cities. If he liked, he could even have the dowry without her.

As people do at the crux of a tragedy though they know the end, the boy willed that all should be well now: that Achilles should relent, that he and Patroklos should go into battle side by side, happy and glorious. But Achilles turned away his face. They still asked too much, he said. "For my goddess mother has told me I bear two death-fates within me. If I stay before Troy and fight, I lose my homecoming, but win everlasting fame. Or, if I go home to my dear fatherland, I lose the height of my glory, but have a long life left me, death will not come for me soon." Now his honor had been blown on, he would choose the second fate, and sail home.

The third envoy had not yet spoken. Now he came forward; old Phoinix, who had known Achilles since he was a child upon his knee. King Peleus had adopted him, after his own father had cursed him out of doors. He had been happy at Peleus' court; but the father's curse had worked, making him forever childless. Achilles was the child he had chosen for his own, so that one day he would keep the hard times from him. Now, if he sailed, he would go along with him; he would never forsake him, even in exchange for being made young again. But he begged Achilles rather to heed his prayers, and lead out the Greeks to battle.

A moral digression followed; the boy, his attention wandering, withdrew into himself. Impatient of delays, he wished to bestow at once on Lysimachos some gift he had always wanted. It seemed to him that he could.

"I'd have said yes, if you had asked me." Scarcely feeling his sprained foot as he moved, he clasped Lysimachos' neck.

Lysimachos embraced him, openly weeping. The boy was undisturbed at it; Herakles allowed such tears. It was great luck to have had the right gift at hand. It was real too, he had not lied at all to him; he truly loved him, would be like his son and keep the hard times from him. If he had come like Phoinix to Achilles, he would have given him what he asked: have led out the Greeks to fight, taking the first of the death-fates, never to come home to the dear fatherland, never to grow old. It was all quite true, and had given happiness. Why add, then, that though he would give consent, it would not be for Phoinix' sake?

He would do it for the everlasting fame.

The great city of Olynthos, on the northeast coast, had fallen to King Philip. His gold got in first, his soldiers later.

The Olynthians had looked askance at his rising power. For years they had harbored two bastard half-brothers of his who claimed his throne; had played him and Athens off against each other whenever it served their turn, and then allied with Athens.

First he took care that his bought men in the town should grow rich, and show it. Their party grew. Down south in Euboia, he fomented a rising to keep the Athenians minding their own business. Meantime he kept exchanging envoys with Olynthos, haggling at length over peace terms, while he reduced strategic country all around.

This done, he sent them an ultimatum. Either they or he would have to go; he had decided they should. If they surrendered, they could leave with a safe-conduct. No doubt their Athenian allies would look after them.

In spite of Philip's party, the vote went for holding out. They gave him some costly fighting, before his clients contrived to lose a couple of battles, and let him through the gates.

Now, he thought, was the time to warn others against giving so much trouble. Let Olynthos be an example. The rebel half-brothers died by the Companions' spears. Soon the chain-gangs of slaves were going down through Greece, driven by the dealers, or men whose usefulness had deserved a gift. Cities which had seen, time out of mind, their heavy work done by Thracians or Ethiops or broad-cheeked Scythians, gazed in outrage at Greek men bearing burdens under the lash, Greek girls sold to the brothels in the open market. Demosthenes' voice rallied all decent men to stand against the barbarian.

The boys of Macedon saw the hopeless convoys pass, the children wailing in the dust as they trudged at their mothers' skirts. It brought the millennial message. This is defeat: avoid it.

At the sea-foot of Mount Olympos stood the town of Dion, the holy footstool of Olympian Zeus. Here Philip held his victory feast, in the god's sacred month, with splendors which Archelaos had never equaled. Distinguished guests came north from all over Greece; kitharists and flautists, rhapsodes and actors, competed for gold wreaths, purple gowns and bags of silver.

Euripides' *Bakchai* was to be staged; Euripides had first put it on in this very theater. The best scene-painter of Corinth was painting the flats with Theban hills and a royal palace; the tragedians were heard each morning in their lodgings, practicing the gamut of all their voices from the boom of gods to maiden trebles. Even the schoolmasters were on holiday. Achilles and his Phoinix (the nickname had stuck at once) had the threshold of Olympos, and the sights of the festival, to themselves. Phoinix had given Achilles his own Iliad, a secret from Timanthes. They gave trouble to no one, absorbed in their private game.

On the god's annual feast-day, the King gave a grand banquet. Alexander was to appear, but to leave before the drinking. He wore a new blue chiton stitched with gold; his heavy loose-waving hair was curled. He sat on the end of his father's supper couch, his own silver bowl and cup beside him. The hall was brilliant with lamps; the lords' sons of the Royal Bodyguard came and went between the King and his guests of honor, bringing them his gifts.

There were some Athenians, of the party which favored peace with Macedon. The boy noticed his father taking care with his accent. The Athenians might have helped his enemies; they might have sunk to intrigue with the Persians their forebears had fought at Marathon; but they still had in their gift the prize of Greekness.

The King, shouting down the hall, was asking some guest why he looked so glum. It was Satyros, the great comedian of Athens. Having got the feed he had worked for, he mimed fear amusingly, and said he hardly dared ask for what he wanted. Only name it, cried the King with extended hand. It turned out to be the freedom of two young girls he had seen among the slaves, daughters of an old Olynthian guest-friend; he wanted to save them from their fate and give them marriage portions. A happiness, cried the King, to grant a request itself so generous. There was a buzz of applause; good feeling warmed the room. The guests who had passed the slave pens found their food taste a little better.

The garlands were coming in, and big wine-coolers packed with Olympian snow. Philip turned to his son, stroked back the moist fair hair, already losing its curl, from his warm brow, gave it a bristly kiss while the guests murmured delight, and bade him run off to bed. He slipped down, said good night to the guard at the door, who was a friend of his; and made his way to his mother's room to tell her all about it.

Before his hand was on the door, some warning reached him from within.

The place was in confusion. The women stood huddled like frightened hens. His mother, still dressed in the robe she had worn for the choral odes, was pacing to and fro. The mirror-table was overturned; a maid was on hands and knees, scrambling for jars and pins. As the door opened she dropped a jar and the kohl spilled out. Olympias strode across, and sent her sprawling with a blow on the head.

"Out, all of you!" she shouted. "Sluts, useless gaping halfwits! Get out, and leave me with my son."

He came in. The flush of the hot hall and his watered wine drained from his face; his stomach clenched itself on its meal. Silently he walked forward. As the women scurried out, she flung herself on the bed, beating and biting the pillows. He came and knelt beside her, feeling the coldness of his own hands as he stroked her hair. He did not ask the trouble.

Olympias writhed round on the bed, and grasped him by the shoulders, calling all gods to witness her injuries and avenge her. She gripped him to her so that they both shook to and fro; the heavens forbid, she cried, that he should ever learn what she suffered from this vilest of all men; it was unfit for the innocence of his years. She always said this at first. He moved his head so that he could breathe. Not a young man this time, he thought; it must be a girl.

It was a proverb in Macedon, that the King took a wife for every war. It was true these matches, always sealed with rites to please the kindred, were a good way of making reliable allies. The boy only knew the fact. He now remembered a sleekness about his father which he had known before. "A Thracian!" his mother cried. "A filthy, blue-painted Thracian!" Somewhere in Dion, then, all this while, the girl had been hidden away. Hetairas went about, everyone saw them.

"I'm sorry, Mother," he said leadenly. "Did Father marry her?"

"Don't call that man your father!" She held him at arms' length, staring into his face; her lashes were matted, the lids streaked with black and blue; her dilated eyes showed white all round the iris. One shoulder of her gown had fallen; her thick dark-red hair stood out all round her face and fell tangled on her bared breast. He remembered the Gorgon's head in the Perseus room, and shook off the thought with horror. "Your father!" she cried to him. "Zagreus be my witness, you are clean of *that!*" Her fingers dug into his shoulders, so that he clenched his teeth with pain. "The day will come, yes it will come, when he will learn what part *he* had in you! Oh

yes, he will learn a greater was here before him!" Letting go, she
flung herself back on her elbows and began to laugh.

She rolled in her red hair, laughing in sobs, catching her breath
with shrill crowing gasps, the pitch of her laughter mounting louder
and higher. The boy, to whom this was new, knelt by her in stifling
terror, pulling at her hands, kissing her sweat-smeared face, calling
in her ear to her to stop, to speak to him; he was here with her, he,
Alexander; she must not go mad or he would die.

At last she moaned deeply, sat up, gathered him in her arms and
stroked her cheek against his head. Weak with relief, he lay against
her with closed eyes. "Poor boy, poor child. It was only the laugh-
ing-sickness; that is what he has brought me to. I should be ashamed,
before anyone but you; but you know what I have to bear. See,
darling, I know you, I am not mad. Though he would gladly see it,
the man who calls himself your father."

He opened his eyes and sat up. "When I'm a man, I'll see right
done you."

"Ah, he does not guess what you are. But I know. I and the god."

He asked no question. Enough had happened. Later, in the night,
when, empty with vomiting, he lay dry-lipped in bed listening to
the distant roar of the feast, her words came back to him.

Next day the games began. The two-horse chariots ran their laps,
the dismounter leaping off and running with the car and vaulting
on again. Phoinix, who had noticed the boy's hollow eyes and
guessed the cause, was glad to see him held by it.

He woke just before midnight, thinking of his mother. He got
out of bed and dressed. He had dreamed she called to him from the
sea, like the goddess mother of Achilles. He would go to her, and ask
her what she had meant last night.

Her room was empty. Only an old crone, belonging to the house,
crept muttering about, picking things up; they had all forgotten
her. She looked at him with a little wet red eye, and said the Queen
had gone to the Hekate shrine.

He slipped out into the night, among the drunks and whores and
soldiers and pickpurses. He needed to see her, whether she saw him
or not. He knew the way to the crossroads.

The city gates stood open for the festival. Far ahead were the
black cloaks and torch. It was a Hekate night, moonless; they did

not see him stalking them. She had to fend for herself, because she had not a son of age to help her. It was his business, what she did.

She had made her women wait, and gone on alone. He skirted the oleanders and the tamarisks, to the shrine with its three-faced image. She was there, with something whining and whimpering in her hands. She set her torch in the sooty socket by the altar-slab. She was all in black, and what she held was a young black dog. She held it up by the nape, and hacked a knife at its throat. It writhed and squealed, the whites of its eyes shone in the torchlight. Now she grasped it by its hind feet, jerking and choking while the blood ran down; when it only twitched, she laid it down on the altar. Kneeling before the image, she beat her fists on the ground. He heard the furious whisper, soft as a snake's, rise to a howl the dog itself might have made; the unknown words of the incantation, the known words of the curse. Her long hair trailed in the puddled blood; when she got up the ends were sticky, and her hands were clotted with black.

When it was over he tracked her home, keeping himself hidden. She looked familiar again, in her black cloak, walking among her women. He did not want to let her out of his sight.

Next day Epikrates said to Phoinix, "You must spare him to me today. I want to take him to the music contest." He had meant to go with friends, with whom he could discuss technique; but the boy's looks disturbed him. Like everyone else, he had heard the talk.

It was the contest for the kitharists. There was hardly a leading artist from the mainland or Greek Asia or the cities of Sicily and Italy, who had not come. The unguessed-at beauty caught the boy up, breaking his mood and throwing him straight into ecstasy. So Hektor, stunned by Ajax' great stone, had looked up at a voice that raised the hair on his head, and found Apollo standing by him.

After this, he took up his life much as before. His mother reminded him often with a sigh or a meaning look; but the shock had passed the worst, his body was strong and his age resilient; he sought healing as nature taught him. On the footslopes of Mount Olympos, he rode with Phoinix through chestnut groves, chanting line for line of Homer, first in Macedonian and then in Greek.

Phoinix would gladly have kept him from the women's rooms. But if once the Queen mistrusted his loyalty, the boy would be lost to him forever. She must not look for her son in vain. At least he seemed now to come away in better spirits.

He had found her busy with some plan which made her almost cheerful. He had waited in dread, at first, for her to come with her midnight torch, and fetch him to the Hekate shrine. She had never yet bade him call down a curse himself upon his father; the night they went to the tomb, he had only had to hold things and stand by.

Time passed; it was clearly no such thing; at last he even questioned her. She smiled, the subtle shadows curving under her cheekbones. He should know in good time, and it would surprise him. It was a service she had vowed to Dionysos; she promised he should be there. His spirits lightened. It must be the dancing for the god. These last two years she had been saying he was too old for women's mysteries. He was eight now. It had been bitter to think that Kleopatra would soon go with her instead.

Like the King, she gave audience to many foreign guests. Aristodemos the tragedian had come not to perform, but as a diplomat, a role often entrusted to well-known actors; he was arranging ransoms for Athenians taken at Olynthos. A slender elegant man, he managed his voice like a polished flute; one could almost see him caress it. Alexander admired the good sense of his mother's questions about the theater. Later she received Neoptolemos of Skyros, a protagonist even more distinguished, who was rehearsing for *The Bakchai*, playing the god. This time, the boy was absent.

He would not have known his mother was working magic, if he had not heard her through the door one day. Though the wood was thick, he caught some of the incantation. It was one he did not know, about killing a lion on the mountain; but the meaning was always the same. So he went away without knocking.

It was Phoinix who roused him at dawn to see the play. He was too young for the chairs of honor; he would sit with his father when he came of age. He had asked his mother if he could sit with her, as he had done till only last year; but she said she would not be watching, she had other business then. He must tell her afterwards how he had liked it.

He loved the theater; waking to a treat which would begin at once; the sweet morning smells, dew-laid dust, grass and herbs bruised by many feet, the smoke of the early workers' torches just quenched at daybreak; people clambering down the tiers, the deep buzz of the soldiers and peasants up at the top, the fuss with cushions and rugs down among the seats of honor, the chatter from the women's block; then suddenly the first notes of the flute, all other sound dying but the morning birdsong.

The play began eerily in the dawn-dusk; the god, masked as a beautiful fair-haired youth, saluting the fire on his mother's tomb, and planning revenge on the Theban King who scorned his rites. His young voice, the boy perceived, was being skillfully done by a man; his maenads had flat breasts, and cool boys' voices; but, this knowledge once stored away, he gave himself to the illusion.

Dark-haired young Pentheus spoke wickedly of the maenads and their rites. The god was bound to kill him. Several friends had described the plot beforehand. Pentheus' death was the most dreadful one could conceive; but Phoinix had promised one did not see it.

While the blind prophet rebuked the King, Phoinix whispered that this old voice from the mask was the same actor's who played the youthful god; such was the tragedian's art. When Pentheus had died offstage, this actor too would change masks, and enact the mad queen Agave.

Imprisoned by the King, the god broke out with fire and earthquake; the effects, set up by Athenian craftsmen, entranced the boy. Pentheus, defying miracles, infatuate for doom, still rejected the divinity. His last chance gone, Dionysos wound him in deadly magic and stole his wits away. He saw two suns in the sky; thought he could move mountains; yet let the mocking god disguise him absurdly as a woman, to spy on the maenad rites. The boy joined in the laughter whose edge was sharpened by the sense of terrors to come.

The King went off to his agony; the chorus sang; then the Messenger brought the news. Pentheus had climbed a tree to spy from; the maenads had seen him, and in their god-crazed strength uprooted it. His mad mother, seeing only a wild beast, had led them to tear him in pieces. It was over, and as Phoinix had said, need not be seen. The mere telling had been enough.

Agave was coming, cried the Messenger, with the trophy of her kill.

They ran in through the parodos in bloody robes. Queen Agave carried the head, spiked on a spear as hunters did it. It was made of the Pentheus mask and wig with stuffing in them, and bits of red rag hanging down. She wore a terrible mad mask, with an agonized brow, deep staring eyes and frenziedly grimacing mouth. From this mouth came a voice. At its first words, he sat as if he too had seen two suns in the sky. He was not far above the stage; his ears and eyes were sharp. The wig of her mask was fair; but in its streaming tresses live hair was spilling through, the dark red showed clearly. The Queen's arms were bare. He knew them; even their bracelets.

The players, enacting shock and horror, drew back to give her the stage. The audience began to buzz; they had heard at once, after the sexless boys, that this was a real woman. Who . . . what . . . ? The boy seemed to himself to have been hours alone with his knowledge, before questions began to get answers and the word ran round. It spread like a brush fire; good eyes insisting to dim ones, the women's high chatter and outraged sibilance; the deep ebb-shoal murmur from the men above; from the seats of honor, a stunned dead silence.

The boy sat as if his own head had been transfixed. His mother tossed her hair and gestured at the bleeding trophy. She had grown into the dreadful mask, it had become her face. He broke his nails, gripping the edge of his stone seat.

The flautist blew on his double pipes; she sang:

> *I am exalted,*
> *Great upon earth!*
> *Let men praise me—*
> *This hunt was mine!*

Two rows down, the boy saw his father's back, as he turned towards a guest beside him. His face was out of sight.

The curse in the tomb, the black dog's blood, the thorn-pierced mammet, had all been secret rites. This was the Hekate spell by daylight, a sacrifice for a death. The head on the Queen's spear was her son's.

It was the voices all around that roused him from the nightmare. They waked him into another. They rose like the hum of flies disturbed from carrion, almost drowning the actors' lines.

It was of her they were talking, not of Queen Agave in the play.

[65]

They were talking of her! The southerners who said Macedon was barbarous; the lords and farmers and peasants. The soldiers were talking.

A sorceress they might call her. The goddesses worked magic. This was another thing; he knew these voices. So the men of the phalanx talked in the guardroom, about a woman half of them had had; or some village wife with a bastard.

Phoinix too was suffering. A steady man rather than a quick one, he had been stunned at first; he had not thought even Olympias capable of such wildness. Without doubt, she had vowed this to Dionysos while giddy with wine and dancing at her rites. He began to put out a hand for comfort; looked again and refrained.

Queen Agave came out of frenzy to knowledge and despair; the relentless god appeared above, to close the play. The chorus sang the tag-lines.

> *The gods have many faces,*
> *And many fates fulfill,*
> *To work their will.*

> *The end expected comes not;*
> *God brings the unthought to be,*
> *As here we see.*

It was finished; but no one stirred to go. What would she do? She made a reverence to the cult-statue of Dionysos in the orchestra, before sweeping out with the others; some extra picked up the head; it was clear she would not return. From high up in the faceless crush of men came a long shrill whistle.

The protagonist came back to take absent-minded applause. He had not been at his best, with this freak on his mind; however, it had been made well worth his while.

The boy rose, without looking at Phoinix. Chin up, looking straight ahead, he thrust his way through the lingering, chattering crowd. All along their way, talk stopped for them; but not soon enough. Just outside the propylon, he turned round, looked Phoinix in the face, and said, "She was better than the actors."

"Yes indeed. The god inspired her. It was her dedication to do him honor. Such offerings are very pleasing to Dionysos."

They came out into the square of tramped earth outside the theater. The women, in twittering groups, were drifting homeward, the men standing about. Close by, exempt from convention, stood a cluster of well-dressed hetairas, expensive girls from Ephesos and Corinth, who served the officers at Pella. One said in a sweet carrying voice, "Poor dear little lad, you can see he feels it." Without turning, the boy walked on.

They were nearly out of the press; Phoinix was starting to breathe more easily, then found him gone. How not, indeed? But no; there he was not twenty feet off, near a huddle of talking men. Phoinix heard their laughter; he ran, but was still too late.

The man who had spoken the last and unambiguous word, had been aware of nothing amiss. But another, whose back was to the boy, felt a quick low tug at his sword belt. Looking about at man-height, he was only just in time to knock up the boy's arm. The man who had spoken got the dagger along his side, instead of straight in his belly.

It had been so swift and silent, no bystander had turned. The group stood stock-still; the stabbed man with a snake of blood running down his leg; the dagger's owner, who had grabbed the boy before he saw who it was, gazing blankly at the stained weapon in his hand; Phoinix behind the boy, both hands on his shoulders; the boy staring into the face of the wounded man, and finding it one he knew. The man, clutching the warm ooze from his side, stared back in astonishment and pain; then with a shock of recognition.

Breath was drawn in all round. Before anyone spoke, Phoinix lifted his hand as if he had been at war; his square face grew bull-like, they would hardly have known him. "It will be better for you all to keep your mouths shut." He pulled at the boy, breaking off the exchange of looks still unresolved, and led him away.

Knowing nowhere else to hide him, he took him to his own lodging in the one good street of the little town. The small room was frowsty with old wool, old scrolls, old bedding, and the ointment Phoinix rubbed on his stiff knees. On the bed, with its blanket of blue and red squares, the boy fell face down and lay soundless. Phoinix patted his shoulders and his head, and, when he broke into convulsive weeping, gathered him up.

Beyond this instant and its needs, the man saw no call to look.

His love, being sexless, seemed to him proved selfless. Certainly he would have given all he had, shed his own blood. Much less was wanted now, only comfort and a healing word.

"A filthy fellow. Small loss if you had killed him. No man of honor could let it pass . . . A godless fellow who mocks a dedication . . . There, my Achilles, don't weep that the warrior came out in you. He'll mend, it's more than he deserves; and keep quiet if he knows what's good for him. No one shall hear a word from me."

The boy choked into Phoinix' shoulder. "He made me my bow."

"Throw it out, I'll get you a better."

There was a pause. "It wasn't said to me. He didn't know I was there."

"And who wants such a friend?"

"He wasn't ready."

"Nor were you, to hear him."

Gently, with a careful courtesy, the boy disengaged himself, and lay down again with his face hidden. Presently he sat up, wiping his hand across his eyes and nose. Phoinix wrung out a towel from the ewer and cleaned his face. He say staring, saying "Thank you" now and then.

Phoinix got out his best silver cup from his pillow-box, and the last of his breakfast wine. The boy drank, with a little coaxing; it seemed to run straight through to his skin, flushing his drawn face, his throat and breast. Presently he said, "He insulted my kin. But he wasn't ready." He shook out his hair, pulled down his creased chiton, retied a loosened sandal string. "Thank you for having me in your house. Now I am going to ride."

"Now that's foolish. You've had no breakfast yet."

"I have had enough, thank you. Goodbye."

"Wait, then, I'll change and go with you."

"No, thank you. I want to go alone."

"No, no; let's be quiet awhile, read, or go walking—"

"*Let me go.*"

Phoinix' hand withdrew like a scared child's.

Later, going to see, he found the boy's riding-boots gone, his pony, his practice javelins. Phoinix hurried about for word of him. He had been seen above the town, riding towards Mount Olympos.

It still wanted some hours to noon. Phoinix, waiting his return, heard people agree that the Queen had done this outlandish thing as an offering. Epirotes were mystai with their mothers' milk, but it would do her no good with Macedonians. The King had put the best face he could on it for the guests, and been civil to Neoptolemos the tragedian. And where was young Alexander?

Oh, gone riding, answered Phoinix, hiding his mounting fear. What had possessed him, to let the boy walk off like a grown man? He should not have let him a moment out of his sight. No use to follow; in the huge Olympian massif, two armies could be hidden from one another. There were fathomless crags, whose feet were inaccessible; there were boar, wolves, leopards; even lions lived there still.

The sun westered; the steep eastern faces, under which Dion stood, grew darker; cloud swirled round the hidden summits. Phoinix rode about, quartering the cleared land above the town. At the foot of a sacred oak he stretched up his arms to the ever-sunlit peak, King Zeus' throne bathed in its clear aether. Weeping he prayed and vowed his offerings. When night came, he would be able to hide the truth no longer.

The great shadow of Olympos crept beyond the shoreline, and quenched the sea's evening glow. Dusk filled the oak grove; further in, the woods were already black. Between the dusk and the night, something moved. He flung himself on his horse, his stiff joints stabbing him, and rode towards it.

The boy came down through the trees, walking at the pony's head. The beast, bone-weary, head down, plodded beside him, pecking a little with one foot. They moved steadily down the glade; when the boy saw Phoinix, he raised his hand in greeting, but did not speak.

His javelins were tied across his saddlecloth; he did not yet own a holster. The pony like a conspirator leaned its cheek to his. His clothes were torn, his knees grazed and caked with dirt, his arms and legs scribbled with scratches; he seemed, since morning, visibly to have lost weight. His chiton was darkened all down the front with blood. He came calmly forward between the trees, his eyes hollow and dilated; walking lightly, floatingly; inhumanly tranquil and serene.

Phoinix dismounted by him, grasping, scolding, questioning. The

[69]

boy ran his hand over the pony's nose and said, "He was going lame."

"I have been running about here, half out of my mind. What have you done to yourself? Where are you bleeding? Where have you been?"

"I'm not bleeding." He held out his hands, which he had rinsed in some mountain stream; there was blood around the nails. His eyes dwelt on Phoinix', revealing only the impenetrable. "I made an altar and a shrine, and sacrificed to Zeus." He lifted his head; his white brow under the springing peak of hair looked transparent, almost luminous. His eyes widened and glowed in their deep sockets. "I sacrificed to the god. And he spoke to me. *He spoke to me.*"

3

KING ARCHELAOS' STUDY was more splendid than the Perseus Room, having been nearer his heart. Here he had received the poets and philosophers whom his open-handed hospitality and rich guest-gifts had tempted up to Pella. On the sphinx-headed arms of the chair from Egypt had rested the hands of Agathon and of Euripides.

The Muses, to whom the room was dedicated, sang round Apollo in a vast mural which filled the inner wall. Apollo, as he played his lyre, gazed out inscrutably at the polished shelving with its precious books and scrolls. Tooled binding, cases gilded and jeweled; finials of ivory, agate and sardonyx; tassels of silk and bullion; from reign to reign, even during the succession wars, these treasures had been dusted and tended by well-trained slaves. It was a generation since anyone else had read in them. They were too valuable; the real books were in the library.

There was an exquisite Athenian bronze of Hermes inventing the lyre, bought from some bankrupt in the last years of the city's greatness; two standing lamps, in the form of columns twined with laurel boughs, stood by the huge writing-table inlaid with lapis and chalcedony, and supported on lions' feet. All this was little changed since Archelaos' day. But through the door at the far end, the painted walls of the reading-cell had vanished behind racks and shelves, stuffed with the documents of administration; its couch and table given place to a laden desk, where the Chief Secretary was working through the day's letter-bag.

It was a sharp bright March day with a northeast wind. The fretted shutters had been closed to keep the papers from blowing about; a cold dazzling sun came splintering through, mixed with icy drafts. The Chief Secretary had a heated brick hidden in his cloak to warm his hands on; his clerk blew enviously on his fingers, but silently lest the King should hear. King Philip sat at ease. He had just come back from campaign in Thrace; after winter there, he thought his Palace a Sybaris of comfort.

As his power reached steadily towards the immemorial corn route of the Hellespont, the gullet of all Greece; as he encircled colonies, wrested from Athens the allegiance of tribal lands, laid siege to her allies' cities, the southerners counted it among their bitterest wrongs that he had broken the old decent rule of abandoning war in wintertime, when even bears holed up.

He sat at the great table, his brown scarred hand, chapped with cold and calloused from reins and spear-shaft, grasping a silver stylos he kept to pick his teeth with. On a cross-legged stool, a clerk with a tablet on his knees waited to take a letter to a client lord in Thessaly.

There he could see his way; it was business of the south had brought him home. At last his foot was in the door. In Delphi, the impious Phokians were turning like mad dogs on one another, worn out with war and guilt. They had had a good run for the money they had melted down, coining the temple treasures for soldiers' pay; now far-shooting Apollo was after them. He knew how to wait; on the day they had dug below the Tripod itself for gold, he had sent the earthquake. Then panic, frantic mutual accusations, exilings, torturings. The losing leader now held with his outcast force the strongpoints of Thermopylae, a desperate man who could soon be treated with. Already he had turned back a garrison relief from Athens, though they were the Phokians' allies; he feared being handed over to the ruling faction. Soon he would be ripe and ready. Leonidas under his heavy grave-mound, thought Philip, must be tossing in his sleep.

Go tell the Spartans, traveler passing by . . . Go tell them all Greece will obey me within ten years, because city cannot keep faith with city, nor man with man. They have forgotten even what you could show them, how to stand and die. Envy and greed have conquered them for me. They will follow me, and be reborn from it; under me they shall win back their pride. They will look to me to lead them; and their sons will look to my son.

The peroration reminded him he had sent for the boy some time ago. No doubt he would come when found; at ten years, one did not expect them to be sitting still. Philip returned his thoughts to his letter.

Before he was through it, he heard his son's voice outside, greeting the bodyguard. How many score—or hundred—men did the boy know by name? This one had only been in the Guard five days.

The tall doors opened. He looked small between them, shining and compact, his feet bare on the cold floor of figured marble, his arms folded inside his cloak, not to warm them, but in the well-drilled posture of modest Spartan boyhood, taught him by Leonidas. In this room served by pale bookish men, father and son had the gloss of wild animals among tame: the swarthy soldier, tanned almost black, his arms striped with pink cockled war-scars, the forehead crossed with the light band left by the helmet-rim, his blind eye with its milky fleck staring out under the half-drooped lid; the boy at the door, his brown silky skin flawed only with the grazes and scratches of a boy's adventures, his heavy tousled hair making Archelaos' gildings look dusty. His homespun clothes, softened and bleached by many washings and beatings on the river stones, long since subdued to their wearer, now carried his style as if he had chosen them himself in a willful arrogance. His grey eyes, which the cold slanting sun had lightened, kept to themselves some thought he had brought with him.

"Come in, Alexander." He was already doing so; Philip had spoken only to be heard, resenting this withdrawal.

Alexander came forward, noting that like a servant he had been given leave to enter. The glow of the wind outside ebbed from his face, the skin seemed to change its texture, becoming more opaque. He had been thinking at the door that Pausanias, the new bodyguard, had the sort of looks his father liked. If anything came of it, for a time there might be no new girl. There was a certain look one came to know, when they met one's eyes, or did not; it had not happened yet.

He came up to the desk and waited, his hands disposed in his cloak. One part of the Spartan deportment, however, Leonidas had never managed to impose; he should have been looking down till his elders spoke to him.

Philip, meeting the steady eyes, felt a stab of familiar pain. Even hate might have been better. He had seen such a look in the eyes of men prepared to die before they would yield the gate or the pass; not a challenge, an inward thing. How have I deserved it? It is that witch, who comes with her poison whenever my back is turned, to steal my son.

Alexander had been meaning to ask his father about the Thracian battle-order; accounts had differed, but he would know . . . Not now, however.

Philip sent out the clerk, and motioned the boy to the empty stool. As he sat straight-backed on the scarlet sheepskin, Philip felt him already poised to go.

It pleased Philip's enemies, hate being blinder than love, to think his men in the Greek cities had all alike been bought. But though none lost by serving him, there were many who would have taken nothing from him, had they not first been won by charm. "Here," he said, picking up from the desk a glittering tangle of soft leather. "What do you make of this?"

The boy turned it over; at once his long square-ended fingers began to work, slipping thongs under or over, pulling, straightening. As order came out of chaos his face grew intent, full of grave pleasure. "It's a sling and a shot-bag. It should go on a belt, through here. Where do they do this work?"

The bag was stitched with gold plaques cut out in the bold, stylized, flowing forms of stags. Philip said, "It was found on a Thracian chief, but it comes from far north, from the plains of grass. It's Scythian."

Alexander pored over this trophy from the edge of the Kinnerian wilderness, thinking of the endless steppes beyond the Ister, the fabled burial grounds of the kings with their rings of dead riders staked around them, horses and men withering in the dry cold air.

His longing to know more was too much for him; in the end he asked all his stored-up questions. They talked for some time.

"Well, try the sling; I brought it for you. See what you can bring down. But don't go off too far. The Athenian envoys are on the way."

The sling lay in the boy's lap, remembered only by his hands. "About the peace?"

"Yes. They landed at Halos and asked for safe-conduct through the lines, without waiting for the herald. They are in a hurry, it seems."

"The roads are bad."

"Yes, they'll need to thaw out before I hear them. When I do, you may come and listen. This will be serious business; it is time you saw how things are done."

"I'll stay near Pella. I'd like to come."

"At last, we may see action out of talk. They have been buzzing like a kicked bee-skep ever since I took Olynthos. Half last year they were touting the southern cities, trying to work up a league against us. Nothing came of it but dusty feet."

"Were they *all* afraid?"

"Not all; but all mistrusted each other. Some trusted men who trusted me. I shall redeem their trust."

The fine inner ends of the boy's light-brown eyebrows drew together, almost meeting, outlining the heavy bone-shelf over his deep-set eyes. "Wouldn't even the Spartans fight?"

"To serve under Athenians? They won't lead, they've had their bellyful; and they'll never follow." He smiled to himself. "And they're not the audience for a speechmaker beating his breast in tears, or scolding like a market-woman shortchanged of an obol."

"When Aristodemos came back here about that man Iatrokles' ransom, he told me he thought the Athenians would vote for peace."

It was long since such remarks had had power to startle Philip. "Well, to encourage them, I had Iatrokles home before him, ransom free. Let them send me envoys by all means. If they think they can bring Phokis into their treaty, or Thrace either, they are fools; but so much the better, they can be voting on it while I act. Never discourage your enemies from wasting time . . . Iatrokles will be an envoy; so will Aristodemos. That should do us no harm."

"He recited some Homer at supper, when he was here. Achilles and Hektor, before they fight. But he's too old."

"That comes to us all. Oh, and Philokrates will be there, of course." He did not waste time in saying that this was his chief Athenian agent; the boy would be sure to know. "He will be treated like all the others; it would do him no good at home to be singled out. There are ten, in all."

"*Ten?*" said the boy staring. "What for? Will they all make speeches?"

"Oh, they need them all to watch each other. Yes, they will all speak, not one will consent to be passed over. Let us hope they agree beforehand to divide their themes. At least there will be one showpiece. Demosthenes is coming."

The boy seemed to prick his ears, like a dog called for a walk. Philip looked at his kindling face. Was every enemy of his a hero to his son?

Alexander was thinking about the eloquence of Homer's warriors. He pictured Demosthenes tall and dark, like Hektor, with a voice of bronze and flaming eyes.

"Is he brave? Like the men at Marathon?"

Philip, to whom this question came as from another world, paused to bring round his mind to it, and smiled sourly in his black beard. "See him and guess. But do not ask him to his face."

A slow flush spread up from the boy's fair-skinned neck into his hair. His lips met hard. He said nothing.

In anger he looked just like his mother. It always got under Philip's skin. "Can't you tell," he said impatiently, "when a man is joking? You're as touchy as a girl."

How dare he, thought the boy, speak of girls to me? His hands clenched on the sling, so that the gold bit into them.

Now, Philip thought, all the good work was undone. He cursed in his heart his wife, his son, himself. Forcing ease into his voice, he said, "Well, we shall both see for ourselves, I know him no more than you." This was less than honest; through his agents' reports, he felt he had lived with the man for years. Feeling wronged, he indulged a little malice. Let the boy keep himself to himself, then, and his expectations too.

A few days later, he sent for him again. For both, the time had been full; for the man with business, for the boy with the perennial search for new tests on which to stretch himself, rock-clefts to leap, half-broke horses to ride, records to beat at throwing and running. He had been taught a new piece, too, on his new kithara.

"They should be here by nightfall," Philip said. "They will rest in the morning; after luncheon I shall hear them. There is a public dinner at night; so time should limit their eloquence. Of course, you will wear court dress."

His mother kept his best clothes. He found her in her room, writing a letter to her brother in Epiros, complaining of her husband. She wrote well, having much business she did not trust to a scribe. When he came she closed the diptych, and took him in her arms.

"I have to dress," he told her, "for the Athenian envoys. I'll wear the blue."

"I know just what suits you, darling."

"No, but it must be right for Athenians. I'll wear the blue."

"T-tt! My lord must be obeyed. The blue, then, the lapis brooch . . ."

"No, only women wear jewels in Athens, except for rings."

"But my darling, it is proper you outdress them. They are nothing, these envoys."

"No, Mother. They think jewels barbarous. I shan't wear them."

She had begun lately to hear this new voice sometimes. It pleased her. She had never yet conceived of its being used against her.

"You shall be all man, then, my lord." Seated as she was, she could lean on him and look up. She stroked his windblown hair. "Come in good time; you are as wild as a mountain lion, I must see to this myself."

When evening came, he said to Phoinix, "I want to stay up, please, to see the Athenians come."

Phoinix looked out with distaste at the lowering dusk. "What do you expect to see?" he grumbled. "A parcel of men with their hats pulled down to their cloaks. With this ground-mist tonight, you'll not know master from servant."

"Never mind. I want to see."

The night came on raw and dank. The rushes dripped by the

[77]

lake, the frogs trilled ceaselessly like a noise in the head. A wind-less mist hung round the sedge, winding with the lagoon till it met the breeze off the sea. In the streets of Pella, muddy runnels carried ten days' filth and garbage down to the rain-pocked water. Alexander stood at the window of Phoinix' room, where he had gone to rouse him out. He himself was dressed already in his riding-boots and hooded cloak. Phoinix sat at his book with lamp and brazier, as if they had the night before them. "Look! There are the outriders' torches coming round the bend."

"Good, now you can keep your eye on them. I shall go out in the weather when it is time, and not a moment sooner."

"It's hardly raining. What will you do when we go to war?"

"I am saving myself for that, Achilles. Don't forget Phoinix had his bed made up by the fire."

"I'll set light to that book of yours, if you don't hurry. You've not even got your boots on." He hung in the window; small with dark-ness and furred with mist, the torches seemed to creep like glow-worms on a stone. "Phoinix . . . ?"

"Yes, yes. There's time enough."

"Does he mean to treat for peace? Or just to keep them quiet till he's ready, like the Olynthians?"

Phoinix laid down his book on his knee. "Achilles, dear child." He dropped artfully into the magic rhythm. "Be just to royal Peleus, your honored father." Not long ago, he had dreamed he stood on a stage, robed to play Leader of the Chorus in a tragedy, of which only one page had yet been written. The rest was already on the wax, but not fair-copied, and he had begged the poet to change the ending; but when he tried to recall it, he remembered only his tears. "It was the Olynthians who first broke faith. They treated with the Athenians, and took in his enemies, both against their oath. Everyone knows a treaty is made void by oath-breaking."

"The cavalry generals gave up their own men in the field." The boy's voice rose a tone. "He paid them to do it. *Paid them.*"

"It must have saved a good many lives."

"They are slaves! I would rather die."

"If all men would rather, there would be no slaves."

"I shall never use traitors, never, when I'm King. If they come to me I shall kill them. I don't care whom they offer to sell me, if he's my greatest enemy, I shall still send him their heads. I hate them like the gates of death. This man Philokrates, he's a traitor."

"He may do good in spite of it. Your father means well by the Athenians."

"If they do as he tells them."

"Come, one might suppose he meant to set up a tyranny. When the Spartans conquered them in my father's day, then indeed they had one. You know your history well enough, when you've a mind. As far back as Agamemnon the High King, the Hellenes have had a war-leader; either a city or a man. How was the host called out to Troy? How were the barbarians turned in Xerxes' war? Only now in our day they snap and bicker like pi-dogs, and no one leads."

"You don't make them sound worth leading. They can't have changed so soon."

"Two generations running, there has been a great killing of their best. In my opinion, the Athenians and the Spartans have both drawn Apollo's curse, since they hired out troops to the Phokians. They knew well enough what gold was used to pay them. Wherever that gold has gone, it has brought death and ruin, and we have not seen the end of it. Now your father, he took the god's part, and look how he has prospered; it is the talk of Greece. Who is more fit for the leader's scepter? And one day, it will come to you."

"I had rather—" the boy began slowly. "Oh, look, they're past the Sacred Grove, almost in town. Hurry, get ready."

As they mounted in the muddy stable yard, Phoinix said, "Keep your hood well down. When they see you at the audience, you don't want them to know you were out in the street, staring at them like a peasant. What you expect from this outing is more than I can guess."

They backed their horses into a little grassy patch before a hero-shrine. Overhanging chestnut buds, half unfurled, looked like worked bronze against the pale watery clouds which filtered the moonlight. The outriders' torches, burned almost to the sockets, danced to the mules' pacing in the quiet air. They showed the leading envoy escorted by Antipatros; Alexander would have known the general's big bones and square beard, even if he had been muffled like the others; but having just come from Thrace, he thought it a warm night. The other must be Philokrates. The body shapeless in its wraps, the face peering between cloak and hat, looked the soul of evil. Riding after, he recognized the grace of Aristodemos. So much for those. His eye raked through the train of riders, mostly craning under their limp hat-brims to see where their horses' feet were going in the muck. Not far from the tail, a tall well-built man was sitting up like a soldier. He was short-bearded, seemed neither old nor young; the torchlight showed up a bold bony profile. When he had passed, the boy looked after, fitting the face upon his dreams. He had seen great Hektor, who would not be old before Achilles was ready.

Demosthenes son of Demosthenes, of Paiania, woke at first light in the royal guest-house, pushed up his head a little from the clothes, and looked around him. The room was grandiose, with a green marble floor; the pilasters at door and window had gilded capitals; the stool for his clothes was inlaid with ivory; the chamber-pot was Italian ware with garlands in relief. The rain was over, but the gusty air felt freezing. He had three blankets and could have done with as many more. Need for the pot had waked him; but it was at the far side of the room. The floor was rugless. He lingered in discomfort, hunched in his folded arms. Swallowing, he felt a soreness in his throat. His fears, first formed during the ride, were realized; on this day of all days, he was starting a cold in the head.

He thought with longing of his snug house in Athens, where Kyknos, his Persian slave, would have fetched more blankets, brought up the pot, and brewed the hot posset of herbs and honey which soothed and toned his throat. Now he lay like the great Euripides who had met his end here, sick among barbaric splendors. Was he to be one more sacrifice to this harsh land, breeder of pirates and tyrants; the crag of that black eagle which hung ravening over Hellas, ready to swoop on any city which flagged, stumbled or bled? Yet with the pinions darkening the sky above them, they would straggle after petty gains or feuds and scorn the shepherd's warning. Today he would meet the great predator face to face; and his nose was thickening.

On the ship, on the road, he had been over and over his speech. It would come last; for to settle contested precedence on the way,

[80]

they had agreed it should go by age. Eagerly, while others thrust forward evidence of seniority, he had proclaimed himself the youngest, hardly believing they could be so blind to what they were giving away. Not till the final list had been drawn up, had he seen his handicap.

From the distant pot, his eye moved to the other bed. His roommate, Aischines, slept soundly on his back; his height had pushed his feet nearly through the bedclothes, his broad chest gave resonance to his snores. When he woke, he would run briskly to the window, do the showy voice exercises he kept up from his theater days, and, if one mentioned the cold, say it had been worse in some army bivouac or other. He would speak ninth, Demosthenes tenth. No good, he felt, seemed ever to reach him unalloyed. He had the final word, an asset beyond price in the law courts, and no price could buy it. But some of the best arguments had been claimed by earlier speakers; and then he must follow this man's portentous presence, his deep voice and artful sense of timing, his actor's memory which could keep him going a run of the water-clock without a note, and—most enviable gift of the unjust gods—his power to speak extempore at need.

A mere nobody, pinchpenny reared, his schoolmaster father beating enough letters into him to give him a pittance from clerking; his mother a priestess of some immigrant back-street cult, which ought to be put down by law; who was he to swagger in the Assembly, amongst men taught in the schools of rhetoric? No doubt he kept going on bribes; but nowadays one heard forever about his forebears, eupatrids of course—that worn-out tale!—ruined in the Great War, his military record in Euboia, and his tedious mention in dispatches.

A kite screamed in the raw air, a piercing gust blew round the bed. Demosthenes clutched the blankets round his meager frame, recalling bitterly how last night, when he had complained of the marble floor, Aischines had said offhandedly, "I should have thought you'd mind it the least, with your northern blood." It was years since anyone had brought up his grandfather's metic marriage to his Scythian grandmother; only his father's wealth had scraped him citizenship, but he had thought it all forgotten long ago. Staring down his cold nose at the sleeping form, putting off a moment longer the urgent walk to the pot, he murmured viciously, "You were an usher, I was a student; you were an acolyte, I was an initiate; you copied the minutes, I moved the motion; you were third actor, I sat in front." He had never in fact seen Aischines play; but his wishes added, "You were booed off, I hissed."

The marble was green ice underfoot, his urine steamed in the air. His bed would be cold already; he could only dress now, keep moving and stir his blood. If Kyknos were only here! But the Council had bidden them hurry; the others had stupidly offered to dispense with attendants; it would have been worth a thousand words to any hostile orator, if he alone had brought one.

A pale sun was rising; the wind grew less; it might be warmer out than in this marble tomb. The paved garden-court was empty, but for one slave-boy loitering. He would take his roll with him, and run over his speech again. Doing it here would wake Aischines, who would express surprise at his still needing a script, and boast of having always been a quick study.

No one stirred in the house but slaves. He glanced at each, in search of Greeks; many Athenians had been caught in the siege of Olynthos, and all the envoys had commissions to arrange ransoms where they could. He had resolved to redeem any he found, if it had to be at his own cost. In the bitter cold, in this haughty and boastful Palace, he warmed his heart at the thought of Athens.

His childhood had been pampered, his boyhood wretched. His rich merchant father had died leaving him to uncaring guardians. He had been a puny lad, exciting no one's desire but readily excited; in the boys' gymnasium this had been starkly exposed, and the dirty nickname had stuck to him for years. In his teens he had known his guardians were robbing his inheritance; he had no one to fight his lawsuit but himself, with his nervous stutter. He had trained stubbornly, wearily, in secret, copying actors and rhetors, till he was ready; but when he won, the money was two-thirds gone. He had made a living at the one thing he had skill in, building up capital from such pickings as were half-respectable; and at last had begun to taste the great wine of power, when the crowd on the Pnyx was one ear, one voice, and his. All these years, he had armored his tender bruised pride in the pride of Athens. She should be great again; it should be his victor's trophy, one to last till the end of time.

He hated many men, some with good cause, others from envy; but more than them all he hated the man, still unseen, in the heart of this old hubristic Palace, the Macedonian tyrant who would debase her to a client city. In the hallway, a blue-tattooed Thracian slave was scrubbing. The sense of being an Athenian, inferior to no other breed on earth, sustained him now as always. King Philip should learn what it meant. Yes, he would sew up the man's mouth, as they said in the law courts. He had assured his colleagues of that.

If the King could be defied, there would have been no embassy. Yet subtly, with reminders of old bonds, one could prick out neatly enough his broken promises, reassurances meant only to gain him time, his playing off of city against city, faction against faction; his comfort to Athens' enemies while he seduced or crushed her friends. The preamble was word-perfect; but he had a telling little anecdote to work in just after, which could do with polishing. He had the other envoys to impress, as well as Philip; in the long run they might matter more. He would publish, in any case.

The paved court was scattered with windblown twigs. Against its low wall stood pots of pruned leafless rose trees; was it possible they ever flowered? The far skyline was a blue-white mountain range, split with black gorges, skirted with forests as thick as fur. Two young men ran past, cloakless, beyond the wall, calling to each other in their barbaric patois. Flogging his chest with his arms, stamping his feet, swallowing in a vain hope that his sore throat might be better, he allowed the unwilling thought that men reared in Macedon must be hardy. Even the slave-boy, who should no doubt have been sweeping the twigs away, seemed at ease in his one drab garment, sitting on the wall, warm enough to be idle. His master, though, might at least have given him shoes.

To work, to work. He opened his scroll at the second paragraph, and, pacing to keep from freezing, began to speak, trying it this way and that. The linking of cadence with cadence, rise with fall, attack with persuasion, made each finished speech a seamless garment. If some interjection forced reply, he made it as brief as he could, never happy till he was back with the written script. Only when well rehearsed was he at his best.

"Such," he told the air, "were the generous services of our city to your father Amyntas. But since I have spoken of things which are naturally outside your remembrance since you were unborn, let me speak of kindnesses you witnessed and received yourself." He paused; at this point Philip would be curious. "And kinsmen of yours who are now old will bear out what I say. For after your father Amyntas, and your uncle Alexandros, both were dead, while your brother Perdikkas and yourself were children, Eurydike your mother had been betrayed by those who had claimed to be her friends; and the exiled Pausanias was returning to contest the throne, favored by opportunity, and not without support."

Walking and declaiming together made him pause for breath. He became aware that the slave-boy had jumped down from the wall to walk just behind him. In a moment, he was returned to the years of mockery. He turned round sharply, to catch a grin or lewd gesture; but the boy looked back with a grave open face and clear grey eyes. He must be held by the mere novelty of gestures and inflections, like some young animal by a shepherd's flute. One was used, at home, to servants coming and going while one rehearsed.

"When, therefore, our general, Iphikrates, came into those parts, Eurydike your mother sent for him, and, as all who were there confirm, she led into his arms your elder brother Perdikkas; and you who were only a little child she put on his knee. 'The father of these orphans,' she said, 'while he lived, adopted you as his son . . .'"

He stopped in his tracks. The boy's stare had pierced his back. To be gaped at like a mountebank by this peasant brat was growing tiresome. He made a shooing gesture, as if sending home a dog.

The boy fell back a few steps, and paused looking up, his head tilted a little. In rather stilted Greek, with a strong Macedonian accent, he said, "Do please go on. Go on about Iphikrates."

Demosthenes started. Used to addressing thousands, he found this audience of one, only now disclosed, absurdly disconcerting. Moreover, what did it mean? Though dressed like a slave, this could not be a garden-boy. Who had sent him, and why?

A closer scrutiny showed him clean, even to his hair. One could guess what that meant, when it went with looks like these. This was his master's bedfellow, without a doubt, employed, young as he was, on the man's secret business. Why had he been listening? Demosthenes had not lived among intrigue for thirty years in vain. His mind explored, in moments, half a dozen possibilities. Was some creature of Philip's trying to brief him in advance? But so young a spy was too unlikely. What else, then? A message? Then for whom?

Somewhere, among the ten of them, must be a man in Philip's pay. On the journey the thought had haunted him. He had begun to doubt Philokrates. How had he paid for his big new house, and brought his son a racehorse? His manner had changed, as they got near Macedon.

"What is it?" asked the boy.

He became aware that while he had been engrossed within himself, he had been observed. An unreasoning anger rose in him. Slowly and clearly, in the kitchen Greek one used to foreign slaves, he said, "What do you want? You look someone? Which master?"

The boy tilted his head, began to speak, and seemed to change his mind. In Greek which was quite correct, and less accented than before, he said, "Can you please tell me if Demosthenes has gone out yet?"

Even to himself, he did not admit feeling affronted. His ingrained caution made him say, "We are all envoys alike. You can tell me what you want with him."

"Nothing," said the boy, unmoved it seemed by the voice of inquisition. "I only want to see him."

There seemed no more to be gained by hedging. "I am he. What have you to say to me?"

The boy gave one of those smiles with which civil children meet inept grown-up jokes. "I know which he is. Who are you really?"

These were deep waters indeed! A secret beyond price might be in reach here. Instinctively he looked about him. The house might be full of eyes; he had no one to help, to hold the boy and stop him from crying out, which would stir up a hornets' nest. Often, in Athens, he had stood beside the rack, when slaves were questioned as law allowed; there must be something for them to fear more than their masters, or they would never witness against them. Now and then they had been as young as this; one could not be soft in a prosecution. However, here he was among barbarians, no legal resource at hand. He must do as best he could.

[85]

Just then, from the guest-room window, a deep melodious voice started running up and down the scale. Aischines stood, his bare torso visible to the waist, his broad chest expanded. The boy, who had turned at the sound, cried, "There he is!"

Demosthenes' first feeling was blind fury. His stored envy, goaded and taunted, almost burst him. But one must be calm, one must think, go step by step. There, then, was the traitor! Aischines! He could have wished for no one better. But he must have evidence, a lead; it was too much to hope for proof.

"That," he said, "is Aischines son of Atrometos, an actor by trade till lately. Those are actors' exercises he is doing. Anyone in the guest-house will tell you who he is. Ask, if you wish."

Slowly the boy gazed from man to man. Slowly a crimson flush spread from his chest, dyeing his clear skin up to his brow. He remained quite silent.

Now, thought Demosthenes, we may learn something to the purpose. One thing was certain—the thought thrust in, even while he pondered his next move—he had never seen a handsomer boy. The blood showed like wine poured into alabaster and held up to the light. Desire became insistent, disturbing calculation. Later, later; everything might hang upon keeping one's head now. When he had found out who owned the boy, he might try to buy him. Kyknos had long since lost his looks, and was merely useful. One would need to take care, use a reliable agent . . . This was folly. He should have been pinned down in his first confusion. Demosthenes said sharply, "And now tell me the truth, no lies. What did you want with Aischines? Come, out with it. I know enough already."

He has paused too long; the boy had collected himself; he looked quite insolent. "I don't think you do," he said.

"Your message for Aischines. Come, no lies, what was it?"

"Why should I tell lies? I'm not afraid of you."

"We shall see. What did you want with him?"

"Nothing. Nor with you, either."

"You are an impudent boy. I suppose your master spoils you." He went on to improve on this, for his own satisfaction.

The boy had followed the intention, it seemed, if not the Greek. "Goodbye," he said curtly.

[86]

This would never do. "Wait! Don't run off before I have finished speaking. Whom do you serve?"

Coolly, with a slight smile, the boy looked up. "Alexander."

Demosthenes frowned; it seemed to be the name of every third well-born Macedonian. The boy paused thoughtfully, then added, "And the gods."

"You are wasting my time," said Demosthenes, his feelings getting the better of him. "Don't dare go away. Come here."

He grasped the boy's wrist as he was turning. He drew back the length of his arm, but did not struggle. He simply stared. His eyes in their deep sockets seemed to grow first pale, then dark as the pupils opened. In slow Greek, with fastidious correctness, he said quietly, "Take your hand off me. Or you are going to die. I am telling you."

Demosthenes let go. A frightening, vicious boy; clearly some great lord's minion. No doubt his threats were empty . . . but this was Macedon. The boy though released still paused, brooding intently on his face. A cold creeping moved in his bowels. He thought of ambushes, poison, knives in dark bedrooms; his stomach turned, his skin chilled. The boy stood motionless, gazing from under his mane of tousled hair. Then he turned, vaulted the low wall, and was gone.

From the window, Aischines' voice boomed in its lowest register, and soared, for effect, to a pure falsetto. Suspicion, only suspicion! Nothing one could pin to an indictment. The soreness climbed from Demosthenes' throat to his nose; he gave a violent sneeze. Somehow he must get a hot tisane, even if some ignorant fool would make it. How often, in his speeches, he had said of Macedon that it was a land from which it had never yet been possible even to buy a decent slave.

Olympias sat in her gilded chair carved with palmettes and roses. Noon sun streamed from the window, warming the high room, lacing the floor with shadows of budding branches. A small table of cypress wood was at her elbow; on a stool by her knees sat her son. His teeth were clenched, but low gasps of agony now and then escaped him. She was combing his hair.

"The very last knot, my darling."

"Can't you cut it off?"

"And have you ragged? Do you want to look like a slave? If I did not watch you, you would be lousy. There; all done. A kiss for being good, and you may eat your dates. Don't touch my dress while your hands are sticky. Doris, the irons."

"They are too hot still, madam; hissing-hot."

"Mother, you must stop curling it. None of the other boys have it done."

"What is that to you? You lead, you do not follow. Don't you want to look beautiful for me?"

"Here, madam. I don't think they will scorch now."

"They had better not! Now don't fidget. I do it better than the barbers. No one will guess it's not natural."

"But they see me every day! All but the . . ."

"Keep still, you will get a burn. What did you say?"

"Nothing. I was thinking about the envoys. I think after all I'll wear my jewels. You were right, one shouldn't dress down to the Athenians."

"No, indeed. We will look out something presently, and proper clothes."

"Besides, Father will wear jewels."

"Oh, yes. Well, you wear them better."

"I met Aristodemos just now. He said I'd grown so much he'd hardly have known me."

"A charming man. We must ask him here, by ourselves."

"He had to go, but he presented another man who used to be an actor. I liked him; he's called Aischines, he made me laugh."

"We might ask him too. Is he a gentleman?"

"It doesn't matter with actors. He told me about the theater, how they tour; how they get their own back on a man who's bad to work with."

"You must be careful with these people. I hope you said nothing indiscreet."

"Oh, no. I asked about the war party and the peace party in Athens. He was in the war party, I think; but we're not like he thought. We got on well."

"Don't give any of these men the chance to boast of being singled out."

"He'll not do that."

"What do you mean? Was he familiar?"

"No, of course not. We only talked."

She tilted his head back, to curl the locks above his brow. As her hand passed his mouth he kissed it. There was a scratch upon the door.

"Madam, the King sends to say he has had the envoys summoned. He would like the Prince to enter with him."

"Say he will be there." She stroked out the hair lock by lock, and looked him over. His nails were trimmed, he was freshly bathed, his gold-studded sandals stood ready. She found him a chiton of saffron wool, with a border she had worked herself in four or five colors; a red chlamys for his shoulder and a big gold pin. When the chiton was on, she clasped round his waist a belt of golden filigree. She was leisurely; if he were early, it would be with Philip he would wait.

"Isn't it finished?" he asked. "Father will be waiting."

"He has only just summoned the envoys."

"I expect they were all ready."

"You will find the afternoon quite long enough, with their tedious speeches."

"Well, one must learn how things are done . . . I've seen Demosthenes."

"That great Demosthenes! Well, what did you think of him?"

"I don't like him." She looked up from the golden girdle, raising her brows. He turned towards her, with an effort she noticed. "Father told me, but I didn't listen. He was right, though."

"Put on your cloak. Or do you want it done for you like a baby?"

Silently he threw it round his shoulder; silently, with untender fingers, she drove the pin through the stuff, which gave too quickly. He made no movement. She said sharply, "Did I prick you?"

"No." He knelt to lace his sandals. The cloth fell away from his neck, and she saw blood.

She held a towel to the scratch, kissing his curled head, making peace before he went to meet her enemy. As he went towards the Perseus Room, the smart of the pin was soon forgotten. For the other, it was like a pain he had been born with. He could not remember a time when it had not been.

The envoys stood facing the empty throne, with the great mural behind it of Perseus freeing Andromeda. At their backs were ten ornate hard chairs; it had been made clear, even to the most ardent democrats, that they would sit when, and not before, the King invited them. The leader, Philokrates, looked demurely about him, straight-faced, at pains not to seem at ease. As soon as the order and matter of the speeches had been determined, he had made a brief digest and sent it secretly to the King. Philip was known to speak extempore with force and wit, but would be grateful for the chance to do himself full justice. His gratitude to Philokrates had already been very solid.

Down at the far left (they stood in order of speaking) Demosthenes swallowed painfully, and mopped his nose with the corner of his cloak. Lifting his eyes, he met the painted eyes of a splendid youth, poised wing-footed on blue air. In his right hand he held a sword; in his left, by its hair, the ghastly head of Medusa, aiming its lethal gaze at the sea-dragon in the waves below. Manacled to a leafy rock by her outspread arms, her body shimmering through her thin robe, her fair hair lifted by the breeze which upbore the hero, Andromeda gazed at her savior with soft wild eyes.

It was a masterpiece; as good as the Zeuxis on the Acropolis, and bigger. Demosthenes felt as bitter as if it had been looted in war. The beautiful tanned youth, superbly naked (some Athenian athlete of the great days must have posed for the first cartoon), looked down with hauteur on the heirs of his city's greatness. Once again, as in old years at the palaestra, Demosthenes felt the pause of dread before he stripped his thin limbs; the admired boys strolling by, elaborately careless of their public; for himself, the giggle and the hateful nickname.

You are dead, Perseus; beautiful, brave, and dead. So you need not look at me. You died of malaria in Sicily, you drowned in Syracuse harbor, or parched in the waterless retreat. At Goat River the Spartans bound you and cut your throat. The hangman of the Thirty burned you with his irons and choked you. Andromeda must do

FIRE FROM HEAVEN

without you. Let her take help where she can, for the waves are
parting to show the dragon's head.

With her feet on a cloud, bright-helmed Athene hovered to in-
spire the hero. Grey-eyed Lady of Victories! Take and use me; I am
yours, for what I am. If I have only words to serve you with, your
power can turn them to sword and Gorgon. Let me only guard
your citadel till it brings forth heroes again.

Athene returned him a level stare. As was proper, her eyes were
grey. He seemed to feel again the dawn chill, and his fasting belly
griped with fear.

There was a stir at the inner door. The King came in, with his
two generals, Antipatros and Parmenion; a formidable trio of hard-
bitten warriors, each of whom by himself would have filled the eye.
Along with them, almost lost beside them, walked at the King's
elbow a curly-haired, overdressed boy with downcast eyes. They
disposed themselves in their chairs of honor; Philip greeted the
envoys graciously, and bade them sit.

Philokrates made his speech, full of openings which would be
useful to the King, masked by spurious firmness. Demosthenes' suspicions grew. They had all been given the précis; but could these
weak links be merely slipshod? If only he could keep his mind on it;
if only his eye did not keep straying to the King.

Hateful he had expected Philip to be; but not unnerving. His
speech of welcome, though perfectly courteous, had not wasted a
word, its brevity subtly hinting that smoke-screens of verbiage would
not serve. Whenever a speaker turned to the other envoys for support, Philip would scan the line of faces. His blind eye, which was
as mobile as the good one, seemed to Demosthenes the more bale-
ful of the two.

The day wore on; the steep sun-patches under the windows
stretched along the floor. Speaker after speaker urged Athens' claims
to Olynthos, to Amphipolis, to her old spheres of influence in
Thrace and Chersonesos; referred to the Euboian war, to this naval
brush or that; dragged up old dealings with Macedon in the long
complex wars of her succession; talked of the Hellespont corn route,
of the aims of Persia and the intrigues of her coastal satraps. Every
so often, Demosthenes would see the bright black eye and its
spatchcock yokefellow move his way and linger.

[91]

He was being awaited, he the famous tyrannophobe, as the protagonist is awaited through the opening chorus. How often, in the law
courts and at Assembly, this knowledge had quickened his blood
and wits! Now, it came to him that never before had he so addressed
himself to a single man.

He knew every string of his instrument, could measure the light-
est turn of each key; he could transpose righteousness into hatred;
play on self-interest till it seemed even to itself a self-denying duty;
he knew where thrown mud would stick on a clean man, and white-
wash on a dirty one; even for a lawyer-politician of his day, when
standards of skill were high, he was a first-class professional. And
he had known himself to be more; on great days he had tasted the
pure ecstasy of the artist, when he had kindled them all with his own
dream of Athenian greatness. He was reaching the peak of his powers; he would be better yet; but now it was borne in on him that the
medium of his art was the crowd alone. When it left for home, it
would still be praising his oration; but it would break up into so
many thousand men, not one of whom really liked him. There was
no one at whose side he had locked shields in battle. And when he
wanted love, it cost two drachmas.

They were down to the eighth speaker, Ktesiphon. Soon he himself would be speaking; not to the manifold ear he knew, but to this
one black probing eye.

His nose was blocked again; he had to blow it on his cloak, the
floor looked too pretentiously ornate. What if it ran while he was
speaking? To keep his mind off the King, he looked at red big-boned
Antipatros, and Parmenion with his broad shoulders, brown bush of
beard, and bowed horseman's knees. This was unwise. They had not
Philip's obligations to the speaker, and were frankly appraising the
envoys together. The fierce blue eye of Antipatros brought back, the
moment it met his, the eye of the phylarch under whom he had done
his compulsory army training, as a spindly youth of eighteen.

All this while, the gaudy princeling sat unmoving in his low chair,
his eyes bent towards his knees. Any Athenian lad would have been
looking about him, impertinent perhaps (alas, manners were de-
clining everywhere) but at least alert. A Spartan training. Sparta,
symbol of past tyranny and present oligarchy. It was just what one
would expect in Philip's son.

[92]

Ktesiphon had done. He bowed; Philip spoke a few words of thanks. He had managed to make each speaker feel noticed and remembered. The herald announced Aischines.

He rose to his full height (he had been too tall to do well in women's roles, one cause of his leaving the stage). Would he betray himself? Not a word or tone must be missed. The King must be watched too.

Aischines went into his preamble. Once more, Demosthenes was forced to see how training told. He himself relied much on gesture; he indeed had brought it into public speaking, calling the old sculpted stance a relic of aristocracy; but when warmed up, he tended to do it from the elbow. Aischines' right hand rested easily just outside his cloak; he wore a manly dignity, not trying to old-soldier the three great generals before him, but hinting the respect of one who knows the face of war. It was a good speech, following the scheme arranged. He would give nothing away, whatever he had been up to. Giving up in disgust, Demosthenes blew his nose again, and turned to a mental run-through of his own oration.

"And your elder kinsmen will bear out what I say. For after your father Amyntas, and your uncle Alexandros, had both fallen, while your brother Perdikkas and you were children . . ."

His mind hung suspended in the pause between shock and thought. The words were right. But Aischines, not he, had spoken them.

". . . betrayed by false friends; and Pausanias was coming back from exile to contest the throne . . ."

The voice ran on, unforced, persuasive, expertly timed. Wild thoughts of coincidence rose and died, as word followed word, confirming infamy. "You yourself were only a small child. She put you on his knee, saying . . ."

The early years of anguished struggle to cure his stammer, project his thin voice and temper its shrillness, made him need his own reassurance. Again and again, in audible undertones, script in hand, he must have rehearsed this passage on the journey, on board ship or at inns. This mountebank peddler of others' words; of course he could have mastered it.

The anecdote reached its well-turned close. Everyone looked impressed, the King, the generals, the other envoys; all but the boy, who, growing restless at last after the hours of stillness, had begun to scratch his head.

Demosthenes confronted not only the loss of his most telling passage; that was the least of it. It should have led his theme to the central matter. Now, at this last moment, he would have to recast his speech.

He had never been good extempore, even with the audience on his side. The King's eye had swiveled his way again, expectantly.

Frantically he gathered in mind the fragments of his speech, trying edge against edge for joins, bridging, transposing. But having taken no interest in Aischines' speech, he had no idea how much of it was left, how soon his own turn would come. The suspense scattered his thoughts. He could only remember the times when he had put down Aischines' upstart pretensions, reminding him, and people of influence along with him, that he came of broken-down gentlefolk, that as a boy he had ground ink for his father's school and copied civil service lists; that on the stage he had never played leading roles. Who could have reckoned on his bringing to the noble theater of politics the sleights of his sordid trade?

And he could never be accused of it. To own the truth would make any orator the laughingstock of Athens. One would never live it down.

Aischines' voice had the swell of peroration. Demosthenes felt cold sweat on his brow. He clung to his opening paragraph; its momentum might lead him on. Perseus hovered scornfully. The King sat stroking his beard. Antipatros was muttering something to Parmenion. The boy was raking his fingers through his hair.

Deftly, into his final paragraph, Aischines slipped the key passage of Demosthenes' prepared finale. He bowed, was thanked. "Demosthenes," said the herald, "son of Demosthenes, of Paiania."

He rose and began, advancing as to a precipice; all sense of style had deserted him, he was glad to remember the mere words. Almost at the last, his normal quick sense revived; he saw how to bridge the gap. At this moment, a movement drew his eye. For the first time, the boy had lifted his head.

FIRE FROM HEAVEN

The crimped curls, already loosening before he had begun work on them, had changed to a tousled mane springing strongly from a peak. His grey eyes were wide open. He was very slightly smiling.

"To take a broad view of the question . . . a broad view . . . to take a . . ."

His voice strangled in his throat. His mouth closed and opened; nothing came out but breath.

Everyone sat up and stared. Aischines, rising, patted him solicitously on the back. The boy's eyes were leveled in perfect comprehension, missing nothing, awaiting more. His face was filled with a clear, cold brightness.

"To take a broad view . . . I . . . I . . ."

King Philip, astounded and bewildered, had grasped the one fact that he could afford to be magnanimous. "My dear sir, take your time. Don't be disturbed; it will come back to you in a moment."

The boy had tilted his head a little to the left; Demosthenes recalled the pose. Again the grey eyes opened, measuring his fear.

"Try to think of it little by little," said Philip good-humoredly, "back from the beginning. No need to be put off by a moment's dry-up, like the actors in the theater. I assure you, we can wait."

What cat-and-mouse game was this? It was impossible the boy should not have told his father. He remembered the schoolroom Greek: "You are going to die. I am telling you."

There was a buzz from the envoys' chairs; his speech contained matter of importance, not yet covered. The main headings, if he could find only those . . . In dull panic, he followed the King's advice, stumbling again through the preamble. The boy's lips moved gently, smilingly, silently. Demosthenes' head felt empty, like a dried gourd. He said, "I am sorry," and sat down.

"In that case, gentlemen . . ." said Philip. He signed to the herald. "When you have rested and refreshed yourselves, I will let you have my answer."

Outside, Antipatros and Parmenion were telling each other how they thought the envoys would shape in cavalry. Philip, as he turned towards his study where he had his written speech (he had kept a few spaces for matters arising), became aware of his son looking up at him. He signed with his head; the boy followed him into the garden, where, in reflective silence, they relieved themselves among the trees.

"You could have gone out," said Philip. "I didn't think to tell you."

"I didn't drink anything first. You told me once."

"Did I? Well; what did you make of Demosthenes?"

"You were right, Father. He isn't brave."

Philip let fall his robe and looked round; something in the voice had arrested him. "What ailed the man? Do *you* know?"

"That man's an actor, who spoke before him. He stole his lines."

"However do you know that?"

"I heard him practicing them in the garden. He spoke to me."

"*Demosthenes?* What about?"

"He thought I was a slave and asked if I was spying. Then when I spoke in Greek, he said he supposed I was someone's bedboy." He used the barrack word which came to him most readily. "I didn't tell him; I thought I'd wait."

"*What?*"

"I sat up when he started speaking, and he knew me then."

The boy saw, with unmixed pleasure, his father's slow laughter inform his gap-toothed grin, his good eye, even his blind one. "But why didn't you tell me first?"

"He'd have expected that. He doesn't know what to think."

Philip looked at him glintingly. "Did the man proposition you?"

"He wouldn't *ask* a slave. He just wondered how much I'd cost."

"Well; we may suppose that now he knows."

Father and son exchanged looks, in a moment of perfect harmony; unalienated heirs of bronze-sworded chariot lords from beyond the Ister, who had led their tribes down in past millennia, some driving further to seize the southlands and learn their ways, some taking these mountain kingdoms where they kept old customs on; burying their dead in chamber-tombs alongside their forebears whose skulls were cased in boar-tusk helms and whose hand-bones grasped double axes; handing down, father to son, elaborate niceties of blood-feud and revenge.

Affront had been requited, on a man immune from the sword

and in any case beneath its dignity; with finesse, in terms cut to his measure. It had been as neat, in its way, as the vengeance in the hall at Aigai.

The peace terms were debated at length in Athens. Antipatros and Parmenion, who went to represent Philip, watched fascinated the strange ways of the south. In Macedon, the only thing ever voted on was the putting of a man to death; all other public matters were for the King.

By the time the terms had been accepted (Aischines urging it strongly), and the envoys had journeyed back to ratify, King Philip had had time to reduce the Thracian stronghold of Kersobleptes, and take his surrender on terms, bringing back his son to Pella, as a hostage for his loyalty.

Meantime, in the hill-forts above Thermopylai, the exiled temple-robber, Phalaikos the Phokian, was running out of gold, food and hope. Philip was now treating with him in secret. News that Macedon held the Hot Gates would strike Athenians like an earthquake; they could bear the Phokians' sins (and had indeed an alliance with them) far more lightly than this. It must be hidden till the peace had been ratified by sacred and binding oaths.

Philip was charming to the second embassy. Aischines was most valuable, a man not bought but changed in heart. He accepted gladly the King's assurance that he meant no harm to Athens, which was sincere; and, which he saw as not false, that he would deal mildly with the Phokians. Athens needed Phokis; not only to hold Thermopylai, but to contain the ancient enemy, Thebes.

The envoys were entertained and given conspicuous guest-gifts, which they all took except Demosthenes. He had spoken first this time, but his colleagues had all agreed that he lacked his usual fire. They had in fact been quarreling and intriguing all the way from Athens. Demosthenes' suspicions of Philokrates had reached certainty; he was eager to convince the others, but also to convict Aischines; this charge, being doubted, discredited the other. Brooding on these injuries, he had gone in to dinner; where the guests had been entertained by young Alexander and another boy singing partsongs to the lyre. Across the instrument, two cool grey eyes had lingered on Demosthenes; turning quickly, he had seen Aischines smile.

The oaths were ratified; the envoys went home. Philip escorted them south as far as Thessaly, without revealing that it was on his way. As soon as they had gone, he marched over to Thermopylai, and received the hill-forts from Phalaikos in return for a safe-conduct. The exiles went gratefully, wandering off to hire out their swords in the endless local wars of Greece, dying here and there as Apollo picked them off.

Athens was in panic. They waited for Philip to sweep down on them like Xerxes. The walls were manned, refugees from Attica crowded in. But Philip only sent word that he wished to set in order the affairs of Delphi, so long a scandal, and invited the Athenians to send an allied force.

Demosthenes made a fiery speech against the treachery of tyrants. Philip, he said, wanted the flower of their youth delivered him to use as hostages. No force was sent. Philip was sincerely puzzled; affronted, wounded in his soul. He had shown mercy when none was looked for, and had not even had thanks for it.

Leaving Athens to herself, he pressed on with the Phokian war. He had the blessing of the Sacred League, the states who with the Phokians had been guardians of the shrine.

Affairs in Thrace being settled, he could attack with all his force. Fort after Phokian fort surrendered or fell; soon all was over, and the Sacred League met to decide the Phokians' fate. They had become a detested people, whose god-cursed plunder had ruined all in its path. Most of the deputies wanted them tortured to death, or hurled from the summits of the Phaidriades, or at least sold off as slaves. Philip had long been sickened by the savageries of the war; he foresaw endless further wars for possession of the empty lands. He argued for mercy. In the end, it was decided to resettle the Phokians in their own country, but in small villages they could not fortify. They were forbidden to rebuild their walls, and had to pay yearly reparations to Apollo's temple. Demosthenes made a fiery speech, denouncing these atrocities.

The Sacred League passed a vote of thanks to Philip, for cleansing from impiety the holiest shrine in Greece; and conferred on Macedon the two seats in the Council from which Phokis had been deposed. He had returned to Pella when they sent two heralds after him, inviting him to preside at the next Pythian Games.

After the audience, he stood alone at his study window, tasting his happiness. It was not only a great beginning, but a longed-for end. He was received, now, as a Hellene.

He had been the lover of Hellas since he was a man. Her hatred had burned him like a whip. She had forgotten herself, fallen below her past; but she only needed leading, and in his soul he felt his destiny.

His love had been born in bitterness, when he had been led by strangers from the mountains and forests of Macedon to the dreary lowlands of Thebes, a living symbol of defeat. Though his jailor-hosts were civil, many Thebans were not; he had been torn from friends and kin; from willing girls, and the married mistress who had been his first instructor. In Thebes, free women were barred to him; his comings and goings watched; if he went to a brothel, he had not the price of a whore who did not disgust him.

In the palaestra he had found his only comfort. Here no one could look down on him; he had proved himself an athlete of skill and stubborn fortitude. The palaestra had accepted him, and let him know that its loves were not denied him. Begun at first in mere loneliness and need, they had proved consoling; by degrees, in a city where they had tradition and high prestige, they had grown as natural as any other.

With new friendships had come visits to the philosophers and teachers of rhetoric; and, presently, the chance to learn from experts the art of war. He had longed for home and had returned with gladness; but by then he had been received into the mystery of Hellas, forever her initiate.

Athens was her altar, almost her self. All he asked of Athens was to restore her glories; her present leaders seemed to him like the Phokians at Delphi, unworthy men who had seized a holy shrine. Deep in his mind moved a knowledge that for Athenians freedom and glory went together; but he was like a man in love, who thinks the strongest trait of the loved one's nature will be easily changed, as soon as they are married.

All his policies, devious and opportunist as they had often been, had looked forward to the opening of her door to him. Rather than lose her, in the last resort he would break it down; but he longed for her to open it. Now he held in his hand the elegant scroll from Delphi; the key, if not to her inner room, at least to her gate.

In the end, she must receive him. When he had freed her kindred cities of Ionia from their generations of servitude, he would be taken to her heart. The thought grew in his mind. Lately, he had had like an omen a long letter from Isokrates, a philosopher so old that he had been a friend of Sokrates while Plato was still a school-boy, and had been born before Athens declared war on Sparta, to begin that long mortal bloodletting of Greece. Now in his tenth decade still alert to a changing world, he urged Philip to unite the Greeks and lead them. Dreaming at the window, he saw a Hellas made young again, not by the shrill orator who called him tyrant, but by a truer Heraklid than those effete and bickering Kings of Sparta. He saw his statue set up on the Acropolis; the Great King set down to the proper place of all barbarians, to furnish slaves and tribute; with Philip's Athens once more the School of Hellas.

Young voices broke his thoughts. On the terrace just below, his son was playing knucklebones with the young hostage son of Teres, King of the Agrianoi.

Philip looked down with irritation. What could the boy want with that little savage? He had even brought him to the gymnasium, so had said one of the Companion lords, whose son went there too, and who did not like it.

The child had been treated quite humanely, well clad and fed, never made to work or do anything disgraceful to his rank. Of course none of the noble houses had been prepared to take him in, as they would have done a civilized boy from a Greek city of coastal Thrace; he had had to be found quarters in the Palace, and, since the Agrianoi were a warlike race whose submission might not be lasting, a guard put over him in case he ran away. Why Alexander, with every boy of decent birth in Pella to choose from, should have sought out this one, was past comprehension. No doubt he would soon forget the whim; it was not worth interfering.

The two princes squatted on the flagstones, playing their game in mixed Macedonian and Thracian helped out with mime; more Thracian, because Alexander had learned faster. The guard sat, bored, on the rump of a marble lion.

Lambaros was a Red Thracian of the conquering northern strain which, a thousand years before, had come south to hew out mountain chiefdoms among the dark Pelasgians. He was about a year older than Alexander and looked more, being big-boned. He had a shock of fiery hair; on his upper arm was tattooed an archaic, small-headed horse, the sign of his royal blood—like every high-born Thracian, he claimed direct descent from the demigod Rhesos the Rider. On his leg was a stag, the mark of his tribe. When he came of age and his further growth would not spoil them, he would be covered with the elaborate design of whorls and symbols to which his rank entitled him. Round his neck on a greasy thong was a gryphon amulet in yellow Scythian gold.

He held the leather dice-bag, muttering an incantation over it. The guard, who would have liked to go where he had friends, gave an impatient cough. Lambaros threw a wild look over his shoulder. "Take no notice," said Alexander. "He's a guard, that's all. He can't tell you what to do." He thought it a great dishonor to the house, that a royal hostage should be worse treated in Pella than in Thebes. It had been in his mind, even before the day he had come upon Lambaros crying his heart out with his head against a tree, watched by his indifferent warder. At the sound of a new voice he had turned like a beast at bay, but had understood an outstretched hand. Had his tears been mocked, he would have fought even if they killed him for it. This knowledge had passed between them without words.

There had been red lice in his red hair, and Hellanike had grumbled even at asking her maid to see to it. When Alexander had sent for sweets to offer him, they had been brought by a Thracian slave. "He's only on sentry-go. You're my guest. Your throw."

Lambaros repeated his prayer to the Thracian sky-god, called fives, and threw a two and three.

"You ask him for such little things; I expect he was offended. Gods like to be asked for something great."

Lambaros, who now prayed less often to go home, said, "Your god won for you."

"No, I just try to feel lucky. I save prayer up."

"What for?"

"Lambaros; listen. When we're men, when we're kings—you understand what I'm saying?"

"When our fathers die."

"When I go to war, will you be my ally?"

"Yes. What is an ally?"

"You bring your men to fight my enemies, and I'll fight yours."

From the window above, King Philip saw the Thracian grasp his son's hands, and, kneeling, arrange them in a formal clasp about his own. He lifted his face, speaking long and eloquently; Alexander knelt facing him; holding his folded hands, patient, his whole frame attentive. Presently Lambaros leaped to his feet, and gave a high howl like a forsaken dog's, his treble attempting the Thracian war-yell. Philip, making nothing of the scene, found it distasteful; he was glad to see the guard stop idling and walk over.

It brought back to Lambaros the truth of his condition. His paean stopped; he looked down, sullen with misery.

"What do you want? Nothing is wrong, he is teaching me his customs." The guard, come to separate brawling children, was startled into apology. "Go back. I shall call you if I need you. That's a fine oath, Lambaros. Say the end again."

"I will keep faith," said Lambaros slowly and gravely, "unless the sky fall and crush me, or the earth open and swallow me, or the sea rise and overwhelm me. My father kisses his chiefs when he swears them in."

Philip watched, incredulous, his son take in his hands the red head of the young barbarian, and plant the ritual kiss on his brow. This had gone far enough. It was un-Hellenic. Philip remembered he had not yet given the boy the news about the Pythian Games, to which he intended taking him. That would give him better things to think about.

There was a drift of dust on the flags. Alexander was scribbling in it, with a whittled twig. "Show me how your people form up for battle."

From the library window on a floor above, Phoinix saw with a smile the gold and the rufous head bent together over some solemn game. There was always relief in seeing his charge a child awhile, the bow unbent. The presence of the guard had lightened his duties. He returned to his unrolled book.

"We'll win a thousand heads," Lambaros was saying. "Chop-chop-chop!"

"Yes, but where do the slingers stand?"

The guard, who had had a message, came up again. "Alexander, you must leave this young lad to me. The King your father wants you."

Alexander's grey eyes lifted to his a moment. In spite of himself, he shifted his feet.

"Very well. Don't stop him from doing everything he wants. You're a soldier, not a pedagogue. And don't call him this young lad. If I can give him his rank, then so can you."

He walked up between the marble lions, followed by Lambaros' eyes, to hear the great news from Delphi.

4

"IT IS A PITY," said Epikrates, "that you cannot give more time to it."

"Days should be longer. Why must one sleep? One should be able to do without."

"You would not find it improved your execution."

Alexander stroked the polished box of the kithara with its inlaid scrollwork and ivory keys. The twelve strings sighed softly. He slipped off the sling which let it be played standing (sitting muted its tone) and sat down by it on the table, plucking a string here and there to test the pitch.

"You are right," said Epikrates. "Why should one die? One should be able to do without."

"Yes, having to sleep reminds one."

"Well, come! At twelve years, you are still pretty rich in time. I should like to see you entered for a contest; it would give you an aim to work for. I was thinking of the Pythian Games. In two years, you might be ready."

"What's the age limit for the youths?"

"Eighteen. Would your father consent?"

"Not if music was all I entered for. Nor would I, Epikrates. Why do you want me to do it?"

"It would give you discipline."

[104]

"I thought as much. But then I shouldn't enjoy it."

Epikrates gave his accustomed sigh.

"Don't be angry. I get discipline from Leonidas."

"I know, I know. At your age, my touch was not so good. You started younger, and I may say without hubris that you have been better taught. But you will never make a musician, Alexander, if you neglect the philosophy of the art."

"One needs mathematics in the soul. I shall never have it, you know that. In any case, I could never be a musician. I have to be other things."

"Why not enter the Games," said Epikrates temptingly, "and take in the music contest too?"

"No. When I went to watch, I thought nothing would be so wonderful. But we stayed on after, and I met the athletes; and I saw how it really is. I can beat the boys here, because we're all training to be men. But these boys are just boy athletes. Often they're finished before they're men; and if not, even for the men, the Games is all their life. Like being a woman is for women."

Epikrates nodded. "It came about almost within my lifetime. People who have earned no pride in themselves are content to be proud of their cities through other men. The end will be that the city has nothing left for pride, except the dead, who were proud less easily . . . Well, with music every man's good is ours. Come, let me hear it again; this time, with a little more of what the composer wrote."

Alexander slung and strapped on the big instrument sideways to his breast, the bass strings nearest; he tested them softly with his left-hand fingers, the trebles with the plectrum in his other hand. His head inclined a little, his eyes rather than his ears seemed to be listening. Epikrates watched him with exasperation mingled with love, asking himself as usual whether, if he had refused to understand the boy, he could have taught him better. No; more likely he would simply have given it up. Before he was ten, he had already known enough to strum a lyre at supper like a gentleman. No one would have insisted on his learning more.

He struck three sonorous chords, played a long rippling cadenza, and began to sing.

At an age when the voices of Macedonian boys were starting to roughen, he kept a pure alto which had simply gained more power.

As it went soaring up with the high grace-notes flicked by the plectrum, Epikrates wondered that this never seemed to trouble him. Nor did he hesitate to look bored when other lads were exchanging the obsessive smut of their years. A boy never seen afraid can dictate his terms.

> *God brings all things to pass as he would have them be;*
> *God overtakes the flying eagle, the dolphin in the sea.*
> *He masters mortal men, though their pride be bold;*
> *But to some he gives glory that will never grow old.*

His voice floated and ceased; the strings echoed and re-echoed it, like wild voices in a glen.

Epikrates, sighing, thought, He's off.

As the dramatic, headlong, passionate impromptu swept from climax to climax, Epikrates gazed at leisure; he would not be noticed. He felt bewildered by the misuse to which, with open eyes, he was dedicating his aesthetic life. He was not even in love; his tastes were otherwise. Why did he stay? This performance, at the Odeon of Athens or of Ephesos, would have enraptured the upper tiers and had them booing the judges. Yet nothing here was for show; it was redeemed not indeed by ignorance, Epikrates had seen to that, but by a perfect innocence.

And this, he thought, is why I stay. I feel here a necessity, whose depth and force I cannot measure; and to deny it makes me afraid.

There was a tradesman's son in Pella, whom he had overheard playing once, a real musician; he had offered to teach him for nothing, to redeem his peace of mind. The lad would make a professional, worked hard, was grateful; yet those fruitful lessons engaged Epikrates' mind less than these, when all that was sacred to the god he served was flung like wasteful incense on an unknown altar.

> *Garland the prow with flowers, my song is for the brave . . .*

The music climbed to a rapt crescendo. The boy's lips were parted in the fierce and solitary smile of an act of love performed in darkness; the instrument could not sustain his onslaught, and was going out of tune; he must have heard it, but went on as if his will could compel the strings. He is using it, thought Epikrates, as one day he will use himself.

I must go, it is more than time; I have given him all he will ever take from me. All this he could do alone. In Ephesos, all round the year one can hear good music, and once in a while the best. And I should like to work in Corinth. I could take young Peithon; he ought to be hearing the masters. This one here, I am not teaching him, he is corrupting me. He comes to me for a listener who knows the language, and I listen, though he murders my native tongue. He must play to what gods will hear him, and let me go.

"You have learned your begetting; live as what you are!"

He swept the plectrum across the strings. One snapped, and whipped around the others; there was discord, and silence. He stared at it unbelievingly.

"Well?" said Epikrates. "What did you expect? Did you think it was immortal?"

"I thought it would last till I'd finished."

"You would not treat a horse so. Come, give it me."

He took a new string from his box, and began to put the instrument in order. The boy walked restlessly to the window; what had been about to be revealed would not return. Epikrates worked on the tuning, taking his time. I wish I could make him show what he really does know, before I leave.

"You have never yet played to your father and his guests, except on the lyre."

"The lyre is what people want at supper."

"It is what they get for want of better. Do me a kindness. Work on one piece for me and play it properly. I am sure he would like to see how you have got on."

"I don't think he knows I have a kithara. I bought it myself, you know."

"So much the better, you will show him something new." Like everyone else at Pella, Epikrates knew there was trouble in the women's quarters. The boy was on edge with it, and had been for some time. It was not only his practice he had missed, but a lesson too. As soon as he had walked in, Epikrates had seen how it would be.

Why, in the name of all gods of reason, could the King not be content with paid hetairas? He could afford the best. He had his young men as well; was it too much to ask? Why must he always do his rutting so ceremoniously? He must have gone through at least three such weddings before this last one. It might be an old royal custom in this backward land, but if he wanted to be thought a Hellene, he should remember "Nothing too much." One could not make over barbarians in a generation; it came out in the boy as well; and yet . . .

He was still gazing from the window as if he had forgotten where he was. His mother must have been at him. One could have pitied the woman, if she had not begged for half her troubles, and her son's as well. He must be hers, hers only, and only the gods could say what else, for the King was civilized when set beside his Queen. Could she not see she might cry stinking fish once too often? From any one of these other brides might come a boy glad enough to be his father's son. Why could she not show some policy? Why could she never spare the boy?

There was no hope, thought Epikrates, of his learning anything today. As well put away the kithara . . . Well, but if I myself have learned, what have I learned for? Epikrates put on the instrument, stood up and began to play.

After a while Alexander turned back from the window, and came to sit on the table, fidgeting at first, then quiet, then still, his head tilted a little, his eyes finding a distance for themselves. Presently tears filled their lashes. Epikrates saw it with relief; it had always happened when music moved him, and embarrassed neither of them. When it was over, he wiped his eyes on his palms and smiled. "If you want me to, I'll learn a piece to play in Hall."

Epikrates said to himself as he went away, I shall have to go soon; the turbulence here is too much for any man who wants harmony and balance in his soul.

A few lessons later, Alexander said, "There will be guests at supper; if I'm asked to play, shall I try it?"

"Certainly. Play it just as you did this morning. Will there be a place for me?"

"Oh yes; it will be all men we know, no foreigners. I'll tell the steward."

Supper was late; it had to wait for the King. He greeted his guests with civility, but was rather short with the servants. Though his cheeks were flushed and his eyes injected, he was clearly sober, and anxious to forget whatever had put him out. Slaves passed along the news that he had just come from the Queen.

The guests were old campaigning friends from the Companion Cavalry. Philip looked down the couches with relief; no state envoys to put on a show for, or to complain if they got along early to the wine. Good full-bodied Akanthian, and no water with it; he needed it, after what he had had to endure.

Alexander sat on the end of Phoinix' supper couch and shared his table. He never sat with his father unless invited. Phoinix, who had no ear to speak of but knew all the literary references to music, was pleased to hear of the boy's new piece and cited Achilles' lyre. "And I shall not be like Patroklos, who Homer says was sitting waiting for his friend to leave off."

"Oh, unfair. It only means Patroklos wanted to talk."

"Now, now, boy, what are you up to? That's my cup you're drinking from, not yours."

"Well, I pledge you in it. Try mine. If they rinsed wine round it before they put in the water, that was all."

"It's the proper mixture for boys, one in four. You can pour some in my cup, we can't all take it neat as your father can, but it looks bad to call for the water pitcher."

"I'll drink some to make room, before I pour."

"No, no, boy, stop, that's enough. You'll be too drunk to play."

"Of course not, I only had a mouthful." And indeed he showed no sign beyond a little heightened color. He came of well-seasoned stock.

The noise was rising as the cups were topped up. Philip, shouting above it, invited anyone to give them a tune or a song.

"Here's your son, sir," called Phoinix, "who has learned a new tune for this very feast."

Two or three cups of strong neat wine had made Philip feel much better. It was a known cure for snakebite, he thought with a grim smile. "Come up, then, boy. Bring your lyre and sit up here."

Alexander signed to the servant with whom he had left the kithara. He put it on with care, and went over to stand by his father's couch.

"What's this?" said the King. "You can't play that thing, can you?"

Mary Renault

He had never seen it used by a man not paid to do it; it struck him as unsuitable.

The boy smiled, saying, "You must tell me that when I've finished, Father." He tested the strings and began.

Epikrates, listening down the hall, looked at the boy with deep affection. At this moment he could have posed for a young Apollo. Who knows, this may be the true beginning; he may come to a pure knowledge of the god.

All the Macedonian lords, who had been awaiting the cue to shout a chorus, listened amazed. They had never heard of a gentleman playing like this, or wanting to. What had those schoolmasters been up to with the boy? He had the name of being plucky and game for anything. Were they making a southerner of him? It would be philosophy next.

King Philip had attended many music contests. Though without sustained interest in the art, he could recognize technique. He was aware of it here, together with its lack of fitness. The company, he could see, did not know what to make of it. Why had the teacher not reported this morbid fervor? The truth was plain. *She* had been bringing him again to those rites of hers, steeping him in their frenzies, making a barbarian of him. Look at him now, thought Philip; look at him now.

Out of civility to foreign guests, who always expected it, he had got into the way of bringing the boy to supper in the Hellene fashion; his friends' sons would not appear till they came of age. Why had he broken this good custom? If the boy had a girl's voice still, must he tell the world? That Epirote bitch, that malignant sorceress; he would long since have put her away, had her powerful kin not been like a spear poised at his back when he went to war. Let her not be too sure of herself. He would do it yet.

Phoinix had had no notion the boy could play like this. He was as good as that fellow from Samos a few months back. But he was letting himself get carried away, as he did sometimes with Homer. Before his father, he had always held himself in. He should never have had that wine.

He had reached the cadenzas which led to the finale. The stream of sound cascaded through its gorges, the bright spray glittered above.

Philip gazed, almost unhearing, taken up with what he saw: the brilliant glow of the face, the deep-set eyes unfocused and glittering with unshed tears, the remotely smiling mouth. To him, it mirrored the face he had left upstairs, its cheekbones flushed red, its defiant laughter, its eyes weeping with rage.

Alexander struck the last chord and drew a long deep breath. He had not made one mistake.

The guests broke into uneasy applause. Epikrates joined in eagerly. Phoinix shouted rather too loudly, "Good! Very good!"

Philip banged down his wine cup on the table. His forehead had flushed dark crimson; the lid of his blind eye had dropped a little, showing only the white spot; his good eye started in its socket.

"Good?" he said. "Do you call that music for a man?"

The boy turned slowly, as if waking from sleep. He blinked his eyes clear, and fastened them on his father.

"Never," said Philip, "let me see you make such a show of yourself again. Leave it to Corinthian whores and Persian eunuchs; you sing well enough for either. You should be ashamed."

With the kithara still strapped on to him, the boy stood stock-still for a few moments, his face blank, and, as the blood receded, growing sallow. Looking at no one, he walked out between the couches and left the hall.

Epikrates followed. But he had wasted a few moments thinking what to say, and did not find him.

A few days later, Gyras, a tribal Macedonian from the inland hills, set out along ancient tracks, returning home on leave. He had told his commander, formally, that his father was dying and had begged for a last sight of him. The officer, who had expected it since the day before, told him not to waste time at home when he had done his business, if he wanted to draw his pay. Tribal wars were winked at, unless they showed signs of spreading; they were immemorial; to put down blood-feud would have taken the army all its time, even had it not been itself steeped in tribal loyalties. Gyras' uncle had been killed, the wife raped and left for dead; if Gyras was refused leave he would desert. Some such thing happened once a month or so.

Mary Renault

It was his second day out. He was a light cavalryman with his own horse, small and scrubby but tough, qualities Gyras shared; a gingery brown man, with a broken nose set slightly skew and a short bristly beard, dressed mainly in leather, and armed to the teeth, this being required for the journey as well as for his errand. He had been favoring his horse over grass wherever he could find it, to keep its unshod hooves sound for the work ahead. At about noon, he was crossing a rolling heathland between the mountain ribs of Macedon. In the wooded dips, birches and larches swayed in a gentle breeze; it was late summer, but up here the air was fresh. Gyras, who did not want to be killed, but preferred it to the life of disgrace which followed a failure to take vengeance, looked about him at the world he might shortly have to leave. Meantime, however, there was an oak grove ahead; in its hushed and grateful shade a stream burbled over pebbles and black oak-leaves. He watered and tethered his horse; dipping the bronze cup he carried on his belt, he approved the water's sweetness. From his saddlebag he took goat cheese and black bread, and sat on a rock to eat.

Hoofbeats cantered on the track behind him. At a walk, some stranger entered the wood. Gyras reached for his javelins, already laid at hand.

"Good day to you, Gyras."

Till the latest moment he had not believed his eyes. They were a good fifty miles out from Pella.

"Alexander!" His bread had stuck in his throat; he dislodged and bolted it, while the boy dismounted and led his horse to the stream. "How did you get here? Is no one with you?"

"You are, now." He invoked the god of the stream in proper form, restrained his mount from drinking too much, and tethered it to an oak sapling. "We can eat together." He unpacked food and came over. He wore a man's long hunting-knife on a shoulder-sling; his clothes were tumbled and dirty, his hair had pine-needles in it. Clearly he had slept out. His horse carried, among other things, two javelins and a bow. "Here, take an apple. I thought I should catch up with you about mealtime."

Dazedly Gyras complied. The boy drank from cupped hands and splashed his face. Concerned with his own affairs, for him momentous, Gyras had heard nothing of King Philip's supper party. The thought of this charge on his hands appalled him. By the time he had returned him and set out again, anything might have happened at home. "How did you come so far alone? Are you lost? Were you out hunting?"

"I am hunting what you are hunting," said Alexander, biting into his apple. "That is why I am coming with you."

"But . . . but . . . what notion . . . You don't know what I'm about."

"Of course I do. Everyone in your squadron knows it. I need a war, and yours will do very well. It is quite time, you know, that I got my sword belt. I have come out to take my man."

Gyras gazed transfixed. The boy must have tracked him all this way, keeping out of sight. He was equipped with care and forethought. Also, something had changed his face. His cheeks had sunk and flattened below the cheekbones; his eyes looked deeper under the shelf of his brows, his high-bridged nose stood out more. There was a line across his forehead. It was scarcely a boy's face at all. Nonetheless he was twelve years old, and Gyras would have to answer for him.

"It's not right," he said desperately, "what you've done. You know it's not right. I was needed at home, you know that. Now I'll have to leave them in their trouble, and take you back."

"You can't, you've eaten with me, we're guest-friends." He was reproving, not alarmed. "It's wicked to betray a guest-friend."

"You should have told me the right of it first, then. I can't help it now. Come back you must and will. You're no more than a child. If harm came to you, the King would have me crucified."

The boy got up without haste, and strolled to his horse. Gyras started up, saw he was not untying it, and sat down again.

"He won't kill you if I come back. If I die, you'll have plenty of time to run away. I don't suppose he'd kill you anyway. Think about me, instead. If you do anything to get me sent home before I'm ready, if you try to ride back or send a message, then I shall kill you. And that you can be sure of."

He had turned from the horse with lifted arm. Gyras looked along a javelin, balanced and poised. The narrow leaflike blade shone blue with honing, the point looked like a needle.

"Keep still, Gyras. Sit just as you are, don't move. I'm quick, you

[113]

know, everyone knows it. I can throw before you can do anything.
I don't want you for my first man. It wouldn't be enough, I should
still have to take another in battle. But you will be, if you try to
stop me now."

Gyras looked at his eyes. He had faced such eyes through helmet-
slits. He said, "Now, come, now, you don't mean that."

"No one will even know I did it. I shall just leave your body in
that thicket, for the wolves and kites. You'll never be buried, or
given your rites to set you free." His voice grew rhythmic. "And
the shades of the dead will not let you cross the river to join their
company, but you will wander alone forever before the wide gates
of Hades' house. No, don't move."

Gyras sat immobile. It gave him time to think. Though ignorant of
the supper party, he knew about the King's new wedding, and
those before. There was already a boy from one of them. Folk said
it had started bright enough, but had turned out an idiot, no doubt
poisoned by the Queen. Maybe she had only bribed the nurse to
drop it on its head. Maybe it was just a natural. But there might be
others. If young Alexander wanted to make himself a man ahead of
time, one could see why.

"Well?" said the boy. "Will you pledge yourself? I can't stand
like this all day."

"What I've ever done to deserve this of the gods, they only know.
What do you want me to swear to?"

"Not to get word to Pella of me. To tell no one my name without
my leave. Not to keep me from going into battle, or get anyone
else to do it. You must swear all that, and call down a death-curse
on yourself if you break your oath."

Gyras felt himself flinch. He wanted no such compacts with a
witch's son. The boy lowered his weapon but kept the thong in his
fingers, twisted for a throw. "You'll have to do it. I don't want you
creeping up to bind me when I'm asleep. I could sit up to watch,
but it would be stupid before a battle. So if you want to come out
of this wood alive, you'll have to swear."

"And what's to become of me after?"

"If I live I'll see you right. You must chance my dying, that's
war." He reached into his leather saddlebag, looking over his shoulder at the still unsworn Gyras, and took out a piece of meat. It

smelled high, not having been fresh when it left Pella. "This is from a haunch of sacrifice," he said, slapping it down upon a boulder. "I knew we should have to do this. Come here. Lay your hand on it. Have you respect for oaths before the gods?"

"Yes." His hand was so chilly that the dead goat-flesh felt quite warm.

"Then say this after me."

The oath was elaborate and exact, the death-fate invoked was ghastly. The boy was well versed in such things, and had on his own account a ready awareness of loopholes. Gyras finished binding himself as he was told, and went to swill his bloody hand in the running stream. The boy sniffed at the meat. "I don't think this is fit to eat, even if we were to waste time making fire." He tossed it away, holstered his javelin, and came back to Gyras' side. "Well, that's done, now we can go on like friends. Let's finish eating, while you tell me about the war."

Passing his hand across his brow, Gyras began to recite his kinsmen's injuries. "No, I know about that. How many are you, how many are they? What kind of country is it? Have you horses?"

Their track threaded green hills, steadily rising. Grass gave way to bracken and thyme, the track wound past pine woods and thickets of arbutus. The ranges heaved up all round them; they met mountain air, with its life-giving holy pureness. They entered the open secrecy of the heights.

Gyras traced back the feud three generations. The boy, his first questions once answered, proved a good listener. Of his own affairs, he said only, "When I've taken my man, you must be my witness at Pella. The King didn't take his man till he was fifteen. Parmenion told me so."

Gyras planned to spend the last night of the journey with distant kinsmen, half a day's ride from home. He pointed out their village, clinging to the edge of a gorge, with rocky slopes above it. There was a mule-track along the precipice; Gyras was for taking a good road round the slope, one of King Archelaos'; but the boy, having learned that the pass was just usable, insisted on going that way to see what it was like. Between the steep bends and giddy drops, he said, "If these are your clansmen, it's no use our saying I'm your kin. Say I'm your commander's son, come to learn about war. They can never claim you lied to them."

Gyras readily agreed; even this would hint that the boy must be kept an eye on. He could do no more, on account of the death-fate. He was a believing man.

On a flattish shelf a few furlongs round about, between a broken hillside and the gorge, was the hamlet of Skopas, built of the brown stone which lay loose all round it, looking like an outcrop itself. On its open side was a stockade of boulders filled in with thorn-brush. Within, the coarse grass was full of cow-pats from the cattle that spent the night there. One or two small hairy horses were at graze; the rest would be out with the herders and hunters. Goats and some ragged sheep moved on the hill; a goat-boy's piping sounded from above, like the call of some wild bird.

Above the pass, on a gnarled dead tree, was spiked a yellow skull, and a few bones left of a hand. When the boy asked about it, Gyras said, "That was a long time back, when I was a child. That was the man killed his own father."

Their coming was the news of half a year. A horn was blown to tell the herdsmen; the oldest Skopian was carried in from the lair of still older rags and skins where he was waiting to die. In the headman's house they were offered sweet small figs, and some tur-bid wine in the best, least chipped cups; people waited with ritual courtesy till they had done, before the questions began, about themselves, and the distant world. Gyras said the Great King had Egypt under his heel again; King Philip had been called in to set things to rights down in Thessaly, and was Archon there now, as good as King; it had put the southerners in a taking. And was it true, asked the headman's brother, that he had taken a new wife, and put the Epirote Queen away?

Aware of a stillness more piercing than all the voices, Gyras said that this was a pack of lies. The King as he got new lands in order might honor this lord or that by taking a daughter into his house; to Gyras' mind, they were by way of a kind of hostage. As for Queen Olympias, she stood in high respect as the mother of the King's heir, a credit to both his parents. Having got off this speech, sweated over in silence some hours before, Gyras cut off comment by asking in his turn for news.

News of the feud was bad. Four enemy Kimolians had met in a glen two of Gyras' clansmen, out after deer. One had lived just long enough to creep home and tell them where to find his brother's corpse before the jackals had it. The Kimolians were puffed with pride; the old man had no hold upon his sons; soon no one would be safe from them. Many deeds were milled over, many words quoted which had struck someone as telling, while the livestock was driven in, and the women cooked the goat which had been slaughtered to feast the guests. With the fall of dark, everyone went to bed.

Alexander shared with the headman's son, who had a proper blanket. It was verminous; so was the child, but being in awe of his guest he let him sleep in what peace the fleas allowed.

He dreamed that Herakles came up to the bed and shook him. He looked as he did in the garden shrine at Pella, beardless and young, hooded in the fanged mask of the lion, its mane hanging down behind. "Get up, lazy boy," he said, "or I shall start without you. I have been calling you this long time."

All the people in the room were sleeping; he took his cloak and stepped softly out. A late bright moon lit the wide uplands. No one kept watch but the dogs. One huge wolflike beast ran up to him; he stood still to be smelled, and it let him be. It was movement outside the fence that would have had them baying.

All was quiet, why had Herakles called him? His eye fell on a tall crag, with an easy way up well worn by feet, the village lookout. If a guard was there . . . But no guard was. He scrambled up. He could trace the good road of Archelaos, winding on down the hill; and on it a creeping shadow.

Twenty-odd horsemen, riding light, without burdens. Even in the far-sounding hills, they were too far off to hear; but something twinkled under the moon.

The boy's eyes widened. He raised both hands to the sky, his shining face uplifted. He had committed himself to Herakles, and the god had answered. Not leaving him to find the battle, he had sent the battle to him.

In the light of the gibbous moon, he stood printing on his mind the shape of the place, the vantage points and the hazards. There was nowhere down there to ambush them. Archelaos, a good road-builder, had no doubt planned against ambushes. They would have to be ambushed here; for the Skopians were outnumbered. They must be roused at once, before the enemy got near enough to hear the stir. If he ran about shaking them up, they would forget him in the scramble; they must be made to listen. Outside the headman's hut hung the horn which had called the villagers. He tested it softly, and blew.

Doors opened, men ran out with clouts clutched round them, women squealed to each other, sheep and goats bleated. The boy, standing up on a high boulder against the glimmering sky, called, "War! It is war!"

The gabble hushed. His clear voice cut in. Ever since he left Pella, he had been thinking in Macedonian.

"I am Alexander, King Philip's son. Gyras knows who I am. I have come to fight in your war for you, because the god has warned me. The Kimolians are there on the valley road, twenty-three riders. Listen to me, and before sunup we'll make an end of them." He called up, by name, the headman and his sons.

They came forward in stunned silence, their eyes starting in the gloom. This was the witch's child, the son of the Epirote.

He sat on a boulder, not wishing to part with the height it lent him, and spoke earnestly, aware all the while of Herakles at his shoulder.

When he had done, the headman sent the women indoors, and told the men to do as the boy had said. They argued at first; it went against the grain to strike no blow at the accursed Kimolians till they were in the stockade among the cattle they had come to steal. But Gyras came out too for it. So in the loom of the false dawn the Skopians armed themselves and caught their ponies, and clustered the far side of the houses. It was clear the Kimolians reckoned on attacking when the men had gone out about their work. The bar of thorn-brush which closed the gateway had been thinned enough to let them in, but not to make them think. The shepherd boys and goat-boys were sent up on the hills, to make it look like a common morning.

The peaks stood dark against the sky, in whose deeps the stars were paling. The boy, holding his bridle and his javelins, watched for the first rose of dawn; he might be seeing it once for all. This he had known; for the first time, now, he felt it. All his life he had been hearing news of violent death; now his body told back the tale to him; the grinding of the iron into one's vitals, the mortal pain, the dark shades waiting as one was torn forth to leave the light, forever, forever. His guardian had left his side. In his silent heart he turned to Herakles, saying, "Why have you forsaken me?"

Dawn touched the highest peak in a glow like flame. He had been perfectly alone; so the voice of Herakles, still as it was, reached him unhindered. It said, "I left you to make you understand my mystery. Do not believe that others will die, not you; it is not for that I am your friend. By laying myself on the pyre I became divine. I have wrestled with Thanatos knee to knee, and I know how death is vanquished. Man's immortality is not to live forever; for that wish is born of fear. Each moment free from fear makes a man immortal."

The rose-red on the hilltops changed to gold. He stood between death and life as between night and morning, and thought with a soaring rapture, I am not afraid. It was better than music or his mother's love; it was the life of the gods. No grief could touch him, no hatred harm him. Things looked bright and clear, as to the stooping eagle. He felt sharp as an arrow, and full of light.

The Kimolians' horses sounded on the hard earth of the road. They paused outside the stockade. A goat-boy piped on the hill. In the houses children talked, innocent of guile; a guileful woman was singing. They kicked the thorn-brush aside, and rode in laughing. The cattle they had come for were still within the pound. They would have the women first.

Suddenly came a yell so loud and high that they thought some wild girl had seen them. Then came the shouts of men.

Horse and foot, the Skopians burst out on them. Some were already making for the houses; these were dealt with quickly. Soon numbers were almost even.

For a while there was only chaos, as men dived and stumbled about among the bawling cattle. Then one of the raiders made a bolt for the gate, and was off. Cheers of triumph rose from the Skopians. The boy perceived that this was the beginning of flight; and that the Skopians were going to allow it, content that the day was theirs, not looking to another day when the enemy would come back, sore from defeat and bent on vengeance. Did they take this for victory? With a shout he rode towards the gate, calling fiercely, "Head them off!"; and, drawn by his certainty, the Skopians followed. The gate was blocked. Cattle still milled about; but men were facing men; there had formed, in little, opposing battle-lines.

Now! thought the boy. He looked at the man across from him.

He had on a war-cap of greasy black old leather, stitched with crudely forged plates of iron, and a corselet of goat's hide with the hair on, worn bald here and there. His red beard was young, his face freckled and peeled with sunburn. He was frowning deeply, not in anger but like a man charged with some work he is not skilled in, who has time for no one's concerns except his own. Nonetheless, thought the boy, that is an old war-cap, often used; and he's a grown man, quite tall. One must take the first comer, that is the proper thing.

He had his two javelins, the first to throw, the second to fight with. Spears were flying, and one Skopian had jumped on a house-roof with a bow. A horse neighed and reared, a shaft sticking in its neck; the rider fell, and scrambled off hopping on one leg; the horse bolted round the houses. Much time seemed to pass in these beginnings. Most of the spears had missed, through impatience, distance or lack of skill. The red-haired man's eyes shifted, waiting for the melee to throw up his own enemy he must fight. Before long, someone else would have him.

The boy poised his throwing-spear as he kicked his pony forward. An easy mark; there was a black patch on the goatskin over the heart. No; this was his first man, it must be hand to hand. Alongside was a dark, stocky, swarthy man with a black beard; the boy jerked back his arm, and threw almost without looking; his fingers reaching for the second shaft the moment the first was gone, his eyes seeking the red-haired man's. The man had seen him, their eyes met. The boy shouted a wordless battle-yell, and urged on his horse with his spear-butt. It leaped forward jerkily over the broken ground.

The man leveled his spear, a longer one, peering about. His eyes passed over the boy, shifting and seeking. He was waiting for someone; for a grown man, whom he must heed.

The boy threw up his head, and shouted at his lungs' full pitch. The man must be roused, made to believe in him, or it would not be a proper killing; it would be like taking him in the back, or half asleep. It must be perfect, there must be nothing that could ever be said against it. He yelled again.

The raiders were a big-made tribe. To the red-haired man, it seemed a child who came riding. He gazed in unease, disliking the need to keep an eye on him, fearing that while he beat him off some man would rush in and take him off guard. His eyesight was only middling; though the boy had seen him clearly, he took some moments to make out the approaching face. It was not a child's. It raised the hair on his neck.

The boy set his face into a warrior's, that he might be believed in and challenge death. In a perfect singleness, free from hatred, anger, or doubt, pure in dedication, exultant in victory over fear, he swooped towards the red-haired man. With this face of inhuman radiance; with this being, whatever it was, eerie, numinous, uttering its high hawklike cries, the man wanted no more to do. He swerved his horse; a burly Skopian was nearing, perhaps to single him out; someone else should deal with the matter. His eye had strayed too long. With a shrill "Ahii-i!" the shining man-child was on him. He thrust with his spear; the creature swung past it; he saw deep sky-filled eyes, a mouth of ecstasy. A blow struck his breast, which at once was more than a blow, was ruin and darkness. As sight faded from his eyes, it seemed to him that the smiling lips had parted to drink his life.

The Skopians cheered the boy, clearly a luck-bringer; it had been the quickest kill of the fight. The raiders were shaken; this was the favorite son of their headman, who was old and would get no more. They struggled in bad order to the gate-gap, forcing their horses through the cattle and the men; not all the Skopians were resolute. Horses squealed, cows bawled and trampled the fallen; there was a stink of fresh-dropped dung, crushed herbage, sweat and blood.

As the flight cohered, it was seen to head for the road. The boy, steering his horse through goats, remembered the lie of the land, seen from the lookout. He burst out of the press, with an ear-piercing yell of "Stop them! The pass! Head them for the pass!" He never looked back; had the spellbound Skopians not streamed after him, he would have confronted the Kimolians all alone.

They were in time; the raiders were contained, all ways but the one. In full panic now, unfit for a wise choice of evils, scared of the precipices, but ignorant of the goat-ways on the rocky hill, they crowded onto the narrow track above the gorge.

At the back of the rout, a single man wheeled round to face the pursuers. Straw-haired, darkly tanned, hawk-nosed, he had been first in attack and last to fly; last, too, to give up struggling to reach the road. Knowing the choice of evils had been wrong, he waited where the mouth of the pass grew narrow. He had planned and led the raid; his youngest brother had fallen, at the hand of a boy who should still have been herding goats; he would have to face their father with it. Better redeem shame in death; the odds were on death in any case; a few might escape, if he could hold the pass awhile. He drew the old iron sword which had been his grandfather's, and, dismounting, straddled the rough way.

The boy, riding up from his place in the dragnet, saw him hold his own against three, take a head blow, give at the knees. The chase broke over him. Ahead, the raiders were strung along the ledge. Yelling with joy, the Skopians hurled rocks at them, the archer loosed his bow. Horses fell screaming down the cliff, men followed the horses. They had lost half their strength, before the remnant turned out of range.

It was over. The boy reined in his pony. Its neck had been cut, it began to feel the pain and be plagued by flies. He caressed and reassured it. He had only come to take his man, and he had won a battle. This the god had given him from the sky.

The Skopians crowded round him, those who had not climbed down to strip the bodies in the gorge. Their heavy hands were on his back and shoulders, the air round him steamed with their strong breath. He was their general, their fighting quail, their little lion, their luck-piece. Gyras walked by him with the air of a man whose status is changed forever.

Someone shouted, "This whore's son is moving still." The boy, not to miss anything, shoved in. The straw-haired man lay where he had been beaten down, bleeding from his torn scalp, trying to struggle up on one arm. A Skopian grasped him by the hair, so that he cried out with pain, and pulled back his head to cut his throat. The others gave scarcely a second glance to this natural action.

"No!" said the boy. They all turned, surprised and puzzled. He ran up and knelt by the man, pushing aside the knife. "He was brave. He did it for the others. He was like Ajax at the ships."

The Skopians broke into lively argument. What did he mean? Something about some sacred hero, about an omen, that it would be bad luck to kill the man? No, said another, it was just some fancy of the boy's, but war was war. Laughing, pushing aside the first comer, he came knife in hand to the man upon the ground.

"If you kill him," said the boy, "I will make you sorry. I swear it by my father's head."

The knife-bearer looked round with a start. A moment ago, the lad had been all sunshine. Gyras muttered, "You had better do as he says."

He stood up, saying, "You must let this man go. I claim him as my battle-prize. He is to have his horse; I will give you the horse of the man I killed, to make good." They listened open-mouthed; but, he thought looking round, they were reckoning he would soon forget and they could finish the man off later. "Get him mounted now, at once, and put him on the road. Gyras, help them."

The Skopians escaped into laughter. They bundled the man along to his horse, amusing themselves till the sharp young voice behind them called, "Stop doing that." They slashed the horse's rump and it went walloping off along the road, its limp rider clinging to its mane. The boy turned back, the frown-line smoothed from his brow. "Now," he said, "I must find my man."

No living wounded were left upon the field. The Skopians had been carried home by their women, the raiders butchered, mostly by the women too. Now they had come to their dead, flinging themselves across the bodies, beating their breasts, clawing at their faces, wrenching their loosened hair. Their keening hung in the air like the voices of wild things native to the place, young wolves or crying birds or goats at yeaning-time. White clouds sailed the sky, calmly, sending dark wings over the mountains, touching far forest-tops with black.

The boy thought, This is a battlefield. This is what it is like. The enemy dead lay littered and bundled about, forsaken, ungainly, sprawling. The women, clustered like crows, hid the fallen victors. Already, balanced swaying on high air, by one and one vultures appeared.

[123]

The red-haired man lay on his back, one knee bent up, his young beard cocked at the sky. The iron-patched war-cap, two generations older than he, had been taken already; it would serve many other men. He was not bleeding much. There had been a moment, while he was falling, when the javelin had stuck in him, and the boy had thought he would have to let go or be dragged off too. But he had tugged once more and it had pulled free, just in time.

He looked at the white face, already growing livid, the gaping mouth, and thought again, This is a battlefield, a soldier must learn to know it. He had taken his man, and must show a trophy. There was no dagger, not even a belt; the goatskin corselet was gone. The women had been quickly over the field. The boy was angry in himself, but knew that complaint would bring no redress and would lose him face. He must have a trophy. Nothing was left, now, except . . .

"Here, little warrior." A Skopian youth with black tangled hair stood over him, showing broken teeth in a friendly smile. In his hand was a cleaver with half-dry blood over it. "Let me have off the head for you. I know the knack."

Between the grinning and the gaping face, the boy paused silent. The cleaver, light in the youth's big hand, looked heavy for his own. Gyras said quickly, "They only do that in the back country now, Alexander."

"I had better have it," he said. "There's nothing else." The youth came forward eagerly. Gyras might be citified, but for the King's son old customs were good enough; that was the way of quality. He tried the edge on his thumb. But the boy had found himself too glad to have this work done for him. "No. I must cut it off myself." While the Skopians laughed and swore admiringly, the cleaver, warm, sticky, slimy, raw-smelling, was put in his hand. He knelt by the corpse, forcing himself to keep his eyes open, doggedly chopping at the neckbone, spattering himself with bloody shreds, till the head rolled free. Grasping a handful of dead hair—for there must be nothing he could know after in his most secret soul that he had feared to do—he stood upright. "Fetch me my gamebag, Gyras."

Gyras unstrapped it from the saddlecloth. The boy dropped the head in, and rubbed his palms on the bag. There was still blood between his fingers, sticking them together. The stream was a hun-

dred feet down, he would wash them going home. He turned to
bid his hosts farewell.

"Wait!" shouted someone. Two or three men, carrying something,
were running and waving. "Don't let the little lord go. Here, we
have his other trophy for him. Two, yes, look, he killed two."

The boy frowned. He wanted to go home now. He had only
fought one combat. What did they mean?

The foremost man ran up panting. "It's true. This one here"—he
pointed to the raw-necked trunk—"that was his second man. He
took the first with a javelin-throw, before ever we closed with them.
I saw it myself; he pitched straight down stuck like a pig. He was
creeping about awhile, but he was finished before the women got
to him. Here you are, little lord. Something to show your father."

The second man displayed the head, holding it up by its black
hair. The strong bushy beard hid the shorn neck. It was the head of
the man he had thrown his first javelin at, before he fought hand to
hand. There had been an eye-blink moment, when he had seen
this was the man to have it. He had forgotten, his mind had shut
on it as if it had never been. Held by the forelock, it had an arrogant
upward tilt; rigor had set a gap-toothed grin on it; the skin was
swarthy, one of the eyes was half closed, showing only the white.

The boy looked at the face confronting his. A coldness spread in
his belly; he felt a great heave of nausea, a clammy sweat in his
palms. He swallowed, and fought to keep from vomiting.

"I didn't kill him," he said. "I never killed that man."

They began all three at once to reassure him, describing the body,
swearing it had no other wound, offering to take him there, thrusting the head towards him. Two men at his first blooding! He could
tell his grandsons. They appealed to Gyras; the little lord was over-
done, and no wonder; if he left his prize behind, when he was himself again he would be sorry; Gyras must keep it for him.

"No!" The boy's voice had risen. "I don't want it. I didn't see him
die. You can't bring him to me if the women killed him. You can't
tell what happened. Take it away."

They clicked their tongues, sorry to obey him to his later loss.
Gyras took aside the headman, and whispered in his ear. His face
changed; he took the boy kindly round the shoulders, and said he
must be warmed with a drop of wine before the long ride home.

The boy walked with him quietly, his face with its clear pallor remote and gentle, a faint blueness under his eyes. Presently with the wine the color came back into his skin; he began to smile, and before long joined in the laughter.

Outside there was a buzz of praise. What a fine boy! Such pluck, such a head on his shoulders; and now such proper feeling. Not much of a likeness, yet it had moved his heart. What father would not be proud of such a son?

"Look well at the horn of the hoof. A thick horn makes for much sounder feet than a thin one. Take care, too, to see the hoofs are high front and back, not flattened; a high hoof keeps the frog clear of the ground."

"Is there any of that book," asked Philotas, Parmenion's son, "that you don't know by heart?"

"One can't know too much of Xenophon," Alexander said, "when it comes to horses. I want to read his books about Persia, too. Are you buying anything today?"

"Not this year. My brother's buying one."

"Xenophon says a good hoof ought to make a ringing noise like a cymbal. That one there looks splay to me. My father wants a new battle-charger. He had one killed under him, fighting the Illyrians last year." He looked at the dais beside them, run up as usual for the spring horse-fair; the King had not yet arrived.

It was a sharp brilliant day; the lake and the lagoon were ruffled and darkly gleaming; the white clouds that skimmed across to the distant mountains had edges honed blue, like swords. The bruised turf of the meadow was green from the winter rains. All morning the soldiers had been buying; officers for themselves, tribal chiefs for the vassals who made up their squadrons (in Macedon, the feudal and the regimental always overlapped) tough stocky thick-maned beasts, lively and sleek from the winter grazing. By noon, this common business was done; now the bloodstock was coming out, racers and parade show-horses and chargers, curried and dressed up to the eyes.

The horse fair at Pella was a rite not less honored than the sacred feasts. Dealers came from the horse-lands of Thessaly, from Thrace, from Epiros, even across Hellespont; these would always claim their stock was crossed with the fabled Nisaian strain of the Persian kings.

Important buyers were only now arriving. Alexander had been there most of the day. Following him about, not yet at ease with him or with one another, were half a dozen boys whom Philip had lately collected from fathers he wished to honor.

It was long since a Prince's Guard had been formed in Macedon for an heir just come of age. The King himself had never been heir apparent. In the wars of succession before that, no heir for generations had had time to come of age before he was murdered or dispossessed. Records revealed that the last Prince of Macedon to have his Companions chosen for him in proper form had been Perdikkas the First, some fifty years before. One ancient man survived of them; he had tales as long as Nestor's about border wars and cattle-raids, and could name the grandchildren of Perdikkas' bastards; but he had forgotten everything about procedure.

The Companions should have been youths of about the Prince's age, who had also passed the test of manhood. No such boy was now to be found in the royal lands. Fathers put forward eagerly the claims of sons sixteen or seventeen years old, who already looked and talked like men. They argued that most of Alexander's current friends were even older. It was natural, they added tactfully, with so brave and forward a boy.

Philip endured the compliments with a good grace, while he lived with the remembered eyes which had met his when the head, already stinking from its journey, was laid before him. During the days of waiting and seeking news, it had been clear to him that if the boy never came back, he would have to have Olympias killed before she could kill him. All this was tough meat to feast on. Epikrates, too, had left, telling him the Prince had decided to give up music, and not meeting his eyes. Philip bestowed lavish guest-gifts, but could see an unpleasant tale going round the odeons of Hellas; these men went everywhere.

In the upshot, no real attempt had been made to muster a formal Prince's Guard. Alexander took no interest in this dead institution; he had picked up for himself the group of youths and grown men who were already known everywhere as Alexander's Friends.

[127]

They themselves were apt to forget that he was only thirteen last summer.

The morning, however, of the horse fair, he had been spending with the boys attached to him by the King. He had been pleased to have their company; if he treated them all as his juniors, it was not to assert himself or put them down, but because he never felt it otherwise. He had talked horses untiringly, and they had done their best to keep up. His sword belt, his fame, and the fact that with all this he was the smallest of them, bewildered them and made them awkward. They were relieved that now, for the showing of the bloodstock, his friends were gathering, Ptolemy and Harpalos and Philotas and the rest. Left on one side, they clumped together and, with their pack-leader gone, started edging for precedence like a chance-met group of dogs.

"My father couldn't come in today. It's not worth it; he imports his horses straight from Thessaly. All the breeders know him."

"I shall need a bigger horse soon; but my father's leaving it till next year, when I've grown taller."

"Alexander's a hand shorter than you, and *he* rides men's horses."

"Oh, well, I expect they trained them specially."

The tallest of the boys said, "He took his boar. I suppose you think they trained a boar for him."

"That was set up, it always is," said the boy with the richest father, who could count on having it set up for him.

"It was not set up!" said the tall boy angrily. The others exchanged looks; he reddened. His voice, which was breaking, gave a sudden startling growl. "My father heard about it. Ptolemy tried to set it up without his knowing, because he was set on doing it, and Ptolemy didn't want him killed. They cleared the wood except for a small one. Then when they brought him there in the morning, overnight a big one had got in. Ptolemy went as white as a fleece, they said, and tried to make him go home. But he saw through it then; he said this was the boar the god had sent him, and the god knew best. They couldn't budge him. They were in a sweat with fright, they knew he was too light to hold it, and the net wouldn't hold it long. But he went straight for the big vein in the neck; no one had to help him. Everyone knows that's so."

"No one would dare spoil the story, you mean. Just look at him now. My father would belt me, if I stood in the horse-field letting men make up to me. Which of them does he go with?"

One of the others put in, "No one, my brother says."

"Oh? Did he try?"

"His friend did. Alexander seemed to like him, he even kissed him once. But then when he wanted the rest, he seemed surprised and quite put out. He's young for his age, my brother says."

"And how old was your brother when he took his man?" asked the tallest boy. "And his boar?"

"That's different. My brother says he'll come to it all of a sudden, and be mad for girls. His father did."

"Oh, but the King likes—"

"Be quiet, you fool!" They all looked over their shoulders; but the men were watching two racehorses whose dealer had set them to run round the field. The boys ceased squabbling, till the Royal Bodyguard began to form up around the dais, in readiness for the King.

"Look," whispered someone, pointing to the officer in command. "That's Pausanias." There were knowing looks, and inquiring ones. "He was the King's favorite before the one who died. He was the rival."

"What happened?"

"Shsh. Everyone knows. The King threw him over and he was madly angry. He stood up at a drinking-party and called the new boy a shameless whore who'd go with anyone for pay. People pulled them apart; but either the boy really cared for the King, or it was the slight to his honor; it gnawed at him, and in the end he asked a friend, I think it was Attalos, to give the King a message when he was dead. Then next time they fought the Illyrians, he rushed straight in front of the King among the enemy, and got hacked to death."

"What did the King do?"

"Buried him."

"No, to Pausanias?"

There were confused whispers. "No one really knows if . . ." "Of course he did!" "You could be killed for saying that." "Well, he can't have been sorry." "No, it was Attalos and the boy's friends, my brother says so."

[129]

Mary Renault

"What did they *do?*"

"Attalos got Pausanias dead drunk one night. Then they carried him out to the grooms and said they could enjoy themselves, he'd go with anyone without even being paid. I suppose they beat him up as well. He woke in the stable yard next morning."

Someone whistled softly. They stared at the officer of the Guard. He looked old for his years, and not strikingly handsome. He had grown a beard.

"He wanted Attalos put to death. Of course the King couldn't do it, even if he'd wanted; imagine putting *that* to the Assembly! But he had to do something, Pausanias being an Orestid. He gave him some land, and made him Second Officer of the Royal Guard."

The tallest boy, who had heard the whole tale in silence, said, "Does Alexander get to know of things like this?"

"His mother tells him everything, to turn him against the King."

"Well, but the King insulted him in Hall. That's why he went out to take his man."

"Is that what he told you?"

"No, of course he wouldn't speak of it. My father was there; he often has supper with the King. Our land's quite near."

"So you've met Alexander before, then?"

"Only once, when we were children. He didn't know me again, I've grown too much."

"Wait till he hears you're the same age, he won't like that."

"Who said I was?"

"You told me you were born the same month."

"I never said the same year."

"You did, the first day you came."

"Are you calling me a liar? Well, come on, are you?"

"Hephaistion, you fool, you can't fight here."

"Don't call me a liar, then."

"You do look fourteen," said a peacemaker. "In the gymnasium, I thought you were more."

"You know who Hephaistion has a look of? Alexander. Not really *like*, but, say, like his big brother."

"You hear that, Hephaistion? How well does your mother know the King?"

He had counted too much on the protection of place and time. Next moment, with a split lip, he was on the ground. In the stir of the King's approach, few people saw it. Alexander all this while had kept the tail of his eye on them, because he thought of himself as their commanding officer. But he decided not to notice it. They were not precisely on duty, and the boy who had been knocked down was the one he liked the least.

Philip rode up to the stand, escorted by the First Officer of the Guard, the Somatophylax. Pausanias saluted and stepped aside. The boys stood respectfully, one sucking his lip, the other his knuckles.

The horse fair was always easy-going, an outing where men were men. Philip in riding-clothes lifted his switch to the lords and squires and officers and horse-dealers; mounted the stand, shouted to this friend or that to join him. His eye fell on his son; he made a movement, then saw the little court around him and turned away. Alexander picked up his talk with Harpalos, a dark lively good-looking youth with much offhand charm, whom fate had cursed with a clubfoot. Alexander had always admired the way he bore it.

A racehorse came pounding by, ridden by a little Nubian boy in a striped tunic. Word had gone round that this year the King was only in the market for a battle-charger; but he had paid the sum, already a legend, of thirteen talents for the racer that had won for him at Olympia; and the dealer had thought it worth a try. Philip smiled and shook his head; the Nubian boy, who had hoped to be bought with the horse, to wear gold earrings and eat meat on feast-days, cantered back, his face a landscape of grief.

The chargers were led up, in precedence fiercely fought over by the dealers all the forenoon, and settled in the end by substantial bribes. The King came down to peer into mouths and at upturned hooves, to feel shanks and listen to chests. The horses were led away, or kept by in case nothing better turned up. There was a lag. Philip looked impatiently about. The big Thessalian dealer, Philonikos, who had been fuming for some time, said to his runner, "Tell them I'll have their guts for picket ropes, if they don't bring the beast *now*."

"Kittos says, sir, they can *bring* him, but . . ."

"I had to break the brute myself, must I show him too? Tell

[131]

Kittos from me, if I miss this sale, they won't have hide enough left between them for a pair of sandal soles." With a sincere, respectful smile, he approached the King. "Sir, he's on his way. You'll see he's all I wrote you from Larissa, and more. Forgive the delay; they've just now told me, some fool let him slip his tether. In prime fettle as he is, he was hard to catch. Ah! Here he comes now."

They led up, at a careful walk, a black with a white blaze. The other horses had been ridden, to show their paces. Though he was certainly in a sweat, he did not breathe like a horse that had been running. When they pulled him up before the King and his horse-trainer, his nostrils flared and his black eye rolled sidelong; he tried to rear his head, but the groom dragged it down. His bridle was costly, red leather trimmed with silver; but he had no saddlecloth. The dealer's lips moved viciously in his beard.

A hushed voice beside the dais said, "Look, Ptolemy. Look at *that.*"

"There, sir!" said Philonikos, forcing rapture into his voice. "There's Thunder. If there ever stepped a mount fit for a King . . ."

He was indeed, at all points, the ideal horse of Xenophon. Starting, as he advises, with the feet, one saw that the horns of the hooves were deep before and behind; when he stamped, as he was doing now (just missing the groom's foot) they made a ringing sound like a cymbal. His leg-bones were strong but flexible; his chest was broad, his neck arched, as the writer puts it, like a gamecock's; the mane was long, strong, silky and badly combed. His back was firm and wide, the spine well padded, his loins were short and broad. His black coat shone; on one flank was branded the horned triangle, the Oxhead, which was the mark of his famous breed. Strikingly, his forehead had a white blaze which almost copied its shape.

"That," said Alexander with awe, "is a perfect horse. Perfect everywhere."

"He's vicious," Ptolemy said.

Over at the horse-lines, the chief groom Kittos said to a fellow slave who had watched their struggles, "Days like this, I wish they'd cut my throat along with my father's, when they took our town. My back's not healed from last time, and he'll be at me again before sundown."

"That horse is a murderer. What does he want, does he want to kill the King?"

"There was nothing wrong with that horse, I tell you nothing, nothing beyond high spirits, till he lost his temper when it took against him. He's like a wild beast in his drink; mostly it's us men he takes it out of, we come cheaper than horses. Now it's anyone's fault but his; he'd kill me if I told him its temper's spoiled for good. He only bought it from Kroisos a month ago, just for this deal. Two talents he paid." His hearer whistled. "He reckoned to get three, and he well might if he'd not set out to break its heart. It's held out well, I'll say that for it. He broke mine long ago."

Philip, seeing the horse was restive, walked round it a few paces away. "Yes, I like his looks. Well, let's see him move."

Philonikos took a few steps towards the horse. It gave a squeal like a battle-trumpet, forced up its head against the hanging weight of the groom, and pawed the air. The dealer swore and kept his distance; the groom got the horse in hand. As if dye were running from the red bridle, a few drops of blood fell from its mouth.

Alexander said, "Look at that bit they've put on him. Look at those barbs."

"It seems even that can't hold him," said big Philotas easily. "Beauty's not everything."

"And still he got his head up." Alexander had moved forward. The men strolled after, looking out over him; he barely reached Philotas' shoulder.

"You can see his spirit, sir," Philonikos told the King eagerly. "A horse like this, one could train to rear up and strike the enemy."

"The quickest way to have your mount killed under you," said Philip brusquely, "making it show its belly." He beckoned the leathery bow-legged man attending him. "Will you try him, Jason?"

The royal trainer walked round to the front of the horse, making cheerful soothing sounds. It backed, stamped and rolled its eyes. He clicked his tongue, saying firmly, "Thunder, boy, hey, Thunder." At the sound of its name it seemed to quiver all over with suspicion and rage. Jason returned to noises. "Keep his head till I'm up," he told the groom, "that looks like one man's work." He approached the horse's side, ready to reach for the roots of the mane; the only means, unless a man had a spear to vault on, of getting up. The saddlecloth, had it been on, would have offered comfort and show, but no kind of foothold. A hoist was for the elderly, and Persians, who were notoriously soft.

At the last moment, his shadow passed before the horse's eyes. It gave a violent start, swerved, and lashed out, missing Jason by inches. He stepped back and squinted at it sideways, screwing up one eye and the side of his mouth. The King met his look and raised his eyebrows.

Alexander, who had been holding his breath, looked round at Ptolemy and said in a voice of anguish, "He won't buy him."

"Who would?" said Ptolemy, surprised. "Can't think why he was shown. Xenophon wouldn't have bought him. You were quoting him only just now, how the nervous horse won't let you harm the enemy, but he'll do plenty of harm to you."

"Nervous? He? He's the bravest horse I ever saw. He's a fighter. Look where he's been beaten, under the belly too, you can see the weals. If Father doesn't buy him, that man will flay him alive. I can see it in his face."

Jason tried again. Before he got anywhere near the horse it started kicking. He looked at the King, who shrugged his shoulders.

"It was his shadow," said Alexander urgently to Ptolemy. "He's shy of his own, even. Jason should have seen."

"He's seen enough; he's got the King's life to think of. Would you ride a horse like that to war?"

"Yes, I would. To war most of all."

Philotas raised his brows, but failed to catch Ptolemy's eye.

"Well, Philonikos," said Philip, "if that's the pick of your stable, let's waste no more time. I've work to do."

"Sir, give us a moment. He's frisky for want of exercise; too full of corn. With his strength, he—"

"I can buy something better for three talents than a broken neck."

"My lord, for you only, I'll make a special price."

"I'm busy," Philip said.

Philonikos set his thick mouth in a wide straight line. The groom, hanging for dear life on the spiked bit, began to turn the horse for the horse-lines. Alexander called out in his high carrying voice, "What a waste! The best horse in the show!"

Anger and urgency gave it a note of arrogance that made heads turn. Philip looked round startled. Never, at the worst of things, had the boy been rude to him in public. It had best be ignored till later. The groom and the horse were moving off.

"The best horse ever shown here, and all he needs is handling." Alexander had come out into the field. All his friends, even Ptolemy, left a discreet space round him; he was going too far. The whole crowd was staring. "A horse in ten thousand, just thrown away."

Philip, looking again, decided the boy had not meant to be so insolent. He was a colt too full of corn, ever since his two precocious exploits. They had gone to his head. No lesson so good, thought Philip, as the one a man teaches to himself. "Jason here," he said, "has been training horses for twenty years. And you, Philonikos; how long?"

The dealer's eyes shifted from father to son; he was on a tightrope. "Ah, well, sir, I was reared to it from a boy."

"You hear that, Alexander? But you think you can do better?"

Alexander glanced, not at his father but at Philonikos. With an unpleasant sense of shock, the dealer looked away.

"Yes. With this horse, I could."

"Very well," said Philip. "If you can, he's yours."

The boy looked at the horse, with parted lips and devouring eyes. The groom had paused with it. It snorted over its shoulder.

"And if you can't?" said the King briskly. "What are you staking?"

Alexander took a deep breath, his eyes not leaving the horse. "If I can't ride him, I'll pay for him myself."

Philip raised his dark heavy brows. "At three talents?" The boy had only just been put up to a youth's allowance; it would take most of this year's, and the next as well.

"Yes," Alexander said.

"I hope you mean it. I do."

"So do I." Roused from his single concern with the horse, he saw that everyone was staring: the officers, the chiefs, the grooms and dealers, Ptolemy and Harpalos and Philotas; the boys he had spent the morning with. The tall one, Hephaistion, who moved so well that he always caught the eye, had stepped out before the others. For a moment their looks met.

Alexander smiled at Philip. "It's a bet, then, Father. He's mine; and the loser pays." There was a buzz of laughter and applause in the royal circle, born of relief that it had turned good-humored. Only Philip, who had caught it full in the eyes, had known it for a battle-smile, save for one watcher of no importance who had known it too.

Philonikos, scarcely able to credit this happy turn of fate, hastened to overtake the boy, who was making straight for the horse. Since he could not win, it was important he should not break his neck. It would be too much to hope that the King would settle up for him.

"My lord, you'll find that—"

Alexander looked round and said, "Go away."

"But, my lord, when you come to—"

"Go away. Over there, down wind, where he can't see you or smell you. *You've* done enough."

Philonikos looked into the paled and widened eyes. He went, in silence, exactly where he was told.

Alexander remembered, then, that he had not asked when the horse was first called Thunder, or if it had had another name. It had said plainly enough that Thunder was the word for tyranny and pain. It must have a new name, then. He walked round, keeping his shadow behind, looking at the horned blaze under the blowing forelock.

"Oxhead," he said, falling into Macedonian, the speech of truth and love. "Boukephalos, Boukephalos."

The horse's ears went up. At the sound of this voice, the hated presence had lost power and been driven away. What now? It had lost all trust in men. It snorted, and pawed the ground in warning.

Ptolemy said, "The King may be sorry he set him on to this."

"He was born lucky," said Philotas. "Do you want to bet?"

Alexander said to the groom, "I'll take him. You needn't wait."

"Oh, no, sir! When you're mounted, my lord. My lord, they'll hold me accountable."

"No, he's mine now. Just give me his head without jerking that bit . . . I said, give it me. *Now.*"

He took the reins, easing them at first only a little. The horse snorted, then turned and snuffed at him. The off forefoot raked restlessly. He took the reins in one hand, to run the other along the moist neck; then shifted his grip to the headstall, so that the barbed bit no longer pressed at all. The horse only pulled forward a little. He said to the groom, "Go that way. Don't cross the light."

He pushed round the horse's head to face the bright spring sun. Their shadows fell out of sight behind them. The smell of its sweat and breath and leather bathed him in its steam. "Boukephalos," he said softly.

It strained forward, trying to drag him with it; he took in the rein a little. A horsefly was on its muzzle; he ran his hand down, till his fingers felt the soft lip. Almost pleadingly now, the horse urged them both onward, as if saying, "Come quickly away from here."

"Yes, yes," he said stroking its neck. "All in good time, when I say, we'll go. You and I don't run away."

He had better take off his cloak; while he spared a hand for the pin, he talked on to keep the horse in mind of him. "Remember who we are. Alexander and Boukephalos."

The cloak fell behind him; he slid his arm over the horse's back. It must be near fifteen hands, a tall horse for Greece; he was used to fourteen. This one was as tall as Philotas' horse about which he talked so much. The black eye rolled round at him. "Easy, easy, now. I'll tell you when."

With the reins looped in his left hand he grasped the arch of the mane; with his right, its base between the shoulders. He could feel the horse gather itself together. He ran a few steps with it to gain momentum, then leaped, threw his right leg over; he was up.

The horse felt the light weight on its back, compact of certainty; the mercy of invincible hands, the forbearance of immovable will; a nature it knew and shared, transfigured to divinity. Men had not mastered it; but it would go with the god.

The crowd was silent at first. They were men who knew horses, and had more sense than to startle this one. In a breathing hush they waited for it to get its head, taking for granted the boy would be run away with, eager to applaud if he could only stick on and ride it to a standstill. But he had it in hand; it was waiting his sign to go. There was a hum of wonder; then, when they saw him lean forward and kick his heel with a shout, when boy and horse went racing down towards the water-meadows, the roar began. They vanished into the distance; only the rising clouds of wildfowl showed where they had gone.

They came back at last with the sun behind them, their shadow thrown clear before. Like the feet of a carved pharaoh treading his beaten enemies, the drumming hooves trampled the shadow triumphantly into the ground.

At the horse-field they slowed to a walk. The horse blew and shook its bridle. Alexander sat easy, in the pose which Xenophon commends: the legs straight down, gripping with the thigh, relaxed below the knee. He rode towards the stand; but a man stood waiting down in front of it. It was his father.

He swung off cavalry style, across the neck with his back to the horse; considered the best way in war, if the horse allowed it. The horse was remembering things learned before the tyranny. Philip put out both arms; Alexander came down into them. "Look out we don't jerk his mouth, Father," he said. "It's sore."

Philip pounded him on the back. He was weeping. Even his blind eye wept real tears. "My son!" he said choking. There was wet in his harsh beard. "Well done, my son, my son."

Alexander returned his kiss. It seemed to him that this was a moment nothing could undo. "Thank you, Father. Thank you for my horse. I shall call him Oxhead."

The horse gave a sudden start. Philonikos was coming up, beaming and full of compliments. Alexander looked round, and motioned with his head. Philonikos withdrew. The buyer was never wrong.

A surging crowd had gathered. "Will you tell them to keep off, Father? He won't stand people yet. I'll have to rub him down myself, or he'll catch a chill."

He saw to the horse, keeping the best of the grooms beside him for it to know him another time. The crowd was still in the horse-field. All was quiet in the stable yard when he came out, flushed from the ride and the work, tousled, smelling of horse. Only one loiterer was about; the tall boy Hephaistion, whose eyes had wished him victory. He smiled an acknowledgment. The boy smiled back, hesitated, and came nearer. There was a pause.

"Would you like to see him?"

"Yes, Alexander . . . It was just as if he knew you. I felt it, like an omen. What is he called?"

"I'm calling him Oxhead." They were speaking Greek.

"That's better than Thunder. He hated that."

"You live near here, don't you?"

"Yes. I can show you. You can see from over here. Not that first hill there, the second, the one behind it—"

"You've been here before. I remember you. You helped me fix a sling once, no, it was a quiver. And your father hauled you off."

"I didn't know who you were."

"You showed me the hills before; I remembered then. And you were born in Lion Month, the same year as me."

"Yes."

"You're half a head taller. But your father's tall, isn't he?"

"Yes he is, and my uncles too."

"Xenophon says you can tell a tall horse when it's foaled, by the length of leg. When we're men you'll still be taller."

Hephaistion looked into the confident and candid eyes. He recalled his father saying that the King's young son might have more chance to make his growth, if that stone-faced tutor would not overwork and underfeed him. He should have been protected, some friend should have been there. "You'll still be the one who can ride Boukephalos."

"Come and look at him. Not too near just yet; I shall have to be here at first every time they groom him, I can see that."

He found he had fallen into Macedonian. They looked at each other and smiled.

They had been talking some time, before he remembered he had meant to go straight up from the stable, just as he was, and bring the news to his mother. For the first time in his life, he had forgotten all about her.

A few days after, he made a sacrifice to Herakles.

The hero had been generous. He deserved something richer than a goat or a ram.

Olympias agreed. If her son thought nothing too good for Herakles, she thought nothing too good for her son. She had been writing letters to all her friends, and her kindred in Epiros, relating that Philip had tried again and again to mount the horse, and had been thrown with indignity before all the people; how it was as savage as a lion, but her son had tamed it. She opened her new bale of stuffs from Athens, inviting him to choose stuff for a new festal chiton. He chose plain, fine white wool, and, when she said it was too mean for so great a day, answered that it was proper for a man.

He brought his offering in a gold cup to the hero-shrine in the garden. His father and mother were present; it was a court occasion.

Having made the proper invocation to the hero, with his praises and his epithets, he thanked him for his gifts to mankind, and finished, "As you have been to me, so remain; be favorable to me in what I shall henceforth undertake, according to my prayers."

He tilted the cup. A translucent stream of incense, like grains of amber, shone in the sunlight, and fell on the glowing wood. A cloud of sweet blue smoke rose to heaven.

All the company, but one, pronounced amen. Leonidas, who had come to watch because he thought it his duty, compressed his lips. He was leaving soon; another was taking up his charge. Though the boy had not yet been told, his good spirits were offensive. The Arabian gum was still showering from the chalice; the cost must run into scores of drachmas. This after his constant training in austerity, his warnings against excess!

Among the cheerful pieties, his voice said tartly, "Be less wasteful of such precious things, Alexander, till you are master of the lands they grow in."

Alexander turned from the altar, with the emptied cup in his hand. He looked at Leonidas with an alert kind of surprise, followed by grave attention. At length he said, "Yes. I will remember."

As he came down the steps from the shrine, his eyes met the waiting eyes of Hephaistion, who understood the nature of omens. There was no need for them to speak of it after.

5

"I KNOW NOW who it will be. Father's had a letter, he sent for me this morning. I hope this man will be bearable. If not, we must make a plan."

"You can count on me," said Hephaistion, "even if you want to drown him. You've put up with more than enough. Is he a real philosopher?"

They were sitting in the trough between two of the Palace gables; a private spot, since only Alexander had climbed there till he showed Hephaistion the route.

"Oh, yes, from the Academy. He was taught by Plato. You'll come to the lessons? Father says you can."

"I'd only hold you back."

"Sophists teach by disputation, he wants my friends. We can think later who else to have. It won't just be logic-chopping, he'll have to teach things I can use, Father told him that. He wrote back that a man's education should be suited to his station and his duties. That doesn't tell us much."

"At least this one can't beat you. He's an Athenian?"

"No, a Stagirite. He's the son of Nikomachos, who was my grandfather Amyntas' doctor. My father's too I suppose, when he was a child. You know how Amyntas lived, like a wolf in hunting-country, throwing out his enemies or trying to get back himself. Nikomachos must have been loyal. I don't know how good a doctor he was. Amyntas died in bed; that's very rare in our family."

"So this son—what's he called—?"

"Aristotle."

"He knows the country, that's something. Is he very old?"

"About forty. Not old for a philosopher. They live forever. Isokrates, who wants Father to lead the Greeks, is ninety-odd, and *he* applied for the job! Plato lived to over eighty. Father says Aristotle had hoped to be head of the School, but Plato had chosen a nephew of his. That's why Aristotle left Athens."

"So then he asked to come here?"

"No, he left when we were nine. I know the year, because of the Chalkidian war. And he couldn't go home to Stagira, Father had just burned it and enslaved the people. What is it pulling my hair?"

"It's a stick from the tree we came up." Hephaistion, who was not very neat-handed, unwound with anxious care the walnut twig from its shining tangle, which smelled of some expensive wash used on it by Olympias, and of summer grass. This done, he slid his arm down to Alexander's waist. He had done it the first time almost by accident; though not rebuffed, he had waited two days before daring to try again. Now he watched his chance whenever they were alone; it had become a thing he thought about. He could not tell what Alexander thought, if he thought at all. He accepted it contentedly, and talked, with ever more ease and freedom, about other things.

"The Stagirites," he said, "were confederates of Olynthos; he made examples of those who wouldn't treat with him. Did your father tell you about the war?"

"What? . . . Oh yes. Yes, he did."

"Listen, this is important. Aristotle went off to Assos, as Hermeias' guest-friend; they'd met at the Academy. He's tyrannos there. You know where Assos is; it's opposite Mytilene, it controls the straits. So, as soon as I thought, I saw why Father chose this man. This is only between us two."

He looked deeply into Hephaistion's eyes, as always before a confidence. As always, Hephaistion felt as if his midriff were melting. As always, it was some moments before he could follow what he was being told.

". . . who were in other cities and escaped the siege, have been begging Father to have Stagira restored and the citizens enfranchised. That's what this Aristotle wants. What Father wants, is an alliance with Hermeias. It's a piece of horse-trading. Leonidas came for politics, too. Old Phoinix is the only one who came for *me*."

Hephaistion tightened his arm. His feelings were confused; he wanted to grasp till Alexander's very bones were somehow engulfed within himself, but knew this to be wicked and mad; he would kill anyone who harmed a hair of his head.

"They don't know I've seen this. I just say Yes, Father. I've not even told my mother. I want to make my own mind up when I've seen the man, and do what I think good without anyone knowing why. This is only between us two. My mother is entirely against philosophy."

Hephaistion was thinking how fragile his rib cage seemed, how terrible were the warring desires to cherish and to crush it. He continued silent.

"She says it makes men reason away the gods. She ought to know I would never deny the gods, whatever anyone told me. I know the gods exist, as surely as I know that you do . . . I can't breathe."

Hephaistion, who could have said the same, let go quickly. Presently he managed to reply, "Perhaps the Queen will dismiss him."

"Oh, no, I don't want that. That would only make trouble. I've been thinking, too, he may be the kind of man who'll answer questions. Ever since I knew a philosopher was coming, I've been writing them down, things nobody here can tell me. Thirty-five already, I counted yesterday."

He had not withdrawn, but, backed to the sloping gable-roof, sat propped lightly against Hephaistion, trustful and warm. This thought Hephaistion, was the true perfection of happiness; it ought to be; it must be. He said restlessly, "I should like to kill Leonidas, do you know that?"

"Oh, I thought that once. But now, I think he was sent by Herakles. A man doing one good against his will, that shows the hand of a god. He wanted to keep me down, but he taught me to put up with hardship. I never need a fur cloak, I never eat after I'm full, or lie in bed in the morning. It would have come harder, to start learning now, as I'd have had to do, without him. You can't ask your men to put up with things you can't bear yourself. And they'll all want to see if I'm softer than my father."

His ribs and their muscle layer had knit together; his side felt like armor. "I wear better clothes, that's all. I like to do that."

"You'll never wear this chiton again, I'm telling you. Look what you did in the tree, I can get my whole hand inside it . . . Alexander. You won't ever go to war without me?"

Alexander sat up staring; Hephaistion was jolted into taking his hand away. "Without *you?* What do you mean, how could you even think of it? You're my dearest friend."

Hephaistion had known for many ages that if a god should offer him one gift in all his lifetime, he would choose this. Joy hit him like a lightning bolt. "Do you mean it?" he said. "Do you really mean it?"

"*Mean* it?" said Alexander, in a voice of astonished outrage. "Did you doubt I meant it? Do you think I tell everyone the things I've told to you? Mean it—what a thing to say!"

Only a month ago, Hephaistion thought, I should have been too scared to answer. "Don't fight me. One always doubts great good fortune."

Alexander's eyes relented. Raising his right hand, he said, "I swear by Herakles." He leaned and gave Hephaistion a practiced kiss; that of a child who is affectionate by nature, and fond of grown-up attention. Hephaistion had hardly time to feel the shock of delight before the light touch had gone. By the time he had nerved himself to return the kiss, Alexander's attention had been withdrawn. He seemed to be gazing at heaven.

"Look," he said pointing. "You see that Victory statue, on the top gable of all? I know how to get up there."

From the terrace, the Victory looked as small as a child's clay doll. When the dizzy climb had brought them to its base, it turned out to be five feet tall. Its hand held a gilded laurel wreath, extended over the void.

Hephaistion, who had questioned nothing all the way because he had not dared think, clasped in his left arm, at Alexander's bidding, the bronze waist of the goddess. "Now hold my wrist," Alexander said.

Thus counterpoised, he leaned out, off balance, into empty space, and broke two leaves from the wreath. One came easily; the second he had to worry at. Hephaistion fet clammy sweat in his palms; the dread that it would make his grip slide off turned his belly to ice, and crept in his hair. Through this terror he was aware of the wrist he held. It had looked delicate, against his own big frame; it was hard, sinewy, the fist clenched on itself in a remote and solitary act of will. After a short eternity, Alexander was ready to be pulled back. He climbed down with the leaves in his teeth; when they were back on the roof, he gave one to Hephaistion, saying, "Now do you know we shall go to war together?"

The leaf sat in Hephaistion's hand, about the size of a real one. Like a real one it was trembling; quickly he shut his fingers on it. He felt now the full horror of the climb, the tiny mosaic of great flagstones far below, his loneliness at the climax. He had gone up in a fierce resolve to face, if it killed him, whatever ordeal Alexander should set to test him. Only now, with the gilt-bronze edges biting his palm, he saw that the test had not been for him. He was the witness. He had been taken up there to hold in his hand the life of Alexander, who had been asked if he meant what he had said. It was his pledge of friendship.

As they climbed down through the tall walnut tree, Hephaistion called to mind the tale of Semele, beloved of Zeus. He had come in a human shape, but that was not enough for her; she had demanded the embrace of his divine epiphany. It had been too much, she had burned to ashes. He would need to prepare himself for the touch of fire.

It was some weeks before the philosopher arrived; but his presence came before him.

Hephaistion had underrated him. He not only knew the country, but the court, and his knowledge was up-to-date; he had family guest-ties at Pella, and many traveled friends. The King, well aware, of this, had written offering to provide, if it seemed of use, a precinct where the Prince and his friends could study undisturbed.

The philosopher read, approvingly, between the lines. The boy was to be taken from his mother's claws; in return, the father too would let well alone. It was more than he had dared hope; he wrote back promptly, suggesting the Prince and his fellow students be lodged at some distance from the court's distractions, and adding, as an afterthought, a recommendation of pure upland air. There were no sizable hills within miles of Pella.

On the footslopes of Mount Bermion, west of the Pella plain, was a good house which had gone downhill in the wars. Philip bought it, and put it in order. It was more than twenty miles out; it would do very well. He added a wing and a gymnasium; and, since the philosopher had asked for somewhere to walk about, had a garden cleared; nothing formal, a pretty editing of nature, what the Persians called a "paradise." It was said that the legendary pleasance of King Midas had been thereabouts. Everything flourished there.

These orders given, he sent for his son; his wife would hear of them from her spies within the hour, and somehow twist their meaning to the boy.

In the talk which followed, much more was exchanged than was said in words. This was the self-evident training of a royal heir. Alexander saw his father took it as a matter of course. Had all the rebuffs, ambiguous double-edged words, been more than sparring in the endless war with his mother? Had all the words really been said? Once he had believed she would never lie to him; but he had known for some time that this was vanity.

"In the next few days," said Philip, "I'd like to know which friends of your own you want to spend your time with. Think it over."

"Thank you, Father." He remembered the hours of tortuous stifling talk in the women's rooms, the reading of gossip and rumor, the counterintrigues, the broodings and guessings over a word or look; cries, tears, declarations before the gods of outrage; smells of incense and magic herbs and burning meat; the whispered confidences that kept him awake at night, so that next day he was slower in the race or missed his aim.

"Those you go about with now," his father was saying, "if their fathers agree, will all be quite acceptable. Ptolemy, I suppose?"

"Yes, Ptolemy of course. And Hephaistion. I asked you about him before."

"I remember. Hephaistion by all means." He was at pains to sound easy; he had no wish to disturb a state of things which had taken a load off his mind. The erotic patterns of Thebes were engraved on it; a youth and a man, to whom the youth looked for example. Things being as it began to seem they were, there was no one he wished to see in this place of power. Even Ptolemy, brotherly and a man for women, had been throwing too long a shadow. What with the boy's startling beauty, and his taste for grown-up friends, he had been an anxiety for some time. It was of a piece with his oddness, suddenly to throw himself into the arms of a boy his own age almost to a day. They had been inseparable now for weeks; Alexander, it was true, was giving nothing away, but the other could be read like an open book. However, here there was no doubt at all who looked for example to whom. An affair, then, not to be interfered with.

There was trouble enough outside the kingdom. The Illyrians had had to be thrown back last year on the west border; it had cost him, as well as much grief, trouble and scandal, a sword-slash on the knee from which he was still limping.

In Thessaly, all was well; he had put down a dozen local tyrannies, made peace in a score of blood-feuds, and everyone, except a tyrant or two, was grateful. But he had failed with Athens. Even after the Pythian Games when, because he was presiding, they had refused to send competitors, he had still not given them up. His agents all said that the people could be reasoned with, if the orators would let them be. Their first concern was that the public dole should not be cut; no policy was ever passed if it threatened that, not even for home defense. Philokrates had been indicted for treason, and got away just ahead of a death sentence, to enjoy a generous pension; Philip rested his best hopes now on men never for sale, who yet favored the alliance because they thought it best. They had seen for themselves that, his first aim being the conquest of Asian Greece, the last thing he wanted was a costly war with Athens in which, win or lose, he must stand as Hellas' enemy, for no better reward than to secure his back.

He had sent therefore this spring another embassy, offering to revise the peace treaty, if reasonable amendments were put up. An Athenian envoy had been sent back, an old friend of Demosthenes, a certain Hegesippos known to his fellow citizens as Tufty, from his effeminate topknot of long curls tied in a ribbon. At Pella it became clear why he had been chosen; to unacceptable terms he added, on his own account, uncompromising rudeness. No risk had been taken of Philip winning him over; he was the man who had arranged Athens' alliance with the Phokians, his mere presence was an affront. He came and went; and Philip, who had not yet enforced the Phokians' yearly fine to the plundered temple, gave them notice to start paying up.

Now there was a war of succession boiling up in Epiros, where the King had lately died. He had been scarcely more than one chieftain among many; soon there would be chaos, unless a hegemon could be set up. Philip meant to do so, for the good of Macedon. For once he had his wife's blessing on his work, since he had chosen her brother Alexandros. He would see where his interest lay and be a curb on her intrigues; he was eager for support and should be a useful ally, Philip thought. It was a pity that, the affair being so urgent, he could not stay to welcome the philosopher. Before he limped out to his war-horse, he sent for his son and told him this. He said no more; he had been using his eyes, and had been many years a diplomat.

"He will be here," said Olympias ten days later, "about noon tomorrow. So remember to be at home."

Alexander was standing by the little loom on which his sister was learning fancy border-work. She had newly mastered the egg-and-dart pattern and was anxious to be admired for it; they were friends just now and he was generous with applause. But now he looked round, like a horse when it pricks its ear.

"I shall receive him," said Olympias, "in the Perseus Room."

"I shall receive him, Mother."

"Of course you must be there, I said so."

Alexander walked away from the loom. Kleopatra, forgotten, stood with the shuttle in her hand, and looked from face to face with a familiar dread.

Her brother patted his sword belt of polished chestnut leather. "No, Mother, it's for me to do it, now that Father's away. I shall make his apologies, and present Leonidas and Phoinix. Then I shall bring Aristotle up here, and present him to you."

Olympias stood up from her chair. He had grown faster lately; she was not so much the taller as she had thought. "Are you saying

to me, Alexander," she said in a swelling voice, "that you do not
want me there?"

There was a short, unbelievable silence.

"It's for little boys, to be presented by their mothers. It's no way
to come to a sophist, when one is grown up. I'm nearly fourteen,
now. I shall start with this man in the way I mean to go on."

Her chin rose, her back stiffened. "Did your father tell you this?"

The moment found him unprepared, but he knew it for what it
was. "No," he said. "I didn't need Father to tell me I'm a man. It
was I who told him."

There was a flush on her cheekbones; her red hair seemed to rise
by itself from its central peak. Her grey eyes had widened. He gazed
transfixed, thinking no other eyes in the world could look so dangerous. No one had yet told him otherwise.

"So, you are a man! And I, your mother, who bore you, nursed
you, suckled you, who fought for your rights when the King would
have thrown you off like a stray dog to set up his bastard—" She
had fixed him with the stare of a woman who drives home a spell.
He did not question her; that she willed his hurt was truth sufficient.
Word followed word like a flight of burning arrows. "I who have
lived for you each day of my life since you were conceived, oh, long
before you saw the light of the sun; who have gone through fire and
darkness for you and into the houses of the dead—! Now you plot
with him to beat me down like a peasant wife. Now I can believe
that you are his son!"

He stood silent. Kleopatra dropped her shuttle and cried urgently,
"Father's a wicked man. I don't love him, I love Mother best."
Neither of them looked at her. She started to cry, but no one heard.

"The time will come when you look back upon this day." Indeed,
he thought, it would not soon be forgotten. "Well? Have you no
answer?"

"I am sorry, Mother." His voice had been breaking for some time;
it betrayed him, cracking upward. "I have done my tests of manhood. Now I must live like a man."

For the first time, she laughed at him as he had heard her laugh
at his father. "Your tests of manhood! You silly child. Come and
tell me that when you have lain with a woman."

A shocked pause fell between them. Kleopatra, unheeded, ran

Mary Renault

outside. Olympias flung herself back into her chair, and burst into a storm of tears.

He went up presently, as so often before, and stroked her hair. She wept on his breast, murmuring of the cruelties she suffered, crying that she would no longer wish to see the light of day if he turned against her. He said that he loved her, that she knew it well enough. Much time passed in such words. In the end, he hardly knew how, it was decided he should receive the sophist himself, with Leonidas and Phoinix; and a little after, he went away. He felt neither defeated nor victorious, merely drained.

At the stair-foot Hephaistion was waiting. He happened to be there, as he happened to have a ball handy if Alexander wanted a game, or water if he was thirsty; not by calculation, but in a constant awareness by which no smallest trifle was missed. Now, when he came down the stairs with a shut mouth and blue lines under his eyes, Hephaistion received some mute signal he understood, and fell into step beside him. They went up along the path which wandered into the wood; in an open glade was an old fallen oak-bole with orange fungus and a lace of ivy. Hephaistion sat down with his back to it. Alexander, in a silence unbroken since setting out, came and settled into his arm. After a while he sighed; no other word was spoken for some time.

"They claim to love you," he said at length. "And they eat you raw."

Words made Hephaistion anxious; it had been simpler and safer to do without. "It's that children belong to them, but men have to go away. That's what my mother says. She says she wants me to be a man, and yet she doesn't."

"Mine does. Whatever she likes to say." He edged himself closer; like an animal, Hephaistion thought, which is reassured by handling. It was nothing more for him. No matter, whatever he needed he must have. The place was solitary, but he spoke softly as if the birds were spies. "She needs a man to stand up for her. You know why."

"Yes."

"She's always known I shall do that. But I saw today, she thinks when my time comes I shall let her reign for me. We didn't speak of it. But she knows that I told her no."

Hephaistion's back prickled with danger, but his heart was full of

[150]

pride. He had never hoped to be called in alliance against this mighty rival. He expressed his allegiance, but without risking words.

"She cried. I made her cry."

He was still looking quite pale. Words must be found. "She cried too when you were born. But it had to be. So has this."

There was a long pause; then, "You know that other thing I told you?"

Hephaistion assented. They had not spoken of it since.

"She promised to tell me everything one day. Sometimes she says one thing, sometimes another . . . I dreamed I caught a sacred snake and I was trying to make it speak to me, but it kept escaping and turning away."

Hephaistion said, "Perhaps it wanted you to follow it."

"No, it had a secret, but it wouldn't speak . . . She hates my father. I think I'm the only one she ever truly loved. She wants me all hers, none of me his. Sometimes I've wondered . . . is that *all?*"

In the sun-steeped wood, Hephaistion felt a fine tremor running through him. Anything he needed, he must have. "The gods will reveal it. They revealed it to all the heroes. But your mother . . . in any case . . . *she* would be mortal."

"Yes, that's true." He paused, turning it over. "Once when I was by myself on Mount Olympos, I had a sign. I vowed to keep it forever between me and the god." He made a little movement, asking to be released, and stretched his whole frame in a long shuddering sigh. "Sometimes I forget all this for months on end. Sometimes I think of it day and night. Sometimes I think, unless I find out the truth of it, I shall go mad."

"That's stupid. You've got me now. Do you think I'd let you go mad?"

"I can talk to you. As long as you're there . . ."

"I promise you before God, I'll be there as long as I'm alive."

They looked up together into the tall clouds, whose scarcely visible drift was like stillness in the sky of the long summer day.

Aristotle, son of Nikomachos the physician of the line of the Asklepiads, gazed round him as the ship rowed into harbor, trying to recall the scenes of boyhood. It was a long time; everything looked strange. He had had a quick smooth voyage from Mytilene, sole passenger in a fast war-galley sent to fetch him. It was no surprise, therefore, to see a mounted escort waiting on the wharf.

He hoped to find its leader helpful. He was well informed already, but no knowledge was ever trivial; truth was the sum of all its parts.

A gull swooped over the ship. With the reflex of many years' self-training, he noted its species, the angle of its flight, its wingspread, its droppings, the food it dived for. The lines of the vessel's bow-wave had changed with its lessening speed; a mathematical ratio formed in his mind, he stored it where he would find it again when he had time. He never needed to carry tablets and stylos with him.

Through the cluster of small craft, he could not see the escort clearly. The King would have sent someone responsible. He prepared his questions; those of a man formed by his era, when philosophy and politics were totally engaged, when no man of intellect could conceive for his thought a higher value than that of being physician to Hellas' sickness. Barbarians, by definition, were hopeless cases; as well try to make a hunchback straight. Hellas must be healed to guide the world.

Two generations had seen each decent form of government decay into its own perversion: aristocracy into oligarchy, democracy to demagogy, kingship to tyranny. With mathematical progression, according to the number who shared the evil the deadweight against reform increased. To change a tyranny had lately been proved impossible. To change an oligarchy called for power and ruthlessness, destructive to the soul. To change a demagogy, one must become a demagogue and destroy one's mind as well. But to reform a monarchy, one need only mold one man. The chance to be a king-shaper, the prize every philosopher prayed for, had fallen to him.

Plato had risked death for it in Syracuse, once with the tyrant father, again with the trivial son. He had thrown away half his last harvest-time, sooner than refuse the challenge he himself had first defined. It was the aristocrat and soldier in him; or maybe the dreamer. Far better have collected reliable data first, and saved the journey . . . Yet even this crisp thought evoked that formidable brooding presence; the old unease, the sense of something eluding the tools of measurement, defeating category and system, came hauntingly back with the summer scents of the Academy garden.

Well, in Syracuse he had failed. Maybe for want of good stuff to work on; but his failure had resounded through all Greece. And before the end, his mind must have been failing too, to bequeath the School to Speusippos, that barren metaphysician. At all events, Speusippos had been eager to give up even that, and come to Pella. The King cooperative, the boy intelligent and strong-willed, without known vices, the heir to yearly increasing power; no wonder that Speusippos had been tempted, after the squalors and miseries of Syracuse. But Speusippos had been turned down. Demosthenes and his faction had achieved this if nothing else, that no one from Athens had stood a moment's chance.

Good friends in Mytilene had praised his courage in braving the backward and violent northland; he had brushed it aside with his astringent smile. His roots were here; in the air of these mountains he had known childhood happiness, tasting their beauty while his elders' minds were clenched in the cares of war. As for violence, he was no novice, having lived under the shadow of Persian power. If there he had succeeded in making of a man with so dark a past a friend and a philosopher, he need hardly fear failure with an unformed boy.

As the galley threaded the shipping, backing oars to let through a troop-trireme, he thought with affection of the hillside palace at Assos, looking out to the wooded mountains of Lesbos, and the strait he had crossed so often; the terrace with its burning cresset on summer nights; debate or thoughtful silence, or a book read together. Hermeias read well, his high voice was musical and expressive, never shrill. Its epicene pitch did not reflect his mind; as a boy he had been gelded, to prolong the beauty his master prized; he had been through the depths, before he made himself ruler, but like a smothered sapling he had grown through to the light. He had been persuaded to visit the Academy, and from there he had never fallen back.

He had adopted a niece, being condemned to childlessness. For their friendship's sake, Aristotle had married her; the fact that she adored him had come as a surprise. He was glad to have shown gratitude, for she was lately dead; a thin dark studious girl, who had held his hand, gazed at him dimly with nearsighted eyes already beginning to wander, and begged that her ashes and his might share one urn. He had vowed it to her, and added of his own accord that he would never take another wife. He had brought the urn with him, in case he should die in Macedon.

There would of course be women. He took some pride, not improper, he thought, to a philosopher, in his own healthy normality. Plato, in his opinion, had committed too much to love.

The galley was docking, turning in with the suddenness of such maneuvers in crowded harbors. Ropes were flung and hitched, the gangplank clattered. The escort stood dismounted, five or six men. He turned to his two servants to make sure of all his baggage. Some stir among the seamen made him look up. At the top of the gangplank stood a boy gazing about. His hands were poised on the man's sword belt round his waist, his bright heavy hair was ruffled in the offshore breeze. He looked as alert as a young hunting-dog. As their eyes met he jumped down, not waiting for the sailor who ran to help, landing so lightly that it did not check his pace.

"Are you Aristotle the philosopher? May you live happy. I am Alexander son of Philip. Be welcome to Macedon."

They exchanged the formal courtesies, taking stock of one another.

Alexander had planned his expedition at short notice, adjusting his strategy to events.

Instinct had made him watchful. His mother was taking it too well. He had known her agree with his father on this or that, only to cover her next move. Going to her room in her absence, he had seen a state gown laid out. A new battle would be bloodier than the last, and still indecisive. He had bethought him of the admirable Xenophon, who, when cornered in Persia, had decided to steal a march.

It must be done correctly, not turned into an escapade. He had gone to Antipatros, his father's Regent in Macedon, and asked him to come too. He was a King's man of unshaken loyalty; he read the lie of the land with satisfaction, which he was not fool enough to show. He was here now on the quay; the reception was an official one; and here was the philosopher.

He was a lean smallish man, not ill-proportioned, who yet gave at first sight the effect of being all head. His whole person was commanded by his wide bulging brow, a vessel stretched by its contents. Small piercing eyes were busy recording, without prejudgment or error, just what they saw. The mouth was closed in a line precise as a definition. He had a short neat beard; his thinning hair looked as if its roots had been forced apart by the growth of the massive brain.

A second glance revealed him to be dressed with some care and with the elegance of Ionia, wearing one or two good rings. Athenians thought him rather foppish; in Macedon, he looked tasteful and free from harsh austerity. Alexander offered him a hand to mount the gangplank, and tried the effect of a smile. When the man returned it, it could be seen that smiling was what he would do best; he would not often be caught with his head back laughing. But he did look like a man who would answer questions.

Beauty, thought the philosopher; the gift of God. And it moved with mind; in that house there was someone living. This enterprise was no such forlorn hope as poor Plato's trips to Syracuse. He must take care that Speusippos had the news.

Presentations went forward, the Prince performing them with address. A groom led up a mount for the philosopher, offering a leg up, Persian style. This seen to, the boy turned round; a taller boy moved forward, his hand on the headstall of a magnificent black charger with a white blaze. All through the formalities, Aristotle had been aware of the creature fretting; he was surprised therefore to see the youth release it. It trotted straight to the Prince, and muzzled the hair behind his ear. He stroked it, murmuring something. With neatness and dignity, the horse sank its crupper on its haunches, waited while he mounted, and at his finger-touch straightened up. There was a moment in which the boys and the beast seemed like initiates, who have exchanged in secret a word of power.

The philosopher swept aside this fantasy. Nature had no mysteries, only facts not yet correctly observed and analyzed. Proceed from this sound first principle, and one would never miss one's way.

The spring of Mieza was sacred to the Nymphs. Its waters had been led into an old stone fountain-house, where they tinkled hollowly; but the ferny pool below had been carved by the falling stream itself, swirling between the rocks. Its brown surface caught the sun; it was a pleasant place to bathe in.

Runnels and conduits threaded about the gardens, glittering streamlets sprang out in jets, or tumbled in little falls. Bay and myrtle and rowan grew there; in rough grass beyond the tended orchard, old gnarled apple trees and crabs still bloomed in spring. Fine green turf had been laid where the scrub had been cleared away; from the pink-washed house, paths and rough steps meandered, circling some rock with its small wiry mountain flowers, or crossing a wooden bridge, or widening round a stone seat with a view. In summer, the woods beyond were a tangle of huge wild roses, the gift of the Nymphs to Midas; the night dews were full of their briery scent.

The boys would ride out at cocklight, to go hunting before the day's school began. They would set up their nets in the coverts, and get their buck or their hare. Under the trees the smells were dank and mossy; on the open slopes, spicy with crushed herbs. At sunup there would be smells of wood-smoke and roasting meat, horse-sweat on leather, dog-smells as the hounds came coaxing up for scraps. But if the quarry was rare or strange, they would go fasting home and save it for dissection. Aristotle had learned this skill from his father; it was the Asklepiad heritage. Even insects, they found, he did not disdain. Most of what they brought in he knew already; but now and then he would say sharply, "What's this, what's this?" then get out his notes with their fine pen-drawings, and be in good humor for the day.

Alexander and Hephaistion were the youngest boys. The philosopher had made it clear that he wanted no children under his feet, however great their fathers. Many youths and older boys who had been friends of the Prince's childhood were now grown men. None of those chosen refused the invitation to join the School. It established them as Companions of the Prince, a privilege which might lead anywhere.

Antipatros, after waiting some time in vain, put forward to the King the claims of his son Kassandros. Alexander, to whom Philip had given this news before he left, had not taken it well. "I don't like him, Father. And he doesn't like me, so why does he want to come?"

"Why do you suppose? Philotas is going."

"Philotas is one of my friends."

"Yes, I said your friends should go, and as you know I have not refused one of them. But I did not promise to let in no one else. How can I admit Parmenion's son, and reject Antipatros'? If you're on bad terms, now's the time to mend it. It will be of use to me. And it is an art that kings must learn."

Kassandros was a youth with bright-red hair, and a bluish-white skin patched with dark freckles; thickly built, and fond of exacting servility from anyone he could frighten. He thought Alexander an insufferable young show-off, spoiling for a good setdown, but protected by his rank and the ring of toadies it brought him.

Kassandros had not wanted to go to Mieza. Not long before, he had been beaten up by Philotas, to whom he had said something ill-advised, unaware that Philotas' chief concern just then was to get accepted in Alexander's set. No exploit of Philotas' was likely to lose in the telling. Kassandros found himself cut by Ptolemy and Harpalos; Hephaistion looked at him like a leashed dog at a cat; Alexander ignored him, but was charming in his presence to anyone he was known to dislike. Had they ever been friends it could have been righted; Alexander was fond of reconciliations, and, to refuse one, had to be very angry indeed. As it was, casual dislike had become hostility. Kassandros would see them all rot, before he came fawning to that vain little whelp, who, in the proper course of nature, ought to be learning a wholesome respect for him.

He had pleaded in vain to his father that he could not learn philosophy; that it was known to turn men's brains; that he wanted only to be a soldier. He dared not confess that he was disliked by Alexander and his friends; he would have had a belting for letting it happen. Antipatros valued his own career and was ambitious for his son's. As it was, he fixed Kassandros with a fierce blue eye, whose bristling brows had once been as red as his, and said, "Behave yourself there. And be careful with Alexander."

Kassandros said dismissively, "He's only a little boy."

"Don't make yourself out a bigger fool than you were born. Four or five years between you, it's nothing once you're men. Now pay heed to what I tell you. That boy has his father's wits about him; and if he doesn't turn out as bad to cross as his mother, then I'm an

Ethiop. Don't cross him. The sophist is paid to do it. You I'm sending to improve yourself, not to make enemies. If you stir up brawls
there, I'll tan your hide."

So Kassandros went to Mieza, where he was homesick, bored,
lonely and resentful. Alexander was civil to him, because his father
had said it was the art of kings, and because he had more serious
things to think about.

The philosopher had turned out not only willing, but eager to
answer questions. Unlike Timanthes, he would do this first, and only
afterwards explain the value of system. The exposition, however,
when it came was always rigorous. He was a man who hated loose
ends and cloudy edges.

Mieza faced east; the tall rooms with their faded frescoes were
sun-drenched all morning, and cool from noontime on. They worked
indoors when they needed to write or draw or study specimens;
when they discoursed or were lectured to, they walked the gardens.
They talked of ethics and politics, the nature of pleasure and of justice; of the soul, virtue, friendship and love. They considered the
causes of things. Everything must be traced to its cause; and there
could be no science without demonstration.

Soon a whole room was full of specimens: pressed flowers and
plants, seedlings in pots; birds' eggs with their embryos preserved
in clear honey; decoctions of medicinal herbs. Aristotle's trained
slave worked there all day. At night they observed the heavens; the
stars were stuff more divine than any other thing man's eye could
reach, a fifth element not to be found on earth. They noted winds
and mists and the aspect of the clouds, and learned to prognosticate
storms. They reflected light from polished bronze, and measured the
angles of refraction.

For Hephaistion, it was a new life. Alexander was his own in the
sight of everyone. His place was recognized even by the philosopher.

The school discussed friendship often. It is, they learned, one of
the things man can least afford to lack; necessary to the good life,
and beautiful in itself. Between friends is no need of justice, for
neither wrong nor inequality can exist. He described the degrees
of friendship, up from the self-seeking to the pure, when good is

willed to the friend for the friend's own sake. Friendship is perfect when virtuous men love the good in one another; for virtue gives more delight than beauty, and is untouched by time.

He went on to value friendship far above the shifting sands of Eros. One or two of the young men argued this. Hephaistion, who was not very quick at shaping his thoughts into words, usually found that someone else got in before him. He preferred this to making a fool of himself. Kassandros, for one thing, would count it as a score against Alexander.

Hephaistion was quickly growing possessive. Everything led him that way: his nature, the integrity of his love and his own sense of it; the tenet of the philosopher that for each man there was only one perfect friend; the certainty of his unspoiled instincts that Alexander's loyalty matched his own; and their acknowledged status. Aristotle was a man to proceed from facts. He had seen at once the attachment already fixed for good or ill; one of real affection, not of incontinence or flattery. It should not be opposed, but molded in its innocence. (Had some wise man only done as much for the father . . . !) When therefore he spoke of friendship, he let his eyes fall kindly on the two handsome boys unfailingly side by side. In the stolen intimacies of Pella, Hephaistion had only had eyes for Alexander; now he saw refracted, as clearly as in the optics class, the fact that they made a very good-looking pair.

There was nothing to do with Alexander of which he was not proud; this included his rank, for he could not be imagined without it. Had he lost it, Hephaistion would have followed him to exile, prison or death; this knowledge gave self-respect to his pride. He was never jealous over Alexander, since he never doubted him; but he was jealous of his own standing, and liked to have it recognized.

Kassandros at least was well aware of it. Hephaistion, who had eyes for him in the back of his head, knew that though Kassandros wanted neither of them, he hated in both their closeness, their trust, their beauty. He hated Alexander because with Antipatros' soldiers he came before Antipatros' son; because he had won his belt at twelve, because Oxhead sat down for him. Hephaistion he hated for not being after Alexander in hope of gain. All this Hephaistion knew, and mirrored back his deadly knowledge to Kassandros, whose self-esteem craved assurance that he hated Alexander for his faults alone.

Most hateful of all was his going to Aristotle for private lessons in statecraft. Indeed, Hephaistion offered Kassandros' envy to cheer Alexander up, when he complained that he found the lessons boring.

"I thought they'd be the best. He knows Ionia and Athens and Chalkidike, and even Persia a little. I want to know what men are like there, their customs, how they behave. What he wants, is to fit me out with answers beforehand to everything. What would I do if this happened, or that? I'd see when it happened, I said; happenings are made by men, one would need to know them. He thought I was being obstinate."

"The King might let you drop it?"

"No, I've a right to it. Besides, disagreeing makes one think. I know what's wrong. He thinks it's an inexact science, but still a kind of science. Put a ram to a ewe and you get a lamb each time, even if not identical; heat snow and it melts. That's science. Your demonstrations should be repeatable. Well, say in war, now; even if one could repeat all other conditions, which is impossible, one could still not repeat surprise. Nor the weather. Nor the mood the men are in. Armies and cities, they're all made up of men. Being a king . . . being a king is like music."

He paused, and frowned. Hephaistion said, "Has he been asking you again to play?"

"'With mere listening, half the ethical effect is lost.'"

"When he's not as wise as a god, he's as silly as some old henwife."

"I told him I'd learned the ethical effect by an experiment, but it was not repeatable. I suppose he took the hint."

The matter was indeed never raised again. Ptolemy, who did not deal in hints, had taken the philosopher aside and explained the facts.

The young man had borne without rancor the rise of Hephaistion's star. Had the new friend been adult, a clash would have been certain; but Ptolemy's fraternal role remained untrespassed on. Though still unmarried, he was several times a father, with a sense of duty to his scattered offsprings; into this feeling, his friendship for Alexander began to merge. The world of passionate adolescent friendship was unknown country to him; he had been entranced by girls since puberty. He had lost nothing to Hephaistion; except that he no longer came first of all. This being not the least of human losses, he was inclined not to take Hephaistion more seriously than he had to. No doubt they would soon grow out of it. But meantime, Alexander should get the boy to be less quarrelsome. One could see the two of them never fell out, one soul in two bodies as the sophist put it; but Hephaistion on his own could be pugnaciously assertive.

There was just then some excuse for this. Mieza, sanctuary of the Nymphs, was a shelter too from the court with its turmoil of news, events, intrigues. They lived with ideas, and with one another. Their minds were ripening, a growth they were daily urged to hasten; less was said about the fact that their bodies were ripening too. At Pella, Hephaistion had lived in a cloud of vague, inchoate longings. They had become desires, and no longer vague.

True friends share everything; but Hephaistion's life was filling with concealments. It was Alexander's nature to love the proofs of love, even when he was sure of it; in this spirit he welcomed and returned his friend's caresses. Hephaistion had never dared do anything which could tell him more.

When one so quick-minded was so slow to understand, he must lack the will. When he delighted in giving, what he did not offer he might not possess. If then the knowledge was forced home to him, one would have made him fail. His heart might forgive it; his soul would never forget.

And yet, thought Hephaistion, sometimes one could swear . . . But it was no time to trouble him, he had trouble enough.

Every day they had formal logic. The King had forbidden, and the philosopher did not want, the quibbling logomachy of eristics, that science which Sokrates had defined as making the worse cause look the better. But the mind must be trained to detect a fallacy, a begged question, false analogy or undistributed middle; all science hung on knowing when two propositions excluded one another. Alexander had picked up logic quickly. Hephaistion kept his misgivings to himself. He alone knew the secret of impossible alternatives, avoided by half-believing two things at once. At night, for they shared a room, he would look across to his bed and see him

[161]

open-eyed in the moonlight, confronted by the syllogism of his own being.

For Alexander, their sanctuary was not inviolate. Half a dozen times a month would come his mother's courier, with a gift of sweet figs, a riding-hat or a pair of worked sandals (the last pair too small, for his growth was quickening); and a thick letter, thread-bound and sealed.

Hephaistion knew what the letters contained. He read them. Alexander said that true friends share everything. He did not try to hide that he needed to share his trouble. Sitting on the edge of his bed, or in one of the garden arbors, with an arm around him to read over his shoulder, Hephaistion would be scared by his own anger, and shut his teeth on his tongue.

The letters were full of secrets, detraction and intrigue. If Alexander wanted news of his father's wars, he had to question the courier. Antipatros had been left again as Regent, while Philip campaigned in the Chersonesos; Olympias thought she herself should have been governing, with the general as garrison commander. He could do nothing right for her; he was Philip's creature; he was plotting against her, and against Alexander's succession. She always ordered the courier to await his answer; and he would do no more work that day. If he seemed lukewarm against Antipatros, a letter full of reproaches would come back; had he supported her accusations, he knew her not above showing Antipatros his letter, to score in their next quarrel. In time came the inevitable day when news reached her that the King had a new girl.

This letter was terrible. Hephaistion was amazed, even dismayed, that Alexander should let him read it. Halfway through he drew back; but Alexander reached for him and said, "Go on." He was like someone with a recurring illness, who feels the familiar grip of the pain. At the end he said, "I must go to her."

He had grown chilly to the touch. Hephaistion said, "But what can you do?"

"Only be there. I'll come back tomorrow, or the day after."

"I'll go with you."

"No, you'd be angry, we might quarrel. It's enough without that."

The philosopher, when told that the Queen was sick and her son must visit her, was nearly as angry as Hephaistion, but did not say so. The boy did not look like a truant going off to a party; nor did he come back looking as if he had had one. That night he woke Hephaistion by shouting "No!" in his sleep. Hephaistion went over and got in with him; Alexander grasped his throat with savage strength, then opened his eyes, embraced him with a sigh of relief that was like a groan, and fell asleep again. Hephaistion lay awake beside him, and just before daybreak returned to his own cold bed. In the morning, Alexander remembered nothing of it.

Aristotle too, in his way, attempted consolation, making next day a special effort to draw back his charge into the pure air of philosophy. Grouped round a stone bench with a view of clouds and distances, they discussed the nature of the outstanding man. Is self-regard a flaw in him? Certainly yes, in respect of common greeds and pleasures. But then, what self should be regarded? Not the body nor its passions, but the intellectual soul, whose office it is to rule the rest like a king. To love that self, to be covetous of honor for it, to indulge its appetite for virtue and noble deeds; to prefer an hour of glory closed by death, to a slothful life; to reach for the lion's share of moral dignity: there lies the fulfilling self-regard. The old saws are wrong, said the philosopher, which tell man to be forever humble before his own mortality. Rather he should strain his being to put on immortality, never to fall below the highest thing he knows.

On a grey boulder before a laurel bush, his eyes upon the skyline, Alexander sat with his hands clasping his knees. Hephaistion watched him, to see if his soul was being calmed. But he seemed more like one of those young eagles which, they had read, were trained by their parents to stare into the noonday sun. If they blinked, the books said, they were thrown out of the nest.

Afterwards Hephaistion took him away to read Homer, having more faith in this remedy.

They now had a new book for it. Phoinix' gift had been copied some generations back, by an untalented scribe from a corrupt text. Asked about one unclear passage, Aristotle had compressed his lips over the whole, had sent to Athens for a good recension, and gone over it himself for errors. Not only did it contain some lines the old book had dropped out, but it now scanned everywhere and made sense. Here and there it had also been edited for moral tone; a footnote explained that when Achilles called "Lively!" for the wine, he wanted it soon, not strong. The pupil was keen and grateful; but to the teacher, this time, the causes of things were not revealed. He had been concerned to make an archaic poem edifying; Alexander, that a sacred scripture should be infallible.

The philosopher felt less easy when, at one of the feasts, they rode into town and went to the theater. To his regret, it was Aischylos' *Myrmidons,* which showed Achilles and his Patroklos as more (or in his own view less) than perfect friends. In the midst of his critical concerns, when the news of Patroklos' death had reached Achilles, he became aware that Alexander was sitting trance-bound, tears streaming from his wide-open eyes, and that Hephaistion was holding his hand. A reproving stare made Hephaistion let go, red to the ears; Alexander was unreachable. At the end they vanished; he ran them down backstage, with the actor who had played Achilles. He was unable to stop the Prince from actually embracing this person, and giving him a costly arm-ring he had on, which the Queen was sure to inquire for. It was most unsuitable. All next day's work was devoted to mathematics, as a healthy antidote.

No one had informed him that his school, when not required to discuss law, rhetoric, science or the good life, was busy debating whether those two did anything, or not. Hephaistion knew it well, having lately thrashed someone for asking him outright, because there was a bet on it. Was it possible for Alexander not to know? If he did, why did he never speak of it? Was it loyalty to their friendship, lest anyone should think it incomplete? Did he, even, think they were lovers already, as he understood it himself? Sometimes in the night Hephaistion wondered if he was a fool and coward, not to try his luck. But the oracle of instinct signed against it. They were being daily told that all things were open to reason; he knew better. Whatever it was that he was waiting for—a birth, a healing, the intervention of a god—he would have to wait, if he waited forever. Only with what he had, he was rich beyond his dreams; if, reaching for more, he lost it, he would as soon be dead.

In the month of the Lion, when the first of the grapes were harvested, they had their birthdays and turned fifteen. In the week of the first frosts the courier brought a letter, not from the Queen but from the King. He greeted his son; expected he would like a change from sitting down with the philosophers; and invited him to visit his headquarters. It was none too soon, since he was forward in such matters, for him to see the face of war.

Their road led by the shore, skirting the mountains when marsh or river-mouth drove it inland. The armies of Xerxes had first leveled it, moving westward; the armies of Philip had repaired it, moving east.

Ptolemy came, because Alexander thought it due to him; Philotas, because his father was with the King; Kassandros because if the son of Parmenion came, Antipatros' could not be left behind; and Hephaistion as a matter of course.

The escort was commanded by Kleitos, Hellanike's younger brother. The King had detailed him for it, because Alexander had known him so long. This was indeed one of the first beings he could remember, as a dark thickset young man who would walk into the nursery and talk to Lanike across him, or come roaring across the floor playing bears. He was now Black Kleitos, a bearded captain of the Companion Cavalry; highly reliable, and with an archaic forthrightness. Macedon had many such survivals from a Homeric past, when the High King had to take, if his chieftains chose to give it, a wholesome piece of their minds. Now, escorting the King's son, he was hardly aware of harking back to the rough teasing of the nursery; Alexander scarcely knew what it was he half-remembered; but there was an edge to their sparring, and though he laughed, he took care to give as good as he got.

They forded streams which, it was said, had been drunk dry by the Persian hordes; crossed the Strymon by King Philip's bridge, and climbed Pangaios' shoulder to the terraced city of Amphipolis. There at the Nine Ways, Xerxes had buried nine boys and nine girls alive, to please his gods. Now between mountain and river stood a great fortress shining with new squared ashlar; gold-smelters' furnaces smoked within its walls; it was a strongpoint Philip did not mean to lose, the first of his conquests beyond the river which had once been Macedon's furthest boundary. Above them towered Pangaios, dark with forests and scarred with the workings of the mines, its white marble outcrops gleaming in the sun; the rich womb of the royal armies. Wherever they went, Kleitos pointed out to them the spoor of the King's wars; weed-covered siege works, ramps where his towers and his catapults had been reared against city walls still laid in ruins. There was always a fort of his along the way, to take them in for the night.

"What's to become of us, boys," said Alexander laughing, "if he leaves us nothing to do?"

When the coastal plain was firm, the boys would wheel off at a gallop, and charge back with streaming hair, splashing along the seashore, shouting to each other above the crying of the gulls. Once, when they were singing, some passing peasants took them for a wedding party, bringing the bridegroom to the house of the bride.

Oxhead was in high spirits. Hephaistion had a fine new horse, red with a blond mane and tail. They were always giving each other things, on impulse, or at the feasts, but they had been boys' small keepsakes; this was the first costly and conspicuous gift he had had from Alexander. The gods had only made one Oxhead; but Hephaistion's mount must excel all others. It handled well. Kassandros admired it pointedly. After all, then, Hephaistion was making a good thing out of his sycophancy. Hephaistion felt the meaning, and would have given much for the chance of vengeance; but nothing had been said in words. Before Kleitos and the escort, it was unthinkable to make a scene.

The road ran inland to skirt a brackish swamp. Perched on a spur of hill to command the passage, towering proudly above the plain, was the citadel rock of Philippi. Philip had taken it, and sealed it with his name, in a famous year.

"My first campaign," Kleitos said. "I was there when the courier brought the news. Your father, Philotas, had pushed back the Illyrians and run them halfway to the western sea; the King's horse had won at Olympia; and you, Alexander, had come into the world —with a great yell as we were told. We were issued a double wine-ration. Why he didn't make it a treble one, I don't know."

"I do. He knew how much you could hold." Alexander trotted ahead, and murmured to Hephaistion, "Since I was three I've been hearing that story."

Philotas said, "All this used to be Thracian tribal land."

"Yes, Alexander," said Kassandros. "You'll need watch your blue-painted friend, young Lambaros. The Agrianoi"—he waved his hand northwards—"must be hoping to make something of this war."

"Oh?" Alexander raised his brows. "They've kept their pledges. Not like King Kersobleptes, who made war as soon as we'd given his hostage back." It was known that Philip had had enough of this chief's false promises and brigand raids; the aim of the war was to make his lands a province of Macedon.

"These barbarians are all alike," Kassandros said.

"I heard from Lambaros last year. He got a merchant to write for him. He wants me to visit their city as his guest."

"I don't doubt it. Your head would look well on a pole at the village gate."

"As you just now said, Kassandros, he's my friend. Will you remember that?"

"And shut your mouth," said Hephaistion audibly.

They were to sleep at Philippi. The tall acropolis flamed like a cresset in the red light of the westering sun. Alexander gazed long in silence.

The King, when at last they reached him, was camped before the fort of Doriskos, on the near side of the Hebros valley. Beyond the river was the Thracian city of Kypsela. Before investing that, he must take the fort.

It had been built by Xerxes, to guard his rear after he had crossed the Hellespont. On the flat sea-meadow below it, he had rough-reckoned the number of his host, too vast for counting, by marching troop after troop into a square drawn around the first ten thousand men. The fort was solid; he had had no lack of slaves. But it had grown ramshackle in its century and a half of Thracians; cracks were filled in with rubble, the battlements patched with thorn like a goat pen in the mountains. It had withstood Thracian tribal wars; till now, no more had been asked of it.

Dusk was falling as they came near. From within the walls rose the smell of cook-fires and the distant bleat of goats. Just out of arrow-shot was the camp of the Macedonians, a workmanlike shantytown of hide tents, lean-tos roughly thatched with reeds from the Hebros River, and propped upturned carts. Drawn geometric and black against the sunset sky stood a sixty-foot wooden siege tower; its guards, shielded by thick ox-hide housing against missiles

[167]

from the ramparts, were cooking supper within its base. In the cavalry lines, the horses whinnied at their pickets. The platforms had been set up for the catapults; the great engines seemed to crouch like dragons about to spring, their timber necks extended, their massive bolt-firing bows outspread from their sides like wings. The outlying scrub stank of ordure; the nearer air smelled of wood-smoke, grilling fish, and the unwashed bodies of many men and women. The camp-followers were busy with supper; here and there one of their incidental children chirped or wailed. Someone was playing a lyre in need of tuning.

A little hamlet of huts, its people fled to the fort or mountains, had been cleaned out for the officers. The headman's place, two stone rooms and a lean-to, housed the King. They saw his lamp at some distance.

Alexander moved into the lead, lest Kleitos take it on himself to deliver him like a child. His eyes and nose and ears took in the presence of war, the difference from barracks or home camp. When they reached the house, Philip's square shape darkened the doorway. Father and son embraced, and viewed each other in the light of the watch-fire. "You're taller," said the King.

Alexander nodded. "My mother," he said for the escort's ears, "sends you greeting and hopes you are in good health." There was a loaded pause; he went on quickly, "I've brought you a sack of apples from Mieza. They're good this year."

Philip's face warmed; Mieza apples were famous. He clapped his son on the shoulder, greeted his companions, directed Philotas to his father's lodging, and said, "Well, come in, come in and eat."

Joined presently by Parmenion, they ate at a trestle, waited on by the royal squires, youths in their mid-teens whose fathers' rank entitled them to learn manners and warfare by acting as bodyservants to the King. The sweet golden apples were brought in a silver dish. Two lamps stood on bronze standards. The King's weapons and armor leaned in a corner. An ancient smell of humanity sweated out from the walls.

"Only a day later," said Philip, "and we might have lodged you inside." He gestured with his apple-core at the fort.

Alexander leaned forward across the table. The long ride had sunburned him; the clear color glowed in his cheeks, his hair and eyes caught the lamplight brilliantly; he was like kindling caught with the spark.

"When do we attack?"

Philip grinned across at Parmenion. "What can one do with such a boy?"

They were to go in just before dawn.

After supper, the officers came in for briefing. They were to approach the fort in darkness; then flame-arrows were to be shot at the brushwood in the walls, the catapults and siege tower would open covering fire to clear the ramparts while scaling-ladders were set up. Meantime the ram, slung in its mighty cradle, would be swung against the gates, the siege tower would thrust out its drawbridge; the assault would begin.

It was an old story to the officers, only small details imposed by the site were new. "Good," Philip said. "Time for a little sleep, then."

The squires had brought in a second bed to the room behind. Alexander's eyes had followed it for a moment. Just before bedtime, when he had honed his weapons, he went out to find Hephaistion, to tell him he had arranged they should be posted together for the assault, and to explain that he himself had to share his father's lodging. For some reason he had not thought to expect it.

When he got back, his father had just stripped, and was handing a squire his chiton. Alexander checked a moment in the doorway, then entered, saying something to seem at ease. He could not, indeed, account for the deep distaste and shame the sight of his father gave him. As far as he could remember, he had never seen him naked before.

By sunup the fort had fallen. A pure, clear golden light came lifting from behind the hills that hid the Hellespont. A fresh breeze blew from the sea. Over the fort hung the acrid smells of smoke and smolder, the stink of blood and entrails and grimy sweat.

The ladders, solid structures of undressed pine which would take two men abreast, still leaned against the fire-stained walls, with here and there a broken rung where the rush had overloaded one. Before the burst splintered gates hung the ram in its hide-roofed cradle; the gangway from the siege tower lolled on the ramparts like a great tongue.

Inside, the Thracian men who survived were being fettered for their march to the slave market at Amphipolis; the clink sounded musical, at a little distance. An example, Philip thought, might encourage the Kypselans to surrender when their turn came. All round the huts and hovels that clung like swallows' mud nests to the inside of the walls, the soldiers were on the hunt for women.

The King stood, with Parmenion and a couple of runners by whom he was sending orders, up on the ramparts; solid, workman-like, relaxed, like an able farmer who has plowed a big field and got it sown before the rain. Once or twice, when a shriek rose shrilling to hurt the ears, Alexander looked towards him; but he went on talking to Parmenion, undisturbed. The men had fought well, and deserved what meager spoils the place could offer. Doriskos should have surrendered; then no one would have been hurt.

Alexander and Hephaistion were by themselves in the gatehouse, talking about the battle. It was a small stone room, containing besides themselves a dead Thracian, a slab carved with the name and styles of Xerxes, King of Kings; some rough wooden stools; half a loaf of black bread; and, by itself, a man's forefinger with a black broken nail. Hephaistion had kicked it aside; it was a trifle to what they had seen already.

He had won his sword belt. One man he had killed for certain, dead on the spot; Alexander thought it might well be three.

Alexander had taken no trophies, nor counted his men. As soon as they were on the walls, the officer who led their party had been hurled down. Alexander, giving no one else time to think, had shouted that they must take the gatehouse, whence missiles were being showered on the ram below. The appointed second-in-command, an untried man, had wavered, and in that moment had lost his men to Alexander's certainty; they were already running after him, clambering, scrambling, stabbing and thrusting along Xerxes' old ragged masonry, with its wild blue-stained defenders and clefts of crackling fire. The entry to the gatehouse was narrow; there had been a minute, after Alexander had hurled himself inside, when the following press had jammed in it, and he had been fighting alone.

He stood now with the blood and dust of combat on him, looking down on the other face of war. But, Hephaistion thought, he was not really seeing it. He talked quite clearly, remembered every detail where for Hephaistion things were already flowing together like a dream. For him it was fading; Alexander was living in it still. Its aura hung about him; he was in a mode of being he did not want to leave, as men linger on in a place where they saw a vision.

He had a sword-cut across his forearm. Hephaistion had stopped the bleeding with a strip of his kilt. He looked out at the pale clean sea, saying, "Let's go down and bathe, to wash off the muck."

"Yes," said Alexander. "I ought to see Peithon first. He put out his shield to cover me when two of them were at me, and that man with the forked beard caught him under it. But for you he'd have been killed outright." He took off his helmet (they were both armed, at short notice, from the common stock of the Pella armory) and ran his hand through his damp hair.

"You ought to have waited, before you dashed in alone, to see if we'd come up with you. You know you run faster than anyone else. I could have killed you for it, when we were milling in the doorway."

"They were going to drop that rock there, look at the size of it. I knew you weren't far off."

Hephaistion was feeling the reaction, not only to his fears for Alexander, but to all he had seen and done. "Rock or no rock, you'd have gone in. It was written all over you. It's only luck you're alive."

"It was the help of Herakles," said Alexander calmly. "And hitting them quickly, before they could hit me."

He had found this easier than he had foreseen. The best he had hoped from his constant weapon-practice had been some lessening of disadvantage, against seasoned men. Hephaistion, reading his thought, said, "These Thracians are peasants. They fight two or three times a year, in a cattle-raid or a brawl. Most of them are stupid, none of them are trained. Real soldiers, like your father's men, would have cut you down before you were well inside."

"Wait till they do it," said Alexander sharply, "and tell me about it then."

"You went in without me. You didn't even look."

[171]

Suddenly transformed, Alexander gave him a loving smile. "What's the matter with you? Patroklos reproached Achilles for *not* fighting."

"He was listened to," said Hephaistion in a different voice.

From below in the fort, the wail of a woman keening rhythmically over some dead man broke off in a shriek of terror.

"He should call the men in," Alexander said. "It's enough. I know there was nothing else worth taking, but—"

They looked along the wall; but Philip had gone off on some other business.

"Alexander. Listen. It's no use to be angry. When you're a general, you'll not be able to expose yourself like that. The King's a brave man, but he doesn't do it. If you'd been killed, it would have been like a battle won for Kersobleptes. And later, when you're King . . ."

Alexander turned round, and riveted on him that gaze of peculiar intensity with which he told a secret. Dropping his voice, a needless caution in so much noise, he said, "I can never not do it. I know it, I've felt it, it's the truth of the god. It's then that I—"

A sound of panting breath, catching in shrill sobs, broke in on them. A young Thracian woman rushed in from the ramparts and, without looking right or left, dashed towards the wide parapet above the gate. It was some thirty feet from the ground. As she got her knee on the sill, Alexander jumped after and grasped her arm. She screamed, and clawed at him with her free hand, till Hephaistion caught it back. She stared into Alexander's face with the fixity of a cornered animal, writhed suddenly free, crouched down and clutched his knees.

"Get up, we won't harm you." Alexander's Thracian had been improved by his talks with Lambaros. "Don't fear, get up. Let go."

The woman gripped harder, pouring out a stream of half-smothered words as she pressed her face with its running eyes and nose against his bare leg.

"Get up," he said again. "We won't . . ." He had never learned the essential word. Hephaistion supplied a gesture of universal meaning, followed by a strongly negative sign.

The woman let go and sat back on her heels, rocking and wailing. She had red matted hair, and a dress of some coarse raw wool, torn at the shoulder. The front was splashed with blood; there were damp patches of leaked milk over the heavy breasts. She wrenched at her hair, and began to wail again. Suddenly she started, leaped to her feet, and flattened herself against the wall behind them. Footsteps approached; a thick breathless voice called, "I saw you, you bitch. Come here. I saw you." Kassandros entered. His face was crimson, his freckled brow beaded with sweat. He charged blindly in, and stopped dead.

The girl, shouting out curses, entreaties, and the incomprehensible tale of her wrongs, ran up behind Alexander and grabbed his waist, holding him like a shield. Her hot breath was in his ear; her wet softness seemed to seep even through his corselet; he was half stifled with the rank female smell of dirty flesh and hair, blood, milk and sex. Pushing her arms away, he gazed at Kassandros with mystified repugnance.

"She's mine," panted Kassandros, with an urgency hardly capable of words. "You don't want her. She's mine."

Alexander said, "No. She's a suppliant, I've pledged her."

"She's *mine*." He spoke as if the word must produce effect, staring across at the woman. Alexander looked him over, pausing at the linen kilt below his corselet. In a withdrawn distaste he said, "No."

"I caught her once," Kassandros insisted. "But she got away." His face was plowed down one side with scratches.

"So you lost her. I found her. Go away yourself."

Kassandros had not quite forgotten his father's warnings. He kept his voice down. "You can't interfere here. You're a boy. You know nothing about it."

"Don't dare call him a boy!" said Hephaistion furiously. "He fought better than you did. Ask the men."

Kassandros, who had blundered and hacked his way through the complex obstacles of battle, confused, harassed, and intermittently scared, recalled with hatred the enraptured presence cleaving the chaos, as lucid as a point of flame. The woman, supposing all this to be concerned with her, began to pour out another flood of Thracian. Above it Kassandros shouted, "He was looked after! Whatever fool thing he did, they were bound to follow him! He's the King's son. Or so they say."

Stupid with anger, and looking at Hephaistion, he was an instant too late for Alexander, whose standing leap at his throat took him off balance and hurled him to the rugged floor. He threshed and flailed; Alexander, intent on choking him, took kicks and blows with indifference. Hephaistion hovered, not daring to help without leave. Something rushed past him from behind. It was the woman, whom they had all forgotten. She had snatched up a three-legged stool; missing Alexander by an inch, she brought it down in a side-sweep on Kassandros' head. Alexander rolled out of the way; with a frenzied rage she began to beat Kassandros over the body, slamming him back whenever he tried to rise; taking both hands to it, as if she were threshing corn.

Hephaistion, who was becoming overwrought, burst out laughing. Alexander, regaining his feet, stood looking down, stone-cold. It was Hephaistion who said, "We must stop her. She'll finish him off."

Without moving, Alexander answered, "Someone killed her child. That's its blood on her."

Kassandros had begun to roar with pain. "If he dies," said Hephaistion, "she'll be stoned. The King couldn't refuse. You pledged her."

"Stop!" said Alexander in Thracian. Between them they got the stool away. She burst into wild weeping, while Kassandros rolled about on the cobbled floor.

"He's alive," said Alexander, turning away. "Let's find someone reliable, and get her out of the fort."

A little later, rumors reached King Philip that his son had thrashed Antipatros' son in a fight over a woman. He said offhandedly, "Boys will be men, it seems." The note of pride was too clear for anyone to risk taking it further.

Hephaistion, walking back with Alexander, said grinning, "He can hardly complain to Antipatros that you stood by and let a woman beat him."

"He can complain where he likes," said Alexander. "If he likes." They had turned into the gate. A sound of groaning came from a house within the wall. Here on makeshift bedding the wounded lay; the doctor and his two servants were going to and fro. Hephaistion said, "Let him see properly to your arm." It had started to bleed again, after the brawl in the gatehouse.

"There's Peithon," Alexander said, peering into the gloom with its buzzing flies. "I must thank him first."

[174]

He picked his way between mats and blankets, by the light from holes in the roof. Peithon, a youngish man who in battle had looked stern and Homeric, lay with his bandage seeping, limp with loss of blood. His pale face was pinched, his eyes shifted anxiously. Alexander knelt by him and clasped his hand; presently, as his exploits were recalled to him, his color livened a little, he bragged, and essayed a joke.

When Alexander got up, his eyes had grown used to the shadows. He saw they were all looking at him, jealous, despondent, hopeful; feeling their pain, and wanting their contribution recognized. In the end, before he left, he had spoken to every one of them.

It was the hardest winter old men remembered. Wolves came down to the villages and took the watchdogs. Cattle and herd-boys died of cold on the low slopes of the winter grazing. The limbs of fir trees cracked under their weight of snow; the mountains were blanketed so thick that only great cliffs and clefts in them still showed dark. Alexander did not refuse the fur cloak his mother sent him. Taking a fox among the stark black tangle of the rose-thorns near Mieza, they found that its pelt was white. Aristotle was very pleased with it.

The house was pungent and smoky with its braziers; nights were so bitter that the young men doubled up together, only for warmth. Alexander was anxious to keep well hardened (the King was still in Thrace, where winter blew down straight from the Scythian steppes). He thought he should get through the cold spell without such coddling; but gave way to Hephaistion's view that people might suppose they had quarreled.

Ships were lost at sea, or land-bound. Even from as near as Pella, the roads were sometimes snowed up. When the mule train got through, it was like a feast-day.

"Roast duck for supper," said Philotas.

Alexander smelled the air and nodded. "Something's wrong with Aristotle."

"Has he gone to bed?"

"No, it's bad news. I saw him in the specimen room." Alexander went there often; he was now apt to set up his own experiments. "My mother sent me some mitts; I don't need two pairs, and no

[175]

one sends him presents. He was there with a letter. He looked dreadful; like a tragic mask."

"I daresay some other sophist has contradicted him."

Alexander held his peace, and went off to tell Hephaistion.

"I asked him what the trouble was, if I could help. He said no, he'd tell us about it when he was more composed; and that womanishness would be unworthy of a noble friend. So I went off, to let him weep."

At Mieza, the winter sun went down quickly behind the mountain, while the eastward heights of Chalkidike still caught its light. Around the house, the dusk was whitened by the snow. It was not yet time to eat; in the big living-room with its peeling frescoes of blue and rose, the young men hung round the fire-basket on the hearth, talking about horses, women or themselves. Alexander and Hephaistion, sharing the wolfskin cloak sent by Olympias, sat near the window because the lamps were not yet lit. They were reading Xenophon's *The Upbringing of Kyros,* which, next to Homer, was just then Alexander's favorite book.

"*And she could not hide her tears,*" read Hephaistion, "*falling all down her robe to her feet. Then the eldest man of us said, 'Don't be afraid, Lady; we know your husband was noble, but we are choosing you out for one who is not below him in beauty, or mind, or power. We believe that if any man is admirable, it is Kyros; and to him you will belong.' When the lady heard this, she rent her peplos from top to bottom, crying aloud, while her servants wept with her; and we then had a sight of her face, her neck and arms. And let me tell you, Kyros, it seemed to me and all of us that there was never so beautiful a woman of mortal birth in Asia. But you must be sure to see her for yourself.'*

"'*No, by God,' said Kyros. 'Especially if she is as lovely as you say.'*

"They keep asking me," said Hephaistion, looking up, "why Kassandros doesn't come back."

"I told Aristotle he fell in love with war and forsook philosophy. I don't know what he told his father. He couldn't have come back with us; she broke two of his ribs." He pulled another roll out of the cloak. "This part I like. *Bear in mind that the same toils do not bear equally on the general and the common soldier, though their bodies are of the same kind; but the honor of the general's rank, and his knowing that nothing he does will go unnoticed, make his hardships lighter to endure.* How true that is. One can't bear it in mind enough."

"Can the real Kyros have been quite so much like Xenophon?"

"The Persian exiles used to say he was a great warrior and a noble king."

Hephaistion peered into a roll. *"He trained his companions not to spit or blow their noses in public, not to turn round and stare . . ."*

"Well, the Persians were rough hill-people in his day. They must have seemed to the Medes like, say, Kleitos would to an Athenian . . . I like it that when his cooks served him something good, he sent pieces round to his friends."

"I wish it were suppertime. I'm clemmed."

Alexander edged more of the cloak around him, remembering that at night he was always drawing close because of the cold. "I hope Aristotle will come down. It must be icy upstairs. He ought to have some food."

A slave came in with a hand-lamp and tinder-stick, and kindled the tall standing lamps, then reached his flame to the hanging lamp-cluster. The raw young Thracian he was training closed up the shutters, and gingerly pulled the thick wool curtains across.

"A ruler," read Alexander, *"should not only be truly a better man than those he rules. He should cast a kind of spell on them . . ."*

There were footsteps on the stairs, which paused till the slaves had gone. Into the evening snugness, Aristotle came down like a walking corpse. His eyes were sunken; the closed mouth seemed to show beneath it the rigid grin of the skull.

Alexander threw off the cloak, scattering the scrolls, and crossed the room to him. "Come to the fire. Bring a chair, someone. Come and get warm. Please tell us the trouble. Who is dead?"

"My guest-friend, Hermeias of Atarneus." Given a question of fact to answer, he could bring out the words. Alexander shouted in the doorway for some wine to be mulled. They all crowded round the man, grown suddenly old, who sat staring into the fire. For a moment he stretched his hands to warm them; then, as if even this stirred some thought of horror, drew them back into his lap.

[177]

"It was Mentor the Rhodian, King Ochos' general," he began, and paused again. Alexander said to the others, "That's Memnon's brother, who reconquered Egypt."

"He has served his master well." The voice too had thinned and aged. "Barbarians are born so; they did not make their own base condition. But a Hellene who sinks to serve them . . . Herakleitos says, *The best corrupted is the worst.* He has betrayed nature itself. So he sinks even below his masters."

His face looked yellow; those nearest saw his tremor. To give him time, Alexander said, "We never liked Memnon, did we, Ptolemy?"

"Hermeias brought justice and a better life to the lands he ruled. King Ochos coveted his lands, and hated his example. Some enemy, I suspect Mentor himself, carried to the King tales he gladly believed. Then Mentor, pretending a friend's concern, warned Hermeias of danger, and invited him to come and take counsel on it. He went, believing; in his own walled city he could have held out a long time, and was in reach of help from . . . a powerful ally, with whom he had agreements."

Hephaistion looked at Alexander; but he was fixed in entire attention.

"As a guest-friend he came to Mentor; who sent him, in fetters, to the Great King."

The young men made sounds of outrage, but briefly, being eager to learn what next.

"Mentor took his seal and fixed it to forged orders, which opened all the strongpoints of Atarneus to Mentor's men. King Ochos now owns them, and all the Greeks within them. As for Hermeias . . ."

A brand fell out of the hearth; Harpalos picked up the fire-iron and shoved it back. Aristotle wetted his lips with his tongue. His folded hands did not move, but their knuckles whitened.

"From the first his death had been determined; but that was not enough for them. King Ochos wished first to know what secret treaties he might have made with other rulers. So he sent for the men whose skill it is to do such things, and told them to make him speak. It is said they worked on him a day and a night."

He went on to tell them what had been done; forcing his voice, when he could, into the tone of his lectures on anatomy. The young men listened wordless; their breath hissed as they sucked it in through their shut teeth.

"My pupil Kallimachos, whom you know, sent me the news from Athens. He says that when Demosthenes announced to the Assembly that Hermeias had been taken, he numbered it among the gifts of fortune, saying, 'The Great King will now hear of King Philip's plots, not as a complaint from us, but from the lips of the man who worked them.' *He* knows, none better, how such things are done in Persia. But he rejoiced too soon. Hermeias told them nothing. At the end, when after all they could do he was still alive, they hung him on a cross. He said to those in hearing, 'Tell my friends I have done nothing weak, nor unworthy of philosophy.'"

There was a deep-voiced murmuring. Alexander stood rooted and still. Presently, when no one else spoke, he said, "I am sorry. Indeed I am truly sorry." He came forward, put his arm around Aristotle's shoulders and kissed his cheek. He stared on into the fire.

A servant brought the warmed wine; he sipped it, shook his head, and put it aside. Suddenly he sat up, and turned towards them. In the upward glow of the fire, the lines of his face looked as if carved in clay, ready for casting in the bronze.

"Some of you will command in war. Some of you will have the ruling of lands you conquer. Always remember this: as the body is worth nothing without the mind to rule it, as its function is to labor that the mind may live, such is the barbarian in the natural order God ordained. Such peoples may be bettered, as horses are, by being tamed and put to use; like plants or animals, they can serve purposes beyond what their own natures can conceive. That is their value. They are the stuff of slaves. Nothing exists without its function; that is theirs. Remember it."

He stood up from the chair, giving as he turned a haunted look at the fire-basket, whose bands were reddening. Alexander said, "If I ever take the men who did this to your friend, the Persians or the Greek, I swear I will avenge him."

Without looking back, Aristotle walked to the dark staircase and went up it out of their sight.

The steward came in, to announce that supper was ready.

Talking loudly of the news, the young men made for the dining-room; there was not much formality at Mieza. Alexander and Hephaistion lingered, exchanging looks. "So," said Hephaistion, "he did arrange the treaty."

"My father and he caused this between them. What must he feel?"

"At least he knows his friend died faithful to philosophy."

"Let's hope he believes it. A man dies faithful to his pride."

"I expect," said Hephaistion, "the Great King would have killed Hermeias in any case, to get his cities."

"Or he did it because he doubted him. Why was he tortured? They guessed there was something he knew." The firelight burnished his hair and the clear whites of his eyes. He said, "If ever I get my hands on Mentor, I shall have him crucified."

With a complex inward shudder, Hephaistion pictured the beautiful vivid face watching unmoved. "You'd better go in to supper. They can't start without you."

The cook, who knew how young men eat in cold weather, had allowed a whole duck to each. First helpings, with the breast, were being carved and handed; a warm aromatic smell enriched the air.

Alexander picked up the plate they had put before him, and swung down his feet from the dining-couch he was sharing with Hephaistion. "Everyone eat, don't wait. I'm only going to see Aristotle." To Hephaistion he said, "He must eat before night. He'll fall sick if he lies fasting in the cold, in all that grief. Just tell them to get me something, anything will do."

The plates were being wiped with bread when he came back. "He took a little. I thought he would once he got the smell of it. I daresay he'll have more, now . . . There's too much here, you've been giving me yours." Presently he added, "Poor man, he was half out of his mind. I could tell, when he made us that speech about the nature of barbarians. Imagine calling a great man like Kyros the stuff of slaves, only because he was born a Persian."

The pale sun rose earlier and gained strength; steep mountain faces let slip their snow-loads, roaring, to flatten great pines like grass. Torrents foamed down their gorges, grinding boulders with thunderous sound. Shepherds waded thigh-deep through wet snow to rescue the early lambs. Alexander put his fur cloak away, in case he should come to depend on it. The young men who had been doubling up went back to sleep alone; so he put away Hephaistion too, though not without some regret. Secretly Hephaistion exchanged their pillows, to take with him the scent of Alexander's hair.

King Philip came back from Thrace, where he had deposed King Kersobleptes, left garrisons in his strongpoints, and planted the Hebros valley with Macedonian colonists. Those who applied for lands in these uncouth wilds were mostly men unwanted, or wanted too much, elsewhere; the wits of the army said he should have called his new city, not Philippopolis, but Knavestown. However, the foundation would serve its purpose. Pleased with his winter's work, he returned to Aigai to celebrate the Dionysia.

Mieza was abandoned to its slaves. The young men and their teacher packed up their things, and rode along the track which skirted the ridge to Aigai. Here and there they had to descend to the plain, to ford swollen streams. A long while before they sighted Aigai, on the forest trail they felt the earth below them shudder with the pounding of the falls.

The old rugged castle was full of lights and bright stuffs and beeswax polish. The theater was being readied for the plays. The half-moon shelf Aigai stood on was like a great stage itself, looked down on by wild hills whose audience one could only guess at, when in the windy spring nights they cried to each other over the sounds of water, in defiance, terror, loneliness or love.

The King and Queen were installed already. Reading as he crossed the threshold those signs in which the years had made him expert, Alexander judged that, publicly at least, they were on speaking terms. But they were unlikely to be found together. This had been his first long absence; which should be greeted first?

It ought to be the King. Custom decreed it; to omit it would be an open slight. Unprovoked too; in Thrace, Philip had gone to trouble to keep things decent before him. No girl about the place; never a glance too many at the handsomest of the body-squires, who thought himself a cut above the rest. His father had commended him handsomely after the battle, and promised him his own company when next he went into action. It would be boorish to insult him. Indeed, Alexander found that he wished to see him; he would have much to tell.

Mary Renault

The King's business room was in the ancient tower which had been the first core of the castle, filling its upper floor. A ponderous wooden ladder, mended through the centuries, still had beside it the heavy ring to which earlier kings, whose bedchamber it had been, had chained a watchdog of the great Molossian breed that could rear up taller than a man. King Archelaos had hung a smoke-hood over the hearth; but he had made few changes at Aigai, the Palace at Pella had been his love. Philip's clerks had the anteroom below the ladder. Alexander had one of them announce him, before he went up.

His father got up from his writing-table, to thump him on the shoulders. Their greetings had never been so easy. Alexander's questions burst from him. How had Kypsela fallen? He had been sent back to school while the army still sat before it. "Did you go in from the river side, or breach that blind bit next the rocks?"

Philip had been saving him a reprimand for visiting, without leave, the wild eyrie of young Lambaros on his journey home, but this was now forgotten. "I tried a sap on the river side, but the soil was sandy. So I built a siege tower for them to think about, while I sapped the northeast wall."

"Where did you put the tower?"

"On that rise where—" Philip looked for his tablet, found it filled with notes, and made gestures in the air to sketch the site.

"Here." Alexander ran to the log-basket by the hearth, and came back with both hands full of kindling. "Look, this is the river." He laid down a stick of pine. "Here's the north watchtower." He stood a log on its end. Philip reached for another, and made a wall next the tower. They began eagerly to push bits of wood about.

"No, that's too far out, the gate was here."

"Look, but Father, your siege tower . . . Oh, there, I see. And the sap was here?"

"Now the ladders, give me those sticks. Now here was Kleitos' company. Parmenion—"

"Wait, we left out the catapults." Alexander dived into the basket for fir-cones. Philip set them up.

"So Kleitos was partly covered, while I—"

Silence fell like a sword-stroke. Alexander, whose back was to the door, needed only to read his father's face. It has been easier to leap

[182]

into the gatehouse at Doriskos than now it was to turn; so he turned at once.

His mother was dressed in a robe of purple bordered with white and gold. Her hair was bound with a gold fillet, and draped with a veil of byssos silk from Kos, through which its red showed like fire through wood-smoke. She did not glance at Philip. Her burning eyes sought not the enemy, but the traitor.

"When you have done your game, Alexander, I shall be in my room. Do not hurry. I have waited half a year; what are a few hours more?"

She turned rigidly and was gone. Alexander stood unmoving. Philip read into this what he wished to see. He raised his brows with a smile, and turned again to the battle-plan.

"Excuse me, Father. I had better go along."

Philip was a diplomat; but the rancor of years, the present exasperation, robbed him of his instinct for the moment when generosity would pay. "You can stay, I suppose, till I have finished speaking."

Alexander's face changed to that of a soldier awaiting orders. "Yes, Father?"

With a folly he would never have shown in parley with his enemies, Philip pointed to a chair and said, "Sit down." Challenge had been offered, beyond recall.

"I am sorry. I must see Mother now. Goodbye, Father." He turned towards the door.

"Come back," barked Philip. Alexander looked round from where he was. "Do you mean to leave all this filth on my table? You put it there; clear it up."

Alexander walked back to the table. Crisply, precisely, he put the wood in a pile, strode with it to the log-basket, and flung it in. He had knocked a letter off the table. Ignoring it, he gave one deadly look at Philip and left the room.

The women's quarters had been the same since the first days of the castle. From here they had been summoned, in Amyntas' day, to greet the Persian envoys. He went up the narrow stairs to the little anteroom. A girl he had not seen before was coming out, looking over her shoulder. She had fine feathery dark hair, green eyes, a clear pale skin, and a deep bosom over which her thin red dress was tightly bound; her lower lip was caught a little, in a natural line.

[183]

Mary Renault

At the sound of his step she started. Her long lashes swept up; her face, as frank-looking as a child's, showed admiration, realization, fright. He said, "Is my mother there?" and knew there had been no need to ask the question, he had done it from choice. "Yes, my lord," she said, dipping nervously. He wondered why she looked scared, though a mirror might have told him; felt sorry for her and smiled. Her face changed as if a pale sun had touched it. "Shall I tell her, Alexander, that you are here?" "No, she expects me, you need not stay." She paused a moment, looking at him earnestly, as if not satisfied that she had done enough for him. She was a little older than he, perhaps a year. Then she went on down the stairs.

He paused a moment outside the door, staring after. She had looked fragile and smooth to touch, like a swallow's egg; her mouth had been unpainted, pink and delicate. She had been a sweet taste after a bitter one. From outside the window came drifting the sound of a men's chorus, practicing for the Dionysia.

"You have remembered, then, to come," said his mother as soon as they were alone. "How soon you have learned to make your life without me!"

She stood by the window in the thick stone wall; a slanting light touched the curve of her cheek and shone in her thin veil. She had dressed for him, painted; intricately done her hair. He saw it; as she saw that he had grown again, that the bones of his face had hardened, his voice lost the last flaws of boyhood. He had come back a man, and faithless like a man. He knew that he had longed for her; that true friends share everything, except the past before they met. If only she would weep, even that, and let him comfort her; but she would not humble herself before a man. If only he would run to her side and cling to her; but his manhood was hard-won, no mortal should make him a child again. So, blinded by their sense of their own uniqueness, they fought out their lovers' quarrel, while the roar of the Aigai falls pounded in their ears like blood.

"How shall I be anything, without learning war? Where else can I learn it? He is my general; why affront him without a cause?"

"Oh, you have no cause now. Once you had mine."

"What? What has he done?" He had been gone so long, Aigai itself had looked changed, like the promise of some new life. "What is it, tell me."

[184]

"Never mind, why should you be troubled? Go and enjoy yourself with your friends. Hephaistion will be waiting."

She must have been questioning someone, he had always been careful. "I can see them any time. All I wanted was to do the proper thing. For your sake too, you know that. One would think you hated me."

"I only counted on your love. Now I know better."

"Tell me what he's done."

"Never mind. It is nothing, except to me."

"*Mother.*"

She saw the crease drawn across his forehead, deeper now; two little new lines came down between his brows. She could no longer look down at him; his eyes, drawn at the inner corners, met hers level. She came forward and laid her cheek to his. "Never be so cruel to me again."

Once through this rising river, and she would forgive him everything, all would be rendered back. But no. He would not give her this. Before she could see his tears, he broke from her and ran down the narrow stair.

At the turn, his eyes blurred, he collided with someone head-on. It was the dark-haired girl. "Oh," she cried, fluttering and soft like a pigeon, "I am sorry, I am sorry, my lord."

He took her slender arms in his hands. "My fault. I hope I did not hurt you?"

"No, no indeed." They paused a moment, before she swept down her thick lashes and went on up the stairs. He touched his eyes, in case there had been anything to notice; but they were scarcely wet.

Hephaistion, who had been looking for him everywhere, found him an hour later in a little old room which looked towards the falls. Their sound was deafening here when the water was in spate; the very floor seemed to shudder with the grinding of the rocks below. The room was lined with chests and shelves of old musty records and title deeds, treaties, and long family trees going back to heroes and gods. There were a few books too, left there by Archelaos or by the accidents of time.

Alexander sat curled in the small deep window-hole, like an animal in a cave. A handful of scrolls was strewed around him.

[185]

"What are you doing here?" Hephaistion asked.

"Reading."

"I'm not blind. What's the matter?" Hephaistion came up nearer, to see his face. It had the fierce secretiveness of a wounded dog which will bite the hand that strokes it. "Someone said you went up here. I've never seen this room before."

"It's the archives room."

"What are you reading?"

"Xenophon on hunting. He says the tusk of the boar is so hot that it singes dogs' fur."

"I never knew that."

"It's not true. I put a hair on one to see." He picked up the scroll. "It will soon be dark in here."

"Then I'll come down."

"Don't you want me to stay?"

"I just want to read."

Hephaistion had come to tell him that their sleeping-quarters had been set out in the archaic manner, the Prince in a small inner room, the Companions in a dormitory outside it, devoted to that purpose immemorially. Now, without asking, Hephaistion could see that the Queen would take notice if this arrangement were changed. The groan of the waterfall, the lengthening shadows, spoke of grief.

Aigai was in its yearly bustle for the Dionysia, enhanced by the presence of the King, so often absent at war. The women ran from house to house, the men met to practice their phallic dances. Mule trains of wine came in from the vineyards and up from the castle storerooms. The Queen's rooms were a buzzing secret hive. Alexander was barred from them, not in disgrace but because he was a man. Kleopatra was inside, though she was not yet a woman. She must know nearly all the secrets now. But she was too young yet to go with them up the mountain.

On the day before the feast, he woke early and saw dawn glimmer in the window. The first birds were chirping; the water sounded more distantly here. He could hear a woodman's ax, and cattle lowing for the milkers. He rose and dressed, thought of waking Hephaistion, then looked at the little postern stair which would let him out alone. It was built within the wall, so that the Prince could have women brought in discreetly. It could have told some tales, he thought as he stepped quietly down and, at the bottom, turned the key in its massive lock.

There was no garden at Aigai, only an old orchard enclosed in the outer wall. On the black bare trees, one or two buds were splitting at the thrust of unfolding flowers. Dew was heavy in the long grass; it hung in the spiders' webs like crystal beads. The peaks, still snowbound, were flushed with pink. The cold air was quickened with spring and violets.

He traced them by their scent to the bank where they grew deep in rank grass. When he was a child, he had gathered them for his mother. He would pick some now, and bring them while the women were doing her hair. It was as well he had come alone; even with Hephaistion, he could not very well have done it.

His hands were full of the cold wet flowers, when he saw something gliding through the orchard. It was a girl, with a thick brown wrap over a pale filmy gown. He knew her at once, and went towards her. She was like the plum buds, the light enfolded in the dark. When he came out from the trees, she gave a great start, and went as white as her linen. What a shy girl she was. "What is it? I shan't eat you. I only came to say good day." "Good morning, my lord." "What's your name?" "Gorgo, my lord."

She still looked quite blanched with fright; she must be extremely modest. What should one say to girls? He knew only what his friends, and the soldiers, claimed that they had said. "Come, smile for me, Gorgo, and you shall have some flowers." She gave him with dropped lashes a little smile, fragile, mysterious, like a hamadryad slipping out briefly from her tree. He almost found himself dividing the flowers in two, to keep some for his mother; what a fool he would have looked. "Here," he said, and, as she took them, bent and kissed her cheek. She leaned it a moment to his lips, then drew back, not looking at him, softly shaking her head. Opening her thick cloak she tucked the violets between her breasts, and slipped away through the trees.

He stood looking after her, seeing again the cold crisp stems of the violets going down into the warm silky crease. Tomorrow was the Dionysia. *And holy Earth made fresh young grass grow under them, dewy clover and crocuses and hyacinths, a thick soft bed between them and the hard ground.*

[187]

Mary Renault

He said nothing of it to Hephaistion.

When he went to greet his mother, he saw that something had happened. She was raging like a banked-down fire; but from her looks he was not the offender. She was asking herself whether or not to tell him of it. He kissed, but did not question her. Yesterday had been enough.

All day his friends were telling each other about the girls they meant to have next day, if they could catch them on the mountain. He threw back the old jokes, but kept his own counsel. The women would be setting out from the sanctuary, long before the dawn.

"What shall we do tomorrow?" Hephaistion asked him. "I mean, after the sacrifice?"

"I don't know. It's unlucky to make plans for the Dionysia."

Hephaistion gave him a secret, startled glance. No, it was not possible; he had been moody since he got here, and cause enough. Till he got over it, one must let him be.

Supper was early; everyone would be up next day before cock-light; and on the eve of Dionysos no one, even in Macedon, sat late over the wine. The spring twilight fell early, when the sun sank under the western ridges; there were corners in the castle where lamps were kindled half through afternoon. The meal in Hall had a transit air; Philip made use of its sobriety to seat Aristotle by him, a compliment less convenient on other nights, for the man was a poor drinker. After supper, most people went straight to bed.

Alexander was never fond of sleeping early. He decided to look up Phoinix, who often read late; he was lodged in the western tower.

The place was a warren; but he knew the short-cuts from childhood. Beyond an anteroom, where spare furniture for guests was kept, was the well of a little stair which took one straight there. The lobby was unlit, but a wall-cresset from beyond shone through. He was almost inside, when he heard a sound, and saw a movement.

Silent and motionless, he stood in shadow. In the patch of light, the girl Gorgo faced towards him, wriggling and squirming in the arms of a man who stood behind her, one dark square hairy hand squeezing her groin and the other her breast. Breathless soft giggles stirred her throat. The dress slid off her shoulder under the working hand; a couple of dead violets fell out on the flagstones. The man's

[188]

face, muzzling for her ear, appeared from behind her head. It was his father's.

Stealthily as in war, his footfalls covered by her squeaking, he drew back, and went through the nearest door into the cold, water-loud night.

Upstairs, in the lodging of the Prince's Guard, Hephaistion lay awake, waiting for Alexander to come to bed so that he could go in and say good night. Other nights here, they had all gone up together; but tonight, no one had seen him since supper. To go searching about for him might make people laugh; Hephaistion lay in the darkness, staring at the line of light under the thick old door of the inner room, watching for the shadows of feet to cross it. No shadow stirred. He drifted into sleep, but dreamed he was watching still.

In the dark small hours, Alexander went up by the postern to change his clothes. The lamp, nearly burned out, flickered dimly. Stripping in the bitter cold, his fingers almost too numb to fasten things, he got into the dressed leather tunic, boots and leggings he used for hunting. He would get warm when he began to climb.

He leaned from the window. Already here and there, wavering among trees, twinkling like stars in the down-drafts from the snows, the first torches shone.

It was long since he had followed them to the grove. Never, at any time of his life, had he followed them to the rites upon the mountain. He could have given no reason now, except that it was the only thing. He was returning, though it was unlawful. There was nowhere else to go.

He had always been a quick, light-footed hunter, impatient of others' noise. Few men were astir so early; they were easily heard, laughing and talking with time in hand to find in the footslopes the willing tipsy stragglers who would be their prey. He slipped past unseen; soon he had left them all below him, going up through the beech woods along the immemorial track. Long ago, the day after an earlier Dionysia, he had traced this path in secret, all the way to the trodden dancing-place, by footprints, threads caught on thorns, fallen sprays of vine and ivy, torn fur and blood.

She should never know; even in after years, he would never tell her. Forever possessed in secrecy, this would belong only to him.

He would be with her invisibly, as the gods visit mortals. He would know of her what no man had known.

The mountainside grew steep, the path doubled to and fro; he threaded its windings quietly, lit by the sinking moon and the first glimmer of dawn. Down in Aigai, the cocks were crowing; the sound, thinned by distance, was magical and menacing, a ghostly challenge. On the zigzag path above him, the line of torches twined like a fiery snake.

Dawn rose up out of Asia and touched the snow-peaks. Far ahead in the forest he heard the death-squeal of some young animal, then the bacchic cry.

A steep bluff was split by a timbered gorge; its waters spread from their narrow cleft in a chuckling bed. The path turned left; but he remembered the terrain, and paused to think. This gorge went right up till it flanked the dancing-place. It would be a hard climb through virgin woods to the other edge, but it would make a perfect hide, out of reach yet near; the cleft was narrow there. He could hardly reach it before the sacrifice; but he would see her dance.

He forded the fast ice-cold water, clinging to the rocks. The pine woods above were thick, untouched by man, dead timber lying where time had felled it; his feet sank in the black sheddings of a thousand years. At last he glimpsed the torches flitting, small as glow-worms; then, as he drew nearer, the bright clear flame from the altar fire. The singing too was like flames, shrilling and sinking and rising in some new place as one voice kindled another.

The first shafts of sunlight shone ahead, at the open edge of the gorge. Here grew a fringe of small sun-fed greenery, myrtle and arbutus and broom. On hands and knees, stealthily as if stalking leopard, he crept behind their screen.

On the far side it was clear and open. There was the dancing-place, the secret meadow screened from below, exposed only to the peaks and the gods. Between its rowan trees it was scattered with small yellow flowers. Its altar smoked from the flesh of the victim and blazed with resin; they had thrown the butts of their torches on it. Below him the gorge plunged a hundred feet, but across it was only a javelin-cast. He could see their dew-dabbled, blood-stained robes and their pine-topped wands. Even from so far, their faces looked emptied for the god.

His mother stood by the altar, the ivy-twined thyrsos in her hand. Her voice led the hymn; her unbound hair flowed over her robe and fawnskin and her white shoulders, from under her ivy crown. He had seen her, then. He had done what men must not do, only the gods.

She held one of the round wine flasks proper to the festival. Her face was not wild or blank, like some of the others', but bright, clear and smiling. Hyrmina from Epiros, who knew most of her secrets, ran up to her in the dance; she held the flask to her mouth and spoke in her ear.

They were dancing round the altar, running out and back from it, then in on it with loud cries. After a while, his mother threw away her thyrsos, and sang out a magic word in Old Thracian, as they called the unknown tongue which was the language of the rites. They all threw their wands away, left the altar, and joined hands in a ring. His mother beckoned to a girl along the line, to come out in the middle. The girl came slowly, urged on by the others' hands. He stared. Surely, he knew her.

Suddenly, she ducked under their joined arms, and started running towards the gorge, taken no doubt by the maenad frenzy. As she came nearer, he saw it was certainly the girl Gorgo. The divine frenzy, like terror, had made her eyes start and stretched her mouth. The dance stopped, while some of the women ran after her. Such things, no doubt, were common at the rites.

She ran furiously, keeping well ahead, till her foot tripped on something. She was up again in a moment, but they caught her. In her bacchic madness, she began to scream. The women ran her back towards the others; on her feet at first, till her knees gave way and they pulled her along the ground. His mother waited, smiling. The girl lay at her feet, neither weeping nor praying; only shrieking on and on, a thin shrill note like a hare in a fox's jaws.

It was past noon. Hephaistion walked about the footslopes, calling as it seemed to him he had been doing for many hours, though it was not so long; earlier he had been ashamed to search, not knowing what he might find. Only since the sun was high had misery changed to fear.

"Alexander!" he called. A cliff-slab at the head of the glade flung ". . . ander!" back and forth. A stream ran out from a gorge, spreading through scattered rocks. On one of them Alexander sat, looking straight before him.

Hephaistion ran to him. He did not rise, scarcely looked round. It's true, thought Hephaistion, it's done. A woman, he is changed already. Now it will never be.

Alexander looked at him strainingly, with sunken eyes, as if feeling it urgent to remember who he was.

"Alexander. What is it? What happened, tell me. Did you fall, have you hurt your head? Alexander!"

"What are you doing," said Alexander in a flat clear voice, "running about on the mountain? Are you looking for a girl?"

"No. I was looking for you."

"Try the gorge up there, you'll find one. But she's dead."

Hephaistion, sitting down on the rock beside him, almost said, "Did you kill her?" for nothing seemed impossible to this face. But he dared not speak.

Alexander rubbed the back of a dirt-crusted hand across his brow, and blinked. "I didn't do it. No." He gave the dry rictus of a smile. "She was a pretty girl, my father thought so, my mother too. It was the frenzy of the god. They had a wildcat's kittens, and a fawn, and something else one couldn't tell. Wait if you like, she'll come down with the stream."

Speaking quietly, watching him, Hephaistion said, "I'm sorry you saw that."

"I shall go back and read my book. Xenophon says, if you lay the tusk of a boar on them, you can see it shrivel. It's the heat of their flesh. Xenophon says it scorches violets."

"Alexander. Drink some of this. You've been up since yesterday. I brought you some wine along . . . Alexander, look, I brought some wine. Are you sure you're not hurt?"

"Oh no, I didn't let them catch me, I saw the play."

"Look. Look here. Look at me. Now drink this, do as I tell you. Drink it." After the first swallow, he took the flask from Hephaistion's hand, and emptied it thirstily.

"That's better." Instinct told Hephaistion to be common and plain. "I've some food too. You shouldn't follow the maenads, everyone knows it's unlucky. No wonder you feel bad. You've a great thorn in your leg here, hold still while I get it out." He grumbled on, like a nurse sponging a child's bruises. Alexander sat docile under his hands.

"I've seen worse," said Alexander suddenly, "on a battlefield."

"Yes. We have to get used to blood."

"That man on the wall at Doriskos, his entrails fell out and he tried to put them back."

"Did he? I must have looked away."

"One must be able to look at anything. I was twelve when I took my man. I cut off the head myself. They'd have done it for me, but I made them give me the ax."

"Yes, I know."

"She came down from Olympos to the plain of Troy, walking softly, that's what the book says, walking softly with little steps like a quivering dove. Then she put on the helm of death."

"Of course you can look at anything, everyone knows you can. You've been up all night . . . Alexander, are you listening? Can you hear what I say?"

"Be quiet. They're singing."

He sat with hands on knees, his eyes upturned towards the mountain. Hephaistion could see white below the iris. He must be found, wherever he was. He ought not to be alone.

Quietly, insistently, without touching him, Hephaistion said, "You're with me now. I promised you I'd be here. Listen, Alexander. Think of Achilles, how his mother dipped him in the Styx. Think how black and terrible, like dying, like being turned to stone. But then he was invulnerable. Look, it's finished, it's over now. Now you're with me."

He put out his hand. Alexander's came out and touched it, deathly cold; then closed on it crushingly, so that he caught his breath with mingled relief and pain. "You're with me," Hephaistion said. "I love you. You mean more to me than anything. I'd die for you any time. I love you."

For some time they sat like this, with their clasped hands resting on Alexander's knee. After a while the vise of his grip relaxed a little; his face lost its masklike stiffness, and looked only rather ill. He gazed vaguely at their joined hands.

"That wine was good. I'm not so very tired. One should learn to do without sleep, it's useful in war."

"Next time, we'll stay up together."

"One should learn to do without anything one can. But I should find it very hard to do without you."

"I'll be there." The warm spring sun, slanting now towards afternoon, slid into the glade. A thrush was singing. Hephaistion's omens spoke to him, telling him there had been a change: a death, a birth, the intervention of a god. What had been born was bloodstained from a hard passage, still frail, not to be handled. But it lived, it would grow.

They must be getting back to Aigai, but there was no hurry yet, they were well enough as they were; let him have some quiet. Alexander rested from his thoughts in a waking sleep. Hephaistion watched him, with the steadfast eyes and tender patience of the leopard crouched by the pool, its hunger comforted by the sound of light distant footfalls, straying down the forest track.

6

THE PLUM-BLOSSOM had fallen, and lay beaten with spring rain; the time of violets was done, and the vines were budding.

The philosopher had found some of his students a little scatter-brained after the Dionysia, a thing not unknown even in Athens; but the Prince was studious and quiet, doing well at ethics and logic. He remained sometimes unaccountable; when found sacrificing a black goat to Dionysos, he evaded questions; it was to be feared philosophy had not yet rid him of superstition; yet this reticence showed, perhaps, a proper self-questioning.

Alexander and Hephaistion stood leaning on one of the small rustic bridges which spanned the stream of the Nymphs.

"Now," Alexander said, "I think I have made my peace with the god. That's why I've been able to tell you everything."

"Isn't it better?"

"Yes, but I had to master it first in my own mind. It was the anger of Dionysos pursuing me, till I made my peace with him. When I think about it logically, I see it would be unjust to be shocked at what my mother did, only because she's a woman, when my father has killed men by thousands. You and I have killed men who never injured us except for the chance of war. Women can't issue challenges to their enemies, as we can; they can only be avenged like women. Rather than blame them, we ought to be thankful to the gods for making us men."

"Yes," said Hephaistion. "Yes, we should."

"So then I saw it was the anger of Dionysos, because I profaned his mystery. I've been under his protection, you know, ever since I was a child; but lately I've sacrificed more to Herakles than to him. When I presumed, he showed his anger. He didn't kill me, like Pentheus in the play, because I was under his protection; but he punished me. It would have been worse, but for you. You were like Pylades, who stayed with Orestes even when the Furies came for him."

"Of course I stayed with you."

"I'll tell you something else. This girl, I'd thought, perhaps, at the Dionysia . . . But some god protected me."

"He could protect you because you'd a hold over yourself."

"Yes. All this happened because my father couldn't be continent, even for decency in his own house. He's always been the same. It's known everywhere. People who should be respecting him, because he can beat them in battle, mock him behind his back. I couldn't bear my life, to know they talked like that of me. To know one's not master of oneself."

"People will never talk like that about you."

"I'll never love anyone I'm ashamed of, that I know." He pointed to the clear brown water. "Look at all those fish." They leaned together over the wooden rail, their heads touching; the shoal shot like a flight of arrows into the shadow of the bank. Presently straightening up Alexander said, "Kyros the Great was never enslaved by women."

"No," said Hephaistion. "Not by the most beautful woman of mortal birth in Asia. It's in the book."

Alexander had letters from both his parents. Neither had been much disturbed by his unwonted quiet after the Dionysia, though each, at parting, had been aware of a certain scrutiny, as if from a window in a doorless wall. But the Dionysia left many young lads changed; there would be more cause for concern if it passed them by.

His father wrote that the Athenians were pouring colonists into the Greek coastal lands of Thrace, such as the Chersonesos; but, faced with a cut in the public dole, had refused to maintain the supporting fleet, which kept going perforce on piracy and inshore raids, like the reivers of Homer's day. Macedonian ships and steadings had been looted; they had even seized a Macedonian envoy sent to ransom prisoners, tortured him, and extracted nine talents' ransom for his life.

Olympias, for once almost at one with Philip, had a similar tale to tell. A Euboian dealer, Anaxinos, who imported southern goods for her, had been seized in Athens on the orders of Demosthenes, because the house of his host had been visited by Aischines. He was tortured till he confessed to being a spy of Philip, on which he was put to death.

"I wonder how long," Philotas said, "before it comes to war."

"We are at war," said Alexander. "It's only a matter of where we shall fight the battle. It would be impious to lay Athens waste; like sacking a temple. But sooner or later, we shall have to deal with the Athenians."

"Will you?" asked crippled Harpalos, who saw in the fighters round him a friendly but alien race. "The louder they bark, the more you can see their rotten teeth."

"Not so rotten that we can do with them in our backsides when we cross to Asia."

The war for the Greek cities of Asia was no longer a vision; its essential strategy had begun. Each year saw the causeway of conquered lands pushed nearer to the Hellespont. The strongpoints of the narrow seas, Perinthos and Byzantion, were the last great obstacles. If they could be taken, Philip would need only to secure his rear.

This fact being plain, the Athenian orators were touring Greece again in search of allies whom Philip had not yet persuaded, scared or bought. The fleet off Thrace was sent a little money; an island base was garrisoned in Thasos, close at hand. In the garden of Mieza, the young men debated together how soon they would get another taste of fighting, or, under the eye of the philosopher, discussed the nature and attributes of the soul.

Hephaistion, who had never imported anything in his life before, had gone through the complex business of ordering from Athens a copy of *The Myrmidons*, which he gave to Alexander.

Under a flower-bowed lilac beside the pool of the Nymphs, they discussed the nature and attributes of love.

It was the time when the wild beasts mated in the woods. Aristotle was preparing a thesis on their coupling and the generation of their young. His pupils, instead of hunting, hid in the coverts and made notes. Harpalos and a friend of his amused themselves by inventing far-fetched procedures, carefully doctored with enough science to secure belief. The philosopher, who thought himself too useful to mankind to risk a chill crouching for hours on wet ground, thanked them warmly and wrote all of it down.

One beautiful day, Hephaistion told Alexander he had found a vixen's earth, and thought she was mating. An old tree near by had been uprooted in the storms, leaving a deep hollow; one could watch from there. In the late sunlight, they went into the forest, not crossing the paths of their friends. Neither remarked on this, or offered the other any reason.

The dead roots of the fallen tree sheltered the hollow; its bottom was soft with last year's deep-drifted leaves. After some time the vixen, heavy with young, came slipping through the shadows with a partridge chick in her mouth. Hephaistion half-raised his head; Alexander, who had closed his eyes, heard the rustle of her passage but did not open them. She took fright at their breathing, and ran like a red streak into her lair.

Soon after, Aristotle expressed the wish to dissect a pregnant fox bitch; but they spared the guardian of their mystery. She grew used to them, after a while, would bring out her cubs without fear, feed them and let them play.

Hephaistion liked the cubs, because they made Alexander smile. After love he would grow silent, drifting into some private darkness; if recalled he was not impatient, but too gentle, as if with something to hide.

Both agreed that all this had been ordained by their destinies before their birth. Hephaistion still felt an incredulous sense of miracle; his days and nights were lived in a glittering cloud. It was only at these times that a shadow pierced it; he would point to the fox cubs playing, the deep brooding eyes would move and lighten, and all was well again. The pools and streams were fringed with forget-me-not and iris; in sunny copses the famous dog-roses of

Mieza, blessed by the Nymphs, opened their great bland faces and spread their scent.

The young men read the signs with which their youth made them familiar, and paid up their bets. The philosopher, less expert and not so good a loser, while they all walked or sat in the rose-starred gardens looked doubtfully at the two handsome boys unfailingly side by side. He risked no questions; there was no place in his thesis for the answers.

The olives were powdered with fine pale-green flowers, whose faint sweet waxy scent blew everywhere. The apple trees let fall their false fruit; small and green the true apples began to set. The vixen led her cubs into the forest; it was time they learned the craft by which they would live.

Hephaistion, too, became a patient and skillful hunter. Till his prey first came to his lure, he had not doubted that the passionate affection bestowed on him so freely held the germ of passion itself. He found matters less simple.

Once more he told himself that when the gods are bountiful, man must not cry for more. He thought how, like the heir of great wealth who is happy at first only to know his fortune, he had gazed at the face before him; the wind-tossed hair springing loosely from its peak, the forehead already traced with faint creases by the eyes' intensity; the eyes in their beautiful hollows, the firm yet feeling mouth, the aspiring arch of the golden eyebrows. It had seemed he could sit forever, content simply with this. So it had seemed at first.

"Oxhead wants exercise, let's go riding."

"Has he thrown the groom again?"

"No, that was just to teach him. I'd warned him, too." The horse had consented, by degrees, to be mounted for the routine of the stables. But once his headstall was on with its buckles and plaques of silver, his collar worked with filigree, and his fringed saddlecloth, then he knew himself the seat of godhead, and avenged impiety. The groom was still laid up.

They rode through red new-leaved beech woods to the grassy uplands, at an easy pace set by Hephaistion, who knew Alexander would not let Oxhead stand in a sweat. At a coppice edge they dismounted, and stood looking out to the Chalkidian mountains beyond the plain and the sea.

"I found a book at Pella," Alexander said, "last time we were there. It's one by Plato, that Aristotle never showed us. I think he must have been envious."

"What book?" Hephaistion smiling tested the hitch of his horse's bridle.

"I learned some, listen. *Love makes one ashamed of disgrace, and hungry for what is glorious; without which neither a people nor a man can do anything great or fine. If a lover were to be found doing something unworthy of himself, or basely failing to resent dishonor, he would rather be exposed before family or friends or anyone, than before the one he loves.* And somewhere it says, *Suppose a state or an army could be made up only of lovers and beloved. How could any company hope for greater things than these, despising infamy and rivaling each other in honor? Even a few of them, fighting side by side, might well conquer the world.*"

"That's beautiful."

"He was a soldier when he was young, like Sokrates. I expect Aristotle was envious. The Athenians never founded a lovers' regiment, they left it to the Thebans. No one's yet beaten the Sacred Band, did you know that?"

"Let's go in the wood."

"That's not the end, Sokrates ends it. He says the best, the greatest love can only be made by the soul."

"Well," said Hephaistion quickly, "but everyone knows he was the ugliest man in Athens."

"The beautiful Alkibiades threw himself at his head. But he said that to make love with the soul was the greatest victory, like the triple crown at the games."

Hephaistion stared out in pain to the mountains of Chalkidike. "It would be the greatest victory," he said slowly, "to the one who minded most."

Knowing that in the service of a ruthless god he had baited his trap with knowledge gained in love, he turned to Alexander. He stood staring out at the clouds, in solitude, conferring with his daimon.

Guilt-troubled, Hephaistion reached out and grasped his arm. "If you mean that, if it's what you really want . . ."

He raised his brows, smiled, and tossed back his hair. "I'll tell you something."

"Yes?"

"If you can catch me."

He was always the quickest off the mark. While his voice still hung in the air he was gone. Hephaistion threaded light birches and shadowy larches to a rocky scarp. At its foot Alexander lay motionless with closed eyes. Distraught and breathless Hephaistion clambered down, knelt by him, felt him for injuries. Nothing whatever was wrong. He eyed Hephaistion smiling. "Hush! You'll scare the foxes."

"I could kill you," said Hephaistion with rapture.

The sunlight, sifting through the larch boughs, had moved westward a little, striking glints like topaz from the wall of their rocky lair. Alexander lay watching the weaving tassels with his arm behind his head.

"What are you thinking of?" Hephaistion asked him.

"Of death."

"It does leave people sad sometimes. It's the vital spirits that have gone out of one. I'd not have it undone; would you?"

"No; true friends should be everything to one another."

"It *is* what you really want?"

"You should know that."

"I can't bear you to be sad."

"It soon goes by. It's the envy of some god perhaps." He reached up to Hephaistion's head, bent anxiously above him, and settled it on his shoulder. "One or two of them were shamed by unworthy choices. Don't name them, they might be angry; still, we know. Even the gods can be envious."

Hephaistion, his mind freed from the clouds of longing, saw in a divining moment the succession of King Philip's young men: their coarse good looks, their raw sexuality like a smell of sweat, their jealousies, their intrigues, their insolence. Out of all the world, he had been chosen to be everything which those were not; between his hands had been laid, in trust, Alexander's pride. As long as he should live, nothing greater could ever happen to him than this; to have more, one would need to be made immortal. Tears burst from his eyes, and trickled down on the throat of Alexander, who, believing he too felt the after-sadness, smilingly stroked his hair.

In the next year's spring, Demosthenes sailed north to Perinthos and Byzantion, the fortified cities on the narrow seas. Philip had negotiated a peace treaty with each: if let alone, they would not impede his march. Demosthenes persuaded both cities to denounce the treaties. The Athenian forces based on Thasos were conducting an undeclared war with Macedon.

On the drill-field of the Pella plain, a sea-flat left bare in old men's living memory, the phalanxes wheeled and countermarched with their long sarissas, graded so that the points of three ranks, in open order, should strike the enemy front in a single line. The cavalry did their combat exercises, gripping with the thighs, the knees, and by the mane, to help them keep their seats through the shock of impact.

At Mieza, Alexander and Hephaistion were packing their kit to start at dawn next day, and searching each other's hair.

"None this time," said Hephaistion, laying down the comb. "It's in winter, with people huddling together, that one picks them up."

Alexander, sitting at his knees, shoved off a dog of his that was trying to lick his face, and changed places. "Fleas one can drown," he said as he worked, "but lice are like Illyrians creeping about in the woods. We'll have plenty on campaign, one can at least start clean. I don't think you've . . . no, wait . . . Well, that's all." He got up to reach a stoppered flask from a shelf. "We'll use this again, it's far the best. I must tell Aristotle."

"It stinks."

"No, I put in some aromatics. Smell." During this last year, he had been taken up with the healing art. Among much theory, little of which he thought could issue well in action, this was a useful thing, which warrior princes had not disdained on the field of Troy; the painters showed Achilles binding Patroklos' wounds. His keenness had somewhat disconcerted Aristotle, whose own interest now was academic; but the science had been his paternal heritage, and he found after all a pleasure in teaching it. Alexander now kept a notebook of salves and draughts, with hints on the treatment of fevers, wounds and broken limbs.

"It does smell better," Hephaistion conceded. "And it seems to keep them off."

"My mother had a charm against them. But she always ended in picking them out by hand."

The dog sat grieving by the baggage, whose smell it recognized. Alexander had been in action not many months before, commanding his own company as the King had promised. All of today the house had sounded with shrill susurrations, like crickets' chirping; the scrape of whetstones on javelins, daggers and swords, as the young men made ready.

Hephaistion thought of the coming war without fear, erasing from his mind, or smothering in its depths, even the fear that Alexander would be killed. Only so was life possible at his side. Hephaistion would avoid dying if he could, because he was needed. One must study how to make the enemy die instead, and beyond that trust in the gods.

"One thing I'm scared of," said Alexander, working his sword about in its sheath till the blade glided like silk through the well-waxed leather. "That the south will come in before I'm ready." He reached for the brush of chewed stick with which he cleaned the goldwork.

"Give me that, I'll do it along with mine." Hephaistion bent over the elaborate finial of the sheath, and the latticed strap-work. Alexander always rid himself of his javelins quickly, the sword was already his weapon, face to face, hand to hand. Hephaistion muttered a luck-charm over it as he worked.

"Before we march into Greece, I hope to be a general."

Hephaistion looked up from rubbing the hilt of polished sharkskin. "Don't set your heart on it; time's looking short."

"They'd follow me already, in the field, if it came to a push in action. That I know. They'd not think it proper to appoint me yet, though. A year, two years . . . But they'd follow me, now."

Hephaistion gave it thought; he never told Alexander what he wished to hear, if it could cause him trouble later. "Yes, they would. I saw that last time. Once they thought you were just a luck-bringer. But now they can tell you know what you're about."

"They've known me a long time." Alexander took down his helmet from the wall-peg, and shook out its white horsehair crest.

"To hear some of them talk, one would think they'd reared you." Hephaistion dug too hard with the brush, broke it, and had to chew a new end.

"Some of them have." Alexander, having combed the crest, went over to the wall-mirror. "I think it will do. It's good metal, it fits, and the men can see me." Pella had no lack of first-class armorers. They came north from Corinth, knowing where good custom was. "When I'm a general, I can have one to show up."

Hephaistion, looking over his shoulder at his mirrored face, said, "I'll bet on that. You're like a gamecock for finery."

Alexander hung back the helmet. "You're angry, why?"

"Get made a general, then you'll have a tent of your own. We'll never be out of a crowd from tomorrow till we get back."

"Oh . . . Yes, I know. But that's war."

"One has to get used to it. Like the fleas."

Alexander came swiftly over, struck with remorse at having forgotten. "In our souls," he said, "we'll be more than ever united, winning eternal fame. *Son of Menoitios, great one, you who delight my heart.*" He smiled deeply into Hephaistion's eyes, which faithfully smiled back. "Love is the true food of the soul. But the soul eats to live, like the body, it mustn't live to eat."

"No," said Hephaistion. What he lived for was his own business, part of which was that Alexander should not be burdened with it.

"The soul must live to *do.*"

Hephaistion put aside the sword, took up the dagger with its dolphin hilts and agate pommel, and agreed that this was so.

Pella rang and rattled with sounds of war. The breeze brought Oxhead the noise and smell of war-chargers; he flared his nostrils and whinnied.

King Philip was on the parade ground. He had had scaling-ladders rigged up against tall scaffolding, and was making the men climb up in proper order, without crowding, jostling, pinking each other with their weapons, or undue delay. He sent his son a message that he would see him after maneuvers. The Queen would see him at once.

When she embraced him, she found he was the taller. He stood five foot seven; before his bones set, he might make another inch or so, not more. But he could break a cornel spear-shaft between his hands, walk thirty miles in a day over rough country without food (for a test, he had done it once without drink either). By gradual unnoticed stages, he had ceased to grieve that he was not tall. The tall men of the phalanx, who could wield a twenty-foot sarissa, liked him very well as he was.

His mother, though there was only an inch between them, laid her head on his shoulder, making herself soft and tender like a roosting dove. "You are a man, really a man now." She told him all his father's wickedness; there was nothing new. He stroked her hair and echoed her indignation, his mind upon the war. She asked him what kind of youth was this Hephaistion; was he ambitious, what did he ask for, had he exacted any promises? Yes. That they should be together in battle. Ah! Was that to be trusted? He laughed, patted her cheek, and saw the real question in her eyes, which sought, like wrestlers, for a moment's failure of nerve which would let her ask it. He faced her out, and she did not ask. It made him fond of her and forgiving; he leaned to her hair to smell its scent.

Philip was in the painted study at a littered desk. He had come straight from the drill-field, the room smelled acridly of his horse's sweat and his own. At the kiss of greeting, he noticed that his son, after a ride of less than forty miles, had already bathed to wash off the dust. But the real shock was to perceive on his jaw a fine golden stubble. With astonishment and dismay, Philip perceived that the boy was not, after all, behindhand with his beard. He had been shaving.

A Macedonian, a king's son, what could have possessed him to make him ape the effete ways of the south? Smooth as a girl. For whom was he doing this? Philip was well informed about Mieza; Parmenion had arranged this secretly with Philotas, who made regular reports. It was one thing to take up with Amyntor's son, a harmless and comely youth whom Philip, indeed, could himself have fancied; it was another to go about looking like someone's

minion. He cast his mind back to the troop of young men he had
seen arriving; it now occurred to him that there had been older
chins there, beardless too. It must be a fashion among them. A
vague feeling of subversion stirred under his skin; but he pushed it
out of the way. In spite of the boy's oddities, he was trusted by the
men; and, since business stood where it did, this was no time
to cross him.

Philip waved his son to the seat beside him. "Well," he said, "as
you see, we're well forward here." He described his preparations;
Alexander listened, elbows on knees, hands clasped before him;
one could see his mind running a step ahead. "Perinthos will be
tough to crack, but we shall have Byzantion on our hands as well;
openly or not they'll support Perinthos. So will the Great King. I
doubt he's in a state to make war, from what I hear; but he'll send
supplies. He has a treaty for that with Athens."

For a moment, their faces shared a single thought. It was as if
they spoke of some great lady, the strict mentor of their childhood,
now found to be plying the streets in a seaport town. Alexander
glanced at the beautiful old bronze by Polykleitos, of Hermes inventing the lyre. He had known it all his life; the too-slender youth
with his fine bones and runner's muscles had always seemed, under
the divine calm imposed by the sculptor, to conceal a deep inward
sadness, as if he knew it would come to this.

"Well, then, Father; when do we march?"

"Parmenion and I, seven days from now. Not you, my son. You
will be at Pella."

Alexander sat bolt upright staring; he seemed to stiffen all over.
"At Pella? What do you mean?"

Philip grinned. "You look for all the world like that horse of
yours, shying at his shadow. Don't be so quick off the mark. You
won't be sitting idle."

From his scarred and knotted hand he drew a massive ring of
antique goldwork. Its signet of sardonyx was carved with a Zeus
enthroned, eagle on fist; it was the Royal Seal of Macedon.

"You will look after this." He flipped it up and caught it. "Do
you think you can?"

The fierceness left Alexander's face; for a moment it looked almost stupid. In the King's absence, the Seal was held by his Regent.

"You've had a good grounding in war," his father said. "When you're old enough to be upgraded without a fuss, you can have a cavalry brigade. Let's say two years. Meantime, you must learn administration. It's worse than useless to push out frontiers, if the realm's in chaos behind you. Remember, I had to deal with that before I could move anywhere, even against the Illyrians who were inside our borders. Don't think it can't come back again. Moreover, you'll have to protect my lines of communication. This is serious work I'm giving you."

Watching the eyes before him, he saw a look in them he had not met since the day of the horse fair, at the end of the ride. "Yes, Father. I know it. Thank you; I'll see that you don't repent of it."

"Antipatros will stay too; if you've sense you'll consult him. But that's your own choice; the Seal's the Seal."

Each day till the army marched, Philip held councils: with the officers of the home garrisons, the tax-collectors, the officers of justice, the men whom the tribal chiefs, enrolled with the Companions, had left to rule their tribes; the chiefs and princes who for reasons historic, traditional or legal remained at home. Amyntas was one, the son of Perdikkas, Philip's elder brother. When his father fell he had been a child. Philip had been elected Regent; before Amyntas came of age, the Macedonians had decided they liked Philip's work and wanted to keep him on. Within the royal kin, the throne was elective by ancient right. He had dealt graciously with Amyntas, giving him the status of a royal nephew, and one of his own half-legal daughters for a wife. He had been conditioned to his lot from infancy; he came now to the councils, a thickset, dark-bearded young man of five-and-twenty, whom any stranger might have picked out of a crowd as Philip's son. Alexander, sitting on his father's right at the conference, would steal a look sometimes, wondering if such inertia could be real.

When the army marched, Alexander escorted his father to the coast road, embraced him, and turned for Pella. Oxhead, as the cavalry went off without him, blew restively down his nose. Philip was pleased he had told the boy he would be in charge of the communication lines. A happy thought; it had delighted him; and in fact the route was very well secured.

The first act of Alexander's regency was a private one; he bought a thin slip of gold, which he wound round the hoop of the royal signet to make it fit his finger. He knew that symbols are magical, in perfection and in defect.

Antipatros proved most helpful. He was a man for acting on facts, not wishes. He knew his son had fallen foul of Alexander, disbelieved Kassandros' version of it, and had been keeping him well out of the Prince's way; for here, if Antipatros had ever seen one, was a boy needing only a clumsy push at a crucial moment to discover in himself a very dangerous man. He must be served and served well, or else destroyed. In Antipatros' youth, before Philip secured the kingdom, a man might find himself any day standing siege in his own home against a vengeful neighbor prince, a horde of Illyrian raiders, or a brigand band. His choice had long since been made.

Philip had sacrificed his useful Chief Secretary, to take care of the young Regent. Alexander thanked him politely for the digests he had prepared, then asked for the original correspondence; he wished, he explained, to get the feel of the men who wrote. When he met anything unfamiliar, he asked questions. After everything was clear in his mind, he consulted with Antipatros.

They had no differences, till one day when a certain soldier was accused of rape, but swore to the woman's willingness. Antipatros was inclined to accept his well-argued case; but since a blood-feud threatened, he felt obliged to consult the Regent. With some diffidence he laid the unsavory tale before the fresh-faced youth in Archelaos' study, who answered without a pause that Sotion, as all his phalanx knew, when sober could talk his way out of a wolf-trap, but in drink he'd not know a farrow sow from his sister, and either would do as well.

A few days after the King marched east, the whole garrison force around Pella was called out on maneuver. Alexander had had some thoughts about the use of light cavalry against flanking infantry. Besides, he said, they must not be allowed to gather moss.

Relieved or frustrated at being left behind, in either case the men were inclined to take things easy. Before the trim well-burnished

FIRE FROM HEAVEN

youth on his sleek black horse had ridden half down the line, they were dressing ranks with nervous care and trying, with scant success, to conceal defects. One or two were sent in disgrace straight back to barracks. The rest spent a strenuous morning. Afterwards, the veterans who beforehand had grumbled loudest jeered at raw men's complaints; the youngster might have sweated them, but he knew how many beans make five.

"They shaped quite well," said Alexander to Hephaistion. "The chief thing is, they know now who's in command."

It was not, however, the troops who first tested this.

"My darling," said Olympias, "there is a little thing you must do for me before your father comes back; you know how he crosses me in everything. Deinias has done me so many kindnesses, looked after my friends, kept me warned of enemies. Your father has held back his son's promotion, just out of spite. Deinias would like him to have a squadron. He is a most useful man."

Alexander, half whose mind had been on mountain maneuvers, said, "Is he? Where is he serving?"

"Serving? It is Deinias, of course, I meant is useful."

"Oh. What's the son's name, who's his squadron commander?"

Olympias looked reproach, but referred to her notes and told him.

"Oh, Heirax. He wants *Heirax* to have a squadron?"

"It's a slight to a distinguished man like Deinias; he feels it is."

"He feels this is the time to say so. I expect Heirax asked him."

"Why not, when your father has taken against him for my sake?"

"No, Mother. For mine."

She swept round to face him. Her eyes seemed to explore some dangerous stranger.

"I've been in action," he said, "with Heirax, and I told Father what I saw of him. That's the reason he's here instead of in Thrace. He's obstinate, he resents men who are quicker-thinking than he is; and then when things go wrong he tries to shift the blame. Father transferred him to garrison duty, rather than demote him. I'd have demoted him, myself."

"Oh! Since when is it Father this and Father that? Am I no one to you now, because he gives you the Seal to wear? Do you take his part against me?"

"I take the men's part. They may have to be killed by the enemy;

[209]

that's no reason to have them killed by a fool like Heirax. If I gave him a squadron, they'd never trust me again."

She struck back at the man in him, with love and hatred. Once long ago, in the torchlit cave of Samothrace, when she was fifteen, she had met the eyes of a man before she knew what men were. "You are growing absurd. What do you think it means, that thing stuck on your finger? You are only Antipatros' pupil; it was to watch him govern, that Philip left you here. What do you know of men?"

She was ready for the battle, the tears and the bloodstained peace. For a moment he said nothing. Suddenly he grinned at her. "Very well, then, Mother. Little boys should leave affairs to the men, and not interfere."

While she still stared, he took three quick strides across and put his arm round her waist. "Dearest Mother! You know I love you. Now leave all these things and let me deal with them. I can see to them. You're not to be troubled with them any more."

For a moment she stood rigid. Presently she told him he was a wicked cruel boy, and she could not think what she would say to Deinias. But she had softened in his arm; and he knew she had been glad to feel its strength.

He gave up his hunting-trips to stay near Pella. In his absence, Antipatros would feel justified in taking decisions without him. Feeling short of exercise, and rambling through the stables, he found a chariot fitted up for the dismounters' race. Years ago he had meant to learn the trick, but then had come Mieza. The chariot was a synoris, a two-horse racer of walnut and pearwood; the bronze handgrip for the dismounter was about the right height; it was not a race for big men. He had two Venetian ponies yoked to it, called for the royal charioteer, and began to practice jumping down in mid-course, running with the car and leaping up again. Besides being good exercise, it was Homeric; the dismounter was the last heir of the chariot-borne hero, who drove to the fray in order to fight on foot. His spare hours were given to acquiring this archaic skill; he became very fast at it. Old chariot sheds were rummaged, so that friends could give him a race; this he enjoyed, but never arranged a formal one. He had disliked set contests, from as soon as he had been old enough to perceive that there were people who would let him win.

Dispatches came from Propontis, where Philip, as he had foretold, was finding Perinthos hard to crack. It stood on a headland impregnable from the sea, and strongly walled inland. The Perinthians, prospering and increasing on their steep rocks, had for years been building upward; four- and five-story houses, rising in tiers like theater benches, overlooked the ramparts, and now harbored slingers and javelineers to repel assaults. Philip, to give his men covering fire, had built hundred-foot siege towers, and mounted a platform of catapults; his sappers had brought down part of the wall, only to find an inner one, made from the first row of houses packed solid with rock, rubble and earth. As he had expected, too, the Byzantines were supplying the enemy; their fast triremes, with pilots expert in local waters (Macedon had never been a strong naval power), brought in crack troops, and kept open the way for the Great King's store-ships. He was fulfilling his pact with Athens.

King Philip, who dictated these reports, was a crisp and clear expositor. After reading one, Alexander would pace about, aware of the great campaign he was missing. Even the Seal was scant amends.

He was on the race-track one morning, when he saw Harpalos waving. A Palace messenger had passed the word to someone who could stop him without disrespect; it must be urgent. He jumped down from the car, ran with it a few steps to keep his balance, and came over, plastered with track-dust which coated his legs to the knee as thick as buskins. Through the mask of sweat-striped dirt shone his eyes, looking by contrast turquoise-blue. His friends stood well away, not from good manners but to keep him off their clothes. Harpalos murmured behind him, "It's an odd thing; have you noticed he never stinks, when anyone else would be rank as a dog-fox?" "Ask Aristotle," said someone. "No, I think he must burn it up."

The messenger reported that a courier was in from the northeast border, awaiting the Prince's leisure.

He sent a servant running to fetch him a fresh chiton; stripped and scraped down under the horse-yard fountain; and appeared in the audience room just before Antipatros, the scroll still correctly sealed, had finished questioning the courier, who had more to tell. He had barely got back with his life from the highlands up the

Mary Renault

Strymon River, where Macedon knit with Thrace in a mesh of disputed gorges, mountains, forests and grazing-grounds.

Antipatros blinked with surprise at Alexander's uncanny promptness; the messenger blinked with exhaustion, his eyes gummed by lack of sleep. Having asked his name, Alexander said, "You look dead tired; sit down." Clapping his hands he ordered wine for the man; while it came, he read the dispatch to Antipatros. When the man had drunk, he asked him what he knew.

The Maidoi were hillmen of a strain so ancient that Achaians, Dorians, Macedonians and Celts had all, in their southward drift, passed by the tribe's savage homeland in hope of better things. They had survived in the mountains and the Thracian weather, tough as wild goats, keeping up customs older than the age of bronze, and, when in spite of human sacrifice their food-gods were still unkind, raiding the settled lands. Philip had conquered them long ago, and taken their oaths of fealty; but with time he had grown dim to them and faded into legend. Their numbers had increased; boys come to manhood needed to blood their spears; they had broken south like a flash flood in a river bed. Farms had been stripped and burned; Macedonian settlers and loyal Thracians had been cut up alive, their heads taken for trophies, their women carried away.

Antipatros, for whom this was a second hearing, watched the youth in the chair of state, waiting kindly to meet his need with reassurance. He remained, however, with his eyes fixed on the messenger, sitting forward eagerly.

"Rest awhile," he said presently. "I want a few things in writing." When the scribe appeared, he dictated, checking them with the messenger, the Maidoi's movements and the main features of the country; adding, himself, a sketch-map worked up in the wax. Having checked this too, he ordered that the man be bathed, fed and put to bed, and sent out the clerk.

"I thought," he said scanning the tablets, "we should get all this from him now. A night's sleep should set him up, but one never knows, he might die. I want him well rested till I start out, so that I can take him as a guide."

Antipatros' brows with their foxy grizzle met over his fierce nose. He had felt this coming, but decided not to believe in it.

"Alexander, you know how gladly I would have you with me. But

[212]

you know too it is impossible we should both be out of Macedon, with the King at war."

Alexander sat back in his chair. His hair, streaked with dust and damp from his makeshift bath, hung limply on his brow; his nails and his toes were grimy. His eyes were cool, and made no pretense at naivety. "But of course, Antipatros. I should never think of such a thing. I shall leave you the Seal, while I am gone."

Antipatros opened his mouth, breathed deep and paused. Alexander cut in ahead, with inflexible courtesy. "I haven't it on me, I've been at exercise. You shall have it when I leave Pella."

"Alexander! Only consider . . ."

Alexander, who had been watching him like a duelist, made a small gesture to say he had not done speaking. After a crucial instant, Antipatros' voice tailed off. With stately formality, Alexander said, "Both my father and I know our great good fortune, in having such a man to entrust the realm to." He stood up, feet apart, hands on his belt, and tossed back his tousled hair. "I'm going, Antipatros. Settle your mind to it, because we're short of time. I shall start at dawn tomorrow."

Antipatros, who perforce had risen too, tried to use his height but found it ineffectual. "If you will, you will. But just think first. You're a good field officer, that's common knowledge. The men like you, agreed. But you've never mounted a campaign, or kept it in supplies, or planned its strategy. Do you know what that country's like?"

"By this time they'll be down in the Strymon valley; that's what they came for. We'll discuss supplies at the war council. I'm calling one in an hour."

"Do you realize, Alexander, that if you lose, half Thrace will blaze up like a fire of myrtle-brush? Your father's lines will be cut; and once the news is out, I'll be holding the northwest against the Illyrians."

"What troops would you need for that?"

"If you lose, there wouldn't be enough in Macedon."

Alexander tilted his head a little to the left; his gaze, floating beyond Antipatros' head, went slightly out of focus. "Also, if I lose, the men won't trust me again and I shall never be a general. Also, my father may well say I'm no son of his, and I shall never be a king. Well, I shall have to win, it seems."

Mary Renault

Antipatros thought, Kassandros should never have crossed him
. . . The eggshell was cracking indeed. One must already be very
careful. "What about me? What will he say to me for letting you go?"

"If I lose, you mean? That I should have taken your advice. Write
it down, and I'll sign to say you gave it me; win or lose, it goes to
my father. How's that for a fair bet?"

Antipatros looked sharply from under his shaggy brows. "Ah. But
you'd hold it against me after."

"Oh yes," said Alexander blandly. "Of course I should; what do
you suppose? You make your bet, Antipatros. You can't expect to
hedge it. I can't hedge mine."

"I think the stakes as they stand are high enough." Antipatros
smiled, remembering that already one must be careful. "Let me
know what you want, then. I've bet on worse horses in my time."

Alexander was on his feet all day, except during the war council.
He could have sat while he was sending out orders, but he could
think more quickly pacing to and fro; perhaps it came from the
walking discussions at Mieza. He had meant to see his mother
earlier, but there had been no time. He went when he had settled
everything, but did not stay very long; she was inclined to make a
fuss, though surely this was what she had been wanting. She would
see that later. Meantime he had Phoinix to say goodbye to; and it
was important to get some sleep.

It was a quiet morning in the camp before Perinthos; there had
been an engagement on the wall the night before, and the men were
being rested. The noises were those of lull: mules whinnied, men
serviced the engines with shouts and clanks, a man with a head
wound shouted insanely from the hospital shed; a captain of ar-
tillery, detailed to see the besieged did not take a holiday, shouted
to his crew to lift her up a chock, and grease the bolt-track; there
was a clang from the pile of massive boltheads, each stamped with
the laconic message, FROM PHILIP.

Philip had had a large timbered hut put up for him; when not
on the move, there was no sense in using the royal tent, to sweat
under stinking leather. He had made himself snug like an old
campaigner; local straw matting covered the floor, his baggage train

had carried chairs, lampstands, a bath, and a bed broad enough for company. At a pinewood table, made by the camp carpenters, he sat with Parmenion, reading a dispatch.

"*Having summoned also the troops from Pydna and Amphipolis, I marched north to Therma. I had planned to go by the Great East Road to Amphipolis, to learn the enemy's movements, and to make whatever dispositions seemed best, before going north up river.*

"*But at Therma, a rider met me, from the country of the Agrianoi. He had been sent by Lambaros, my guest-friend, in fulfillment of a vow.*

"Guest-friend?" said Philip. "Guest-friend? What does he mean? The boy was a hostage. You remember, Parmenion. I'd have bet a talent the Agrianoi would have joined the Maidoi."

"What was it you told me," said Parmenion, "about the Prince slipping off for a jaunt among the tribesmen, after you'd sent him back to school? I well remember you swearing when you heard."

"That's so, that's so. It slipped my memory. A crazy escapade, he was lucky not to have had his throat cut. I don't take hostages from tribes I think are safe. Guest-friend! Well, let's see.

"*Having heard you were in the east, he sent me word that the Maidoi were in the upper Strymon valley, laying everything waste. They had invited his people to join them in the war; but King Teres respected the oaths exchanged when you returned his son to him.*

"Wouldn't burn his fingers. But it was the boy who sent the message. How old will he be now? About seventeen.

"*He advised me to march quickly up river to Rushing Gate, as they call the steep throat of the gorge, and reinforce the old fort there, before they came down into the plain. I therefore decided not to lose time myself by going to Amphipolis, but to send Koinos with my orders to bring on the troops from there; I would lead the men I had straight up over the Krousia range by the trackways, and ford the Strymon at Siris, where Koinos would meet me with men, fresh horses and supplies, we ourselves traveling light. When I told the men what kind of dangers threatened our colonists in the plain, they made good going; the tracks being difficult, I went on foot with them, encouraging them to hurry.*"

Philip looked up. "Some secretary polished this. But touches of nature show.

Mary Renault

"*We crossed over Krousia and forded Strymon by noon on the third day.*"

"What?" said Parmenion staring. "Over Krousia? It's sixty miles."

"He moved light, and encouraged them to hurry."

"*Koinos met me promptly with all orders carried out. This officer acted with speed and address, and I commend him highly. Also he talked sense to Stasandros commanding at Amphipolis, who thought I should have wasted three days marching out that way and asking him what to do.*"

"Added," said Philip with a grin, "in his own hand."

"*Through Koinos' good management of his mission, I got the forces I had asked for, one thousand men . . .*"

Parmenion's jaw dropped. He did not attempt comment.

"*. . . which, though it left Amphipolis undermanned, still seemed to me most prudent, since for every day the Maidoi went undefeated, the chance grew greater of their being joined by other tribes. I had lookouts and beacons between me and the coast, to warn me if the Athenians should attack by sea.*"

"Ah," mused Parmenion. "Still, I wonder he got a steady man like Koinos to take it on."

"*But before we reached the Strymon, the Maidoi had already overrun the fort at Rushing Gate, had reached the plain and begun to ravage the farms. Some had crossed the Strymon westward to the silver mine, killed the guards and slaves, and carried home the bar silver through the river-pass. This decided me that it would not be enough to beat them off the farmlands; their own settlement ought to be reduced by war.*"

"Did he know," asked Parmenion incredulously, "where it is?"

"*When I had looked over the troops, I sacrificed to the appropriate gods, and to Herakles, and was given good auguries by the diviners. Also, one of the loyal Paionians told me that while hunting early, he had seen a wolf, as it fed upon a carcass, taken by a young lion. The soldiers were pleased with the omen, and I rewarded the man with gold.*"

"He deserved it," said Philip. "The shrewdest of the diviners."

"*Before starting my advance, I sent five hundred chosen hillmen to go under cover of the woods and surprise the fort at the Gate. Lambaros, my guest-friend, had advised me that it would be held*" *by the worst of the enemy, since none of their foremost warriors would forgo his share of the loot to secure their rear. My men found this to be true. They found also the bodies of our garrison, and saw that our wounded had been maltreated. As I had ordered should this be so, they threw the Maidoi down the cliffs into the rapids. They then manned the fort and both flanks of the gorge. Kephalon led; an energetic officer.*

"In the valley, some of our colonists had sent off their families to safety, and stayed themselves to fight off the enemy. I commended them for their courage, issued them with arms, and promised them a year's tax remission.

"Young men never know where money comes from," said the King. "You can be sure he never thought to ask what their tax was worth.

"I now led all my forces north up the valley, with my right flank advanced to deny the high ground to the enemy. Where we came on dispersed bands looting, these we destroyed; the rest we worked northeast, worrying them like herd-dogs getting the flock together, lest they should scatter off into the hills without giving us battle. Thracians trust everything to their first headlong rush, and do not like to stand.

"They collected where I had hoped, in a tongue of land where the river makes an elbow with the lake. They reckoned, as I thought they would, on the river securing their backs; I reckoned to push them into it. There was a ford at their rear, known for being deep and treacherous. By the time they had wet their bowstrings and lost their heavy arms, they should be ready to make for home through the pass, not knowing that my men held it.

"This, then was the order of battle . . ."

A workmanlike summary followed. Philip muttered through it, forgetting to recite aloud to Parmenion, who craned forward to hear. Lured out, rolled up, and thrown into confusion, the Maidoi had duly struggled off through the river, into the iron trap of the gorge. Alexander had returned to Amphipolis most of its borrowed garrison, in charge of his many prisoners.

"Next day I pressed on up river beyond the pass; a number of the Maidoi had crossed the mountains by other ways, and I did not want to give them leisure to re-form. So I came to the country of

the Agrianoi. Here Lambaros, my guest-friend, met me with a troop of horse, his friends and kinsmen. He had asked leave of his father to ride to war with us, in fulfillment of a vow. They showed us the easiest passes; later they did very well in battle.

"Teres saw which way the cat was jumping," said Philip. "Yet the boy didn't wait. Why? A child when he was at Pella, I can't even remember what he looked like."

He muttered his way through the breakneck mountain campaign that followed. Guided by his allies to the enemy's craggy nest, Alexander had attacked its main approach, while his mountaineers crept up the sheer side left unguarded.

"The men of the valley, wanting to revenge their wrongs, were about to kill everyone they found; but I ordered them to spare the women and the children, who had injured no one. These I sent to Amphipolis; do with them as you think best."

"Sensible lad," said Parmenion. "Those strong hill-women always fetch good prices; work better than the men."

Philip skimmed on, through rounding-up operations and commendations (*Hephaistion son of Amyntor, of Pella, fought with great distinction*), his voice fading to the murmur of routine business. Suddenly, making Parmenion jump, he shouted, *"What?"*

"Well, what, then?" asked Parmenion presently.

Philip, looking up from the roll, said in a measured voice, "He has stayed on there to found a city."

"It must be the clerk's writing."

"The clerk writes like a book. The Maidoi had some good grazing-lands, and the footslopes will grow vines. So he is refounding their city, in counsel with Lambaros, his guest-friend. I reckon they can notch up thirty-three years between them."

"If as much," Parmenion grunted.

"He has considered suitable colonists. Agrianoi of course; loyal Paionians; some landless Macedonians he knows of, and . . . Yes, wait. An afterthought, this. Have I any good men I would like to reward with a gift of land? He thinks he could take twenty."

Parmenion, deciding that only a fool would open his mouth, cleared the back of his throat to fill the pause.

"Of course he has named the city. Alexandropolis."

He stared down at the parchment. Parmenion looked at the shrewd, scarred, ageing face, the grizzled black brows and beard; the old bull snuffing the new spring air, tilting his battle-frayed old horns. I'm getting on too, Parmenion thought. They had shared the Thracian winters, stood together through the Illyrian battle-rush; they had shared muddy water in drought, wine after the battle; they had shared a woman, when they were young; she had never known for sure which had fathered her child; they had shared the joke. Parmenion cleared the black of his throat again.

"The boy's forever saying," he brought out brusquely, "that you'll leave him nothing to do, to make his name on. He's taking what chance he can."

Philip brought down his fist on the table. "I'm proud of him," he said decisively. "Proud of him." He pulled a blank tablet towards him, and with deep quick strokes sketched the battle. "That's a pretty plan, nice dispositions. But let them get out of touch; let a gap open, now, say, *here;* and where would he have been then, eh? Or if the cavalry pressed on out of hand? But no, he kept his hand on everything, there in the front line. And when they broke the wrong way, he changed his movement like *that.*" He snapped his fingers. "We shall see things, Parmenion, with this boy of mine. I'll find him those twenty settlers for his Alexandropolis, by God I will."

"I'll ask about, then. Why don't we drink to it?"

"Why not?" He called for wine, and began rolling up the letter. "What's this, wait, what's this? I never finished it.

"*Since I have been in the north, I hear everywhere of the Triballoi who live on the heights of Haimon, how they are unruly and warlike and a threat to the settled lands. It seems to me that while I am at Alexandropolis, I could carry the war up there, and bring them into order. I would like to ask your leave before drawing the troops I would need from Macedon. I propose . . .*"

The wine came and was poured. Parmenion took a great gulp, forgetting to wait for the King, who forgot to notice it. "The Triballoi! What does the boy want, does he want to push on up to the Ister?"

Philip, skipping the requisitions, read, "*These barbarians might annoy us, if they came on our rear when we cross to Asia; and if*

[219]

they were subdued, we could push our frontiers as far north as the Ister, which is a natural defense wall; being, as men say, the greatest river on earth after the Nile and the Encircling Ocean."

The two weathered men searched one another's faces, as if consulting omens. Philip broke the pause, throwing back his head in a great laugh full of broken teeth, and slapping his knee. Parmenion joined in with the loudness of relief.

"Simmias!" called the King at length. "Look after the Prince's courier. A fresh horse tomorrow." He threw back his wine. "I must get off his recall at once, before he starts to mobilize; I don't want to disappoint the lad. Ah, I know. I'll propose he consults with Aristotle over the constitution of his city. What a boy, eh? What a boy!"

"What a boy!" echoed Parmenion. He gazed into his cup, seeing his own image in the dark face of the wine.

The long train of men marched south, by phalanxes and squadrons, along the Strymon plain. Alexander led, at the head of his personal squadron. Hephaistion rode beside him.

The air was loud with sound; thin harsh crying and keening, deep creaks as of strained wood. It was the call of kites, hovering and stooping and fighting for choice shreds, mixed with the croak of ravens.

The settlers had buried their dead, the soldiers burned theirs on ceremonial pyres. At the rear of the column, behind the straw-bedded hospital wagons, a cart trundled along with straw-packed urns of local pottery, each painted with a name.

Losses had been light, for victory had come quickly. The soldiers talked of it as they marched, gazing at the enemy's scattered thousands, lying where they had fallen to receive the rites of nature. By night the wolves and jackals had gorged on them; with daylight the village pi-dogs, and the birds which clustered in a moving pall. When the column passed near, they rose in a screaming cloud and hovered angrily over their meal; only then could one see the raw bones, and the rags torn by wolves in haste to reach the entrails. The stench, like the noise, shifted with the breeze.

In a few days they would be picked clean. Whoever owned the land, the worst of the work done for him, would burn the bones in a heap, or shovel them into a pit.

Over a dead horse danced vultures, bouncing up and down with half-opened wings, scrawking at one another. Oxhead gave a smothered squeal, and shied away. Alexander signed to the column to proceed, dismounted, and led the horse gently towards the mound of reeking flesh; stroking his muzzle, going ahead to scare off the vultures, and, when they scolded and flapped, returning with soothing words. Oxhead stamped and blew, disgusted but reassured. When they had stood there a few moments, Alexander mounted and cantered back to his place. "Xenophon says," he told Hephaistion, "one should always do that with whatever scares a horse."

"I didn't know there were so many kites in Thrace. What do they live on when there's no war?" Hephaistion, who felt sick, was talking to keep his mind off it.

"There's never no war in Thrace. But we'll ask Aristotle."

"Are you still sorry," said Hephaistion dropping his voice, "that we didn't fight the Triballoi?"

"Why, of course," said Alexander, surprised. "We were halfway there. They'll have to be dealt with in the end; and we'd have seen the Ister."

A small cavalry detail on the flank cantered ahead at his signal; there were some bodies blocking the road. They were raked into a hunting net, and dragged out of the way.

"Ride on ahead," Alexander ordered, "and see it's clear . . . Yes, I'm sorry still, of course; but I'm not angry. It's true, as he says, his forces are stretched just now. He sent me a very handsome letter; I read it too quickly, when I saw it was a recall."

"Alexander," said Hephaistion, "I think that man there's alive."

A council of vultures was considering something out of sight; bouncing forward, then recoiling as if offended or shocked. There came into view a feebly flailing arm.

"So long?" said Alexander wondering.

"It rained," Hephaistion said.

Alexander turned and beckoned the first rider whose eye he met. The man cantered up smartly, and gazed at the wonderful boy with fervent affection.

"Polemon. If that man's not past help, have him picked up. They fought well, hereabouts. Or else finish him quickly."

"Yes, Alexander," said the man adoringly. Alexander gave him a slight approving smile; he went radiant off on his mission. Presently he remounted; the vultures, with satisfied croaks, closed in together.

Far on ahead of them shone the blue sea; soon, thought Hephaistion with relief, they would be past the battlefield. Alexander's eyes wandered over the bird-haunted plain, and beyond it skywards. He said,

*"Many brave men's souls it flung down to the house of Hades,
While their flesh made a feast for dogs, and all the birds of the air.
And the will of Zeus was fulfilled."*

The rhythm of the hexameters matched itself smoothly to Oxhead's pacing. Hephaistion gazed at him silent. He rode on, at peace with his unseen companion.

The Seal of Macedon stayed some time with Antipatros. Alexander had been met by a second courier, bidding him come to his father's siege-lines, to be commended. He turned east to Propontis, taking his companions with him.

In the King's lodging before Perinthos, a well-lived-in home by now, father and son would sit at the pinewood trestle, over a tray of sea-sand and stones; heaping up mountains, digging out defiles with their fingers, drawing with writing-sticks the disposition of cavalry, skirmishers, phalanxes and archers. Here no one disturbed their game, except sometimes the enemy. Philip's handsome young squires were decorous; bearded Pausanias with his ruined beauty, now promoted to Somatophylax, Commander of the Guard, watched impassively, never interrupting except for an alarm. Then they would buckle on their armor, Philip with veteran curses, Alexander eagerly. The troops whose section he joined would raise a cheer. Since his campaign he had a nickname: Basiliskos, the Little King.

His legend had run before him. Leading a scouting party against the Maidoi, he had walked round a crag straight into two of them, and dispatched them both while the men behind him were still catching their breath; neither had had time to shout a warning. He had kept a twelve-year-old Thracian girl in his tent all night, because she had run to him when the men were after her; had never laid a finger on her, and had given her a marriage dower. He had run between four big Macedonians brawling with their swords already out, and shoved them apart with his bare hands. In a mountain storm which had rained thunderbolts, so that it seemed the gods had resolved to destroy them all, he had read luck into it, kept them moving, made them laugh. Someone had had his wound stanched with the Basiliskos' own cloak, and been told his blood was a dye more honorable than purple; someone had died in his arms. Someone else, who had thought him raw enough to try old soldiers' tricks on, was sorry and sore. You would need to watch out, if he took against you. But put a fair case to him straight, he would see you right.

So, when in the light of the falling fires they saw him running towards the ladders, burnished like a dragonfly, greeting them as if they had all been bidden to a feast, they would call to him, and race for places near him. It was well to keep your eye on him; he would think quicker than you.

For all this, the siege went badly. Making an example of Olynthos had cut two ways; the Perinthians had decided that at the pinch they would rather die. And the pinch was still far off. The defenders, well supplied by sea, met assaults in strength and often went over to attack. They were setting their own example. From the Chersonesos, just south of the Great East Road, word came that the subject cities were taking heart. The Athenians had long urged revolt on them; but they would not take in Athenian troops, who were seldom paid and forced to live off the country. Now the cities had been emboldened. Macedonian outposts had been seized, and strongpoints threatened. War had begun.

"I swept one side of the road for you, Father," Alexander said as soon as the news arrived. "Now let me sweep the other."

"So I will, as soon as the new troops come. I'll use them here; you'll need men who know the country."

He was planning a surprise assault upon Byzantion, to stop their aid to Perinthos; as well deal with them now as later. He was committed, more deeply than he liked, to this costly war, and had needed to hire more mercenaries. They were coming up from Argos and Arkadia, states friendly to his power because for generations they had lived under the threat of Sparta; they did not share the anger and dread of Athens. But they cost money; which had been swallowed by the siege like water poured in sand.

At length they came, square stocky men of Philip's own build; his Argive descent still showed in him, bridging the generations. He reviewed them and conferred with their officers, from whom for better or worse hired troops would never be divided; it made a weak link in the chain of command. However, they were trained men who would earn their pay. Alexander and his troops marched west; already the men who had served with him in Thrace were patronizing the others.

His campaign was rapid. Revolt was still in the bud; several towns took fright, exiled their rash insurgents and pledged their loyalty. Those already committed, however, rejoiced to hear that Philip, the gods having sent him mad, had trusted his forces to a boy of sixteen years. They sent defiances. Alexander rode to their citadels, sat down before them one by one, looked for the flaws in their defenses, or, if there were none, created them with saps or ramps or breaches. He had learned his lessons at Perinthos, and improved on some of them. Resistance soon died out; the remaining towns opened their gates on his terms.

Riding out from Akanthos he viewed Xerxes' Ditch, the ship canal through the isthmus neck of Athos, cut for the Persian fleet to bypass its mountain storms. Its great snowy peak reared up from its shaggy buttresses. The army turned north, along the curve of a pleasant bay. Perched on the footslopes below the wooded hills stood a long-ruined town. Brambles grew on its fallen walls; the terracing of its vineyards was collapsing from the winter rains; its weed-grown olive groves were forsaken, but for a herd of goats nibbling the bark, and some naked little boys tearing off low branches. Alexander asked, "What place was this?"

A trooper rode to ask, and, when all the boys fled yelling at the sight of him, grabbed up the slowest, who struggled like a netted lynx. Dragged before the general, and finding him no older than his own brother, he was struck dumb. When the portent let him know that all they wanted of him was the name of the spot they stood on, he answered, "Stagira."

The column rode on. Alexander said to Hephaistion, "I must speak to Father. It's time for the old man to have his fee."

Hephaistion nodded. He had seen that schooldays were over.

When the treaties had been signed, the hostages delivered, the strongpoints manned, Alexander went back to Philip, still sitting before Perinthos.

The King had waited for him, before moving against Byzantion; he had needed to know that all was well. He was marching himself, leaving Parmenion here; for Byzantion would be tougher than Perinthos, three sides protected by Propontis and Golden Horn, the land side by massive walls. He set his hopes upon surprise.

They mulled over the campaign together, over the pinewood trestle. Often Philip would forget it was not a grown man he was talking to, till some careless bluntness would set up the boy's back. It was rarer now; rough, wary, touchy, their contact was warmed by a secret, mutual pride in one another's acceptance.

"How are the Argives shaping?" asked Alexander not long after, over a midday meal.

"I shall leave them here. Parmenion must cope with them. They came here I suppose to swagger about before half-trained citizen levies, as they can in the southern cities. Our men think them raw hands, and let them know it. But what are they, soldiers or bridesmaids? Fair pay, good rations, good quarters; yet nothing's right for them. They sulk at drill; they don't like the sarissa; all they mean is they're clumsy still and our own men laugh. Well, they can stay here and use the short spear, for this work it's well enough. When I've marched with my people, and they're cocks of the walk, they'll pick up, their officers tell me."

Alexander, scooping up fish sauce with his bread, said, "Listen." His first question had been prompted by half-heard sounds of discord. They were getting louder.

"Hades take them," said the King. "What now?"

Shouted insults, in Greek and Macedonian, could now be heard.

"Anything looses it off, when they're at odds like this." Philip pushed back his chair, wiping off his fingers on his bare thigh. "A cockfight, a squabble over a boy . . . Parmenion's on reconnaissance." The noise was growing; each side was being reinforced. "Nothing for it, I shall have to sort them myself." He walked with his stolid limp towards the doorway.

"Father. They sound ugly. Why not get armed?"

"What? No, that would make too much of it. They'll give over when they see me. They won't heed one another's officers, there's the mischief."

"I'll come too. If the officers can't quiet them . . ."

"No, no; I don't need you. Finish your food. Simmias, keep mine hot."

He went out as he was, unarmed but for the sword he always wore. Alexander got up and looked after him from the door.

Between the town, and the straggling village of the siege-lines, was a wide space through which slit trenches ran out to the siege towers, and fortified guard-posts stood. Here between men on duty or changing guard the brawl must have begun, visible all along the lines, so that the factions had gathered quickly. There were already some hundreds; Greeks, who had been nearer, outnumbered Macedonians. Racial taunts were flying. Above the din, voices that sounded like officers' were exchanging recriminations, and threatening each other with the King. Philip stumped forward a few paces, looked again; then shouted to a trooper who had been riding towards the crowd. The man dismounted and gave him a leg-up. Provided now with a living rostrum, he cantered purposefully forward, and shouted for silence.

He chose seldom to be formidable. Silence fell; the crowd divided to let him in. As it closed again, Alexander saw that the horse was restive.

The squires who had waited at table were talking in excited undertones. Alexander gave them a look; they should have been waiting for orders. The next hut was the lodging of all the body-squires; the doorway was full of heads. He called out, "Get armed. Be quick."

Philip was wrestling with the horse. His voice, which had carried power, now sounded angry. The horse reared; there was a roar of abuse and cursing; it must have struck a man with its forefeet. Sud-

[226]

denly it gave a great scream, stood almost upright, and sank down, the King still doggedly clinging. Horse and man vanished into a threshing, shouting vortex.

Alexander ran to the armor-pegs on the wall, snatched his shield and helmet—the corselet would take too long—and called to the squires, "They've killed his horse under him. Come." Soon outdistancing all the others, he ran without looking back. The Macedonians were pouring out of barracks. It was the next moments that counted.

At first he simply shoved at the mob, and it let him through. These were sightseers, or mere accretions, easily shifted by anyone who knew his own mind. "Let me pass. Let me through to the King." He could hear the squeals of the dying horse, weakening to groans; no sound from his father. "Back, get back, let me pass. Make way, I want the King."

"He wants his dad." The first defiance; a square-shouldered, square-bearded Argive stood grinning in his way. "Look, here's the cockalorum." The last word choked off. His eyes and mouth gaped, a retch came up from his throat. Alexander with an expert jerk freed his sword.

A gap appeared; he could see the still twitching horse, on its side, his father lying with one leg under it, unmoving; over him stood an Argive with lifted spear, irresolute, waiting for encouragement. Alexander ran him through.

The crowd heaved and swayed, as the Macedonians flung themselves at its edges. Alexander bestrode his father's body, one leg braced against the horse which had stiffened in death; he yelled, "The King!" to guide the rescuers. All round him, uncertain men were urging each other to strike. For anyone behind him, he was a gift.

"This is the King. I will kill the first man who touches him." Some were scared; he fixed his eyes on the man they had been looking at for guidance; he stuck out his jaw and mumbled, but his eyes were flickering. "Get back all of you. Are you mad? Do you think if you kill him or me, you can get out of Thrace alive?" Someone said they had got out of worse places; but no one moved. "Our men are either side of you, and the enemy has the harbor. Are you tired of life?"

[227]

Some warning, a gift of Herakles, made him whip round. He hardly saw the face of the man whose spear was lifted, only the exposed throat. His stab severed the windpipe; the man reeled back, bloody fingers clawing at the hissing wound. He swung back to confront the others; in this instant the scene had changed, he saw instead the backs of the royal squires, shields locked, heaving off the Argives. Hephaistion came breasting through like a swimmer through surf, and stood to shield his back. It was over, in about as long as it would have taken him to finish his half-eaten fish.

He looked round. He had not a scratch; he had been a stroke ahead each time. Hephaistion spoke to him and he answered smiling. He was shining and calm at the center of his mystery, the godlike freedom of killing fear. Fear lay dead at his feet.

Loud voices, expert in command, cleft the confusion; the Argive general, and Parmenion's deputy, roared at their troops in familiar tones. Hangers-on turned swiftly to spectators; the center fell apart, revealing a scatter of dead and wounded; all the men near the fallen King were arrested and led away. The horse was dragged aside. The riot was over. When shouts began again, they came from those on the outskirts who could not see, spreading rumors or asking news.

"Alexander! Where's our boy? Have those whores' sons killed him?" Then, running the other way in a deep bass counterpoint, "The King, they killed the King! The King is dead!" and higher, as if in answer, "Alexander!"

He stood, a point of stillness in all the clamor, looking beyond it into the blue dazzling sky.

There were other voices, down by his knees. "Sir, sir, how are you?" they were saying. "Sir?" He blinked a moment, as if awaking from sleep; then knelt down with the others and touched the body, saying, "Father? Father?"

He could feel at once that the King was breathing.

There was blood in his hair. His sword was half out; he must have felt for it as he was struck, perhaps with a pommel by someone whose nerve had failed him to use the edge. His eyes were closed, and he came limply with their lifting hands. Alexander, remembering a lesson of Aristotle's, pulled back the lid of his good eye. It closed again with a twitch.

"A shield," Alexander said. "Roll him gently. I'll take his head."

The Argives had been marched off; the Macedonians crowded round, asking if the King was alive or dead. "He is stunned," said Alexander. "He will be better presently. He has no other wound. Moschion! The herald is to give that out. Sippas! Order the catapults to fire a volley. Look at the enemy gaping on the wall; I want the fun knocked out of them. Leonnatus, I'll be with my father till he's himself again. Bring anything to me."

They laid the King on his bed. Alexander drew a bloodstained hand from holding his head, to settle it on the pillow. Philip groaned, and opened his eyes.

The senior officers, who had felt entitled to crowd in, assured him all was well, all the men in hand. Alexander standing by the bedhead said to one of the squires, "Bring me water, and a sponge."

"It was your son, King," said someone, "your son who saved you." Philip turned his head and said weakly, "So? Good boy."

"Father, did you see which of them struck you?"

"No," said Philip, his voice strengthening. "He took me from behind."

"Well, I hope I killed him. I killed one there." His grey eyes dwelt deeply on his father's face.

Philip blinked dimly, and sighed. "Good boy. I remember nothing; nothing till I woke up here."

The squire came up with the water-bowl and held it out. Alexander took the sponge, and washed his hand clean of blood, going over it carefully, two or three times. He turned away; the squire paused with the bowl, at a loss, then went round to sponge the King's hair and brow. He had supposed that this was what the Prince had meant it for.

By evening, though sick and giddy if he moved, Philip could give orders. The Argives were marched off on exchange to Kypsela. Alexander was cheered wherever he was seen; men touched him for luck, or for his virtue to rub off on them, or merely for the sake of touching him. The besieged, encouraged by these disorders, came out on the wall at dusk and attacked a siege tower. Alexander led out a party and beat them off. The doctor announced that the King was mending. One of the squires sat up with him. It was midnight before Alexander got to bed. Though he ate with his father, he had his own lodging. He was a general now.

There was a scratch on the door, in a familiar rhythm. He folded back the blanket, and moved over. Hephaistion had known, when this tryst was made, that what Alexander wanted was to talk. He could always tell.

They mulled over the fight, talking softly into the pillow. Presently they fell quiet; in the pause they could hear the sounds of the camp, and, from the distant ramparts of Perinthos, the night watch passing the bell along from man to man, the proof of wakefulness. "What is it?" Hephaistion whispered.

In the dim glimmer of the window, he saw the shine of Alexander's eyes coming close to his. "He says he remembers nothing. He'd already come to himself when we picked him up."

Hephaistion, who had once been hit by a stone from a Thracian wall, said, "He'll have forgotten."

"No. He was shamming dead."

"Was he? Well, who can blame him? One can't even sit up, everything spins round. He hoped they'd be scared at what they'd done, and go away."

"I opened his eye, and I know he saw me. But he gave me no sign, though he knew it was over then."

"Very likely he just went off again."

"I watched him, he was awake. But he won't say he remembers."

"Well, he's the King." Hephaistion had a secret kindness for Philip, who had always treated him with courtesy, even with tact; with whom, too, he shared an enemy. "People might misunderstand, you know how tales get twisted."

"To me he could have said it." Alexander's eyes, glittering in the near-darkness, fastened upon his. "He won't own that he was lying there, knowing he owed his life to me. He didn't want to admit it, he doesn't want to remember."

Who knows? thought Hephaistion. Or ever will? But *he* knows, and nothing will ever shift it. His bare shoulder, crossed by Hephaistion's arm, had a faint sheen like darkened bronze. "Supposing he has his pride? You ought to know what that is."

"Yes, I do. But in his place I'd still have spoken."

"What need?" He slid his hand up the bronze shoulder into the tousled hair; Alexander pushed against it, like a powerful animal consenting to be stroked. Hephaistion remembered his childishness in the beginning; sometimes it seemed like yesterday, sometimes half a lifetime. "Everyone knows. He does; so do you. Nothing can take it away."

He felt Alexander draw a long deep breath. "No; nothing. You're right, you always understand. He gave me life, or he claims so. Whether or not, now I've given it him."

"Yes, now you're quits."

Alexander gazed into the black peak of the rafters. "No one can equal the gifts of the gods, one can only try to know them. But it's good to be clear of debt to men."

Tomorrow he would sacrifice to Herakles. Meantime, he felt a deep wish at once to make someone happy. Luckily he had not far to seek.

"I warned him," said Alexander, "not to put off dealing with the Triballoi." He sat with Antipatros at the great desk of Archelaos' study, over a dispatch full of bad news.

"Is his wound thought dangerous?" Antipatros asked.

"He couldn't sign this; just his seal, and Parmenion's witness. I doubt he even finished dictating it. The last part reads more like Parmenion."

"He has good-healing flesh, your father. It's in the family."

"What were his diviners doing? Nothing's gone right with him since I left. Perhaps we should consult Delphi or Dodona, in case some god needs appeasing."

"It would spread through Greece like wildfire that his luck was out. He'd not thank us for that."

"That's true, no, better not. But look at Byzantion. He did everything right; got there fast, while their best forces were at Perinthos; chose a cloudy night; got up to the very walls. But of a sudden the clouds part, out comes the moon; and all the town dogs start barking. Barking at the crossroads . . . they light the torches . . ."

"Crossroads?" said Antipatros into the pause.

"Or," said Alexander briskly, "maybe he misread the weather, it's changeable on Propontis. But once he'd decided to lift both sieges, why not have rested his men, and let me take on the Scythians?"

"They were there on his flank, and had just denounced their

treaty; but for them he might have hung on at Byzantion. Your
father's always known when to write off his losses. But his troops
had their tails down; they needed a solid victory, and loot; both of
which he got."

Alexander nodded. He could get along well with Antipatros, a
Macedonian of ancient stock, bone-loyal to the King beside whom
he had fought in youth, but to the King before the man. It was
Parmenion who loved the man before the King. "He did indeed. So
there he was, lumbered up with a thousand head of cattle, a slave
train, wagons of loot, on the north border where they can smell
plunder further than buzzards. Tails up or not, his men were tired
. . . If only he'd let me go on north from Alexandropolis; he'd have
had no raid from the Triballoi then." The name was established
now; the colonists had settled. "The Agrianoi would have come in
with me, they'd already agreed . . . Well, done's done. It's lucky his
doctor wasn't killed."

"I should like to wish him well when the courier leaves."

"Of course. Let's not trouble him with business." (If orders came
back, would they be Philip's or Parmenion's?) "We shall have to
shift for ourselves awhile." He smiled at Antipatros, whom he liked
none the worse for being charmable, and amusingly unaware of it.
"War we can deal with well enough. But the business of the south
—that's another thing. It means a great deal to him; he sees it differently; he knows more about it. I should be sorry to act without
him there."

"Well, they seem to be working for him there better than we
could."

"At Delphi? I was there when I was twelve, for the Games, and
never since. Now, once again, to be sure I understand it: this new
offering-house the Athenians put up; they put in their dedications
before it had been consecrated?"

"Yes, a technical impiety. That was the formal charge."

"But the real quarrel was the inscription: SHIELDS TAKEN FROM
PERSIANS AND THEBANS FIGHTING AGAINST GREECE . . . Why *did* the
Thebans Medize, instead of allying with the Athenians?"

"Because they hated them."

"Even then? Well, this inscription enraged the Thebans. So when
the Sacred League of Delphi met, being I suppose ashamed to

come forward themselves, they got some client state to accuse the Athenians of impiety."

"The Amphissians. They live below Delphi, up river."

"And if this indictment had succeeded, the League would have had to make war on Athens. The Athenians had sent three delegates; two went down with fever, and the third of them was Aischines."

"You may remember the man; he was one of the peace envoys, seven years ago."

"Oh, I know Aischines, he's an old friend of mine. Did you know he was an actor once? He must have been good at gagging; because when the Council was about to pass the motion, he suddenly recalled that the Amphissians had been raising crops on some river land which had once been forfeited to Apollo. So he went rushing in, somehow got a hearing, and counteraccused the Amphissians. Is that right? Then, after his great oration, the Delphians forgot Athens, and rushed down pell-mell to wreck the Amphissians' farms. The Amphissians fought; and some of the Councilors had their sacred persons knocked about. This was last autumn after the harvest."

It was now winter. The study was as drafty and cold as ever. The King's son, thought Antipatros, seemed to notice it even less than the King.

"Now the League is meeting at Thermopylai to pass judgment on the Amphissians. It's clear my father won't be fit to go. I am sure what he would like would be for you to represent him. Will you?"

"By all means, yes," said Antipatros, relieved. The boy knew his own limits, eager as he was to stretch them. "I shall try to influence whom I can, and, where I can, postpone decisions for the King."

"Let's hope they've found him a warm house; Thrace in winter is no place for healing wounds. Before long, we shall have to consult him about this. What do you expect will happen?"

"In Athens, nothing. Even if the League condemns Amphissa, Demosthenes will keep the Athenians out. The countercharge was a personal triumph for Aischines, whom he hates like poison, and indicted on a capital charge of treason after their embassy here, as I daresay you know."

[233]

"No one better. Part of the charge was that he was too friendly with me."

"These demagogues! Why, you were only ten years old. Well, the charge failed, and now Aischines comes back from Delphi a public hero. Demosthenes must be chewing wormwood. Also, a larger issue, the Amphissians support the Thebans, whom he won't wish to antagonize."

"But the Athenians hate the Thebans."

"He would like them to hate us more. A war pact with Thebes is what any man of sense would work for, in his place. With the Thebans he may succeed; the Great King has sent him a fortune to buy support against us. It's the Athenians will give him trouble; that feud's too old."

Alexander sat in thought. Presently he said, "It's four generations now since they threw back the Persians; and we Medized, as the Thebans did. If the Great King crossed now from Asia, they'd be intriguing and impeaching one another, while we turned him back in Thrace."

"Men change in less time than that. *We* have come up in one generation, thanks to your father."

"And he's still only forty-three. Well, I shall go out and take some exercise, in case he should leave me anything to do."

On his way to change, he met his mother, who asked the news. He went with her to her room, and told her as much as he thought good. The room was warm, soft and full of color; bright firelight danced on the pictured flames of Troy. His eyes turned to the hearth, he stared unnoticed at the loose stone he had explored in childhood. She found him withdrawn, and accused him of weak compliance with Antipatros, who would stop at nothing to do her harm. This happened often, and he passed it off with the usual answers.

Leaving, he met Kleopatra on the stairs. Now at fourteen she was more like Philip than ever, square-faced, with strong curly hair; but her eyes were not his, they were sad as an unloved dog's. His half-wives had borne him prettier girls; she was plain at the age when, for him, it mattered most; and for her mother she wore the mask of the enemy. Alexander said, "Come with me, I want to speak to you."

In the nursery they had been struggling rivals. Now he was above the battle. She longed for, yet feared, his notice, feeling unequal to anything it could mean. It was unheard of for him to confer with her. "Come in the garden," he said, and, when she shivered and crossed her arms, gave her his cloak. They stood in a leafless rose-plot by the Queen's postern, close against the wall. Old snow lay in the hollows and between the clods. He had spoken to her quietly, he had not wished to frighten her, she saw that in herself she was unimportant; but she was afraid.

"Listen," he said. "You know what happened to Father at Byzantion?" She nodded. "It was the dogs betrayed him. The dogs, and the sickle moon."

He saw the dread in her sad eyes, but read no guilt in it. Neither of Olympias' children looked for innocence in one another. "You understand me. You know the rites I mean. Did you . . . see anything done?"

She shook her head dumbly; if she told, it would come out in one of their dreadful love-quarrels. His eyes searched her like the winter wind; but her fear hid everything. Suddenly he became gentle and grave, and took her hand through the folds of cloak. "I won't tell that you told me. By Herakles. I could never break that oath." He looked round at the garden shrine. "Tell me, you must. I must know."

Her hidden hand shifted in his. "Only the same as other times, when nothing came of it. If there was more, I didn't see it. Truly, Alexander, that's all I know."

"Yes, yes, I believe you," he said impatiently; then grasped at her hand again. "Don't let her do it. She hasn't the right, now. I saved him at Perinthos. He'd be dead now, but for me."

"Why did you?" Much could be left unsaid between them. Her eyes dwelt on the face that was not Philip's, the rough-cut, shining hair.

"It would have been disgraceful not to." He paused, seeking, she thought, some words that would serve for her. "Don't cry," he said, and passed a fingertip gently under her eyes. "That's all I wanted to know. You couldn't help it."

He began to lead her in; but paused at the doorway, and looked about them. "If she wants to send him a doctor, medicines, sweets, anything, you must let me know. I charge you with it. If you don't, it will rest on you."

He saw her face pale with shock. Her surprise, not her distress, arrested him. "Oh, Alexander! No! Those things you spoke of, they've never worked, she must know it. But they're terrible, and when—when she can't contain her soul, they purge it. That's all they are."

He looked at her almost with tenderness, and slowly shook his head. "She meant them." He gave her one of his secret looks. "I remember," he said softly.

He saw her sad dog's eyes, flinching from this new burden. "But that's long ago. I expect it's as you say. You're a good girl." He kissed her cheek, and squeezed her shoulders as he took back his cloak. From the doorway she watched him go shining off through the dead garden.

Winter dragged on. In Thrace the King mended slowly, and could sign letters with the shake of an old man. He had understood the news from Delphi, and directed that Antipatros should support, discreetly, the Amphissian war. The Thebans, though pledged to Macedon, had been doubtful allies, intriguing with the Persians; they were expendable at need. He foresaw the League states voting for the war, each hoping that its burden would be borne by others; Macedon should stand by, without officiousness, in friendly willingness to assume the tiresome duty. It would put the key to the south into his hand.

Soon after midwinter, the Council voted for war. Each state offered only a token force; none would yield leadership to a rival city. Kottyphos, a Thessalian, being President of the Council, had flung in his lap command of this awkward army. Thessalians, whom Philip had rescued from tribal anarchy, remained mostly grateful. There was small doubt where Kottyphos would turn in his hour of need.

"It has begun," said Alexander to his friends, as they sluiced down under the fountain by the stadium. "If one only knew how long."

Ptolemy, pushing his head out of his towel, remarked, "Women say a watched pot never boils." Alexander, dedicated to constant readiness, had been working them hard; Ptolemy had a new mistress, of whom he would have liked to be seeing more.

"They say too," Hephaistion countered, "that when you take your eye off it, it boils over." Ptolemy looked at him with irritation; it was well for him, *he* was getting enough of what he wanted.

He was getting, at least, what he would not have changed for any other human lot; and the world could know it. The rest was his secret; he came to what terms he could with it. Pride, chastity, restraint, devotion to higher things; with such words he made tolerable to himself his meetings with a soul-rooted reluctance, too deep to suffer questioning. Perhaps Olympias' witchcraft had scarred her child; perhaps his father's example. Or, thought Hephaistion, perhaps it was that in this one thing he did not want the mastery, and all the rest of his nature was at war with it; he had trusted his very life much sooner and more willingly. Once in the dark he had murmured in Macedonian, "You are the first and the last," and his voice might have been charged with ecstasy or intolerable grief. Most of the time, however, he was candid, close, without evasions; he simply did not think it very important. One might have supposed that the true act of love was to lie together and talk.

He talked of man and fate; of words heard in dreams from speaking serpents; of the management of cavalry against infantry and archers; he quoted Homer on heroes, Aristotle on the Universal Mind, and Solon on love; he talked of Persian tactics and the Thracian battle-mind; about his dog that had died, about the beauty of friendship. He plotted the march of Xenophon's Ten Thousand, stage by stage from Babylon to the sea. He retailed the backstairs gossip of the Palace, the staff room and the phalanx, and confided the most secret policies of both his parents. He considered the nature of the soul in life and death, and that of the gods; he talked of Herakles and Dionysos, and how Longing can achieve all things.

Listening in bed, in the lee of mountain crags, in a wood at daybreak; with an arm clasping his waist or a head thrown back on his shoulder, trying to silence his noisy heart, Hephaistion understood he was being told everything. With pride and awe, with tenderness, torment and guilt, he lost the thread, and fought with himself, and caught the drift again to find something gone past recall. Bewildering treasures were being poured into his hands and slipping through his fingers, while his mind wandered to the blinding trifle of his own desire. At any moment he would be asked what he thought;

[237]

he was valued as more than a listener. Knowing this he would attend again, and be caught up even against his will; Alexander could transmit imagination as some other could transmit lust. Sometimes, when he was lit up and full of gratitude for being understood, Longing, who has the power to achieve all things, would prompt the right word or touch; he would fetch a profound sigh, dragged up it seemed from the depth of his being, and murmur something in the Macedonian of his childhood; and all would be well, or as well as it could ever be.

He loved giving, to gods or men; he loved achievement here as elsewhere; he loved Hephaistion, whom he forgave for having confronted him, irrevocably now, with his human needs. The profound melancholy after, he bore uncomplaining like a wound. Nothing could be had for nothing. But if later he threw a javelin wide, or won a race by two lengths instead of three, Hephaistion always suspected him, without a word or a look to show it, of thinking that virtue had gone out of him.

In his waking dreams, from which hard clear thought emerged like iron from fire, he would lie back in the grass with his arm behind his head, or sit with his hands loose on the boar-spear across his knees, or pace a room, or stare from a window, his head tilted up and a little leftward, his eyes seeing what his mind conceived. His forgotten face told truths no sculptor would ever catch; behind dropped curtains the secret lamp flared high, one saw the glow, or a dazzling glint through a chink. At times like these, when, Hephaistion thought, even a god could scarcely have kept his hands off him, then above all he must be let alone. But this, after all, one had known from the very beginning.

Once having understood it, Hephaistion could himself achieve, in some degree, Alexander's power to drive the force of sexual energy into some other aim. His own ambitions were more limited; he had already attained the chief of them. He was entirely trusted, constantly and deeply loved.

True friends share everything. One thing, however, he thought well to keep to himself: that Olympias hated him, and her hatred was returned.

Alexander did not speak of it; she must have known that here she would meet with rock. Hephaistion, when she passed him without a greeting, put it down to simple jealousy. It is hard for a generous lover to pity a devouring one; he could not feel much for her, even while he believed that this was all.

It took him time to credit what he saw in front of him, that she was throwing women in Alexander's way. Surely she would hate their rivalry even more? Yet waiting-maids, visiting singers and dancers, young wives not strictly kept, girls who dared not for their lives have risked her anger, now hung about and made eyes. Hephaistion waited for Alexander to talk about it first.

One evening just after lamp-lighting, in the Great Court, Hephaistion saw him waylaid by a young notorious beauty. He flashed his eyes at her languid ones, said something crisp, and walked on with a cool smile, which disappeared at sight of Hephaistion. They fell into step; Hephaistion seeing him on edge said lightly, "No luck for Doris." Alexander looked ahead frowning. The newly lit cressets flung deep shadows and shifting gleams into the painted stoa.

Alexander said abruptly, "She wants me to marry young."

"*Marry?*" said Hephaistion staring. "How could you marry Doris?"

"Don't be a fool," said Alexander irritably. "She's married, she's a whore, she had her last child by Harpalos." They walked on in silence. He paused beside a column. "Mother wants to see me going with women, to know I'm ready."

"But no one marries at our age. Only girls."

"She has her mind on it, and she wishes I had mine."

"But why?"

Alexander glanced at him, not in wonder at his slowness but envy of his innocence. "She wants to bring up my heir. I might fall in battle without one."

Hephaistion understood. He was impeding more than love, more than possession. He was impeding power. The cressets flickered, the night breeze blew coldly down his neck. Presently he said, "And will you do it?"

"Marry? No, I shall suit myself, when I choose, when I've time to think of it."

"You'd have to maintain a household, it's a great deal of business." He glanced at Alexander's creased brows and added, "Girls, you can take or leave whenever you like."

"That's what I think." He looked at Hephaistion with a gratitude not quite aware of itself. Drawing him by the arm into the thick column's shadow, he said softly, "Don't be troubled about it. She would never dare do anything to take you from me. She knows me better than that."

Hephaistion nodded, not liking to admit that he understood what was meant. It was true that he had begun lately to notice how his wine was poured.

A little while later, Ptolemy said in private to Alexander, "I've been asked to give a party for you and invite some girls."

Their eyes met. Alexander said, "I might be busy."

"I'd be grateful if you'd come. I'll see you're not plagued, they can sing and amuse us. Will you? I don't want to be in trouble."

It was not a custom of the north to bring in hetairas at dinner; a man's women were his own concern; Dionysos, not Aphrodite, closed the feast. But lately, among up-to-date young men at private parties, Greek ways were admired. Four guests came to the supper; the girls sat on the ends of their couches, talked prettily, sang to the lyre, filled up their wine cups and patted their wreaths in place; they might almost have been in Corinth. To Alexander his host had allotted the eldest, Kallixeina, an expert and cultured courtesan of some fame. While a girl acrobat was throwing somersaults naked, and on the other couches understandings were being reached with covert tickles and pinches, she talked in her mellow voice about the beauties of Miletos, where she had lately been, and the oppression of the Persians there; Ptolemy had briefed her well. Once, leaning gracefully, she let her dress dip to show him her much-praised breasts; but as he had been promised, her tact was faultless. He enjoyed her company, and at parting kissed the sweetly curving lips from which she took her trade name.

"I don't know," he confided to Hephaistion in bed, "why my mother should want to see me enslaved by women. You'd think with my father she'd have seen enough."

"All mothers are mad for grandchildren," said Hephaistion tolerantly. The party had left Alexander vaguely restless, and receptive to love.

"Think of the great men it has ruined. Look at Persia." His somber mood being on him, he retailed from Herodotos a hideous tale of jealousy and vengeance. Hephaistion expressed a proper horror. His sleep was sweet.

"The Queen was pleased," said Ptolemy next day, "to hear you enjoyed the party." He never said more than enough, a trait Alexander valued. He sent Kallixeina a necklace of gold flowers.

Winter began to break. Two couriers from Thrace, the first having been delayed by swollen streams, arrived together. The first dispatch said that the King could walk a little. He had had news from the south by sea. The League army, after troubles and delays, had won a partial victory; the Amphissians had accepted peace terms, to dismiss their leaders and put in their exiled opposition. This was always a hated condition, since exiles returned bent on settling their old scores. The Amphissians had not fulfilled their agreement yet.

From the second courier's letter, it was clear that Philip was now dealing direct with his southern agents, who had reported the Amphissians still harbored their former government and ignored remonstrances; the opposition dared not return. Kottyphos, the League general, had written to the King in confidence: if the League were forced into action, would Philip be prepared to undertake the war?

With this came a second letter, bound up and double-sealed, addressed to Alexander as Regent. It commended his good government; and informed him that though Philip hoped soon to be fit for the journey home, affairs could not wait so long. He wanted the whole home army mobilized for action; but no one must suspect that his plans led southward; Antipatros alone could share the knowledge. Some other pretext must be sought. There had been tribal musterings in Illyria; it should be given out that the western border was threatened, and the troops were standing by for that. Terse notes on training and staffing were closed with fatherly blessings.

Like a caged bird set free, Alexander flew into action. As he ranged about in search of good country for maneuvers, he could be heard singing to the beat of Oxhead's hooves. If some girl he had loved for years, Antipatros thought, had suddenly been promised him, he could not have glowed more brilliantly.

War councils were called; the professional soldiers conferred with the tribal lords who commanded their own levies. Olympias asked

Alexander what kept him so often away, and why he looked so full of business. He answered that he hoped soon to see action against the Illyrians on the border.

"I have been waiting to speak to you, Alexander. I hear that after Kallixeina the Thessalian entertained you all one evening, you made her a present and never sent again for her. These women are artists, Alexander; a hetaira of that standing has her pride. What will she think of you?"

He turned round, for a moment quite bewildered. He had forgotten the existence of such a person. "Do you think," he said staring, "that I've time now to be playing about with girls?"

She tapped with her fingers on her gilded chair-arm. "You will be eighteen this summer. People may be saying you do not care for them."

He stared at the Sack of Troy, the flames and blood and the shrieking women flung back across warriors' shoulders, waving their arms. After a moment he said, "I shall find them something else to talk about."

"You have always time for Hephaistion," she said.

"He thinks of my work, and helps."

"What work? You tell me nothing. Philip sent you a secret letter; you did not even tell me. What did he say?"

With cool precision, without a pause, he gave her the tale about the Illyrian war. She saw, and was shaken by, the cold resentment in his eyes.

"You are lying to me," she said.

"If you think so, why ask?"

"I am sure you told Hephaistion everything."

Lest Hephaistion should suffer for the truth, he answered, "No."

"People talk. Hear it now from me, if you do not know. Why do you shave, like a Greek?"

"Am I not Greek, then? This is news, you should have told me sooner."

Like two wrestlers who in their grapple reel towards a cliff, and let go in a common fear, they paused and swerved.

"Your friends are known by it, the women point at them. Hephaistion, Ptolemy, Harpalos . . ."

He laughed. "Ask Harpalos why they point."

She was angered by his endurance, when instinct told her she was drawing blood. "Soon your father will be making you a marriage. It is time you showed him it is a husband he has to offer, and not a wife."

After a moment's stillness he walked forward, very slowly, and lightly as a golden cat, till he stood straight before her looking down. She opened her mouth, then closed it; little by little she shrank back into her thronelike chair, till its high back held her and she could retreat no further. Judging this with his eyes, he then said softly, "You will never say that to me again."

She was still there, and had not moved, when she heard Oxhead's gallop thudding away.

For two days he did not come near her; her orders to deny him her door were wasted. Then came a feast; each found a gift from the other. The breach was healed; except that neither spoke of it, or asked forgiveness.

He forgot it, when the news came in from Illyria. Word having spread that King Philip was arming against them, the tribes, which had been settling, were in ferment from the border to the western sea.

"I expected no less," said Antipatros in private to Alexander. "The price of a good lie is that it gets believed."

"One thing's certain, we can't afford to undeceive them. So they'll be over the border any day. Let me think about this; tomorrow I'll tell you what troops I need to take."

Antipatros saved his breath; he was learning when to do so.

Alexander knew what forces he wanted; what most concerned him was how to avoid, without suspicion, committing too many troops to the work they were supposed to be standing by for. Soon fact supplied a pretext. Since the Phokian war, the Thermopylae fort had been held by a Macedonian garrison. It had just been "relieved," in strength and without agreement, by a force of Thebans. Thebes, they explained, had to protect herself from the Sacred League, which, by attacking her allies the Amphissians, was clearly threatening her. This seizure was as near a hostile act as a formal ally could compass. It would be natural, now, to leave a good holding force at home.

The Illyrians were lighting war-fires. Alexander got out his father's old maps and records; questioned veterans about the terrain, which was mountainous and cleft with gorges, and tested his men in marches across country. From one such day he got back at fall of dusk, bathed, greeted friends, had dinner, and, ready for sleep, went straight up to his room. He threw off his clothes at once; with the cold draft from the window came a warm drift of scent. The tall standing lamp shone in his eyes. He stepped past it. On the bed a young girl was sitting.

He stared at her in silence; she gasped and looked down, as if the last thing she had looked for here was an unclothed man. Then slowly she got to her feet, unclasped her hands to let them fall at her sides, and raised her head.

"I am here," she said like a child repeating lessons, "because I have fallen in love with you. Please don't send me away."

He walked steadily across to her. The first shock had passed; one must not be seen to hesitate. This one was not like the painted jeweled hetairas with their easy charm, the patina of much handling. She was about fifteen, a fair-skinned girl, with fine flaxen hair falling unbound over her shoulders. Her face was heart-shaped, her eyes dark blue, her small breasts firm and pointed; the dress of snow-white byssos showed the pink nipples through. Her mouth was un-painted, fresh as flowers. Before he reached her, he felt her steeped in fear.

"How did you get in?" he asked. "There's a guard outside."

She clasped her hands again. "I—I have been trying a long time to come to you. I took the first chance I saw." Her fear shivered like a curtain round her, it almost stirred the air.

He had expected no answer to the purpose. He touched her hair, which felt like thin silk clothing her; she was shaking like the bass string of a kithara lately struck. Not passion, fear. He took her shoulders between his hands and felt her a little calmed, like a scared dog. It was because of him, not of him, she was afraid.

They were young; their innocence and their knowledge spoke to-gether, without their will. He stood holding her between his hands, no longer heeding her, listening. He heard nothing; yet the whole room seemed to breathe.

He kissed her lips, she was just the right height for him. Then he said crisply, "The guard must have gone to sleep. If he let you in, let's make sure there is no one else here."

She grasped him with a clutch of terror. He kissed her again, and gave her a secret smile. Then he went to the far end of the room, shaking the window-curtains loudly on their rings, one after another, looking into the great chest and slamming its lid. He left to the last the curtain before the postern door. When at length he pulled it aside, no one was there. He shot the bronze bolt home.

Going back to the girl, he led her towards the bed. He was angry, but not with her; and he had been offered a challenge.

Her white gauze dress was pinned on the shoulders with golden bees. He loosened them, and the girdle; it all fell on the floor. She was milky as if her flesh never saw the sun, all but the rosy nipples, and the golden fuzz which painters never put in. Poor soft pale thing, for which the heroes had fought ten years at Troy.

He lay down beside her. She was young and scared, she would thank him for time and gentleness, there was no hurry. One of her hands, ice-cold with fright, started traveling down his body; hesitant and inexpert, remembering instruction. It was not enough that she had been sent to learn if he was a man, this child had been told to help him. He found himself handling her with the most delicate care, like a day-old pup, to protect her from his anger.

He glanced at the lamp; but it would be a kind of flight to quench it, shameful to fumble in the dark. His arm lay across her breast, firm, brown, scratched from the mountain brambles; how weak she looked, even a real kiss would bruise her. She had hidden her face against his shoulder. A conscript without doubt, not a volunteer. She was thinking what would become of her if she failed.

And at the best, he thought; at the best? The loom, the bed, the cradle; children, the decking of bride-beds, clacking talk at the hearth and the village well; bitter old age, and death. Never the beautiful ardors, the wedded bond of honor, the fire from heaven blazing on the altar where fear was killed. He turned up her face in his hand. For this lost life, the creature that looked at him with these flax-blue eyes, helpless and waiting, had been created a human soul. Why had it been ordered so? Compassion shocked him, and pierced him with darts of fire.

He thought of the fallen towns, the rafters burning, the women running from the smoke as rats and hares ran out when the last stand of wheat falls to the sickle and the boys wait stick in hand. He remembered the bodies, left behind by men for whom the victor's right of mating, with which wild beasts were content, was not enough. They had something to revenge, some unsated hatred, of themselves perhaps, or of one they could not name. His hand traced softly on her smooth body the wounds he had seen; there was no harm, she did not understand it. He kissed her so that she should be reassured. She was trembling less, knowing now that her mission would not fail. He took her carefully, with the greatest gentleness, thinking of blood.

Later she sat up softly, thinking him asleep, and began to slip out of bed. He had only been thinking. "Don't go," he said. "Stay with me till morning." He would have been glad to lie alone, not crowded by this alien soft flesh; but why should she face her questioning at such an hour? She had not cried, but only flinched a little, though she had been a virgin. Of course, how not? She was to furnish proof. He was angry on her behalf, no god having disclosed to him that she would outlive him by fifty years, boasting to the last of them that she had had the maidenhood of Alexander. The night grew cool, he pulled up the blanket over her shoulders. If anyone was sitting up for her, so much the better. Let them wait.

He got up and snuffed the lamp, and lay looking into the darkness, feeling the lethargy of soul which was the price of going hostage to mortality. To die, even a little, one should do it for something great. However, this might pass for a kind of victory.

He woke to birdsong and first light; he had overslept, some men he had meant to look at would be at drill already. The girl was fast sleeping still, her mouth a little open; it made her look foolish more than sad. He had never asked her her name. He shook her gently; her mouth closed, her deep-blue eyes opened; she looked tumbled, sleek and warm. "We had better get up, I have work to do." Out of courtesy he added, "I wish we could stay longer."

She rubbed her eyes, then smiled at him. His heart lifted; the ordeal was over, and well achieved. There on the sheet was the little red stain the old wives showed the guests on the wedding morrow. It would be practical, but unkind, to suggest she should take it with her. He had a better thought.

He belted on his chiton, went to his casket where his dress jewels were kept, and took out a pouch of soft kidskin, old and worn, with gold embroidery. It was not long ago that, with much solemnity, it had been given him. He slipped it out, a big brooch of two gold swans, their necks entwined in the courtship dance. The work was ancient, the swans wore crowns. "It has come down from queen to queen for two hundred years. Look after it, Alexander; it is an heirloom for your bride."

He tossed the stitched pouch away, his mouth hardening; but he walked over with a smile. The girl had just fastened her shoulder-pins and was tying her girdle. "Here's something for remembrance." She took it wide-eyed, staring and feeling its weight. "Tell the Queen that you pleased me very much, but in future I choose for myself. Then show her this; and remember to say I told you to."

In fresh blowy spring weather they marched west from the coast and up to Aigai. Here on Zeus' ancient altar Alexander offered an unblemished pure-white bull. The seers, poring over the steaming vitals, announced the good portents of the liver.

They passed Lake Kastoria flooded from the snow-streams, half-drowned willows shaking green locks over its wind-ruffled blue water; then wound up through winter-brown scrub, into the rocky heights of the Hills of Lynxes, the Lynkestid lands.

Here he thought well to put on his helmet, and the leather guard for his bridle-arm which he had had made to Xenophon's design. Since old Airopos had died, and young Alexandros had been chief, he had given no trouble, and had aided Philip in the last Illyrian war; nonetheless this was perfect ambush country, and Lynkestids were Lynkestids, time out of mind.

However, they had done their vassal duty; here were all three brothers on strong hairy mountain ponies, armed for campaign with their highlanders behind them; tall brown bearded men, no longer the lads he had met at festivals. They exchanged greetings of scrupulous courtesy, the common heirs of an ancient patched-up feud. For generations their houses had been linked by kinship, war, rivalry and marriage. The Lynkestids had once been kings here; they had contended for the High Kingship more than once through the generations. But they had not been strong enough to hold back the Illyrians. Philip had; and that had settled the matter.

Alexander accepted their formal host-gifts of food and wine, and called them to conference with his chief officers, on a rocky outcrop patched with lichen and flowering moss.

Dressed, themselves, with the rough usefulness of the border, leather tunics stitched with plates of iron, cap-shaped Thracian helmets, they could not take their eyes off the smooth-shaved youth who had chosen, while he outdid men, to keep the face of a boy, and whose panoply glittered with all the refinements of the south. His corselet was shaped to measure over every muscle; elegantly inlaid, but finished so smoothly that no ornament would hold a point. His helmet had a tall white crest, not to give him height but to be seen by his men in battle; they must be ready for change of plan whenever the action called for it. He explained this to the Lynkestids, since they were new to his wars. They had not believed in him before he came; when they saw him, they believed still less; but when they watched the war-scarred faces of warriors forty years old, intent on his every word, they believed at last.

They pressed on, to command the heights above the passes before the enemy; and came to Herakleia, whose fertile valley had been fought for in many wars. The Lynkestids were as familiar here as the storks on the house-roofs; they heartened their people with gnarled country jokes, and saluted shrines of immemorial gods elsewhere unknown. At Alexander the folk gazed as at a fable, and placed his acquisition to the credit of their lords.

The army rode up between vine terraces, stone-edged in good red earth, to the next range; down past Lake Prespa cupped in its rocky hills, and on till Lychnidis smiled blue below them, sky-clear, fringed with its poplars and white acacias and groves of ash, shapely with bays and rocky headlands. From the near side, war-smoke was rising. Illyria had crossed over into Macedon.

At a small hill-fort on the pass, Lynkestid clansmen greeted their chief with loyal cries. To their own kinsmen in the force, they said out of his hearing, "A man only lives once; we'd not have waited so long with that horde so near, only that we heard the witch's son was coming. Is it true that a snake-daimon got him on the Queen? That's he's weapon-proof? Is it true he was born in a caul?" Peasants to whom a visit to the nearest market ten miles off was a thing for the greater festivals, they had never seen a shaved man and asked the easterners if he was a eunuch. Those who had managed to press near reported it false that he was weapon-proof; young as he was, he was already battle-scarred; but they could attest that he was magical, having seen his eyes. Also he had forbidden the soldiers, on the way, to kill a great viper which had slid along the pass in front of them, calling it a messenger of good fortune. They eyed him warily, but with hope.

The battle was fought by the lake, among the ash groves and orchards and glittering poplar trees, on slopes starred with yellow mallows or blue with irises, which the soldiers crushed under trampling feet or stained with blood. The lapis-blue waters were churned and fouled; the storks and the herons fled the reeds; the eaters of carrion watched each his neighbor drop from the sky, and swooped to the glut of corpses heaped on the grassy shores, or floating under the small-flowered rocks.

The Lynkestids obeyed orders, and fought to the honor of their house. They recognized, though they could not have planned, the neat tactics which had trapped the Illyrian raiders between the steeps and the shore. They joined in the pursuit, on into the snow-topped western mountains and down the gorges, where Illyrians who made a stand were dislodged from their fastnesses to die or yield.

The Lynkestids were surprised to see him taking prisoners, after his fierceness in the battle. They had been thinking that those who nicknamed him Basiliskos must have had in mind the crowned dragon whose stare is death. But now, when they themselves would not have spared one of the ancient foes, he was taking oaths of peace as though they were not barbarians.

The Illyrians were tall lean mountaineers, leathery, brown-haired, not unlike the Lynkestids whose forebears had often married with them. Kossos, the chief who had led the raid, had been trapped in a river gorge and taken alive. They brought him bound before Alexander by the rushing stream which foamed brown between the borders. He was a younger son of the great Bardelys, King Philip's old enemy, the terror of the border till he fell spear in hand at ninety years old. Now, the greybeard of fifty, hard and straight as a spear, stared impassively, hiding his wonder, at the boy with a man's eyes, sitting a horse which by itself would have been worth a border raid.

"You have wasted our lands," said Alexander, "driven off the cattle, looted our towns and forced our women. What do you think you deserve?"

Kossos knew little Macedonian, but enough for this. He wanted no interpreter coming between them. He looked long into the young man's face and answered, "What is due to me, we might not agree on. Do with me, son of Philip, what you think is due to yourself."

Alexander nodded. "Unbind him, and give him back his sword."

He had lost in the battle two of his twelve sons; five more had been taken captive. Alexander freed three to him without ransom, and took two as hostages.

He had come to settle the border, not to breed new feuds. Though he had gone deep into Illyria, he did not try to push the frontier beyond Lake Lychnidis, where Philip had won it long ago and where the earth-shaping gods had drawn it. One thing at a time.

This was his first real war in sole command. He had gone into unknown country, and dealt with what he found; everyone thought it a great victory. With him rested the secret that it was the mask for a greater war. Alone with Hephaistion, he said, "It would have been base to take revenge on Kossos."

By the clear lake of Lychnidis, the mud of combat settled, pike and eels picked clean the drifting dead. The crushed lilies slept to sprout green another year; the white acacia flowers fell like snow in the next fresh wind, and hid the blood. Widows mourned, maimed men fumbled at former skills, orphans knew hunger who had never lacked before. The people bowed to fate, as to a murrain on the cattle, or untimely hail stripping the olive trees. They went, even the widows and orphans, to make thank-offerings at the shrines; the Illyrians, notorious pirates and slavers, might have won. Their gods, regarding their offerings kindly, kept from them the knowledge

[250]

that they had been a means and not an end. In grief more than in joy, man longs to know that the universe turns around him.

A few weeks later, King Philip came back from Thrace. With the ships of Athens ranging the coasts, the comfort of a sea-trip had been denied him; he had come most of the way by litter, but, for the last lap to Pella, mounted a horse to show that he could do it. He had to be helped down; Alexander, seeing he still walked with pain, came up to offer his shoulder. They went in together to a muted hum of comment; a sick bent man who had put on ten years and lost ten pounds; and a glowing youth who wore victory like the spring velvet on young stags' horns.

Olympias at her window exulted in the sight. She was less pleased when as soon as the King was rested, Alexander went to his room and stayed two hours.

Some days later the King managed to hobble down for supper in Hall. Alexander, helping him up on his couch, noticed that the smell of pus still clung to him. Himself fastidiously clean, he reminded himself it was the smell of an honorable wound, and seeing everyone's eyes on the ungainly scramble, said, "Never mind, Father, every step you take is the witness of your valor." The company was much pleased. It was five years now since the evening of the kithara, and few of them remembered it.

With home comfort and good doctoring, Philip mended quickly. But his limp was much worse; the same leg had been pierced again, this time in the hamstring. In Thrace the wound had putrefied; he had lain days near to death in fever; when the rotten flesh sloughed off, Parmenion said, there had been a hole you could get your fist into. It would be long before he could mount a horse without a leg-up, if he ever did; but once up, he sat handsomely with the straight-leg grip of the riding schools. In a few weeks he took over the army's training; praised the good discipline he found, and kept to himself the thought that there had been a spate of innovations. Some of them were even worth following up.

In Athens, the marble tablet which witnessed the peace with Macedon had been torn down, in formal declaration of war. Demosthenes had convinced nearly all the citizens that Philip was a

power-drunk barbarian, who looked to them as a source of plunder
and slaves. That they had lain an easy prey five years before, and he
had not harmed them, was credited to anything but himself. He had
offered, later, to treat Athenian troops as allies in the Phokian war;
but Demosthenes had kept them at home by declaring they would
be held as hostages; so many men going to see for themselves could
only come back and confuse the issue. Phokion, the general who had
done best in action against Macedon, declared Philip's offer to be
sincere, and narrowly escaped a treason charge; he was only saved
by a known probity which rivaled that of Aristeides the Just.

Demosthenes found it a constant nuisance. He had no doubt that
he was laying out in the City's interests the gold that the Persians
sent him; but a great deal passed through his hands, he was accountable to no one, and the agent's cut was naturally allowed for. It
freed him from daily cares, and his time for public service; what
object could be worthier? But he had to take care with Phokion.

In the Great War with Sparta, the Athenians had fought for
glory and for empire; they had ended beaten to the dust and stripped
of everything. They had fought for freedom and democracy, and
had finished under the most brutal tyranny of their recorded years.
Old men still lived who had starved through the winter siege; the
middle-aged had heard of it at first hand, mostly from people it had
ruined. They had lost faith in war. If they turned to it again, it
could only be in one cause, for mere survival. Step by step they had
been brought to think that Philip meant to destroy them. Had he
not destroyed Olynthos? So at last they gave up the public dole,
to spend it on the fleet; the tax on the rich was raised above the
old flat rate, in proportion to what they owned.

It was the Athenian navy which made her safer than Thebes. Few
understood that its high command was not just then very talented;
Demosthenes took for granted that mere numbers must be decisive.
Sea-power had saved Perinthos and Byzantion and the corn route
of the Hellespont. If Philip forced his way south it must be by land.
Demosthenes was now the most powerful man in Athens, her
symbol of salvation. Alliance with Thebes was in his grasp; he had
replaced the ancient enmity by a greater.

Thebes paused in doubt. Philip had confirmed her rule over the
Boeotian countryside around her, an age-long issue; where Athens,

declaring it antidemocratic, had sought to weaken her by giving
the Boeotians self-rule. But Thebes controlled the land route into
Attica; this was her value to Philip; all her bargaining power with
him would vanish, if he and Athens made a separate peace.

So they debated, willing things to be as they had always been,
unwilling to know that events are made by men, and that men had
changed.

In Macedon, Philip grew brown and weathered, he could endure
first half a day on horseback, and then a day; on the great horse-
field by Pella lake, the cavalry wheeled and charged in complex
maneuvers. There were now two royal squadrons, Philip's and
Alexander's. Father and son were seen riding together deep in
counsel, the gold head bent towards the grizzled one. Queen Olympias' maids looked pale and fretted; one had been beaten, and
was two days laid up.

In midsummer, when the grain was tall and green, the Council
of Delphi met again. Kottyphos reported the Amphissians still
defaulting, the proscribed leaders unexpelled; it was beyond his
makeshift army to force them to their knees. He proposed in Council
that King Philip of Macedon, who had championed the god against
the impious Phokians, be asked to undertake the holy war.

Antipatros, who was there as envoy, rose to say he was empow-
ered to give the King's consent. What was more, Philip, as a pious
offering, would campaign at his own expense. Votes of thanks and
an elaborate commission were drafted, and inscribed by the local
writing-master; he finished his task about the time when Antipatros'
courier, for whom fresh horses had stood by all the way, arrived at
Pella.

Alexander was in the ball-court, playing odd-man-out with his
friends. It was his turn to stand in the center of the ring, and try
to stop the ball on its way. He had just got it with a four-foot jump,
when Harpalos, condemned as usual to watch others limbering
up, caught a flying rumor from outside, and called that the courier
was here from Delphi. Alexander, in his eagerness to see the letter
opened, brought it in to the King while he was in his bath.

He stood in a broad basin of ornate bronze, steaming his wounded
leg while one of the squires rubbed in a strong-smelling liniment.
His flesh was still sunken, his scars were plowed and knotted all

[253]

Mary Renault

over him; one collarbone, broken long ago when his horse was killed in battle, had knit with a thick callus. He was like some old tree on which the cattle year after year have rubbed their horns. With unthinking instinct, Alexander saw what kind of weapon had made each wound. What scars shall I carry, when I am as old as he?

"Open it for me," said Philip. "My hands are wet." He drooped his eyelid as a sign to hide bad news. But there was no need.

When Alexander ran back to the ball-court, the clean-shaved young men were splashing in the fountain, throwing jars of water at each other to sluice off the dust and cool down. Seeing his face, they paused, arrested in action like a sculpture group by Skopas.

"It has come!" he said. "We are going south."

7

AT THE FOOT of the painted stairway, the bodyguard leaned on his spear. It was Keteus, a stocky iron-bearded veteran rising sixty. It had not been thought seemly for youths to guard the Queen, since the King had ceased to visit her.

The young man in the black cloak paused in the shadowed passage with its floor-mosaic of black and white. He had never been so late to his mother's room.

At his footfall, the guard threw up his shield and pointed his spear, bidding him declare himself. He showed his face, and went up the stairs. When he scratched on the door there was no answer. He drew his dagger, and rapped sharply with the hilt.

A sleepy bustle sounded within, followed by a breathing silence. "It is Alexander," he said. "Open the door."

A blinking rumpled woman, a robe dragged round her, put out her head; behind her the voices rustled like mice. They must have thought, before, that it was the King.

"Madam is sleeping. It is late, Alexander, long past midnight."

His mother's voice from beyond said, "Let him in."

She stood by the bed, tying the girdle of her night-robe, made of wool the color of curded cream edged with dark fur. He could just see her by the flickering night-light; a maid, clumsy from sleep, was trying to kindle with it the wicks of the standing lamp-cluster. The hearth was swept clean, it was summer now.

The first wick of the three burned up. She said, "That is enough."

Her red hair mixed on her shoulders with the dark sleekness of the fur. The slanting lamplight etched the frown-creases between her brows, the lines that framed the corners of her mouth. When she faced the light full, one saw only the fine structure, the clear skin and the firm closed lips. She was thirty-four years old.

The one lamp left the room's edges dark. He said, "Is Kleopatra here?"

"At this hour? She is in her room. Do you want her?"

"No."

She said to the women, "Go back to bed."

When the door closed, she threw the embroidered coverlet over the tumbled bed, and motioned him to sit by her; but he did not move.

"What is it?" she said softly. "We have said goodbye. You should be sleeping, if you march at dawn. What is it? You look strange. Have you had a dream?"

"I have been waiting. This is not a little war, it is the beginning of everything. I thought you would send for me. You must know what brings me here."

She stroked back the hair across her brow, her hand masking her eyes. "Do you want me to make a divination for you?"

"I need no divination, Mother. Only the truth." She had let fall her hand too quickly, his eyes had seized on hers. "What am I?" he said. "Tell me who I am."

She stared. He saw she had expected some other question.

"Never mind," he said, "whatever you have been doing. I know nothing about it. Tell me what I ask."

She saw that in the few hours since they had last met, he had grown haggard. She had nearly said to him, "Is that all?"

It was long past, overlaid with living; the dark shudder, the fiery consuming dream, the shock of waking, the words of the old wise-woman brought by night to this room in secret from her cave. How had it been? She no longer knew. She had brought forth the child of the dragon, and he asked, "Who am I?" It is I who need to ask that of him.

He was pacing, quick and light as a caged wolf, about the room.

Coming to a sudden stop before her, he said, "I am Philip's son.
Isn't it so?"

Only yesterday she had seen them together going to the drill-
field; Philip had spoken grinning, Alexander thrown back his head
and laughed. She grew quiet, and with a long look under her eyelids
said, "Do not pretend you can believe that."

"Well, then? I have come to hear."

"These things cannot be scrambled at, on a whim at midnight.
It is a solemn matter. There are powers one must propitiate . . ."

His searching, shadowed eyes seemed to pass clean through her,
going too deep. "What sign," he said softly, "did my daimon give
you?"

She took both his hands, pulled him near and whispered. When
she had done, she drew back to look. He was wholly within, scarcely
aware of her, wrestling it out. His eyes did not tell the outcome.
"And that is everything?"

"What more? Even now are you not satisfied?"

He looked into the dark beyond the lamp. "All things are known
to the gods. The thing is how to question them." He lifted her to
her feet, and for a few moments held her at arms' length, the corners of his brows pulled together. At last her eyes fell before his.

His fingers tightened; then he embraced her, quickly and closely,
and let her go. When he had left, the dark crept up all around her.
She kindled the other two lamps, and slept at last with all three
burning.

Alexander paused at the door of Hephaistion's room, opened it
quietly and went in. He was fast asleep, one arm thrown out, in a
square of moonlight. Alexander stretched out a hand, and then
withdrew it. He had meant, if his mind had been satisfied, to wake
him and tell him everything. But all was still dark and doubtful, she
too was mortal, one must await the certain word. Why break his
good sleep with that? It would be a long ride tomorrow. The moon
shone straight down on his closed eyes. Softly Alexander drew the
curtain half across, lest the powers of night should harm him.

In Thessaly they picked up the allied cavalry; they came streaming
down over the hills, without formation, yelling and tossing their
lances, showing off their horsemanship. It was a land where men

rode as soon as they could walk. Alexander raised his brows; but Philip said they would do what they were told in battle, and do it well. This show was a tradition.

The army bore southwest, towards Delphi and Amphissa. Some levies from the Sacred League joined them along the way; their generals were made welcome, and swiftly briefed. Used to the confederate forces of small rival states, the edging for precedence, the long wrangles with whichever general had been given chief command, they were drawn amazed into a moving army of thirty thousand foot and two thousand horse, each man of which knew where he had to be, and went there.

There were no forces from Athens. The Athenians had a seat on the League Council; but when it commissioned Philip, no Athenian had been present to dissent. Demosthenes had persuaded them to boycott it. A vote against Amphissa would have antagonized Thebes. He had seen no further.

The army reached Thermopylai, the hot gates between the mountains and the sea. Alexander, who had not passed this way since he was twelve, went with Hephaistion to bathe in the warm springs for which the pass was named. On the grave-mound of Leonidas, with its marble lion, he laid a garland. "I don't think," he remarked after, "that he was really much of a general. If he'd made sure the Phokian troops understood their orders, the Persians could never have turned the pass. These southern states never work together. But one must honor a man as brave as that."

The Thebans still had the fort above. Philip, playing their own game, sent up an envoy, politely asking them to leave so that he could relieve them. They looked down at the long snake of men filling the shore road and thickening into distance; stolidly they picked up their gear, and left for Thebes.

Now the army was on the great southeast road; they saw on their right the stark mountains of Hellas' spine, barer and bleaker, more despoiled by man's axes and man's herds, then the wooded heights of Macedon. In the valleys between these tall deserts, flesh between bones, lay the earth and water that fed mankind.

"Now I see it again," said Alexander to Hephaistion as they rode, "I can understand just why the southerners are as they are. They're land-starved; each man covets his neighbor's, and knows the neighbor covets his. And each state has its fringe of mountains.

Have you seen two dogs by the fence where one of them lives, running up and down barking?"

"But," said Hephaistion, "when dogs come to a gap, they don't rush through and fight, they just look surprised and walk off. Sometimes dogs have more sense than men."

The road towards Amphissa turned due south; an advance party under Parmenion had gone ahead, to take the strongpoint of Kytinion and secure this road, as earnest of Philip's purpose to pursue the holy war. But the main force marched on by the highway, still going southeast, towards Thebes and Athens.

"Look," said Alexander, pointing ahead, "there's Elateia. Look, the masons and engineers are there already. It shouldn't take long to raise the walls, they say all the stone's still there."

Elateia had been a fort of the god-robbing Phokians, pulled down at the end of the previous holy war. It commanded the road. It was two days' fast march from Thebes, and three from Athens.

A thousand slaves, under skilled masons, soon put back the well-squared ashlar. The army occupied the fort and the heights around it. Philip set his headquarters up, and sent an envoy to Thebes.

For years, his message said, the Athenians had made war on him, first covertly, then openly; he could no longer hold his hand. To Thebes they had been hostile even longer; yet now they were trying to draw Thebes, too, into war against him. He must ask the Thebans therefore to declare themselves. Would they stand by their alliance, and give his army passage south?

The royal tent had been put up within the walls; the shepherds who had made hovels in the ruins had fled when the army came. Philip had had a supper couch carted along, to rest his game leg after the day's work. Alexander sat on a chair beside him. The squires had set out wine, and withdrawn.

"This should settle it," said Philip, "once for all. Time comes when one must put down the stake and throw. I think it's long odds against war. If the Thebans are sane, they'll declare for us; the Athenians will wake up and see where their demagogues have brought them; Phokion's party will come in; and we can cross to Asia without a drop of blood shed in Greece."

Alexander turned his wine cup in his hands, and bent to smell the local vintage. They made better wine in Thrace, but Thrace had been given it by Dionysos. "Well, yes . . . but look what hap-

[259]

pened while you were laid up and I was raising the army. We gave
out we were arming against the Illyrians; and everyone believed
it, the Illyrians most of all. Now, what about the Athenians? They've
been told for years by Demosthenes to expect us; here we are. And
what becomes of *him*, if Phokion's party gets the vote?"

"He can do nothing, if Thebes has declared for us."

"They've ten thousand trained mercenaries in Athens."

"Ah, yes. But it's the Thebans who will decide. You know their
constitution. A moderate oligarchy they call it, but the franchise test
is low; it takes in any man who can afford a hoplite panoply. There
you have it. In Thebes, it's the electorate that will fight in any war
it votes for."

He began to talk about his hostage years there, almost with nos-
talgia. Time had misted the hardships; it had the taste of vanished
youth. He had been smuggled once by friends into action under
Epaminondas. He had known Pelopidas. Alexander as he listened
thought of the Sacred Band, which Pelopidas had gathered into one
corps, rather than founded; for their heroic vows were ancient, going
back to Herakles and Iolaos, at whose altar they were sworn. Men
of the Band, having each in his charge a twofold honor, did not
retreat; they advanced, or stood, or died. There was much Alexander would have liked to know of them, and tell Hephaistion, had
there been anyone else to ask.

"I wonder," he remarked instead, "what is going on now in
Athens."

Athens had had the news at sunset, on the day Elateia was occupied.
The City Councilors were at their civic meal in the Council Hall,
with some old Olympic victors, retired generals and other worthies
honored with this privilege. The Agora was clamorous; the courier
from Thebes came only on the heels of rumor. All night the streets
were like market-time, with kindred running to kindred, merchants
to the Piraeus; strangers talking passionately to strangers, women
running with half-veiled faces to the women's rooms of houses
where they had friends. At daybreak the City Trumpeter called
Assembly; in the Agora the hurdles of the stock pens and the market
stalls were set alight to beacon the outer suburbs. The men poured
across to Pnyx Hill with its stone rostrum. They were told the news;

that Philip was expected to march south at once, and that Thebes would make no resistance. Old men recalled a black day of their childhood, the beginning of shame, starvation, tyranny, when the first stragglers had come in from Goat River on the Hellespont, where the fleet had been annihilated; the Great War lost and the death-throes still to come. The crisp cool air of an autumn morning struck to the bone like a winter frost. The presiding Councilor called aloud, "Does anyone wish to speak?"

A long silence followed. All eyes turned one way. Nobody had the folly to come between the people and their choice. When they saw him mount the bema, no one cheered; the chill was too deep for that; there was only a deep murmur, like the sound of prayer.

All night the lamp had burned in Demosthenes' study; men walking the streets, too troubled to go to bed, had been comforted by its light. In the dark before the dawn, the draft of his speech was ready. The city of Theseus, Solon, Perikles, at her crux of fate had turned to him. She had found him ready.

Firstly, he said, they could dismiss their fear that Philip was sure of Thebes. If he were, he would not be sitting in Elateia; he would be here now before their walls, he who had always aimed at their destruction. He was making a show of force, to hearten his bought friends in Thebes and daunt the patriots. Now at last they must resolve to forget the ancient feud, and send envoys to offer generous terms of alliance, before Philip's men had done their evil work there. He himself, if summoned, would not refuse the call. Meantime, let the men of fighting age put on their arms, and march up the Theban road as far as Eleusis, in token of readiness to take the field.

As he ended, the sun rose, and they saw across the dip the Acropolis bathed in splendor; the mellow old marble, the white new shrines, the color and the gold. A great cheer ran over the hill. Those who had been too far to hear all joined in it, sure that salvation had been proclaimed.

Demosthenes went back home, and drafted a diplomatic note to Thebes, heaping scorn on Philip. ". . . acting as might be looked for in one of his race and nature; insolently using his present fortune, forgetful of his unforeseen rise to power from small mean origins . . ." Thoughtfully he chewed his pen; the stylos moved on over the wax.

Mary Renault

Outside his window, young men still new to war, on the way to report to their tribal officers, were shouting to each other; the jokes of the young, whose meaning he no longer knew. A woman was crying somewhere. Surely, it was in the house. It must be his daughter. If she had anyone to weep over, it was the first he knew of it. Angrily he closed his door; the noise was ill-omened, and disturbed his thoughts.

When the Assembly met at Thebes, no man who could stand on his feet was absent. The Macedonians, being formal allies, had first hearing.

They recalled Philip's good offices to Thebes; his help in the Phokian war, his support for her hegemony over Boeotia; rehearsed her ancient injuries from the Athenians, their efforts to weaken her, their alliance with the impious Phokians, paying their troops with Apollo's gold. (With this too, no doubt, they had gilded the Theban shields they had set up, in blasphemous affront to Thebes and to the god.) Philip did not ask that Thebes should take up arms against Athens; Thebans might do so if they chose, and share the fruits of victory; but he would still count them as friends, if they gave him only right of passage.

The Assembly turned it over. They had been angered by Philip's surprise of Elateia; if he was an ally, he was a highhanded one, it was late to consult them now. For the rest, it was true enough. The great issues of power remained unspoken. Once Athens had fallen, what would they be worth to him? And yet, he had power in Thessaly and had done no harm there. They had fought the long Phokian war; Thebes was full of dead men's sons with a family on their shoulders, the widowed mother and the younger ones. Was it not enough?

Antipatros ceased, and sat down. A not unfriendly murmur, almost applause, was heard. The marshal called the Athenian envoys. Demosthenes climbed the rostrum, in a hush of expectation, mostly hostile. Not Macedon, but Athens, had been the threat here for generations. There was no house without a blood-debt from the endless border wars.

He could strike one answering nerve: the common hate for

Sparta. He recalled how after the Great War, when Sparta had imposed on Athens the Thirty Tyrants (traitors like those who wanted peace with Philip now), Thebes had given harbor to the Liberators. Beside Philip, the Thirty were mere schoolboy bullies; let the past be forgotten, only that noble act remembered. With skilled timing, he brought out the Athenian offers. Theban rights over Boeotia should be undisputed; if the Boeotians should rebel, Athens would even send troops to push them down. Plataia too, that old bone of contention. He did not remind his hearers that Plataia, in return for Athens' protection against Thebes, had joined in the stand at Marathon, and been granted Athenian citizenship forever. It was no time for hairsplitting; Plataia should be conceded. Also, if there was war with Philip, Thebes should command all land forces, while Athens would meet two-thirds of the expense.

The burst of applause was missing. Thebans in doubt were looking at other Thebans they knew and trusted, not at him. They were slipping his grip.

Striding forward, lifting his arm, he invoked the heroic dead, Epaminondas and Pelopidas; the glorious fields of Leuktra and Mantinea; the record of the Sacred Band. His ringing voice dropped to a note of silken irony. If these things were no longer of account to them, he had only one request to make on behalf of Athens: right of passage, to oppose the tyrant alone.

He had caught them now. That nip of the old rivalry had done it.

They were shamed, he could hear it in the deep muted sound. Here and there two voices called together for the voting to begin; the men of the Sacred Band were considering their honor. The pebbles rattled into the urns; tally-clerks under close scrutiny flicked their abacuses; a long tedious business, after the efficient slotboxes at home. The Thebans had voted to tear up the treaty with Macedon, and ally with Athens.

He walked back to his lodging, hardly feeling his feet touch ground. Like Zeus with his scales, he had held and tilted the destiny of Greece. If ordeal lay ahead, what new life came forth without birth-pangs? They would say of him now, forever, that the hour had found the man.

They brought Philip the news next day, as he ate his noon meal with Alexander. The King sent his squires out, before even opening the dispatch; like most men of the time, he had not mastered the knack of reading with the eye alone, he needed to hear himself. Alexander, taut with suspense, wondered why his father could not have trained himself, as he had done, to read in silence; it was only a matter of practice; though his lips still moved with the words, Hephaistion had assured him that no sound at all came out.

Philip read levelly, without anger; the lines of his face only deepened into seams. He laid down the scroll by his dish, and said, "Well, if they will have it, they will have it."

"I'm sorry, Father; I suppose it had to be." Could he not see that however the Thebans had voted, Athens would still have hated him? That there was no way he could have entered her gates, but as a victor? How had he nursed so long this insubstantial dream? Better leave him in peace, and think about realities. It would be the second war-plan, now.

Athens and Thebes made ready at fever-heat to meet Philip's southward march. Instead he went west, into the mountain ribs and gorges that fringed the Parnassos massif. He had been commissioned to drive the Amphissians from the sacred plain; this he would do. As for Thebes, let it be said he had only tested a doubtful ally's loyalty, and knew the answer.

The young men of Athens, roused for war, prepared to go north to Thebes. The omens were taken; the fires smoldered, the diviners misliked the entrails. Demosthenes, finding the dead hand of superstition raised against him, declared these portents were meant to reveal the traitors in their midst, paid by Philip to stop the war. When Phokion, back from a mission too late to change events, urged that the city should get an oracle from Delphi, Demosthenes laughed, and said that all the world knew Philip had bought the Pythia.

The Thebans received the Athenians as the Lynkestids had welcomed Alexander, with careful courtesy. The Theban general disposed his joint force to guard the southern passes, and to block Philip from Amphissa. All over the wild stony uplands of Parnassos, and in the gorges of Phokis, the armies scouted and maneuvered. Trees turned brown, then bare; on the tops the first snows fell. Philip took his time. He was busy rebuilding the forts of the impious

Phokians, who gratefully leased them to his men, in exchange for a cut in their fines to the plundered god.

He would not be tempted into a major battle. There was a skirmish in a river gorge, another in an upland pass, both broken off when he saw his troops being drawn into awkward country. Athens hailed them as victories, and thanksgiving feasts were held.

One winter night, Philip's tent was pitched out of the wind against a cliff-face, above a river in snow-spate churning its stony gorge. On the slopes between, a pine wood had been felled for cook-fires. Dusk was falling; eddies of pure mountain air pierced through the heavy mingled smells of wood-smoke, porridge, bean broth, horses, crudely cured tent hides, and many thousand unwashed men. On leather camp-chairs, Philip and Alexander sat warming their wet boots at the glowing crumble of their fire. The steamy reek of his father's feet blended for Alexander with the other homely and familiar scents of war. He himself was no more than fairly dirty; when streams were hard to come at, he would rub himself down with snow. His attention to these things had created a legend, of which he was still unaware, that he was endowed with a natural fragrance. Most of the men had not bathed for months. Their wives would scrub them, when they returned to the marriage bed.

"Well," said Philip, "didn't I tell you Demosthenes' patience would wear out before mine? I heard just now. He's sent them."

"What? How many?"

"The whole ten thousand."

"Is the man mad?"

"No, he's a party politician. The voters didn't like to see paid troops drawing pay and rations in Attica, while citizens went to war. They've been on my mind; trained men, and too mobile where they were, too mobile by far. At the clinch, ten thousand extra men is a good many. Now we can deal with them first; they're being sent direct to Amphissa."

"So we wait till they're there. Then what?"

Philip's yellow teeth grinned in the firelight. "You know how I slipped away at Byzantion? We'll try that again. We'll have bad news, very bad news from Thrace. Revolt, Amphipolis threatened, every man needed to hold the frontier. I shall reply, in good clear writing, that we are marching north with all our forces. My courier will be captured, or maybe sell the letter. The enemy's scouts will see us starting northward. At Kytinion we'll go to ground, lie low, and wait."

"Then over the Grabian Pass, and attack at dawn?"

"A stolen march, as your friend Xenophon says."

They stole it, before spring thaw had drowned the river-crossings. The mercenaries of Athens did their duty, as long as there was hope in it; after that, being professionals, they either got away to the coast, or asked for terms. Most of these last ended by enlisting with Philip, had their wounds dressed, and sat down to a good hot meal.

The Amphissians surrendered without condition. Their government was exiled as the Sacred League had decreed. The holy plain was stripped of their impious husbandry, and left fallow for the god.

In the first warmth of spring, at the theater of Delphi, the steep pale eagle-cliffs of the Phaidriades behind them, the great temple of Apollo before, and the vast gulf beyond, King Philip was crowned by the League with a golden laurel crown. He and his son were eulogized in long speeches and choric odes; a sculptor sketched them, for statues to adorn the temple.

Afterwards, Alexander walked with his friends on the jostling terrace. It hummed and stank with the throng from all over Greece, and as far as Sicily, Italy and Egypt. Rich votaries marched with their offerings displayed on the heads of slaves, goats bleated, doves moaned in wicker cages; faces eager, devout, relieved, drawn with anxiety, came and went. It was one of the days for the oracle.

Under the noise, Hephaistion said in Alexander's ear, "Why don't you, while you're here?"

"Not now."

"It would set your mind at rest."

"No, the time's not right. One should take the seer by surprise, I think, in a place like this."

A sumptuous performance was put on in the theater; the protagonist was Thettalos, renowned for his heroic roles. He was a handsome ardent young man, whose Thessalian blood was mixed with some Celtic strain; his training in Athens had contained his fire in good technique, and his natural rashness in good manners. He had often played in Pella, and was a favorite with Alexander, for whom he conjured some special vision of the hero's soul. Now in Sophokles' *Ajax*, doubling Ajax and Teukros, he made it unthinkable the one should outlive his honor, the other fail in loyalty to the dead. Alexander went round afterwards with Hephaistion to the skene-room. Thettalos had pulled off the mask of Teukros, and was toweling the sweat from his strongly carved face and short curly chestnut hair. At the sound of Alexander's voice he emerged and glowed at him with large hazel eyes, saying, "I am glad if you were pleased. I was playing it all to you."

They talked awhile about his recent travels. At the end he said, "I get about a good deal. If ever you have any business, never mind what, and need someone you can trust, you know it would be a privilege."

He was understood. Actors, the servants of Dionysos, were protected persons; often used as envoys, as secret agents even oftener. Alexander said, "Thank you, Thettalos. There is no one I would sooner ask."

When they were walking away towards the Stadium, Hephaistion said, "You know that man's still in love with you?"

"Well, one can at least be civil. He's sensible, he doesn't misunderstand. Someday I might need to trust him, one never knows."

With good spring weather, Philip moved down to the Gulf of Corinth, and took Naupaktos, which commanded its outer strait. In summer, he moved about in the country behind Parnassos, strengthening strongpoints, keeping alliances warm, making roads, feeding up his cavalry mounts. Now and again he would make feints to the east, where Athenians and Thebans tensely manned the passes. Then he would march away, leaving them flat and stale, and would hold maneuvers or games, to make sure his own men were neither.

Even now, he sent once more envoys to Thebes and Athens, offering to discuss terms for a peace. Demosthenes proclaimed that Philip, twice repulsed by their arms, must be growing desperate; these offers proved it. One good push would finish him in the south.

In late summer, when the barley between the trees in the olive orchards of Attica and Boeotia was yellowing in the ear, he went back to his base at Elateia, but left his strongpoints manned. The forward outposts of Thebes and Athens were at a pass about ten miles south. Till his offers were thrown back, he had done no more than tease them. Now he displayed his strength; they were out-flanked, and could be cut off when he chose. Next day his scouts found them gone; he took and manned the pass.

The men of the cavalry looked happy, polished their gear and made much of their horses. Now, the coming battle would be in the plains.

The barley whitened, the olives ripened. By the calendar of Macedon, it was the month of the Lion. King Philip gave a birthday feast in the fort for Alexander. He was eighteen.

Elateia had been made snug; woven hangings on the wall of the royal quarters, tiles on the floor. While the guests were singing, Philip said to his son, "You've not named your gift yet. What would you like?"

Alexander smiled. "You know that, Father."

"You've earned it, it's yours. It won't be long now. I shall take the right wing, that goes back time out of mind. You will command the cavalry."

Slowly Alexander set down on the table his golden cup. His eyes, shimmering and wide with wine and visions, met Philip's lopsided black glint. "If you ever regret it, Father, I shan't be there to know."

The appointment was cheered, and toasted. Once more the birth-omens were remembered: the Olympic racing win, the Illyrian victory.

"And the third," said Ptolemy. "It's the one I remember best, I was at the age for marvels. It was the day the great Temple of Artemis was burned at Ephesos. A fire in Asia."

Someone said, "I never heard how it came to happen, without a war. Was it a thunderbolt, or did some priest upset a lamp?"

"No, a man did it on purpose. I heard his name once. Heiro— Hero— a longer name than that. Niarchos, can you remember?"

No one could. Niarchos said, "Did they find out why he did it?"

"Oh, yes. He told them all willingly, before they killed him. He did it so that his name should be remembered forever."

Dawn glimmered over the low hills of Boeotia, heather and scrub burned brown with summer, scattered with grey boulders and gravelly stones. Dark and rusty like the heath, weathered like the stones, spiny like the thorn trees, the men poured over the hills towards the plain. They trickled down the slopes and silted in the river valley; the silt thickened, but steadily flowed on.

Along the smoothest inclines the cavalry came ambling, careful of unshod hooves. The horses made only a muffled thudding as they picked their way among the heather, their bare backs gripped by the men's bare thighs. It was the harness of the men that clicked and rattled.

The sky lightened, though the sun still stood behind the great eastward bulk of Parnassos. The valley, scoured out by primeval floods and filled in with their topsoil, began to flatten and widen. Along it burbled through stones the Kephissos River in its summer bed. East of it, low on the terraced slopes, its pink-washed houses still mauve with shadow, stood the village of Cheironeia.

The flood of men slowed its onward course, paused, and spread sideways across the plain. Ahead of it was stretched a dam. Its thick line bristled, and glinted in the first slanting sunbeams; a dam of men.

Between lay a clear space of innocent fields, fed by the river. Mown barley-stubble round the olive trees was pretty with poppies and vetch. There was a noise of crowing cocks, a bleating and lowing of farm-stock, sharp cries of boys and women driving the herds away uphill. The flood and the dam both waited.

In the broad throat of the pass, the northern army made camp along the river. The cavalry went downstream, to water their horses without fouling it for the rest. The men untied their cups from their belts and unpacked their food for the noon meal; flat griddle-cakes, an apple or an onion, a crumble of dirty grey salt from the heel of the bag.

The officers looked about for unsound spear-shafts or javelin thongs, and took the feel of morale. They found a healthy tension, like a drawn bow's; the men had caught the sense of something momentous. They were thirty-odd thousand foot, two thousand horse; the host ahead was as many; this would be the greatest battle of all their lives till now. They were aware too of the men they knew, the captain who was the squire at home, the village neighbor, the fellow tribesmen and kin, who would report their honor or their shame.

Towards afternoon the long baggage train labored down with the tents and bedding. They could sleep well, all but the outposts; the King held all the flanking passes, their position could not be turned. The army ahead could only sit and wait his pleasure.

Alexander rode up to the ox-cart with the royal tents, and said, "Put mine there." A young oak gave shade by the river; under the bank was a clear gravelly pool. Good, thought his servants, it would save carrying water. He liked his bath, not only after a battle but, if he could manage it, even before. Some grumbler had said he would be vain even of his corpse.

The King sat in his tent, giving audience to Boeotians, eager to tell him all they knew of the enemy's plans. The Thebans had oppressed them; the Athenians, their sworn allies, had just sold them publicly to the Thebans; they had nothing much to lose by a leap in the dark. He received them with charm, listened to all their involved and ancient grievances, promised redress, and made notes in his own hand of all they had to tell. Before dusk, he rode up the hill to look for himself, with Alexander, Parmenion, and the next in command, a Macedonian lord called Attalos. The Royal Bodyguard under Pausanias rode behind.

Below them spread the plain which some old poet had called "the dancing-floor of war," so often had armies met there. The confederate troops spread across from the river to the southern foothills, a front of about three miles. The smoke of their evening fires was rising, with here and there a spurt of flame. Not yet in line of battle, they were clumped, like birds of different species, each city and state apart. Their left wing, which would face the Macedonian right, was based firmly on rising ground. Philip narrowed his good eye at it.

"The Athenians. Well, I must have them out of there. Old Phokion, their only general who's good for anything, has been given the navy; he was too canny to please Demosthenes. Our luck; they've sent Chares, who fights by the book . . . Hm, yes; I must put on a good-looking assault before I start falling back. They'll swallow it, from the old general who writes off his losses." He leaned over with a grin to clap Alexander's shoulder. "It wouldn't do for the Little King."

Alexander's brow creased, then cleared. He returned the grin, and went back to considering the long bar of men below, as an engineer who must divert a river considers obstructing rock. Tall lank-cheeked Attalos, with his forked yellow beard and pale blue eyes, had edged his horse up nearer, but now moved quietly back.

"So, then," said Alexander, "in the center we've the odds and ends; Corinthians, Achaians, and so on. And on the right . . ."

"The high command. For you, my son, the Thebans. You see, I've not stinted your dish."

The river gleamed in the light of the paling sky, between tapering poplars and shady planes. Beside it, in orderly patterns, the Theban watch-fires budded into flame. Alexander gazed in deep concentration; for a moment he pictured in this distant firelight the human faces; then they dwindled into the spread of the great design. *And all the gates were opened, and the warriors came pouring out, Foot and horse, and the din of onset resounded.*

"Wake up, lad," said Philip. "We've seen all we need; I want my supper."

Parmenion always ate with them; so tonight did Attalos, newly come in from Phokis. Alexander saw with discomfort that Pausanias was on guard. Those two together in one room always put his teeth on edge. He greeted Pausanias with special warmth.

It was Attalos, friend and kin of the dead rival, who had planned the obscene revenge. It was a mystery to Alexander why Pausanias, a man with no lack of courage, should have come to the King demanding vengeance, rather than take it with his own hand. Could it be that he had wanted a sign of Philip's loyalty? Long ago, before the change, he had had a kind of archaic beauty, which could have housed such an arrogant Homeric love. But Attalos was chief of a powerful clan, a good friend of the King, and useful; the dead boy's loss had been bitter, too. Pausanias had been talked out of it, and his honor patched up with rank. Six years had gone by, he had been laughing oftener, talking more, becoming an easier presence, till Attalos was made a general. Now once more he never met one's eyes, and ten words were a long speech for him. Father shouldn't have done it. It looks like a reward. People say already . . .

His father was talking of the coming battle. He brushed clear his mind; but an aftertaste lingered, as of tainted food.

Alexander had his bath in the gravelly pool, and lay on his bed, going over in his mind the battle-plan, point by point. There was nothing he had forgotten. He got up, dressed, and walked along quietly between the watch-fires, till he reached the tent Hephaistion shared with two or three other men. Before he had touched the flap, Hephaistion had risen soundlessly, thrown on his cloak and come out. They stood for a while talking, then went back to their beds. Alexander slept well till the morning watch.

The din of onset resounded.

Over the barley stubble and round the olive trees, crashing through vineyards half-picked when the laborers fled, knocking down the props and treading the grapes into bloody wine, the press of men swayed and mixed and seethed, their mass swelling and bursting like bubbles, rising and settling like yeast. The noise was deafening. Men yelled to one another, or to the enemy, or to themselves; or screamed in some piercing agony beyond what they had known that flesh could feel. Shields clashed, horses squealed, each corps of the confederate army shouted its own battle-paean at full stretch of its lungs. Officers roared orders, trumpets blew. Over everything hung a great cloud of rusty, choking dust.

On the left, where the Athenians held the foothills which formed the confederates' anchor, the Macedonians shoved their long sarissas doggedly from below, the points of three graded ranks forming one row of weapons, bristling like a porcupine. The Athenians took them on their shields when they could; the bravest pressed between them, stabbing with the short spear or hacking with the sword, sometimes overwhelmed, sometimes denting the line. Along the far flank Philip sat his strong cobby war-horse, his couriers by him, waiting; for what, his men all knew. They heaved and strained in the line, as if their failure to break it was killing them with shame. Though huge noise was everywhere, among them it was somewhat less; they had been told to listen for the word.

In the center, the long front leaned to and fro. The confederate troops, strangers to their neighbors, sometimes rivals, shared the common knowledge that where the line broke disgrace and death would enter. Wounded men fought on till with luck the shields closed before them; or fell, and were trampled on by men who could not drop their guard or pause. The hot press churned in the hot dust, sweating, grunting, cursing, hacking, thrusting, panting, moaning. Where rock broke the ground, the melee heaved round it like sea-foam, and splashed it with crimson spray.

At its north end, where the river guarded its flank, there stretched as evenly as a string of beads the unflawed shield-line of the Sacred Band of Thebes. Now in action the couples were forged into a single bar, each man's shield overlapping the left-hand man. The elder of each pair, the erastes, kept the right, the spear side; the younger, the eromenos, the side of the shield. The right was the side of honor, for a corps or for a man; though the youth might grow up the stronger, he would never ask his friend to cede it. All this was governed by ancient laws. Newly sworn lovers were here, intent upon their proving; and couples who had been in the corps ten years, solid bearded fathers of families, love rendered down to comradeship; the Band was too famous to be renounced at a dream's passing. Its lifelong vows were battle-vows. Even through the dust, it glittered. Its bronze hatlike Boeotian helmets and its round shields edged with cable-work had been burnished to shine like gold. Its weapons were six-foot spears with iron blades, and short stabbing swords, still sheathed, the spear-hedge being unbroken.

Parmenion, whose phalanx faced them, had all he could do to hold them. Now and then they gave a great heave forward, and could have gone further yet, but for fear of breaking contact with the Achaians next to them in the line. They were polished and smooth like some old well-made weapon a man knows the feel of in the dark. Hurry up, Philip; these fellows have been to school. I hope you know what you've given your boy to bite on. I hope he has the teeth for it.

Behind the laboring phalanx, just out of bowshot, the cavalry waited.

They were massed in a thick column like a catapult bolt, with a tapering head, whose point was a single horseman.

The horses fidgeted at the noise, at the drifts of blood-smell on the wind, and the tension in their riders' bodies; they blew from the tickle of the dust. The men talked to neighbors or called to friends, rebuked or fondled the horses, straining to see through the ten-foot dust-cloud how the battle went. They were to charge a line of hoplites, the horseman's nightmare. Cavalry against cavalry, the other man could fall off as easily as you, pushed with the spear, or overreaching himself; he could be outmaneuvered, slashed with the saber. But to run at firm up-pointed spears went against a horse's nature. They fingered the hard-cured bull-hide pectorals on their chargers' breasts. The Companions found their own equipment; but they were glad they had listened to the Boy.

The foremost rider flicked off a fly from his horse's eyelid, feeling with his thighs its strength, its knowledge of the coming fury, its implicit trust, its complicit horse-sense. Yes, yes; we'll be going when I say go. Remember who we are.

Hephaistion in the next short rank felt at his sword belt; should it be one hole tighter? No, nothing makes him so angry as a man fixing his turnout in the line. I must catch him up before he gets there. His color's high. It often is before an action. If it was fever he'd never say. Two days with it before the fort fell, and not a word; I could have carried extra water. A fine night I had of it.

A courier rode through the dusty trampled stubble, and hailed Alexander in the King's name. The message was word of mouth: "They are taking the bait. Be ready."

Up on the hill, above the pink-washed village of Cheironeia, in the tenth row back of the Athenian force, Demosthenes stood with his tribal regiment. The young men held the front; next behind were the strongest of the middle-aged. The whole depth of the line shifted and strained, as a man's whole body does when his right arm alone makes some great effort. The day grew hot. It seemed they had been standing and swaying and staring down for hours; suspense ached in him like a tooth. Ahead men were falling, getting spears in their guts and chests; the shock of the blows seemed to travel all through the thick ranks, back to where he stood. How many fallen already; how many ranks still left between that and him? I should not be here, I am wronging the city by risking myself in war. The milling press made a long shove forward. It was the second in a short time; without doubt now, the enemy was giving ground. There were still nine ranks between him and the long sarissas; and their line was wavering. It is not unknown to you, men of Athens, that I carried shield and spear on the field of Cheironeia, counting as nought my life and my own concerns, though some might have called them weighty, and indeed you might have reproached me with hazarding your welfare in risking mine . . . A choking cry of pain came from the front rank, which had been the second. Men of Athens . . .

The roar of battle changed. An exultant shout ran like fire through the packed mass. It began to move, no longer in labored heaves but like a gathering landslide. The enemy was retreating! The glories of Marathon, of Salamis, of Plataia, flashed before his eyes. Men in front were yelling, "On to Macedon!" He started running with the rest, calling in his high sharp voice, "Catch Philip! Take him alive!" He should be led in chains through the Agora; after that they would make him talk, name every traitor. There would be a new statue on the Acropolis, next to Harmodios and Aristogeiton: DEMOSTHENES THE LIBERATOR. He shouted to those ahead who could run faster, "On to Macedon! Take him alive!" In his haste to be there and see it, he almost stumbled over the bodies of the young men who had fallen in the front line.

Theagenes the Theban, commander-in-chief of the confederate army, urged his horse behind the battle-lines towards the center. The long front fermented with shouted rumor, too garbled to be of use. Here at last came one of his own scouts. The Macedonians were indeed, he reported, in retreat.

How? asked Theagenes. In disorder? In fair order, but getting away pretty fast. They had already fallen right back from the heights, with the Athenians after them. After them? What! Had they left their station, then, without orders? Well, orders or not, they were already in the plain; it was the King himself they were chasing.

Theagenes, cursing, beat his fist on his thigh. Philip! The fools, the misbegotten, fribbling, vainglorious Athenian fools. What had become of the line up there? There must be a gap as long as a hippodrome. He sent off the scout with orders that it must at all costs be filled, and the left flank covered. No sign anywhere else of the enemy falling back; they were laying on harder than ever.

The leader of the Corinthians received the order. How better guard the flank, than get up on the good rising ground where the Athenians had been? The Achaians, left feeling naked, spread out towards the Corinthians. Theagenes stretched out his own troops in turn. Let these Athenian speechmakers see what real soldiers look like. In their place of honor on the right wing, the Sacred Band changed order; briefly, as they moved, they showed in twos.

Theagenes surveyed the long threshing chain of men, now loose at one end, and weaker over all. Before him, the enemy rear was obscured by a tree-tall thicket of sarissas; ranks not engaged held them high, for the safety of those in front. With them and the dust-cloud, one could see nothing. A thought hit him, like a jolt in the midriff. No word of young Alexander. Where is he? On garrison duty in Phokis? Toiling unnoticed in the line? Yes, when iron floats. Then where is he?

There was a lull in the fight before him; almost a stillness, after the noise before; the heavy pause of earthquake weather. Then the deep bristling phalanx swung sideways, ponderously but smoothly, like an enormous door.

It stood open. The Thebans did not go out of it; they waited for what was coming in. The sacred Band, turning face to face before they locked the shield-line and settled their spears, showed up in twos, once and for all.

In the stubble-field among the trampled poppies, Alexander lifted his sword-arm, and yelled the note of the paean.

Strong and sustained, the voice trained by Epikrates rang down the great square of horsemen. They took up the paean; it lost in its passage the sound of words, dinning like the fierce outcry from a cloud of swooping hawks. It goaded the horses more than spurs. Before ever they came in sight, the Thebans had felt their thunder through the ground.

Watching his men like a shepherd on a mountain trail, Philip waited for news.

The Macedonians were plodding back, sullenly, carefully, fighting for every few yards of ground. Philip rode about, directing their retreat just where it should go. Who could believe it, he thought. When Iphikrates was alive, or Chabrias . . . But their orators appoint their generals now. So soon, so soon. A generation . . . He shielded his eyes to scan the line. The charge had begun, he knew no more.

Well, he's alive; if he fell, the news would fly quicker than a bird. Curse this leg, I'd like to take a walk among the men, they're used to it. A spearman all my life. I never thought I'd breed a cavalry general. Ah well, the hammer still needs the anvil. When he can bring off a planned fighting withdrawal like this . . . He understood his briefing. Everything pat. But only half there, he had that look of his mother.

Thought changed to tangled images like a knot of snakes. He saw the proud head lying in blood; the mourning, the tomb at Aigai, the choice of a new heir; idiot Arridaios' jerking face, I was drunk when I got him; Ptolemy, too late now to acknowledge him, I was a boy, what could I do? . . . What's four-and-forty, I've good seed in me yet. A sturdy square dark-haired boy ran up to him, calling, "Father!" . . .

Shouts sounded, nearing, directing a rider to the King.

"He's through, sir. He's broken the line. The Thebans are standing, but they're cut off beside the river, the right wing's rolled up. I didn't speak with him, he said ride straight to you when I saw it, you were waiting for the word. But I saw him there in the van, I saw his white crest."

"The gods be thanked. A bringer of such news deserves something. See me after." He summoned the trumpeter. For a moment, like a good farmer at harvest-time, he viewed the field which through his careful husbandry stood for the reaping just as it ought. His cavalry reserve had appeared upon the heights, before the Corinthians could command them. His withdrawing infantry had spread into the shape of a sickle blade. Enclosed in its curve were the jubilant Athenians.

He gave the order to attack.

The knot of young men was still resisting. They had found a stone sheep-pen, nearly breast high, but the sarissas came thrusting over. In the filth on the ground a lad of eighteen was kneeling, clutching at his eye which was falling down his cheek.

"We should get away," said the older man in the middle, urgently. "We shall be cut off. Look, you can see, look round."

"We're staying here," said the young man who had assumed command. "You go if you want, we'll never notice the difference."

"Why throw away our lives? Our lives belong to the City. We should go back and dedicate our lives to restoring Athens."

[277]

"Barbarians! Barbarians!" yelled the young man to the troops outside. They replied with some uncouth battle-cry. When he had time to spare, he said to the older man, "Restore Athens? Let us rather perish with her. Philip will blot her from the earth. Demosthenes has always said so."

"Nothing is certain, terms can be made . . . Look, they have almost closed us round, are you mad, wasting all our lives?"

"Not even slavery, but annihilation. That's what Demosthenes said. I was there, I heard him."

A sarissa, poking forward out of the thick of the attackers, caught him under the chin and went tearing up through his mouth into his brain-base.

"This is madness, madness," said the middle-aged man. "I'll have no more part in it." Dropping shield and spear, he scrambled over the far wall. Only one man, inactive with a broken arm, was looking when he shed his helmet too.

The rest fought on, till a Macedonian officer came up, calling that if they surrendered the King would spare their lives. At this they laid down their arms. While they were being marched off, between the dying and dead strewed everywhere, to join the herd of captives, one of them said to the rest, "Who was the little fellow who ran away, the one poor Eubios was quoting Demosthenes to?"

The man with the broken arm, who had been a good while silent, answered, "That was Demosthenes."

The prisoners were under guard, the wounded were being carted off on shields, beginning with the victors. This would take many hours, many would be there at nightfall. The defeated lay at the mercy, for good or ill, of those who found them; many, unfound, would be with the dead tomorrow. Among the dead too there was precedence. The conquered would lie till their cities sued for them; their bodies, asked and granted, were formal acknowledgment that the victors possessed the field.

Philip with his staff rode down the long wreck-strewed shore of battle from south to north. The moans of the dying sounded in fitful gusts, like wind in the high woods of Macedon. Father and son said little; sometimes a landmark of the fight would prompt a question.

Philip was trying to make real to himself the event with all its meaning. Alexander had been with Herakles; it took time to come down from that possession. He did his best to attend to his father, who had embraced him when they met, and said everything that was proper.

At length they reached the river. Here by its shore, there was no straggle among the dead of men caught flying. They lay compactly, facing all ways outward, except where the river for a time had guarded their backs. Philip looked at the cable-trimmed shields. He said to Alexander, "You went in here?"

"Yes. Between them and the Achaians. The Achaians stood well; but these died harder."

"Pausanias," called Philip. "Have them counted."

Alexander said, "You will find there is no need."

The count took time. Many were buried under Macedonians they had killed, and had to be disentangled. There were three hundred. All the Band was there.

"I called on them to yield," Alexander said. "They called back that they didn't know the word; they supposed it was Macedonian."

Philip nodded, and sank back into his thoughts. One of the body-guard who had done the counting, a man fond of his own wit, turned one of the bodies over on another and made an obscene joke.

"Let them alone," said Philip loudly. The uncertain titters died. "Perish the man who says they did or bore anything base."

He wheeled round his horse, followed by Alexander. Unseen by either, Pausanias turned and spat on the nearest body.

"Well," Philip said, "the day's work done. I think we have earned a drink."

It was a fine night. The flaps of the royal tent were opened; tables and benches overflowed outside. All the chief officers were there, old guest-friends, tribal chiefs, and various allied envoys who had been following the campaign.

The wine was tempered at first, because people were dry; when thirst was slaked, it went round neat. Everyone who felt happy, or thought it useful, started a new round of toasts, and pledged the King.

[279]

To the rhythm of old Macedonian drinking-songs, the guests began clapping, slapping their thighs, or banging the tables. Their heads were crowned with wreaths from the broken vineyards. After the third chorus, Philip rose to his feet, and proclaimed a komos.

An unsteady line was formed. Anyone in reach of a torch snatched it up and waved it. Those who were giddy grasped the next man's shoulder. Swaying and limping, Philip lurched along at the head of the line, arm in arm with Parmenion. His face glistened red in the shaking torchlight, the lid of his dead eye drooped, he bawled out the song like battle orders. The truth of the wine had lit for him the vastness of his deed; the long plans ended, the vista of power ahead, the downfall of his enemy. Freed from careful southern graces as from a hampering cloak, one in soul with his highland forebears and nomad ancestors, he was a chieftain of Macedon, feasting his clansmen after the greatest of all border raids.

The lilt of the song inspired him. "Hark!" he roared. "Listen to this:

> "Demosthenes decrees!
> Demosthenes decrees!
> Demosthenes of Paiania,
> Son of Demosthenes.
> Euoi Bakchos! Euoi Bakchos!
> Demosthenes decrees!"

It spread down the line like fire in tinder. It was easy to learn, and even easier to sing. Stamping and shouting, the komos wavered out through the moonlit night over the olive fields by the river. A little way downstream, where they would not foul the water for the victors, were the prisoners' pens. Roused by the noise from exhausted sleep or lonely brooding, the drawn grimy men got to their feet and stared silently, or looked at one another. The torches shone on still rows of eyes.

Near the tail of the komos, among the young, Hephaistion slipped from his neighbors' convivial arms, and walked along through the olives' shadows, looking out and waiting. He kept along by the komos till he saw Alexander leave it; he too looked about, knowing Hephaistion would be there.

They stood together under an old tree with a gnarled intricate stem, thick as a horse's body. Hephaistion touched it. "Someone told me they live a thousand years."

"This one," Alexander said, "will have something to remember." He felt at his brow, dragged off the vine-wreath and stamped it under his heel. He was cold sober. Hephaistion had been drunk when the komos started, but that had soon cleared his head.

They walked on together. The lights and noise still meandered before the prisoners' pens. Alexander walked steadily down river. They picked their way over broken spears and sarissas and javelins, round dead horses and dead men. At length Alexander stopped by the riverbank, where Hephaistion had known he would.

No one had stripped the bodies yet. The bright shields, the victors' trophies, glimmered softly under the moon. The smell of blood was stronger here; bleeding men had fought on longer. The river chuckled gently among the stones.

One body lay by itself, face down, feet towards the river; a young man, with dark crisply curling hair. His dead hand still grasped his helmet, which stood by him upside down, with water in it. It was unspilled, because he had been crawling when death overtook him. A blood-spoor, along which he had been returning, led from him to the heap of dead. Alexander picked up the helmet, carrying the water carefully, and followed the trail to its end. This man too was young; he had bled a wide pool, the great vein of his thigh being severed. His open mouth showed the dry tongue. Alexander bent, with the water ready, and touched him, then laid the helmet aside.

"The other had stiffened, but this one is hardly cold. He had a long wait."

"He would know why," Hephaistion said.

A little way on, two bodies lay across each other, both facing upward to where the enemy had been. The elder was a strong-looking man with a fair clipped beard; the younger, on whom he had fallen back in death, was bareheaded. On one side he was bare-skulled; a downward slash of a cavalry saber had flayed off the face to show a bony grin. From the other side, one could see that beauty had been there.

Alexander knelt, and as one might straighten a garment, replaced the flap of flesh. It adhered, sticky with blood. He looked round at Hephaistion and said, "I did this. I remember it. He was trying to spear Oxhead through the neck. I did it."

"He shouldn't have lost his helmet. I suppose the chin-strap was weak."

"I don't remember the other."

He had been speared through the body, and the spear wrenched back in the urgency of battle, leaving a great torn hole. His face was set in a grimace of agony; he had died wide awake.

"I remember him," said Hephaistion. "He came at you after you struck the first one down. You had your hands full already. So I took him on."

There was a silence. Small frogs chirruped in the river shallows. A night bird sang liquidly. Behind them sounded the blurred chant of the komos.

"It's war," said Hephaistion. "They know they'd have done the same to us."

"Oh yes. Yes, it is with the gods."

He knelt down by the two bodies, and tried to compose the limbs; but they were set hard as wood; the eyes, when he had closed the lids, opened again to stare. Finally he dragged the man's corpse over, till it lay by the youth's with one stiff arm across it. Taking off his shoulder-cloak he spread it so that both faces were covered.

"Alexander. I think you should go back to the komos. The King will be missing you."

"Kleitos can sing much louder." He looked round at the still shapes, the dried blood blackened by moonlight, the palely shining bronze. "It is better here among friends."

"It's only right you should be seen. It's a victory komos. You were first through the line. He waited for that."

"Everyone knows what I did. There's only one honor I want tonight, to have it said I wasn't *there*." He pointed at the wobbling torchlight.

"Come, then," said Hephaistion. They went down to the water and washed the blood from their hands. Hephaistion loosened his shoulder-cloak and wrapped it around both of them. They walked on by the river into the hanging shadow of the willows fed by the stream.

Philip finished the evening sober. As he danced before the captives, a certain Demades, an Athenian eupatrid, had said to him with quiet dignity, "When fortune has cast you for Agamemnon, King, aren't you ashamed to play Thersites?"

Philip was not too drunk to feel, through this harshness, a rebuke from Greek to Greek. He stopped the komos, had Demades bathed and freshly clothed, gave him supper in his tent, and, the next day, sent him back to Athens as an envoy. Even in drink, Philip's eye had been good; the man was one of Phokion's party, who had worked for peace but obeyed the call to war. By him, the King's terms were conveyed to Athens. They were proclaimed to an Assembly stunned silent with incredulous relief.

Athens was to acknowledge the hegemony of Macedon; so far the condition was Sparta's of sixty years before. But the Spartans had cut the throats of all their captives at Goat River, three thousand men; they had pulled down the Long Walls to the sound of flutes, and set up a tyranny. Philip would release his prisoners without ransom; he would not march into Attica; he left their form of government to their own choice.

They accepted; and were granted in due form the bones of their dead. They had been burned on a common pyre, since they could not last out the days of peacemaking. The pyre was broad; one party of troops stoked it all day with timber, another fed it with corpses; it smoked up from sunrise to sunset, and both details finished worn out. There were more than a thousand men to burn. The ashes and calcined bones were boxed in oaken chests, awaiting a state cortege.

Thebes, stripped and helpless, had surrendered without condition. Athens had been an open enemy; but Thebes, a faithless ally. Philip garrisoned her citadel, killed or dispossessed her leading anti-Macedonians, and freed the Boeotians from her rule. There being no parleys, her dead were quickly gathered. The Band were given the heroes' right of a common tomb, and remained together; above them the Lion of Cheironeia sat down to its long watch.

When his envoys returned from Athens, Philip let the Athenian prisoners know they were free to go, and went off to his midday meal. He was eating in his tent when a senior officer asked leave to enter. He was in charge of dispatching the convoy. "Yes?" said Philip. "What's wrong?"

"Sir, they're asking for their baggage."

Philip put down his soup-soaked bannock. "Asking for *what?*"

"Their stuff from their camp, bedding-rolls and so on."

Macedonian mouths and eyes fell open. Philip gave a bark of laughter. He grasped his chair-arms, and jutted his black beard. "Do they think," he roared, "that we beat them at a game of knucklebones? Tell them to get out."

As the grumbling exodus was heard, Alexander said, "Why not have marched on? We need not have damaged the city; they'd have left it when you came in sight."

Philip shook his head. "One can't be sure. And the Acropolis has never fallen, so long as it was manned."

"Never?" said Alexander. A dreaming aspiration shone in his eyes.

"And when it did fall, it was to Xerxes. No, no."

"No. That's true." Neither had spoken of the komos, or of Alexander's leaving it; each had welcomed the other's forbearance. "But I wonder you didn't at least make them hand over Demosthenes."

Philip swept his bread around his soup bowl. "Instead of the man, there would be his hero-statue. The man will be truer to life . . . Well, you can see Athens for yourself very shortly. I am sending you as my envoy, to return their dead."

Alexander looked round slowly; he had supposed for a moment he was the object of some obscure joke. He had never thought it possible that, having spared Athens both invasion and occupation, his father would not himself ride in as a magnanimous victor, to receive her thanks. Was it shame for the komos? Policy? Could it be even hope?

"To send you," said Philip, "is a civility. For me to go would be thought hubristic. They have the status of allies now. A more fitting time may come."

Yes, it was still the dream. He wanted the gates opened from within. When he had won the war in Asia and freed the cities, it was in Athens, not as conqueror but honored guest, that he would hold the feast of victory. And he had never even seen it.

"Very well, Father, I'll go." A moment later, he remembered to express thanks.

He rode between the towers of the Dipylon Gate, and into the Kerameikos. On either side were the tombs of the great and noble; old painted grave-steles faded with weather, new ones whose withered grave-wreaths were tasseled with the mourners' hair. Marble knights rode heroically nude, ladies at tiring-tables remembered beauty; a soldier gazed out at the sea that kept his bones. They were quiet people. Among them, the noisy crowds of the living milled to stare.

A pavilion had been built, to house the ossuaries till the tomb was ready; they were lifted in from the train of biers. As he rode on between obsequious faces, a shrill keening swelled up behind him; the women had surged upon the catafalque, to wail the fallen. Oxhead started under him; from behind a grave, someone had hurled a clod. Horse and rider had known worse, and neither deigned to look round. If you were at the fight, my friend, this does not become you; still less if you were not. But if you are a woman, I understand it.

Ahead towered the steep northwest cliffs of the Acropolis. He ran his eye over them, wondering about the other sides. Someone was inviting him to a civic function; he bowed acceptance. By the road, a marble hoplite in antique armor leaned on his spear; Hermes, guide of the dead, bent to offer a child his hand; a wife and husband bade farewell; two friends clasped hands on an altar, a cup beside them. Everywhere Love faced Necessity in silence. No rhetoric here. Whoever had come after, these people had built this city.

He was led through the Agora to hear speeches in the Council Hall. Sometimes far back in the crowd he heard a shouted curse; but the war party, its prophecies made void, mostly kept away. Demosthenes might have vanished into air. Old Macedonia guest-friends and supporters were thrust forward; he did his best with these awkward meetings. Here came Aischines, carrying it off well, but defensive under it. Philip had showed more mercy than even the peace party had dared predict; they were smeared with the odium of men who have been too right. The bereaved, the ruined, watched them Argus-eyed for a gleam of triumph and were sure to find it. Philip's hirelings came too, some cautious, some fawning; these found Philip's son civil, but opaque.

He ate at the house of Demades, with a few guests of honor; the occasion was not one for feasting. But it was very Attic: well-worn spare elegance, couches and tables whose ornament was perfect shaping and silky wood; wine cups of old silver thin with polishing; quiet expert service, talk in which no one interrupted or raised his voice. In Macedon, Alexander's mere lack of greed put his table manners above the common run; but here he took care to observe the others first.

Next day on the Acropolis he made dedications to the City's gods, in earnest of the peace. Here were the fabled glories, towering Athene of the Vanguard whose spear-tip guided ships—where were you, Lady, did your father forbid you the battle, as he did at Troy? This time were you obedient? Here in her temple stood Pheidias' ivory Maiden in her robe of folded gold; here were the trophies and dedications of a hundred years. (Three generations; only three!)

He had been reared in the Palace of Archelaos; fine building was nothing new to him; he talked of history, and was shown Athene's olive, which sprouted green overnight when the Persians had burned it. They had carried off, too, the old statues of the Liberators, Harmodios and Aristogeiton, to adorn Persepolis. "If we can get them back," he said, "we will let you have them. Those were brave men and faithful friends." No one answered; Macedonian boastfulness was a byword. From the parapet he looked for the place where the Persians had climbed up, and found it without help; it had seemed impolite to ask.

The peace party had got a motion passed that, to recognize Philip's clemency, his statue and his son's should be set up in the Parthenon. As he sat for the sculptor's sketch, he thought of his father's image standing there, and wondered how soon the man would follow it.

Was there anything else, they asked, any sight he would like to visit before he left? "Yes; the Academy. Aristotle my tutor studied there. He lives now in Stagira; my father rebuilt the town and brought the people back. But I should like to see where Plato taught."

Along the road there, all the great soldiers of Athens' past were buried. He saw the battle-trophies and his questions delayed the ride. Here, too, men who had died together in famous actions lay in fraternal tombs. A new site was being cleared; he did not ask for whom.

The road petered out into a grove of ancient olives, whose long grass and field-flowers were dried with autumn. Near the altar of Eros was another, inscribed EROS AVENGED. He asked the story. An immigrant, they said, had loved a beautiful Athenian youth, and vowed there was nothing he would not do for him. He had said, "Then go jump off the Rock." When he found he had been obeyed, he made the same leap himself. "He did right," said Alexander. "What does it matter where a man comes from? It's what he is in himself." They changed the subject, exchanging looks; it was natural the son of the Macedonian upstart should have such thoughts.

Speusippos, who had inherited the school from Plato, had died the year before. In the cool, plain white house that had been Plato's, the new head, Xenokrates, received him, a tall big-boned man whose gravity, it was said, cleared a path before him even through the Agora at market-time. Alexander, entertained with the courtesy of eminent teacher to promising student, felt the man to be solid and took to him on sight. They talked a little about Aristotle's methods. "A man must follow his truth," Xenokrates said, "wherever it leads him. It will lead Aristotle, I think, away from Plato, who was a man for making How serve Why. Me it keeps at Plato's feet."

"Have you a likeness of him?"

Xenokrates led him out past a dolphin fountain to Plato's myrtle-shaded tomb; the statue stood near it. He sat scroll in hand, his classic oval head stooped forward from heavy shoulders. To the end of his days he had kept the athlete's short-cut hair of his youth. His beard was cleanly trimmed; his brow was furrowed across and down; from under its weight looked the haunted unwavering eyes of a survivor who has fled from nothing. "Yet still he believed in good. I have some books of his."

"As to the good," said Xenokrates, "he himself was his own evidence. Without that, a man will find no other. I knew him well. I am glad you read him. But his books, he always said, contained the teaching of his master, Sokrates; there would never be a book of Plato, for what he had to teach could only be learned as fire is kindled, by the touch of the flame itself."

Alexander gazed eagerly at the brooding face, as if at a fort on some impregnable rock. But the crag was gone, overthrown by the floods of time, never to be assailed again. "He had a secret doctrine?"

"An open secret. You, who are a soldier, can only teach your wisdom to men whose bodies have been prepared for hardship, and their minds to resist fear; isn't that so? Then the spark can kindle the spark. So with him."

With regret and surmise, Xenokrates gazed at the youth who looked, with surmise and regret, at the marble face. He rode back past the dead heroes to the City.

He was about to change for supper when a man was announced and left alone with him; a well-dressed, well-spoken person, who claimed to have met him at the Council Hall. Everyone, he learned, had praised the modesty and restraint he had shown, so proper to his mission. Many regretted he should have denied himself, from respect for public mourning, the pleasures of a city so well able to provide them. It would be disgraceful were he not offered the chance to taste them in harmless privacy. "Now I have a boy . . ." He described the graces of a Ganymede.

Alexander heard him out without interruption. "What do you mean," he then said, "that you have a boy? Is he your son?"

"Sir! Ah, you will have your joke."

"Your own friend, perhaps?"

"Nothing of the kind, I assure you, entirely at your disposal. Only see him for yourself. I paid two hundred staters for him."

Alexander stood up. "I don't know," he said, "what I have done to deserve you, or your merchandise either. Get out of my sight."

He did so, returning with consternation to the peace party, which had wished the young man to take away grateful memories. A curse on false reports! Too late now to offer a woman.

He rode north next day.

Soon after, the dead of Cheironeia were brought to their common tomb in the Street of Heroes. The people debated who should speak their funeral praises. Aischines was proposed, and Demades. But the one had been too right, the other too successful; to the sore hearts in Assembly, they looked sleek and smug. All eyes returned to the ravaged face of Demosthenes. Perfect defeat, enormous shame had burned out, for the time, all spite from him; the new lines on his tight-drawn skin were of a pain greater than hate. Here was one they could all trust not to rejoice when they were mourning. They chose him to speak the epitaph.

All the Greek states but Sparta sent envoys to the Council at Corinth. They acknowledged Philip supreme war-leader of Hellas against the Persians, for defense. At this first meeting he asked no more. All the rest would follow.

He marched to the frontier of sullen Sparta, then changed his mind. Let the old dog keep its kennel. It would not come out; but if cornered, it would die hard. He had no wish to be the Xerxes of a new Thermopylai.

Corinth, city of Aphrodite, proved readier to please than Athens.

The King and Prince were splendidly entertained. Alexander found time to climb the long path to Acrocorinth, and survey the great walls which, from below, looked narrow as ribbons round the mount's towering brow. With Hephaistion he gazed, the day being clear, south to Athens and northward to Olympos; appraised the walls; saw where one could build better ones and scale those that were there; and was reminded to admire the monuments. At the very top was the small graceful white temple of Aphrodite. Some of the goddess's famous girls, the guide advised them, would certainly at this time have come up from the city precinct to serve her there. He paused expectantly, but in vain.

Demaratos, a Corinthian aristocrat of the ancient Dorian stock, was an old guest-friend of Philip, and played host to him during the Council. At his great house on the footslopes of Acrocorinth, he gave one night a small intimate party, promising the King a guest who would interest him.

It was Dionysios the Younger, son of Dionysios the Greater, late of Syracuse. Since Timoleon had expelled him from his tyranny, he had earned his bread here by running a school for boys. He was a shortsighted, gangling, mouse-colored man of about Philip's age; his new calling, and lack of means, had ended his once notorious dissipations, but he had an old drunkard's broken-veined nose. A combed, scholarly beard masked his weak chin. Philip, who had surpassed the achievements of even his formidable father the elder tyrant, treated him with charming tact, and when the wine had been round was rewarded by his confidences.

"I had no experience, when I inherited from my father, none at all. My father was a very suspicious man. You will have heard the stories; they are mostly true. All the gods could have witnessed, I never had a thought of doing him any wrong; but to the day of his death, I was searched to the skin before I was admitted to his presence. I never saw state papers, never attended a war conference. Now if he had left me, as you did your son, to govern at home while he was on campaign, history might have a different tale to tell."

Philip nodded gravely, and said he could well believe it.

"I would have been content if he had only left me to enjoy a young man's pleasures in peace. He was a hard man; very able, but hard."

"Well, many causes go to these reversals."

"Yes. When my father took power, the people had had a bellyful of democracy; and when it passed to me, they'd had a bellyful of despotism."

Philip had perceived he was not always as foolish as he seemed. "But was Plato no help to you? They say you had two visits from the philosopher."

There was a working in the ineffectual face. "Don't you think I learned some philosophy from Plato, when you see me bear so great a change of fortune?"

The watery eyes had taken on almost dignity. Philip looked at the well-darned splendor of his one good gown, laid a kindly hand on his, and beckoned up the wine-pourer.

On a gilded bed, whose headpiece was carved with swans, Ptolemy lay with Thais the Athenian, his newest girl.

She had come young to Corinth, and had her own house already.

There were wall-paintings of twining lovers; the bed-table held two exquisitely shallow cups, a wine jar, and a round flask of scented oil. A triple lamp, upheld by gilt nymphs, glowed on their pleasures; she was nineteen, and had no need of mystery. Her black hair was feather-soft, her eyes were dark blue; her rose-red mouth was unpainted, though she had tinted like pink shells her nails and nipples and nostrils. Her creamy skin had been polished and plucked as smooth as alabaster. Ptolemy was enchanted with her. Languidly, for the hour was late, he stroked her over, hardly caring whether reminiscence renewed desire.

"We must live together. This is no life for you. I shan't marry for many years. Don't fear that I won't take care of you."

"But, darling man, I have all my friends here. Our concerts, play-readings . . . I should be quite lost in Macedon." Everyone said he was Philip's son. One must never sound too eager.

"Ah, but soon it will be Asia. You shall sit by a blue-tiled fountain, with roses round you; I shall come back from battle and fill your lap with gold." She laughed, and nibbled his ear.

He was a man, she thought, whom one could really put up with every night. When one considered some of the others . . . "Let me think a little longer. Come to supper tomorrow; no, it's today. I'll tell Philetas I'm sick."

"Little finch. What shall I bring you?"

"Only yourself." She had seldom known this to fail. "Macedonians are really men."

"Ah, well, you would move a statue."

"I'm glad you've begun to take your beards off. One can see the handsome faces now." She ran her finger along his chin.

"Alexander set the fashion. He says a beard gives the enemy a handhold."

"Oh, is that why? . . . That beautiful boy. They are all in love with him."

"All the girls but you?"

She laughed. "Don't be jealous. I meant all the soldiers. He's one of us, you know, at heart."

"No. No, there you're wrong. He's as chaste as Artemis; or nearly."

"Yes, that one can see; it's not what I meant." Her feathery brows moved in meditation. She liked her bedfellow, and for the first time bestowed on him her real thoughts. "He is like the great, the famous ones; like Lais or Rhodope or Theodotis they tell tales of in those old days. They don't live for love, you know; but they live upon it. I can tell you, I have seen, they are the very blood of his body, all those men who he knows would run after him through fire. If ever the day comes when they will follow him no longer, it will be the same with him as with some great hetaira when the lovers leave her door and she puts away her mirror. He will begin to die."

A sigh replied to her. Softly she fished up the coverlet and drew it over both of them. He was fast asleep, and it would soon be morning. Let him stay. She might as well start getting used to him.

From Corinth, Philip went homeward to prepare for the war in Asia. When he was ready, he would seek the Council's sanction to begin.

Most of the troops had gone on ahead under Attalos, and dispersed to their homes on leave; Attalos also. He owned an old grey ancestral fort on the footslopes of Mount Pydna; Philip received a message from him, begging the King to honor his rough house by breaking the journey there. The King, who had found him both keen and capable, sent an acceptance back.

As they turned off the high road into the hills, and the sea-horizon widened, Alexander grew taciturn and withdrawn. Presently he rode off from Hephaistion's side, overtook Ptolemy, and beckoned him away from the cavalcade among the heath and scrub of the hillside. Ptolemy followed, puzzled; his mind had been on his own concerns. Would she keep her word? She had made him wait for her answer to the very last.

"What can Father be thinking of," said Alexander, "not to send Pausanias on to Pella? How *can* he bring him here?"

"Pausanias?" said Ptolemy vaguely. His face changed. "Well, it's right to guard the King's person."

"It's his right to be spared this, if he has a right to anything. Don't you know, it was at Attalos' house it happened?"

"He has a house at Pella."

"It was here. I've known that since I was twelve. I was in the stables at home, in one of the stalls, they didn't see me; Attalos' grooms were telling ours. Mother told me too, years later, I didn't tell her it was stale fish. It happened here."

"It's a good while back, now. Six years."

"Do you think one could forget in sixty?"

"He's at least on duty, he needn't feel himself a guest."

"He should have been released from duty. Father should have helped him out."

"Yes," said Ptolemy slowly. "Yes, a pity . . . You know, I'd not recalled the matter till you spoke of it, and I've had less business to think of than the King."

Oxhead, feeling some shock through his rider, snorted and shook his glittering head. "*That* I'd not thought of! Even in our family, there's a limit on what one can remind one's father of. Parmenion should do it, they were young men together. But maybe he's forgotten, too."

"It's only for this one night . . . I've been thinking, if all goes well she may have sold her house by now. You must see her. Wait till you hear her sing."

Alexander rejoined Hephaistion. They rode on in silence till the rock-hewn walls of the fort, a grim relic of the lawless years, came in sight round a bluff. A group of horsemen appeared from the gate, to meet them.

Alexander said, "If Pausanias is sullen, don't fall out with him."

"No. I know."

"Even kings have no right to wrong men and then forget it."

"I don't fancy," said Hephaistion, who had been giving it thought, "that he does forget. You need to bear in mind how many blood-feuds the King has settled, in his reign. Think of Thessaly; the Lynkestids. My father says, when Perdikkas died there wasn't a house or tribe in Macedon without one at least. You know Leonnatos and I should be at feud, his great-grandfather killed mine, I must have told you that. The King often asks our fathers to supper the same night, to prove all's well; they don't mind it now."

"But that was old family business, not their own."

"It's the King's way, Pausanias must know it. That removes the affront."

And when they reached the fort, he did indeed go about his duties as usual. It was his office to keep the door while the King was feasting, not to sit down with the host. His meal would be served him later.

The King's train was hospitably looked after; he himself with his son and a few chief friends were led to the inner rooms. The fort was ruder, and little later, than the castle at Aigai, which was as old as Macedon itself. The Attalids were an ancient clan. Within, the rooms had been well decked out with Persian hangings and inlaid chairs. In supreme compliment to the honored guests, the ladies came in, to be presented and offer sweets.

Alexander, whose eye had been drawn off by a Persian archer on the tapestry, heard his father say, "I never knew, Attalos, that you'd another daughter."

"Nor had I, King, till lately. The gods, who took away my brother, gave her to us. This is Eurydike, poor Bion's child."

"Poor indeed," said Philip, "to watch over such a child and die before her wedding."

Attalos said easily, "We don't yet think of that; we're too pleased with our new daughter to let her go."

At the first sound of his father's voice, Alexander had turned like a house-dog at a stealthy footfall. The girl stood before Philip, with a polished silver sweet-bowl in her right hind. He had taken her left in his, as a kinsman might have done, and now released it, perhaps because he had seen her blush. She had a family look of Attalos, but with his defects all turned to graces: for gaunt cheeks, delicate hollows under fine bones; for straw hair, gold; he was lanky, she was willowy. Philip spoke some praise of her dead father; she made a little reverence, met his eyes and dropped hers; then went on with her silver bowl to Alexander. Her sweet bland smile fixed for a moment; she had looked before he was ready.

Next day, their departure was delayed till noon, Attalos having revealed that it was a feast-day for some local river-nymphs, and the women would be singing. They came with their garlands; the girl's voice was light, childish, but true. The clear water of the nymphs' spring was tasted and praised.

When they set out, the heat of the day was well advanced. A few miles on, Pausanias left the column. Another officer, seeing him go down towards a stream, called after him to wait a mile or two more for better water; here it got staled by cattle. He pretended not to hear, filled his cupped hands and drained them thirstily. He had neither eaten nor drunk, all the while he was at the house of Attalos.

Alexander stood with Olympias under Zeuxis' painting of the sack of Troy. Above her, Queen Hekabe rent her garments; behind his head spread like a crimson nimbus the blood of Priam and Astyanax. Winter firelight leaped in the painted flames, and drew hollows in the living faces.

Olympias' eyes were ringed with black, and her face was lined like a woman's ten years older. Alexander's mouth looked dry and set; he too had been sleepless, but showed it less.

"Mother. Why send for me again? All's said and you know it. What was true yesterday is true today. I shall have to go."

"Expediency! Expediency! He has made a Greek of you. If he kills us for defying him, good, let him kill us. Let us die with our pride."

"You know he'd not kill us. We should be where our enemies want, that's all. If I go to this wedding, if I give it countenance, everyone can see I rate it with all the rest, the Thracians and Illyrian girls and the other nobodies. Father knows that; can't you see that's why he asked me? He did it to save our faces."

"What? When you drink to my disgrace?"

"Would I do so? Accept, since it's true, that he won't forgo this girl. Very well: she's a Macedonian, the family's as old as ours; of course they stand out for marriage. That's why they threw her in his way, I knew it the first moment. Attalos has won this action. If we play into his hands, he'll win the war."

"They will only think you are taking your father's part against me, to keep his favor."

"They know me better." This thought had tormented him half the night.

"Feasting with his whore's kindred."

"A virgin of fifteen. She's only the bait, like the kid in a wolf-trap. Oh, she'll do her part, she's one of them; but in a year or two he'll have seen a younger one. It's Attalos who will use the time. Keep your mind on him."

"That we should come to this!" Though she spoke with bitter reproach, he took it as assent, having had enough.

In his room he found Hephaistion waiting. Here, too, most things had been said. For some time they sat side by side on the bed in silence. At length Hephaistion said, "You will know your friends."

"I know them now."

"The King's own friends should advise him. Can't Parmenion do it?"

"He tried, Philotas tells me . . . I know what Parmenion thinks. What I can't tell Mother is that I understand it."

Hephaistion, after a long wait, said, "Yes?"

"Since Father was sixteen, he's been in love with one who'll never have him. He's sent her flowers, she's thrown them out on the midden; he's sung at her window, she's emptied the chamber-pot on his head; he's offered for her hand, she's flaunted with his rivals. At last he couldn't stand more, and struck her; but he couldn't bear to see her lie at his feet, so he picked her up again. Then, though he'd mastered her, he was ashamed to go to her door; he sent me instead. Well, I went; and when all's done she's an old painted whore. And I pity him. I never thought I'd see the day, but it's true, I pity him. He deserves better. This girl here, I wish she were a dancer or a flute-player, or a boy for that matter; then we'd be out of trouble. But since she's what he wants . . ."

"And *that's* why you're going?"

"Oh, I can find better reasons. But that's why."

The wedding feast was held at Attalos' town house just outside Pella. He had just refurbished it, and not by halves; the columns were twined with gilded garlands, and statues of inlaid bronze had been shipped in from Samos. Nothing had been left out which could show that this marriage of the King's was unlike all others, except the first. As Alexander entered with his friends, and they looked about them, all eyes exchanged one thought. This was the mansion for a King's father-in-law, not the uncle of a concubine.

The bride sat throned among the splendors of her dowry and the groom's gifts; Macedon kept up older customs than the south. Gold and silver cups, rolls of fine weaving, trinkets and necklaces spread out on linen coverlets, inlaid tables on which stood caskets of spices and phials of scent, filled the bridal dais. Robed in saffron and crowned with white roses, she sat looking down at her folded hands. The guests called ritual blessings on her; her aunt beside her spoke thanks on her behalf.

In due time the women bore her off to the house prepared for her. The procession in the wedding car had been left out, as inappropriate. Alexander, viewing the kindred, felt sure that they had hankered for it. He had thought his anger was spent, till he saw their faces watching him.

The meat from the marriage sacrifice, richly dressed, was eaten, and the kickshaws after. Though the chimney had a hood, the hot room grew smoky. He noticed he was being left alone a good deal with his own friends. He was glad to have Hephaistion next him; but it should have been a kinsman of the bride's. Even the younger Attalids were clustered about the King.

Alexander murmured to Hephaistion, "Hurry up, Dionysos, we need you badly."

In fact, however, when the wine came in he drank lightly, as usual, being as moderate in this as in eating. Macedon was a land of good springs with safe pure water. One need never come to table thirsty, as men did in the hot lands of Asia with their deadly streams.

But, with no hosts in hearing, he and Hephaistion allowed themselves the kind of joke guests save for the journey home. The young men of his following, jealous that he had been slighted, read their smiles, and followed their lead with less discretion. The banquet hall became tinged with a scent of faction.

Alexander, growing uneasy at it, murmured to Hephaistion, "We had better make ourselves pleasant," and turned towards the company. When the bridgroom left the feast, they could slip away. He looked at his father; and saw he was already drunk.

His face was glazed and shining, he was bawling out old army songs with Attalos and Parmenion. Grease from the roast was streaked in his beard. He flung back to the company the immemorial jokes of defloration and prowess, showered on the bridegroom as ritually as the earlier raisins and grain. He had won his girl, he was among old friends, good fellowship prevailed, wine made his glad heart gladder. Alexander, scrupulously bathed, almost empty, and nearly sober, though not so sober as if he had eaten more, looked on in a silence which began to be felt around him.

Hephaistion, controlling his own anger, talked to neighbors to draw off notice. No decent master, he thought, would have inflicted this ordeal on a slave. He was angry, too, with himself. How had he not foreseen all this, why had he said nothing to keep Alexander away? He had held his peace, because he had a kindness for Philip, because it had seemed politic, and—he faced it now—in order to spite Olympias. Alexander had made this sacrifice, in one of those flashes of reckless magnanimity for which Hephaistion loved him. He should have been protected; some friend should have stepped in. He had been betrayed.

Through the rising noise he was saying something. ". . . she's one of the clan, but she's had no choice, she's barely out of the nursery . . ."

Hephaistion looked round startled. With all he had on his mind, this was one thing he had never thought of, that Alexander could be angry for the girl.

"It's mostly like this at weddings, you know that; it's custom."

"She was scared when first she met him. She kept a good face, but I could see."

"Well, he'll not be rough with her. It's not like him. He's used to women."

"Imagine it," murmured Alexander into his wine cup. He emptied it quickly and held it out. The boy came with the snow-cooled rhyton; soon after, attentive to his duties, he returned to fill it again.

"Save this one for the toasts," said Hephaistion watchfully.

Parmenion rose on the King's behalf to praise the bride, properly the office of the groom's nearest kinsman. Alexander's ironic smile was noticed by his friends, and returned too openly.

Parmenion had spoken at many weddings, some of them the King's. He was correct, simple, careful and brief. Attalos, a huge ornate gold goblet in his hand, swung down from his supper couch to make the speech of bestowal. It was clear at once that he was as drunk as Philip, and not carrying it so well.

His praise of the King was rambling and wordy, clumsiness defeating fulsomeness; the climaxes were maudlin and badly timed; the applause, which was rapturous, was a tribute to the King. It grew

less carefree as the speech warmed up. Parmenion had wished luck
to a man and woman. Attalos was wishing it, in all but the naked
words, to a King and Queen.

His supporters cheered, and knocked cups on tables. Alexander's
friends talked in undervoices meant to be heard. The uncommitted,
taken by surprise, dismayed, were revealed by silence.

Philip, not too drunk to know what it meant, fixed his bloodshot
black eye on Attalos, wrestling with his own fuddled slowness,
thinking how to stop the man. This was Macedon; he had quieted
plenty of after-dinner brawls; but he had never had to deal before
with a new father-in-law, self-styled or not. The others had known
their places and been grateful. His eye slewed round to his son.

"Don't notice it," Hephaistion was whispering. "The man's soused,
they all know it, they'll all have forgotten by morning." Early on
in the speech he had made his way from his own supper couch
to stand by Alexander's, who, his eyes fixed on Attalos, felt hard
and taut to the touch, like a catapult wound up.

Philip, looking that way, saw under the flushed brow and the gold
hair smoothed for the feast, the wide staring grey eyes pass from
Attalos' face to his. Olympias' rage; no, but that boiled quickly,
this was held in. Nonsense, I'm drunk, he's drunk, we're all drunk,
and why not? Why can't the boy take it easy like anyone else at a
feast? Let him swallow it, and behave.

Attalos was running on about the good old native blood of
Macedon. He had conned his speech well; but lured on by smiling
Dionysos, he knew he could now do better. In the person of this
fair maiden, the dear homeland took back her King to her breast,
with the blessing of the ancestral gods. "Let us pray to them," he
cried in sudden inspiration, "for a lawful, true-born heir."

There was an outbreak of muddled noise; applause, protest, dismay, clumsy efforts to smother danger in jollity. The voices changed,
and checked. Attalos, instead of drinking the toast, had clapped his
other hand to his head; blood showed between his fingers. Something bright, a silver drinking-cup, was clattering along the mosaic
floor. Alexander leaned forward on his supper couch, propped upon
one hand. He had thrown without getting up.

Uproar began, echoing in the high hall. His voice, which had
carried through the din of Cheironeia, called out, "You blackguard,

are you calling me a bastard?" The young men, his friends, yelled out indignant applause. Attalos, perceiving what had hit him, made a choking sound, and hurled his heavy goblet at Alexander, who measured its course and did not trouble to move; it fell short halfway. Friends and kinsmen shouted; it began to sound like a battlefield. Philip, furious and knowing now where to vent his anger, roared over the clamor, "How dare you, boy? How dare you? Behave yourself or go home."

Alexander hardly raised his voice. Like his cup, it struck where it was aimed.

"You filthy old goat. Will you never have any shame? All Hellas can wind your stink; what will you do in Asia? No wonder the Athenians laugh."

For a moment, the only answer was a sound of breathing like a laboring horse's. The red of the King's face deepened to purple. His hand fumbled about the couch. He alone here, in the ceremonial dress of the bridegroom, had a sword.

"Son of a whore!" He swung off the couch, upsetting his taper-legged supper table. There was a crash of cups and dessert plates. He grasped his sword-hilt.

"Alexander, Alexander," muttered Hephaistion desperately. "Come away, quick, come." As if he had not existed, Alexander slid neatly down on the far side of the couch, grasped the wood in both hands, and waited with a cold eager smile.

Panting and limping, drawn sword in hand, Philip stumbled through the mess upon the floor towards his enemy. His foot slipped on a fruit-paring; he came down hard on the lame leg, skidded, and crashed headlong among sweets and sherds.

Hephaistion took a step forward; for a moment, it had been instinct to help him up.

Alexander came round the supper couch. Hands on belt, head tilted, he looked down at the red stertorous cursing man sprawling in spilled wine and reaching about for his sword. "Look, men. Look who is getting ready to cross from Europe into Asia. And he falls flat crossing from couch to couch."

Philip pushed himself up with both hands onto his good knee. He had cut his palm on a broken plate. Attalos and his kinsmen ran, stumbling over each other, to his aid. During the scramble,

Alexander signed to his friends. They all followed him out, silently and promptly, as if in some night action at war.

From his post at the doorway, which through all this he had made no move to leave, Pausanias gazed after Alexander. So might a traveler in a thirsty desert look after the man who gave him a cool delicious drink. No one noticed. Alexander, gathering up supporters, had never given him a thought. From the beginning, he had never been an easy man to talk to.

Oxhead neighed in the courtyard; he had heard his master's war-voice. The young men tossed their festal wreaths upon the midden furred with frost, mounted without waiting for service, and galloped off on the rutted track with its thin-iced puddles towards Pella. In the Palace courtyard, in the glow of the night-flares, Alexander looked them over, reading all their faces.

"I am taking my mother to her brother's house in Epiros. Who will come with me?"

"I for one," said Ptolemy. "And *that* for their true-born heirs."

Harpalos, Niarchos and the others crowded up; from love, from loyalty, from ingrained faith in Alexander's fortune, from fear that the King and Attalos had marked them down; or from shame at being seen by others to hold back.

"No, not you, Philotas; you stay."

"I'll come," said Philotas quickly, looking around. "My father will forgive me, and if not what of it?"

"No, he's a better one than I have, you shan't offend him for me. Listen, the rest of you." His voice took the habit-formed note of brisk command. "We must get away now, before I'm locked up and my mother poisoned. Travel light, bring spare horses; all your weapons, what money you can lay your hands on; one day's food; any good servants fit to bear arms, I'll mount and arm them. All of your meet me here when the horn sounds for the next guard-change."

They dispersed, all but Hephaistion, who looked at him as someone in a sea without horizon looks at the steersman.

"He'll be sorry for this," Alexander said. "He counted on Alex-andros of Epiros. He put him on the throne, he's been to a deal of trouble for that alliance. Now he can go whistle for it, till Mother has her rights."

"And you?" said Hephaistion blankly. "Where are we going?"

"To Illyria. I can do more there. I understand the Illyrians. You remember Kossos? Father's nothing to him, he rebelled once and he would again. It's me he knows."

"You mean . . . ?" said Hephaistion, wishing there were need to ask.

"They're good fighters. They might do better, if they had a general."

Done is done, thought Hephaistion; and what did I do to save him? "Very well, if you think that best."

"The others need not come on beyond Epiros, unless they choose. Today's work today. We'll see how the Supreme Commander of all the Greeks likes to start for Asia with Epiros doubtful and Illyria arming for war."

"I'll pack for you. I know what to put in."

"It's lucky Mother can ride, we've no time for litters."

He found her with her lamp still burning, sitting in her high chair staring before her. She looked at him with reproach, knowing only that he came from the house of Attalos. The room smelled of bruised herbs and burned blood.

"You were right," he said, "and more than right. Get your jewels together; I have come to take you home."

His campaign bag, when he found it in his room, held as Hephaistion had promised all he would need. At the top sat the leather scroll-case of the Iliad.

The high road to the west led by way of Aigai. To avoid it, Alexander led them through the passes he had learned when he was training his men in hill warfare. The oaks and chestnuts on the foothills were black and bare; the tracks above the gorges were wet and slippery with fallen leaves.

In this back country, people seldom saw a stranger. They said they were pilgrims, going to Dodona to consult the oracle. No one who had glimpsed him on maneuver knew him now, in an old traveling hat and sheepskin cloak, unshaven, looking older. Coming down to Kastoria Lake with its willows and marshes and beaver dams, they spruced themselves up, knowing they would be recognized; but their story was the same and was not questioned. That the Queen was at odds with the King was ancient history; if she wanted advice from Zeus and Mother Dione, it was her own affair. They had outstripped rumor. Whether pursuit was following; whether they were being left to stray like unwanted dogs; whether Philip was sitting back in his old way to let time work for him, they could not tell.

Olympias had made no such journey since girlhood. But she had spent that in Epiros, where all journeys were overland because of the pirates from Korkyra with whom its coastline swarmed. The first day out, she was white with fatigue and shivering in the evening chill; they camped in a shepherd's bothy left empty when the flocks went down to the winter grazing-lands, not daring to trust a village so near home; but next day she woke fresh, and soon kept up with them like a man, eyes and cheeks glowing. Till they sighted a village she would ride astride.

Hephaistion rode behind among the others, watching the slight, cloaked figures, their heads together, conferring, planning, confiding. His enemy possessed the field. Ptolemy patronized him, meaning no harm, scarcely aware of it, bearing well the prestige of sacrifice. He had left Thais at Pella, after only a few months' bliss. Hephaistion, on the other hand, had done the only thing that was in him; like Oxhead, he was seen as a limb of Alexander. No one noticed him. It seemed to him they would journey on forever, just like this.

They struck southeast, towards the great watershed ranges between Macedon and Epiros, struggling through swollen streams; making for the hard short way, between the heights of Grammos and Pindos. Before they had climbed to the ridge where the red earth of Macedon peters out, it had begun to snow. The tracks were treacherous, the horses labored; they debated whether to turn back to Kastoria, rather than be benighted in the open. A rider threaded down to them between the beeches, and bade them honor the house of his absent master, who, though detained by duty, had sent word that they be entertained.

"This is Orestid country," said Alexander. "Who is your master, then?"

"Don't be foolish, my dear," Olympias murmured. She turned to the messenger. "We shall gladly be Pausanias' guests. We know he is our friend."

In the massive old fort which stuck out on a spur from the woods behind it, they were given hot baths, good food and wine, warm beds. Pausanias it seemed kept a wife here, though all other court officers brought their wives to Pella. She was a tall strapping mountain girl, born to simplicity but burdened with half-knowledge. Her husband, in some distant place before they met, had once been wronged, in a way never made clear to her; his day was yet to come; these were his friends against his enemies, and must be made welcome. But against whom would Olympias be a friend? Why was the Prince here, when he was a general of the Companions? She lapped them in comfort; but alone at bedtime, in the great room Pausanias visited for two or three weeks a year, she heard an owl hoot and a wolf howl, and round her lamp the shadows thickened. Her father had been killed in the north by Bardelys, her grandfather in the west by Perdikkas. When the guests had gone next day, in charge of a good guide as Pausanias had directed, she went down into the rock-cut cellars, counting over the arrowheads and the stores.

They climbed through a chestnut forest, where even the local bread was of chestnut flour; then up through firs to the head of the pass. The sun gleamed on the fallen snow, and filled the huge horizons; here was the frontier set by earth-shaping gods. Olympias looked back eastward; her lips moved in ancient words she had learned of a witch from Egypt; she whispered them to a stone of the proper shape she had brought along, and cast the stone behind her.

In Epiros the snows were melting; they had to wait three days in a peasant village to cross a flooded river, their horses stabled in a cave. But at last they reached the Molossian lands.

The rolling plateau was famous for hard winters; but their snow-waters made rich pasture. Huge long-horned cattle grazed, the choicest sheep wore leather jackets, to shield their fine wool from thorns; their guard-dogs were as big as they. The towering oaks prized by shipwrights and builders, the sacred wealth of the land, stood bare, weathering themselves for coming centuries. Villages were well built, with crowds of healthy children.

Olympias had dressed her hair, and put on a gold chain. "Achilles' forebears came from here. His son Neoptolemos lived here with Andromache, when he came from Troy. It is through me that their blood comes down to you. We were the first of all the Hellenes. They all took the name from us."

Alexander nodded; he had been hearing this all his life. This was a rich land; it had had no High King till lately; and the King, for all he was Olympias' brother, owed it all to Philip. He rode in thought.

While their courier rode on to announce them, the young men shaved and combed by a rocky pool. It was icy, but Alexander bathed. They all unpacked their best clothes and put them on.

Soon, showing dark and glittering against the half-melted snow, they descried a train of horsemen. King Alexandros was giving them a kinsman's welcome.

He was a tall auburn man, not much over thirty; his strong beard hid the family mouth, but one could see the family nose; his eyes were deep-set, restless, alert. He kissed his sister in greeting and said proper things. He had long been prepared for this unwelcome moment, and brought as good a grace to it as he could. To her marriage he owed his kingdom; but since then, he could not think of much she had left undone to pull him down. From her raging letter, he could not make out if Philip had yet divorced her; in any case he must take her in, and maintain her injured innocence, to keep the family honor out of the dirt. By herself she was trouble enough. He had hoped against certainty that she would not bring along that firebrand son, reputed to have killed his man at twelve and never sat down a day in quiet since.

With distrust, quickly concealed by civil gestures, the King glanced at the troop of young men with firm-boned Macedonian faces, barbered like southern Greeks. They looked tough, watchful, close-knit; what trouble did they mean to brew here? The kingdom was settled, the tribal lords called him hegemon, followed him to war and paid their taxes; the Illyrians kept their own side the border; he had dislodged, only this year, two pirate holds, the local peasants had thanked him with hymns. Who would follow him to war against the might of Macedon, who would bless him after? No one. Philip, if he marched, would march right up to Dodona and make a new High King. Moreover, Alexandros had always liked the man. As he rode between his sister and his nephew and felt the crackling air, he hoped his wife at home would be fit to receive the guests; he had left her in tears, she was pregnant, too.

Coming down to Dodona, a twisting pass strung them out, the King ahead. Alexander, riding close to Olympias, murmured, "Don't tell him what I mean to do. About yourself, what you like. About me, know nothing."

Startled and angry, she said, "What has he done that you doubt him?"

"Nothing. I have to think, I need time."

Dodona sat in a high valley, under a long snow-swept range. A fierce wind crusted them with fine hail like meal. The walled town clasped the hillside; below, the sacred precinct was guarded only by a low fence, and its gods. In the midst of it, dwarfing altars and shrines like toys, a vast oak lifted its bare black labyrinth above the snow. The wind carried up to them a deep booming resonance, rising and falling with the blasts.

The town gates swung open. As they formed up for their entry, Alexander said, "Uncle, I should like to visit the oracle before I go. Will you ask when the next auspicious day is?"

"By all means, yes." He spoke with new warmth, adding the proper well-omened formula, "God and good luck." The auspicious day could not come too soon. He had been a boy when Olympias married; she had always bullied him, he had had no time to outgrow it. Now she must learn he was master of his house. This war-weathered, war-scarred youth, with his mad brooding eyes and his troop of well-groomed outlaws, would not help. Let him go his own way to Hades, and leave sensible men in peace.

The townsmen greeted their King with unforced loyalty. He had led them well against their many enemies, and was less greedy than the warring chiefs had been. A crowd gathered; for the first time since leaving Pella, Oxhead heard the familiar cheers, the shouts of "Alexandros!" His head went up, he fell into his proud parade gait. Alexander sat straight-backed, looking ahead; Hephaistion glancing sidelong saw him pale as if half his blood had been drained away. He kept his countenance, and answered his kinsman calmly; but when they reached the royal house, he was still white about the mouth. The Queen forgot her own sickness, and called to her servants to hurry the mulled wine; only yesterday, a drover had been found frozen on the pass above.

The snow had ceased, but still lay on the ground, frosted over, and brittle to the foot. A pale hard sun glittered on the drifts and the tufted shrubs; a thin icy wind came searching down from the mountains. In the white landscape, like an old cloth, was a cleared space of winter-browned grass and black dank oak-mast. The sanctuary slaves had shoveled the snow away against the oaken palings; it lay in soiled heaps, speckled with leaves and acorn-husks.

A young man in a sheepskin cloak walked up to the doorless gateway of massive, time-blackened beams.

From the lintel, dangling on ropes of hide, hung a deep bronze bowl. He picked up a staff propped by the post, and struck smartly. Long shudders of sound, like rings in water, throbbed on and on; a deep answering hum came from somewhere beyond. The great tree brooded, its crotches and knots and old birds' nests full of snow. Ancient rude altars, the dedications of centuries, stood in the open round it.

It was the oldest oracle in Greece. Its power came from Egyptian Ammon, the father of all oracles, older than time. Dodona had spoken before Apollo came to Delphi.

The wind, which had been quietly keening in the high branches, swept down in a violent gust. A wild clangor broke out ahead; on a marble column stood a bronze boy holding a scourge, with lashes of bronze chain which, whirled by the wind, struck a bronze cauldron with their weighted ends. It was an acoustic vessel like those sometimes used in the theaters. The din was thunderous. All round the sacred tree, standing on tripods, were hollow bronzes; the sound dwindled along them, like thunder rumbling away after a great clap. Before it had died, another gust lifted the scourge. From a little stone house beyond the tree, peering grey heads poked out.

Alexander's mouth smiled as it did when he charged in battle. He strode on towards the thrumming precinct. A third gust blew; a third time the cycle of noise revolved and faded. The former murmurous quiet returned.

From the thatched stone hut, muttering together, mothy fur cloaks clutched round them, came three old women. They were the Doves, the servants of the oracle. As they shuffled forward over the wet black oak-mast, it could be seen that their ankles were wrapped in woolen rags, but their feet were bare, cracked, and ingrained with grime. They drew power from the touch of earth and must never lose it; it was the law of the sanctuary.

One was a strong old woman, big-boned, who looked to have done a man's farm-work most of her life. The second was short, round and severe, with a pointed nose and outthrust lower lip. The third was a tiny bent crone, dry and brown as an old acorn-husk. She was reputed to have been born in the year Perikles died.

Shrugged in their furs, they looked about, their eyes returning, it seemed, in surprise to this single pilgrim. The tall one whispered to the round one. The old one trotted forward on shriveled bird-feet, and fingered him like a curious child. Her eyes had a blue-white film, she was almost blind.

The round one said, in a sharp voice edged with wariness, "How do you wish to question Zeus and Dione? Do you want the name of the god you should offer to, to win your wish?"

Alexander said, "I shall tell my question to the god alone. Give me the things to write with."

The tall one bent towards him with awkward kindness; she moved like a farm animal, and smelled like one. "Yes, yes, only the god will see. But the lots are in two jars; one for the gods to be propitiated; the other for Yes or No. Which shall we set out?"

"Yes or No."

The old one still clutched a fold of his cloak in her tiny fist, with the assurance of a child whose beauty makes it welcome. Suddenly she piped up, from down near his waist, "Take care with your wish. Take care."

He bent down over her, and asked softly, "Why, Mother?"

"Why? Because the god will grant it."

He put his hand on her head, a little shell of bone in a woolen clout, and, caressing it, looked over her at the black depths of the oak. The other two looked at one another. Neither spoke.

He said, "I am ready."

They went off into a low-roofed sanctuary house beside their dwelling, the old one trotting behind squeaking muddled orders, like any great-grandmother who has got into a kitchen to annoy the women at work. They could all be heard bustling and grumbling, as at some inn caught unready by a guest who cannot be turned away.

The huge ancient branches stretched above him, splintering the pale sun. The central trunk was folded and ribbed with age; into its fissures small votives had been thrust by worshippers, in times so remote that the bark had almost engulfed them. A part was crumbled with rot, and wormholed. Summer would reveal what bare winter hid, that some of the main limbs were dead. Its first root had thrust from the acorn while Homer was still alive; it was near its time.

From around its massive center, where the boughs forked, came a sleepy cooing and moaning; in hollows, and little cotes nailed here and there, the sacred doves were huddled, couple by couple, fluffed up and pressed together against the cold. As he came near, one gave from its hidden darkness a loud "Roo-co-coo!"

The women came out, the tall one with a low wooden table, the round one with an ancient jar, painted black on red. They set jar on table under the tree. The old one put into his hands a strip of soft lead, and a bronze stylos.

He laid the strip on an old stone altar, and wrote firmly; the deep letters shone silvery in the dull lead. GOD AND GOOD LUCK. ALEXANDER ASKS ZEUS OF THE SANCTUARY, AND DIONE, WILL THE THING I HAVE IN MY MIND COME TO PASS? Having folded the strip in three, so that the words were hidden, he dropped it in the jar. He had learned what to do, before he came.

The tall woman stood by the table, and lifted her arms. There was a priestess painted on the jar, standing just so. The invocation was in the jargon of some foreign tongue, corrupted long since by time and ignorance; the vowels were drawn out, to mimic a dove. Presently one replied; there was a low murmuring, all round the heart of the tree.

Alexander stood watching, his mind upon his wish. The tall priestess put her hand in the jar, and was beginning to grope about, when the old one came up and twitched her cloak, scolding as shrilly as a monkey. "It was promised me," she chattered. "Promised me." The other stood back, her eyes startled, stealing a glance at him; the round one clucked, but did nothing. The old woman pushed back her robe from her stick-thin arm, like a housewife pot-scouring, and thrust it inside. There was a rattling of the small oak tablets on which the lots were carved.

Through these delays, Alexander stood waiting, his eyes fixed on the jar. The black-painted priestess stood in her stiff archaic posture, showing her lifted palms. At her feet, twined round the leg of her painted table, was a painted snake.

It was drawn with skill and vigor, its head thrust upward. The table-leg was short, like a low bed's, it would climb up easily. It was a house-snake, which knew a secret. While the old woman muttered and scratched about, he frowned at it, trying to trace back, into the darkness from which it had crept forth, a sense of some ancient anger, some enormous wound, some mortal insult unavenged. Images formed. He faced again a giant enemy. The stream of his breath dispersed in the cold air; through a long pause no new breath followed, then a sound escaped him, bitten off into silence. His fingers and teeth had clenched themselves. His memories opened and bled.

The old woman straightened up. In her grimy claw she held the folded lead, and two wooden lots. The others hurried to her; the law was to bring out one lot, that lying nearest to the lead; they hissed at her, like nurses at a child who does an unseemly thing in ignorance. She lifted her head—her backbone was past straightening —and in a younger, commanding voice said, "Stand back! I know what I have to do." For a moment it could be seen that she had once been beautiful.

Leaving the lead on the table, she came towards him, both hands held out, a lot in each. Opening the right, she said, "For the wish in your mind." She opened the left, saying, "And for the wish in your heart."

Each of the little black wood-blocks was carved with "Yes."

8

KING PHILIP's newest wife had had her firstborn. It was a girl.

The downcast midwife brought it from the lying-in room. He took in his hands, with ritual signs of approval, the little red crumpled thing, brought naked to prove it free from blemish. Attalos, who had been haunting the house since the birth-waters broke, craned over, his face red and crumpled too; he must have hoped against hope till he saw the sex for himself. His pale blue eyes followed it with hatred as it was carried back; he would as soon have thrown it in the lake like an unwanted bitch pup, Philip thought. Often it made him feel foolish that he seemed to sire five girls for every boy; but this time he had heard the news with deep relief.

Eurydike was all he liked in a girl, sensual without looseness, eager to please without fuss, never making scenes. Gladly, any day, he would have put her in Olympias' place. He had half-thought, even, of having the witch put out of the way for good; it would solve all problems, she had blood-guilt enough on her hands to make it a rough justice, and there were people to be hired as skilled in such matters as she. But however well it was managed, the boy would know. Nothing would hide it from him; he would pluck the truth from air. And then?

[311]

And now? Well, this girl-child gave breathing-space. Attalos had told him a dozen times that their family ran to boys. Now let him keep quiet awhile. Philip put off decision, as he had been doing these ten months.

His plans for the war in Asia went forward smoothly. Weapons were made and stored, levies came in, horses were broke for cavalry; gold and silver flowed out like water, to contractors, to paymasters, to agents and client rulers. The troops drilled and maneuvered, ready and disciplined, swapping legends about the fabled wealth of Asia and the vast ransoms of captive satraps. But a gloss had gone, a resonance, a crackle and spark, a smile on the face of danger.

There were also rubs more palpable. A savage brawl, which would beget half a dozen blood-feuds, had broken out in a Pella wineshop, between cavalry of Attalos' tribal levy, and those of a corps lately renamed Nikanor's Horse, though no one who valued his life would call it this in hearing of its men. Philip sent for the chief offenders; they glared at each other and were evasive, till the youngest, heir of an ancient house that had helped a dozen kings in or out and well remembered it, lifted his shaven chin and said defiantly, "Well, sir, they were slandering your son."

Philip told them to look after their own households, and leave his to him. Attalos' men, who had hoped to hear him say, "I have no son yet," went grieved away. Soon after, he sent out yet another spy, to learn what was going on in Illyria.

To Epiros he sent none; he knew where he was, there. He had had a letter he perfectly understood; the protest of a man of honor, carried just as far as honor required. One could almost see the drawn line. He replied with equal nicety. The Queen had left him from self-will and sullen temper, having suffered no legal injuries. (He was on good ground here; not every Epirote royal house had been monogamous.) She had turned his son against him; the young man's present exile was her fault alone. The letter contained no mortal insults. It would be understood in its turn. But what was happening in Illyria?

Some few of the young men had ridden home from Epiros, bringing a letter.

Alexander to Philip King of the Macedonians, greeting. I send back to you and to their fathers these men, my friends. They are guilty of no wrong. In kindness they escorted the Queen and me into Epiros; this done, we required no more of them. When the Queen, my mother, is restored to her rights and dignity, we will return. Till then I shall do as I think good, asking no man's leave.

Greet for me the soldiers I led at Cheironeia, and those who served under me in Thrace. And do not forget the man who was saved by my shield, when the Argives mutinied before Perinthos. You know his name. Farewell.

In his private reading-cell, Philip crumpled the letter and threw it down; then, bending stiffly with his lame leg, picked it up, flattened out the creases, and locked it away.

One after another, the spies from the west brought in uneasy news, never facts one could grip on. The names of the small close band were always there. Ptolemy: ah, if I could have bride-bedded his mother it would have been a different tale. Niarchos: a good sea-officer, due for promotion if he'd had sense. Harpalos: I never trusted that limping fox, but the boy would have him. Erigyios . . . Laomedon . . . Hephaistion, well, as soon part a man from his shadow. Philip brooded a moment, in the sad resenting envy of the man who believes himself always to have sought the perfect love, not owning that he has grudged the price.

The names never varied; the news always did. They were at Kossos' fort; at the castle of Kleitos, who was as near a High King as Illyria would stomach; they were on the Lynkestid border. They were on the coast, said to be asking after ships for Korkyra, for Italy, for Sicily, even for Egypt. They had been sighted in the ranges beside Epiros. They were rumored to be buying arms, to be hiring spearmen, to be training an army in some forest lair. Whenever Philip needed to dispose his troops for the war in Asia, one of these alarms would come in, and he must spare a regiment for the border. Without doubt, the boy was in touch with friends in Macedon. On paper, the King's war-plans remained unaltered; but his generals could feel him hanging fire, awaiting the next report.

In a castle perched on a craggy headland by a wooded Illyrian bay, Alexander stared up at the night-shrouded, smoke-black rafters. He had spent the day hunting, like the day before. His bed was of rushes, full of fleas, in the guest-corner of the hall; here, among dogs crunching the bones from old suppers, the bachelors of the household slept. His head ached. A draft of clean air blew from the doorway; the moonlit sky looked bright there. He got up and threw his blanket round him. It was soiled and torn; his good one had been stolen some months before, about the time of his birthday. In a nomad camp near the border, he had turned nineteen.

He steered past sleeping bodies, stumbling on one, which grunted curses. Outside on the bare crag ran a narrow rampart. The cliff plunged straight to the sea; far down, moon-gleaming foam crawled round the boulders. He knew the footsteps behind and did not turn. Hephaistion leaned on the wall beside him.

"What is it? Couldn't you sleep?"

"I woke," Alexander said.

"Have you got the gripes again?"

"It stinks in there."

"Why do you drink that dog-piss? I'd sooner go to bed sober."

Alexander gave him a look like a silent growl. His arm propped on the wall was scored by the claws of a dying leopard. All day he had been in movement; now he was still, looking down the giddy drop to the sea.

At last he said, "We can't keep it up much longer."

Hephaistion frowned at the night. He was glad, however, to be told; it was being asked he had most dreaded. "No," he said. "I doubt we can."

Alexander picked some stone chips from the wall-top, and pitched them down at the shimmering sea. No ripple showed, no sound returned from the depth, even when they struck rock. Hephaistion did nothing. He offered his presence, as his omens had directed him.

"Even a fox," said Alexander presently, "runs through all its tricks in time. And the second time round, the nets are waiting."

"You've often had luck from the gods."

"Time's running out," Alexander said. "It's a feel one gets in war. You remember Polydoros with his dozen men, trying to hold that fort in the Chersonesos. All those helmets propped on the walls; moved, too, now and again. I was fooled into sending for reinforcements, two days, remember? Then a catapult knocked off a helmet and showed the stake. It was bound to happen; his time ran out. Mine will run out when some Illyrian chief crosses the border on his own account, for cattle, or a feud, and Philip hears I wasn't leading. I'll never fool him after that, he knows me too well."

"You could still lead a raid, it's not too late to change your mind. If you pushed a little way in, and withdrew from strength . . . With all he has to do, it's not likely he'd come in person."

"How can I know that? No, I had a warning . . . a kind of warning . . . at Dodona."

Hephaistion stored away this news in silence. It was the most Alexander had ever told him of it.

"Alexander. Your father wants you back. I know it. You should believe me. I've known it all along."

"Good. Then he can do right by my mother."

"No, not only for the war in Asia. You don't want to hear this, but he loves you. You may not like the way it takes him. The gods have many faces, Euripides says."

Alexander laid his hands on the broken stone, and turned on his friend his entire attention. "Euripides wrote for actors. Masks, you can say; yes, masks; some pretty, some not. But one face. Only one."

A meteor flared down with a yellow-green glowing head and fading red trail, and plunged into the distant sea. Hephaistion put happiness briskly by, like a cup drunk down in haste. "It's an omen for you. You must decide tonight. You know; you came out to do it."

"I woke up, and the place stank like a midden." A tuft of pale wallflower had rooted itself among the stones; he fingered it unseeingly. Like a great weight thrown suddenly on his shoulder, Hephaistion felt an awareness of being leaned upon, of being needed for more than love. It brought no joy; it was like glimpsing the first mark of a deadly sickness. Rust; he can bear anything but rust.

"Tonight," he said quietly. "Nothing to wait for, you know it all."

Without movement, Alexander seemed to gather himself together, to grow more compact. "Yes. First, I'm spending time, not using it. This I've never felt before. Second, there are two or three men, and I think King Kleitos is one of them, who once they're sure they can't use me against my father, will want to send him my head. And, third . . . he's mortal, no man knows his hour. If he died, and I away over the border . . ."

"That, too," said Hephaistion calmly. "Well, then, as you say. You want to go home, he wants you back. You've exchanged mortal insults, no one will speak first. So you must find a proper go-between. Who is it going to be?"

Firmly now, as if it had been some time settled, Alexander said, "Demaratos of Corinth. He likes us both, he'll enjoy the importance, he'll do it well. Whom shall we send him?"

It was Harpalos, with his sad graceful limp, his dark vivid face, his quick smile and flattering grave attentiveness, who rode south. They convoyed him to the Epirote border, for fear of robbers; but he carried no letter with him. It was the essence of his mission, that no record of it should exist. He took only his mule, a change of clothing, and his golden charm.

Philip learned with pleasure that his old guest-friend Demaratos had business in the north, and would like to visit him. He was at pains to choose the supper, and hire a good sword-dancer to enliven it. Food and dancer were cleared away; they settled down to their wine. Corinth being the listening-post for all southern Greece, Philip asked at once for news. He had heard of some rub between Thebes and Sparta; what did Demaratos think?

Demaratos, a privileged guest and proud of it, fed with the expected cue, shook his distinguished iron-grey head. "Ah, King! That I should hear you ask if the Greeks are living in harmony! With your own house in the midst of war."

Philip's dark eye, not yet much engorged with wine, slewed sharply round. His trained diplomatist's ear had picked up a certain note, a shade of preparation. He gave no sign of this. "That boy. He flares up at a spark, like pitch. A silly speech from a man in liquor, only worth a laugh next day if he'd kept the sense he was born with. But he runs off in a blaze to his mother; and you know *her*."

Demaratos made sounds of fellow feeling. A thousand pities, he said, that with the mother of such a jealous temper, the young man

should feel his future threatened by her disgrace. He quoted fault-
lessly (having had them ready) some apt elegiacs of Simonides.

"Cutting off his own nose," said Philip, "to spite his face. A boy
with his gifts, the waste of it. We'd get along well enough, but for
that witch. He should know better. Well, by now he'll have paid for
it. He'll have had a bellyful of Illyrian hill-forts. But if he thinks
I'll . . ."

It was not till next morning that the talking began in earnest.

Demaratos was in Epiros, the King's most honored guest. He
would be escorting back to Pella the King's sister and her pardoned
son. Being rich already, he must chiefly be paid in kudos. King
Alexandros toasted him in an heirloom gold cup, and begged him
to accept it as a small memento. Olympias put out for him all her
social graces; if her enemies called her vixenish, let him judge for
himself. Alexander, wearing the one good chiton he had left, was
most attentive; till one evening when a tired stiff old man came
plodding down to Dodona on a weary mule. It was Phoinix. He
had met hard weather on the pass, and almost fell from the saddle
into his foster son's lifted arms.

Alexander demanded a hot bath, sweet oils, and a skilled bath-
man; no one in Dodona, it turned out, had ever heard of such a
calling. He went in to rub Phoinix down himself.

The royal bath was an antique affair of painted clay, much
mended and prone to leak; there was no couch, he had had to send
for one. He worked on the knotted-up thigh muscles, following
their path as Aristotle had shown him, kneading and tapping as,
at home, he had taught his slave to do. In Illyria, he had been
doctor to all the others. Even when, knowledge or memory failing,
he had relied upon omens seen in dreams, they had preferred him
to the local witch-wife.

"Ugh, aah, that's better, that's where it always catches me. Have
you studied with Cheiron, like Achilles?"

"No teacher like necessity. Now turn over."

"Those scars on your arm are new."

"My leopard. I had to give the skin to my host."

"Did the blankets reach you safely?"

"Did you send blankets too? They're all thieves in Illyria. I got the books; they can't read, and by luck they weren't short of tinder. The books were the best. They stole Oxhead, once."

"What did you do?"

"Went after the man and killed him. He'd not gone far, Oxhead wouldn't let him mount." He kneaded Phoinix' hamstring.

"You had us all on edge half a year and more. Here and there like a fox." Alexander laughed shortly, not pausing in his work. "But time went by, and you're not one for putting off. Your father set it down to your natural feeling. As I told him he should." Phoinix screwed round his head to look.

Alexander straightened up, wiping off his oily hands on a towel. "Yes," he said slowly. "A natural feeling, yes, you may call it that."

Phoinix withdrew his steps from the deep water, as he had learned when to do. "And did you see battle, Achilles, in the west?"

"Once, a tribal war. One has to support one's host. We won." He pushed back his steam-moistened hair. His nose and mouth looked pinched. He threw the towel hard into a corner.

Phoinix thought, He has learned to boast of what he suffered under Leonidas; it taught him endurance; I have heard him at Pella and smiled. But these months he will never boast of; and the man who smiles should take care.

As if he had spoken aloud, Alexander said, in sudden anger, "Why did my father demand I should ask his pardon?"

"Well, come, he's a bargaining man. Every bargain starts with asking too much. In the end he didn't press it." Phoinix swung down his stocky wrinkled legs from the couch. By it was a little deep window, with a marten's nest in an upper corner; on the sill, speckled with droppings, lay an ivory comb with chipped teeth, in which clung some reddish hairs from King Alexandros' beard. Combing himself, his face shielded, Phoinix looked his nurseling over.

He has conceived that he could fail. Yes, even he. He has seen there are rivers over which, once the spate has risen, there is no way back. Some dark night in that land of robbers, he has seen himself, who knows what? A strategos of mercenaries, hired out to some satrap at war with the Great King, or to some third-rate Sicilian tyrant; maybe a wandering comet, such as Alkibiades once was, a nine days' wonder every few years, then burnt out in darkness. For a moment he has seen it. He likes to show his war-scars; this scar he will cover like a slave-brand, he hides it even from me.

"Come! The bargain's struck; wipe old scores away and start with the tablet clean. Remember what Agamemnon said to Achilles, when they were reconciled:

"But what could I do? All things come to pass from God.
Blindness of heart is old-born of Zeus, Ate the deadly,
Who fools us all.

Your father has felt it. I have seen it in his face."

Alexander said, "I can lend you a cleaner comb than that." He put it back under the bird's nest, and brushed his fingers. "Well, we know what Achilles said:

"This has been all to the good for Hector, and for the Trojans;
The Greeks, though, I think will long remember our falling out.
Even so, we will put it all by, finished and done with,
Though it hurts us, beating down the inward passion because we
must."

He picked up the fresh chiton creased from Phoinix' saddlebag, dropped it neatly over his head like a well-trained page, and handed him his sword belt.

"Ah, child, you've always been a good boy to me." Phoinix fiddled with the buckle, head down. He had meant these words to open an exhortation; but, the rest failing him, he left them to stand as they were.

Nikanor's Horse was again Alexander's squadron.

The haggling had lasted some time; many couriers between Demaratos and the King had crossed the rough tracks into Epiros. It was the center of the bargain, achieved with much maneuvering, that neither party should claim an outright victory. When father met son at length, both felt that enough had been said already; they excused themselves from going over it again in words. Each eyed the other with curiosity, resentment, suspicion, regret, and a half-hope which each hid too well.

Mary Renault

Under Demaratos' complacent eyes, they exchanged a symbolic kiss of reconcilement. Alexander led up his mother; Philip kissed her too, noting to himself the lines of pride and rancor etched deeper in, and recalling with wonder, for a moment, his youthful passion. Then they all went off to take up their lives as they found them now.

Most men about the court had been able, so far, to avoid taking sides. Only small groups of partisans, Attalids, agents of Olympias, friends and comrades of Alexander, had bickered and intrigued. But the exiles' living presence was like verjuice stirred into milk. Separation began.

The young knew that he was young and had excelled his elders; that when old envious men had tried to put him down, he had stood up to it and won. He was all their own smoldering rebellions, expressed in flame; their hero-victim. Because it was his, they made even Olympias' cause their own. To see one's mother shamed, and one's father, an old man past forty, make a public show of himself with a girl of fifteen; why should one swallow that? When they saw him, therefore, they greeted him with defiant fervor. He never failed to acknowledge it.

His face was thinner. It had been weathered for years, but the closed drawn look was new. Their salutations changed it; his warm confiding smile made them feel rewarded.

Hephaistion, Ptolemy, Harpalos and the rest, the companions of his exile, were treated with awed respect, their stories becoming legend. They did not fail their friend. All the tales were of success; the leopard, the lightning marches to the border, a glorious victory in the tribal war. Their pride was invested in him, besides their love; they would have changed, if they could, his very memories. His thanks, though unspoken, were enough; they felt themselves beloved. Soon they seemed acknowledged leaders, to the young men and to themselves as well; they began to show it, sometimes with discretion, sometimes not.

His party gathered; made up of men who liked him, or had fought beside him; who, perhaps, wounded and half-frozen in Thrace had been given his own place by the fire and a drink from his own wine cup; or whose courage had been damping out when he came along and kindled it; or who had told him tales in the

[320]

guardroom when he was a child: supported by men who looked back to the lawless years, and wanted a strong heir; by men, also, who hated his enemies. The Attalids were daily growing in power and pride. Parmenion, some time widowed, had lately married Attalos' daughter, and the King had stood as groomsman.

The first time Alexander met Pausanias out of others' hearing, he thanked him for his house's hospitality. The bearded lips moved stiffly, as if they would have returned his smile had they not lost the knack. "It was nothing, Alexander. We were honored . . . I would do more than that." For a moment their eyes met, Pausanias' exploring, Alexander's questioning; but he had never been an easy man to understand.

Eurydike had a fine new house on the slope, a short walk from the Palace. A pine wood had been felled to clear the site, and a statue of Dionysos, which had stood in the grove, returned to Queen Olympias, who had set it up. It had not been a shrine of ancient sanctity, only a fancy of hers, to which rumor attached some scandal.

Hephaistion, who had arrived too late to know much about such things, knew like anyone else that a son's legitimacy hangs on his mother's honor. Of course he must defend her, he had no choice; but why with such passion, such bitterness to his father, such blindness to his own good? True friends share everything, except the past before they met.

That she had her faction, everyone knew too well; her rooms were like the meeting-house of some exiled opposition in the southern states. Hephaistion felt his teeth on edge, whenever Alexander went there. Did even he know all she was up to? Whatever it was, if trouble broke the King would believe he knew.

Hephaistion too was young; he had shared the shock when time-servers, once assiduous, now kept their distance. Alexander's very victories were their warning. In Macedon with its history, he was marked dangerous as brightly as the panther. He had always despised servility; but rooted in him was the need to be beloved. Now he was learning which men had known and used it. Watching the lesson, with grim quiet irony, was the King.

"You should try to mend matters," Hephaistion would say. "He must want to, or why recall you? It's always for the younger to come forward first, no disgrace in that."

[321]

"I don't like the way he looks at me."

"He may think the same, you're both on edge. But how can you doubt you're his heir? Who else is there? Arridaios?"

The idiot had been in Pella lately, for one of the great festivals. His mother's kin always brought him, spruced and combed, to pay his respects to his father, who had acknowledged him with pride when, a fine healthy-looking infant, he had been brought out of the birth-room. Now at seventeen he was taller than Alexander, and favored Philip's looks except when his mouth fell open. He was no longer taken to the theater, where he would laugh loudly at the tragic climaxes, nor to solemn rites, in case one of his fits should take him, when he would flap on the ground like a landed fish, wetting and dirtying himself. It was the fits had done some violence to his mind, the doctors said; he had been a likely child before them. He enjoyed the sideshows of the feast, led about by an old family slave like a little boy with his pedagogue. This year his black beard had grown; but he would not be parted from his doll.

"What a rival!" Hephaistion said. "Why can't you be easy?"

After giving this good advice, he would go out, run into some man of the Attalid faction, or even one of Olympias' many enemies; would resent what they said, and hit them in the teeth. All Alexander's friends were doing their share of this; Hephaistion, being quick-tempered, did rather more. True friends share everything, especially their quarrels. Later he might reproach himself; but all of them knew they would get no reproach from Alexander for these proofs of love. It was not that he set them on to make trouble; only that there grew up around him that kind of defiant loyalty from which sparks are struck, as if from flint.

He hunted untiringly, best pleased when the quarry was dangerous, or gave him a long hard chase. He read little, but to the purpose; his restlessness needed action, he was only content when readying his men for the coming war. He seemed everywhere, demanding from the engineers catapults which could be taken apart and carted, not left behind to rot after every siege; in the horse-lines, looking at feet, inspecting the stable floors and discussing fodder. He talked much with traveling men, traders and envoys, actors, paid-up mercenaries, who knew Greek Asia and even the lands beyond. All they told him, he checked stage by stage against Xenophon's *Inland March.*

Hephaistion, whom he shared his studies with, saw all his hopes staked on the war. He was scarred by the months of impotence as if by a fetter; he needed the medicine of command, victory to confound his enemies and heal his pride. He still took for granted he would be sent ahead, alone or with Parmenion, to make good an Asian bridgehead for the main force. Hephaistion, concealing his own uneasiness, asked if he had talked of it with the King. "No. Let him come to me."

The King, though busy himself, was watchful. He saw tactical changes which should have had his sanction and waited to be asked, in vain. He saw the young man's altered face, and his friends as thick as thieves. It had never been easy to read his mind, but once he would have come with all this as soldier to soldier; he could not have kept it in. As a man, Philip was hurt and angry; as a ruler, he was distrustful.

He had just had good news; he had brought off an alliance of priceless strategic value. In his heart, he was longing to boast of it to his son. But, if the boy was too stiff-necked to consult his father and King, he could not expect to be consulted. Let him learn for himself, or from his mother's spies.

It was from Olympias, therefore, that he heard of Arridaios' coming marriage.

The satrapy of Karia, on the southern curve of the Asian coast, was ruled under the Great King by its native dynasts. The great Mausolos, before he was laid in his grandiose Mausoleum, had built himself a little empire, seawards to Rhodes, Kos and Chios, south down the coast to Lykia. The succession, though in dispute, had passed firmly to Pixodoros, his younger brother. He paid tribute and did formal homage; the Great King took care to ask no more. After Syracuse sank back to anarchy, and before the rise of Macedon, Karia had been the greatest power on the Middle Sea. Philip had long been watching her, sending secret envoys, playing her on a silken line. Now he was hauling in. He had betrothed Arridaios to Pixodoros' daughter.

Olympias learned of it one morning at the theater, during a tragedy put on to honor the Karian envoys.

Mary Renault

Alexander, when she sent for him, was not found at once. He had gone backstage with Hephaistion, to congratulate Thettalos. The play had been *The Madness of Herakles*. Hephaistion wondered, after, how he could have missed the omen.

Thettalos was now about forty, at the height of his powers and fame. So versatile that he could give a performance in any mask from Antigone to Nestor, he still triumphed in hero roles. This one had been demanding. His mask only just off, he was careless of his face, which for a moment revealed concern at what he saw; after absence, changes show. He had heard things, too, and took trouble to make it clear that his own loyalty was unshaken.

From the theater, Hephaistion went off to spend an hour with his parents, who had come into town for the feast. When he returned, it was to the center of a hurricane.

Alexander's room was milling with his friends, all talking at once, indignant, guessing, plotting. Seeing Hephaistion at the door, Alexander broke through the crowd to him, grasped him by the arm and shouted the news in his ear. Dazed by his rage, Hephaistion made sounds of sympathy; certainly he should have heard of it from the King, certainly he had been slighted. The truth came piecemeal through the din: he believed this to prove Arridaios had been adopted as heir of Macedon. Olympias was sure of it.

I must get him alone, Hephaistion thought; but he dared not try. Alexander was flushed as if with fever; the young men, recalling his victories, cursing the King's ingratitude, offering wild advice, had felt his need of them and did not mean to leave him. He wanted from Hephaistion what he wanted from all the rest, only more urgently. It would be madness to cross him now.

Illyria, Hephaistion thought. It's like a sickness he can't shake off. Later I'll talk to him. "Who'd be a woman?" he said. "Does she know she's promised to a wittol?"

"What do you think?" said Alexander, his nostrils flaring. "Or her father either." His brows drew together in thought; he began to pace about. Hephaistion recognized the prelude to coming action.

Ignoring the danger signs, falling into step beside him, Hephaistion said, "Alexander, this can't be true unless the King's gone mad. Why, he was elected King himself because the Macedonians wouldn't accept a child. How could he suppose they'd accept a half-wit?"

"I know what he's doing." A dry heat seemed to radiate from him. "Arridaios is a stopgap till Eurydike has a boy. This is Attalos' work."

"But . . . but think! This boy's not even born. Then he has to grow up. Say eighteen years. And the King's a soldier."

"She's pregnant again, didn't you know?" If one touched his hair, Hephaistion thought, one would hear it crackle.

"He can't think he's immortal. He's going to war. What does he think would happen if he died in the next five years? Who is there but you?"

"Unless he has me killed." He threw it off like a commonplace.

"*What?* How can you believe it? His own son."

"They say I'm not. Well, then, I must look out for myself."

"Whoever says so? Do you mean that sottish wedding speech? I think all the man really meant by a true-born heir, was Macedonian blood both sides."

"Oh, no. That's not what they're saying now."

"Listen. Come out awhile. We'll go hunting. Then we'll talk later."

Looking quickly round to be sure no one else could hear, Alexander said in a desperate undertone, "Be quiet, be quiet." Hephaistion went back to the others; Alexander paced, like a caged wolf, to and fro.

Suddenly he faced round to them, and said, "I shall deal with this."

Hephaistion, who had never before heard this voice of decision with less than perfect trust, felt an instant presage of disaster.

"We'll see who wins," Alexander said, "at this marriage-broking." Prompt as a chorus, the others begged to hear. "I shall send to Karia, and tell Pixodoros what kind of bargain he's made."

There was applause. Hephaistion thought, Everyone's gone insane. Over the noise, Niarchos the naval officer called out, "You can't do that, Alexander. You might lose us the war in Asia."

"You might let me finish," Alexander shouted back. "I shall offer for the girl myself."

Almost in silence, they took it in. Then Ptolemy said, "Do it, Alexander. I'll stand by you, here's my hand on it."

Hephaistion stared, appalled. He had counted upon Ptolemy, the big brother, the steady one. He had lately fetched his Thais back from Corinth, where she had spent his time of exile. But now it was clear he was as angry as Alexander. He was, after all, though unacknowledged, the eldest of Philip's sons. Personable and capable, ambitious and turned thirty, he thought he could have managed in Karia very well. It was one thing to uphold a loved and legitimate brother; something else to stand aside for slobbering Arridaios. "What do you say, everyone? Do we all stand by Alexander?"

There were sounds of confused assent. Alexander's certainties were always catching. They exclaimed that this marriage would secure his place, that it would force the King to take care with him. Even the fainthearted, seeing him count heads, joined in; this was no Illyrian exile, there was nothing they need do, all the risks would be taken, they thought, by him.

This is treason, Hephaistion thought. Arrogant with desperation, he took Alexander by the shoulders, with the firmness of one who claims his rights. At once Alexander turned aside with him.

"Sleep on it. Think tomorrow."

"Never put off."

"Listen. What if your father and Pixodoros are swapping stinking fish? What if she's a slut or a hag? Just fit for Arridaios? You'd be a laughingstock."

With an effort he could see, Alexander turned on him dilated glittering eyes, and said with controlled forbearance, "What is it? This will make no difference to us, you know that."

"Of course I know that!" said Hephaistion angrily. "You're not talking to Arridaios, what sort of fool do you . . ." No, no; one of us must keep his head. Suddenly, for no reason that was clear to him, Hephaistion thought, He's proving he can take a woman from his father. She's for Arridaios, that keeps it decent, he need not know. And who dares tell him? No one, not even I.

Alexander, his head tilted defiantly, had started to assess the strength of the Karian navy. Through all this, Hephaistion sensed appeal. He wanted not advice, but the proofs of love. Anything he needed, he must have.

"You know I'm with you, whatever comes of it. Whatever you do."

Alexander pressed his arm, gave him a quick secret smile, and turned back to the rest.

"Whom will you send to Karia?" asked Harpalos. "I'll go, if you want."

Alexander strode over and clasped his hands. "No; no Macedonian; my father could make you pay. It was noble to offer, Harpalos, I'll never forget it." He kissed Harpalos' cheek; he was getting very emotional. Two or three others crowded up, offering to go. This is like the theater, Hephaistion thought.

It was then that he guessed whom Alexander would send.

Thettalos came after dark, and was let in through Olympias' private postern. She had wished to be present at the conference, but Alexander saw him alone. He went away with a gold ring on, and his head held high. Olympias, too, thanked him with the charm she could still sometimes command, and gave him a talent of silver. He replied with grace; he had had practice in making speeches when his mind was on other things.

Some seven days later, Alexander met Arridaios in the Palace courtyard. He came oftener now; the doctors advised he should mix more in company, to stir his wits. He trotted eagerly forward to meet Alexander, the old servant, now half a head shorter, bustling anxiously behind. Alexander, who bore him no more malice than an enemy's horse or dog, returned his greeting. "How's Phryne?" he asked. The doll was missing. "Have they taken her away?"

Arridaios grinned. There was a wet trickle in his soft black beard. "Old Phryne's in the box. I don't need *her*. They're bringing me a real girl, from Karia." He added, like a dull child echoing adults, an obscene boast.

Alexander looked at him with pity. "Take care of Phryne. She's a good friend. You might want her after all."

"Not when I've a wife." He nodded down at Alexander, and added with friendly confidence, "When you're dead I shall be King." His keeper tugged quickly at his belt; he went on towards the stoa, singing to himself a tuneless song.

Philotas was growing concerned. He had seen looks exchanged whose meaning he would have given much to know. Again he had been left outside a secret. Half a month he had scented it, but they were all holding their tongues. Who they were, at least, he knew; they were too pleased with themselves, or too scared, to hide it.

It was an uneasy time for Philotas. Though he had lived for years on the fringe of Alexander's set, he had always failed to reach the inmost ring. He had a good war record; impressive looks, but for rather prominent blue eyes; he was good company at supper, and in the van of fashion; his reports to the King had always been discreet, and he was certain were undetected. Why then was he not trusted? His instincts blamed Hephaistion for it.

Parmenion was badgering him for news. If he missed this, whatever it was, it would set him back, both with his father and the King. It might even have been better to have shared the exile, he could have been useful there, and now he would have been told everything. But it had been too sudden, the choice at the wedding brawl; though brave in the field, he was comfort-loving off it, and in doubtful issues he liked hot chestnuts pulled out of the fire by others.

He wanted no one reporting to Alexander, or to Hephaistion which was the same, that he had been asking dangerous questions. It therefore took him some time, picking up trifles here and there, and seeking the missing pieces where he would least be noticed, before he learned the truth.

It had been agreed that Thettalos was too conspicuous to report, himself, upon his mission. He sent a confidential messenger from Corinth, announcing his success.

Pixodoros had known something, though not enough, about Arridaios; Philip was too old a hand to think a lasting treaty could be won by downright fraud. When, therefore, the satrap learned that at no more cost he could exchange the ass for the racehorse, he was enchanted. In the audience room at Halikarnassos, with its columns of serpentine, Persian wall-tiles and Greek chairs, the daughter was modestly paraded; no one had been at the trouble of telling Arridaios that she was eight years old. Thettalos expressed a proxy's rapture. The marriage, of course, would have to be by proxy too; but once performed, the bridegroom's kin would have to accept it. It only remained to choose someone of proper standing, and send him off.

For the better part of a day, in Alexander's presence and out of it, nothing else was talked of among his friends. When others were about, they endeavored to speak darkly. But that day gave Philotas the last link in his chain.

There was nothing King Philip did better than to act when he was ready, and keep quiet meantime. He wanted no clamor and no rallying-cries; enough harm had been done already. Seldom in his life had he been so angry; this time he was angry cold sober.

The day passed without event. Night came; Alexander went to his room. When he was certainly alone, which meant when Hephaistion left, a guard was put on it. The window was twenty feet up, but there was a guard under that as well.

He knew nothing of it till morning. The men had been chosen with care; they answered no questions. He waited, fasting, till noon.

There was a dagger under his pillow. In the royal house of Macedon, this was as natural as wearing clothes. He slung it on inside his chiton. If food had been brought him, he would have left it; poison was not a fighting death. He waited for the footsteps.

When at last they came, he heard the guard presenting arms. It was not, then, the executioner. He felt no relief; he knew the tread.

Philip came in, with Philotas following.

"I need a witness," said the King. "This man will do."

Out of his sight, behind his shoulder, Philotas gave Alexander a look of shocked concern, mixed with dazed bewilderment. His hand sketched a little gesture, offering in the unknown trouble his helpless loyalty.

Alexander half-perceived it; but the King's presence filled the room. His big mouth was set in his broad face; his thick brows, which had always an outward tilt, flared up from his frown like a hawk's spread wings. Force came from him like heat. Alexander planted his feet and waited; he felt the dagger with the nerves under his skin.

"I knew," said his father, "that you were as headstrong as a wild pig, and as vain as a Corinth whore. Treacherous I knew you could be, as long as you listened to your mother. But one thing I didn't reckon on, that you were a fool."

At "treacherous" Alexander had caught his breath; he began to speak.

"*Be quiet!*" said the King. "How dare you open your mouth? How dared you meddle in my business with your insolence and your ignorant childish spite, you blundering, brainsick fool?"

"It was to hear this," said Alexander into the pause, "that you brought Philotas?" A jar had gone through him, like a wound one does not yet feel.

"No," said the King menacingly. "You can wait for that. You have lost me Karia. Can't you see it, you fool? Before God, since you think so much of yourself, you might have thought better this time. Do you want to be a Persian hanger-on? Do you want to pick up a horde of barbarian marriage-kin, who'll hang about you when war begins, selling the enemy our plans and bargaining for your head? Well, if so your luck's out, for I'll see you to Hades first, you'd be less hindrance there. And after this, do you think Pixodoros will accept Arridaios? Not unless he's a greater fool than you, and small chance of that. I thought I could spare Arridaios better. Well, I was a fool, I deserve to beget fools." He drew a heavy breath. "I have no luck with my sons."

Alexander stood quiet. Even the dagger on his ribs hardly moved against them. Presently he said, "If I am your son, then you have wronged my mother." He spoke without much expression; he was taken up with inward things.

Philip's lower lip thrust out. "Don't tempt me," he said. "I brought her back for your sake. She's your mother; I'm trying to remember it. Don't tempt me before a witness."

In the background, Philotas shifted his tall bulk, and gave a quiet, sympathetic cough.

"And now," said Philip, "attend to me; I am coming to business. First: I am sending an envoy to Karia. He can carry a formal letter from me, refusing my consent to your betrothal, and one from you withdrawing. Or, if you won't write, he can carry one from me telling Pixodoros he is welcome to you, but he'll be getting no son of mine. If that's your choice, tell me now. No? Very well. Then, second: I don't ask you to control your mother, you couldn't do it. I don't ask you to bring her intrigues to me, I've never asked it, I don't ask now. But while you are here in Macedon as my heir, which is while I choose and no longer, you will keep your hands out of her plots. If you meddle in them again, you can go back where you have been, and stay there. To help keep you out of mischief, the young fools you've embroiled so far can go looking for trouble outside the kingdom. Today they are settling their affairs. When they are gone, you may leave this room."

Alexander heard in silence. He had long prepared his mind for torture, lest he should somehow be taken alive in war. But it was his body he had thought of.

"Well?" said the King. "Don't you want to know who they are?" He answered, "You may suppose so."

"Ptolemy: I have no luck with my sons. Harpalos: a sleek greedy fox, I could have bought him if he were worth it. Niarchos: his Cretan kin may have joy of him. Erigyios and Laomedon . . ." The names came slowly. He was watching the face before him whiten. It was time the boy learned once for all who was the master. Let him wait.

Gladly as Philotas would have removed Hephaistion, he had not named him; neither justice nor kindness, but an ineradicable fear, had held his hand. The King for his part had never thought Hephaistion dangerous in himself. Though it was certain that, at the pinch, there was nothing he would not do for Alexander, he was worth taking a risk on. This was the one pardon which would disoblige Olympias. It had another use, besides.

"Concerning Hephaistion son of Amyntor," he said, taking his time, "I have considered that matter by itself." He paused again, while something within him, between contempt and deep secret envy, thought, The man does not live I could feel that for, or the woman either. "You will not pretend, I take it, that he was not told your plans, or that he refused assent to them."

In the distant voice of great pain, Alexander said, "He disagreed, but I overbore him."

"So? Well, be that as it may, I take into account that placed as he is, he could not escape blame either by keeping your counsel or revealing it." His voice was dry, putting Hephaistion where he belonged. "Therefore, at present I have exempted him from exile. If he gives you more good advice, you will do well to take it, both for your own sake and for his. For I am saying this before a witness, in case you should dispute it later: if you are found again in treasonable conspiracy, I shall consider him a party to it, both by

knowledge and consent. I shall accuse him before the Assembly of
the Macedonians, and ask them for his death."

Alexander answered, "I have heard you. You need not have
brought a witness."

"Very well. Tomorrow, if your friends have taken themselves off,
I will dismiss the guard. Today you can give thought to your life.
It is more than time."

He turned. The guard outside presented arms. Philotas, leaving
after him, had meant to look back at Alexander with discreet support and a meaning indignation. But at the last, he went out with
averted face.

Days passed; Alexander, now he was about again, found his following well sifted. It can cost too much to be in fashion, even for the
young. The chaff was all winnowed out now. The solid grain remained. He took note of these faithful ones; they were never
forgotten.

A few days later, he was sent for to the small audience room.
The message only said that the King required his presence.

Philip was in his chair of state, with an officer of justice, some
clerks, and a number of litigants waiting audience. Without speaking, he motioned his son to a seat below the dais, and went on dictating a letter.

Alexander stood a moment, then sat down. Philip said to the
guard at the door, "They can bring him in."

A four-man guard brought in Thettalos. His hands and his legs
were fettered. He walked forward with the heavy shuffling gait
imposed by the leg-irons. His wrists had raw bloody sores, from
the rubbing of the bracelets.

He was unshaven and unkempt, but he kept his head well up.
His bow to the King was not more, nor less, respectful than if he
had been a guest. He made another to Alexander; his eyes held
no reproach.

"So you are here," said the King grimly. "If you were an honest
man, you would have come to give account of your embassy. And
if you were a wise one, you would have run further than to Corinth."

Thettalos inclined his head. "So it seems, King. But I like to fulfill
my contracts."

"It is a pity, then, that your sponsors will be disappointed. You will give your last show in Pella. And you will give it alone."

Alexander stood up. Everyone looked at him; they could see now why he was there.

"Yes," said the King. "Let Thettalos see you. He owes his death to you."

Alexander said in a high taut voice, "He is an artist of Dionysos, his person is sacred."

"He should have kept to his art." Philip nodded to the officer of justice, who began to write something.

"He's a Thessalian," Alexander said.

"He is a citizen of Athens these twenty years. After the peace was signed he has acted as my enemy. He has no rights, and he knows it."

Thettalos looked, with an almost imperceptible shake of the head, at Alexander; but his eyes were fixed on the King.

"If he has his deserts," Philip said, "he will hang tomorrow. If he wants clemency, he must ask me for it. *And so must you.*"

Alexander stood rigid, holding an indrawn breath. Everyone's eyes were on him. He took a step towards the throne.

With a clank, Thettalos advanced one weighted foot. It brought him into the pose of heroic fortitude beloved of audiences. Every eye was drawn his way.

"Let me answer for it all. One should not exceed one's instructions. I was officious in Karia. Rather than your son, I will ask Sophokles to be my pleader." He brought both hands forward in a classic movement which also, to the best advantage, displayed his sores. There was a faint shocked murmur. He had been oftener crowned than any Olympic victor, and Greeks who had scarcely seen a theater knew his name. In his resonant voice which could have reached an audience of twenty thousand, now pitched perfectly to the room, he delivered his supplication.

The lines were fairly appropriate; not that it mattered. It was an exhibition piece. Its real meaning was, "Oh, yes, I know who you are. And you know who I am. Isn't it time to end the comedy?"

Philip narrowed a hard black eye. The message was understood. He was quite startled to see his son, blazing with controlled emotion, come out and stand by the actor's side.

"Certainly, sir, I will ask clemency for Thettalos. It would be far more shameful not to. He has risked his life for me; I shall not grudge him a little of my pride. Please pardon him; all the fault was mine. And you, Thettalos, please forgive me."

Thettalos with his fettered hands made a gesture more exquisite than words. Applause, though unheard, hung in the air.

Philip nodded at Thettalos, like a man who has fulfilled his purpose. "Very well. I hope this has taught you not to hide behind the god when you are making mischief. This time you are pardoned; don't presume on it. Take him away, and strike off his chains. I will hear the other business presently." He went out. He needed time to recover his temper, lest he make mistakes. Between them, they had nearly managed to make a fool of him. Yet they had had no time to concert it. A couple of tragedians, cueing one another to steal his scene.

Thettalos sat that evening at the lodging of his old friend Nikeratos, who had followed him up to Pella in case he needed ransoming, and was rubbing salve on his sores.

"My dear, I bled for the boy. One forgets how little he travels. I tried to signal him, but he swallowed every word. He saw the rope round my neck."

"So did I. Will you never learn sense?"

"Come come, what do you think Philip is, some Illyrian pirate? You should have seen him being Greek at Delphi. He knew already he'd gone too far, before I told him so. A disgusting journey. Let us go home by sea."

"You know the Corinthians are fining you half a talent? Aristodemos got your roles. No one will pay you for acting King Philip off his own stage."

"Oh, not I alone. I never reckoned on the boy being such a natural. What a sense of theater! Wait till he finds himself; I tell you, we shall see something. But it was a monstrous thing to do to him. I bled for him, truly bled."

Hephaistion was whispering in the midnight room, "Yes, I know. I know. But you must get some sleep now. I'll stay with you. Try to sleep."

In a colorless white-hot voice Alexander repeated, "He put his foot on my neck."

"He's getting no praise for it. It's a scandal, his chaining Thettalos; everyone says so. They all say you came off best."

"He put his foot on my neck, to show me he could do it. Before Thettalos; before them all."

"They'll forget. So must you. All fathers are unfair sooner or later. I remember once—"

"*He's not my father.*"

Hephaistion's comforting hands froze in a moment's stillness. "Oh, not in the eyes of the gods; they choose whom—"

"Never use that word again."

"The god will reveal it. You must wait the god's sign, you know that . . . Wait till the war begins. Wait till you win your next battle. He'll be bragging of you then."

Alexander was lying flat on his back, staring upward. Suddenly he grasped Hephaistion in an embrace so fierce that it knocked the breath out of him, and said, "Without you I should go mad."

"I too without you," said Hephaistion with loving ardor. Change the meaning, he thought, and you avert the omen.

Alexander said nothing. His strong fingers gripped into Hephaistion's ribs and shoulder; the bruises would be there a week. Hephaistion thought, I am in the King's gift too, a favor he can take away. Presently, having no more words, he offered instead the sadness of Eros, for this at least brought sleep.

The young slave-girl glided out from the shadow of the column; a black Nubian girl in a scarlet dress. She had been given as a child to Kleopatra in her childhood, to grow up with her, as a puppy might have been given. Her dark eyes with their smoky whites, like the agate eyes of statues, looked left and right before she spoke.

"Alexander, my lady says, please see her in the Queen's garden. By the old fountain. She wants to speak with you."

He looked at her with a sharp alertness, then seemed to draw into himself. "I can't come now. I am busy."

"Please see my lady now. Please come. She is crying." He saw that on her own dark polished face drops were lying like rain on bronze.

"Tell her yes, I'll come."

It was early spring. The old tangled roses were beaded with hard red buds; in the slant evening light they glowed like rubies. An almond tree growing between ancient tilted flagstones looked weightless in its cloud of pink. The shadowed water gushed out from the columned fountain-house into a basin of worn porphyry with ferns growing in its cracks. Seated on its edge, Kleopatra looked up at his footstep. She had dried her tears. "Oh, I am glad Melissa found you."

He rested a knee on the coping and made a quick movement with his hand. "Wait. Before you say anything, wait."

She looked at him blankly. He said, "There was something I asked you once to warn me of. Is it anything like that?"

"Warn you?" She had been full of other things. "Oh, but not—"

"Wait. I am not to interfere with any of her business. In any plot. That was the condition."

"Plot? No, no, please don't go away."

"I am telling you, I release you from the promise. I don't wish to know."

"No, truly. Please stay. Alexander, when you were in Molossia . . . with King Alexandros . . . What is he like?"

"Our uncle? But he was here a few years ago, you must remember him. A big man, red-bearded, young for his age—"

"Yes, I know; but what kind of man?"

"Oh, ambitious, brave in war I'd say, but I'd doubt his judgment. He governs well, though, watches things for himself."

"What did his wife die of? Was he kind to her?"

"How should I know? She died in childbed." He paused and stared, then in a changed voice said, "Why do you ask?"

"I have to marry him."

He stood back. The water from the hidden spring murmured in its columned cave. His first words were, "When did you hear this? I should have been told. The King tells me nothing. Nothing."

She looked at him silently, then said, "He sent for me just now," and turned away.

He crossed over and drew her against his shoulder. He had scarcely embraced her since their childhood, and now it was in Melissa's arms that she had wept. "I am sorry. You need not be frightened. He's not a bad man, he has no name for being cruel. The people like him. And you'll not be too far away."

She thought, *You* took for granted you'd choose the best; when you chose, you had only to lift your finger. When they find you a wife, you can go to her if you choose, or stay away with your lover. But I must be grateful that this old man, my mother's brother, has no name for being cruel. All she said was, "The gods are unjust to women."

"Yes, I have often thought so. But the gods are just; so it must be the fault of men." Their eyes met questioningly, but their thoughts had no point of meeting. "Philip wants to be sure of Epiros, before he crosses to Asia. What does Mother think of it?"

She grasped a fold of his chiton, the gesture of a suppliant. "Alexander. This is what I wanted to ask you. Will you tell her for me?"

"*Tell* her? But of course she must have heard before you."

"No, Father says not. He said I could tell her."

"What is it?" He grasped her wrist. "You are keeping something back."

"No. Only that—I could tell he knows she will be angry."

"So I should think. What an insult! Why go out of his way to slight her, when the thing in itself . . . I should have thought . . ."

Suddenly he released her. His face altered. He began to walk about the pavement, his feet, with a cat's instinct, avoiding the broken edges. She had known he would uncover the secret dread; better he than their mother, she had thought; but now she could scarcely bear the waiting. He turned. She saw a greyness under his skin; his eyes appalled her. He remembered her presence, said abruptly, "I'll go to her," and began to walk away.

"Alexander!" At her cry he paused impatiently. "What does it mean? Tell me what it means?"

"Can't you see for yourself? Philip made Alexandros King of Molossia and hegemon of Epiros. Why isn't that enough? They're brothers-in-law; isn't *that* enough? Why not? Why make him a son-in-law besides? Can't you see? Not besides—instead."

She said slowly, "What?" and then, "Ah, no, God forbid it!"

"What else? What does he mean to do, that would make an enemy

Mary Renault

of Alexandros unless he's sweetened with a new marriage tie? What else, but throw him back his sister? For Eurydike to be Queen."

Suddenly she began to wail, tearing her hair and dress, clawing and beating her bared breast. He pulled back her hands, straightened her clothes and gripped her hard by the arms. "Quiet! Don't tell the world our business. We must think."

She looked up with terror-stretched eyes. "What will she do? She will kill me." The words passed without shock, between the children of Olympias; but he took her in his arms and patted her, as he might have soothed a hurt dog. "No, don't be foolish, you know she won't harm her own. If she killed anyone . . ." He broke off with a violent movement, which in the moment of making it he changed to a clumsy caress. "Be brave. Sacrifice to the gods. The gods will do something."

"I thought," she said sobbing, "if he's not a bad man . . . I can take Melissa . . . at least I would get away. But with *her* there in the house, and after this . . . ! I wish I were dead, I wish I were dead."

Her disheveled hair fell against his mouth, he could taste it damp and salt. Looking past her, he saw behind a laurel bush a glimpse of scarlet, and freed an arm to beckon. The girl Melissa came out flinching. But, he thought, she could have overheard nothing she would not soon have been told. He said to Kleopatra, "Yes, I'll see Mother. I'll go now."

He put his sister into the dark outstretched hands with their pink palms. Looking back on his way to the furnace he was bound for, he saw the slave-girl seated on the rim of the porphyry fountain, bending over the head of the princess crouched by her lap.

News of the betrothal spread quickly. Hephaistion considered what Alexander would think of it, and guessed right. He did not appear at supper; he was said to be with the Queen. Hephaistion, waiting in his room, had fallen asleep on the bed before the sound of the latch aroused him.

Alexander came in. His eyes looked hollow, but full of a feverish exaltation. He walked over, put out his hand and touched Hephaistion, as a man might touch a sacred object for luck or a good omen, while deeply concerned with something else. Hephaistion looked, and was silent.

"She has told me," said Alexander.

Hephaistion did not ask, "What is it now?" He knew.

"She has told me at last." He looked deeply at, and through Hephaistion, including him in his solitude. "She made the conjuration, and asked the god's leave to tell me. He had always signed against it. That I never knew before."

Hephaistion sitting on the edge of the bed, unmoving, watched Alexander with all his being. He had peceived that his being was all he had to give. Men must not be spoken to on their way up from the shades, or they might sink back again forever. This was well known.

With the verge of consciousness, Alexander was aware of the quiet body, the face made beautiful by its intentness, the still dark-grey eyes, their whites lit by the lamp. He gave a deep sigh, and rubbed his hand across his brow.

"I was present," he said, "at the conjuration. For a long time the god did not speak, either yes or no. Then he spoke, in the form of the fire and in the—"

Suddenly he seemed aware of Hephaistion as a presence separate from his own. He sat down by him, and laid a hand on his knee. "He gave me leave to hear, if I vowed not to disclose it. It is the same with all the Mysteries. Anything of mine I would share with you, but this belongs to the god."

No, to the witch, thought Hephaistion; that condition was made for me. But he took Alexander's hand in both of his, and pressed it reassuringly. It felt dry and warm; it rested between his in trust, but sought no consolation.

"You must obey the god, then," said Hephaistion; and thought, not for the first time, nor for the last, Who knows? Aristotle himself never denied that such things have been; he would not be so impious. If it was ever possible, it must be so still. But it is a great burden for the mortal part to carry. He clasped more tightly the hand he held. "Only tell me this, whether you are satisfied."

"Yes." He nodded at the shadows beyond the lamp. "Yes, I am satisfied."

Suddenly his face was drained and drawn; his cheeks seemed to sink in as one looked, and his hand grew chilly. He began to shiver. Hephaistion had seen the same thing after battle, when men's wounds got cold. This needs the same remedy, he thought. "Have you any wine in here?"

Alexander shook his head. He withdrew his hand to hide its tremor, and began to walk about.

Hephaistion said, "We both need a drink. I do. I left supper early. Come and drink with Polemon. His wife's had a boy at last. He was looking for you in Hall. He's always been loyal."

This was true. That night, being happy, he grieved to see the Prince look so worn down by his troubles, and kept his cup well filled. He did grow gay, even noisy; it was a party of friends; most had fought in the charge at Cheironeia. In the end, Hephaistion just got him up to bed on his feet, and he slept on till mid-morning. About noon, Hephaistion went to see how he was getting on. He was reading at his table, with a pitcher of cold water by him.

"What book is it?" asked Hephaistion, leaning over his shoulder; he had been reading so quietly one could hardly make out the words.

He put the book quickly aside. "Herodotas. *Customs of the Persians.* One should understand the kind of man one is going to fight."

The ends of the scroll, curling up together, had met at the place where he had read. A little while after, when he was out of the room, Hephaistion rolled it open.

. . . *the transgressor's services shall always be set against his misdeeds; only if the second are found the greater, shall the wronged party go on to punishment.*

The Persians hold that no one ever yet killed his own father or mother. They are sure that if every such case were fully searched, it would be found out that the child was either a changeling, or born of adultery; for it is inconceivable, they say, that the true father should die by the hands of his child.

Hephaistion let the scroll spring back over the writing. For some time he stood looking out of the window, with his temple pressed against its frame, till Alexander, returning, smiled at the print of the carved laurel leaves stamped into his flesh.

The troops drilled for the war. Hephaistion, long eager for it to begin, now almost craved for it. Philip's threats had angered more than frightened him; like any hostage, he was worth more alive than dead, and the Great King's soldiers would kill him much more readily; yet here it was as if they were all being driven down the funnel of a narrowing gorge, a torrent rushing below them; war beckoned like open country, freedom, escape.

After half a month, an envoy came from Pixodoros of Karia. His daughter, he disclosed, had most unhappily fallen into a wasting sickness. It was no small part of his grief that, besides her expected loss, he must renounce the distinguished honor of a union with the royal house of Macedon. A spy, who arrived by the same ship, reported that Pixodoros had sent the new Great King, Darius, pledges of firm allegiance, and betrothed the girl to one of his most loyal satraps.

Next morning, sitting at the desk of Archelaos, with Alexander standing straight-backed before it, Philip gave this news without any comment, and looked up, waiting.

"Yes," said Alexander evenly. "It has turned out badly. But remember, sir, Pixodoros was content with me. It was not my choice to withdraw."

Philip frowned; yet he had felt something like relief. The boy had been too quiet just lately. This impudence was more like him, except for its restraint. One had always learned from his anger. "Are you trying to excuse yourself, even now?"

"No, sir. I just say what we both know is true."

He had still not raised his voice. Philip, his first fury spent and the bad news long expected, did not shout back. In Macedon, insult was a killing matter, but plain speaking the subject's right. He had taken it from simple men, even from women. Once, when after a long day in the judgment seat he had told some old crone he had no time left to hear her case, she had called out, "Then leave off being King!" and he had stayed to hear it. Now too he listened; it was his business; he was the King. It should have been more; but he put his grief behind him, almost before he knew it for what it was.

"I forbade the match for good reasons which you know." He had kept the best to himself; Arridaios would have been his tool, Alexander could have been dangerous. Karia was powerful. "Blame your mother," he said. "She led you into this folly."

[341]

"Can she be blamed?" Alexander still spoke with calm; there was a kind of searching in his eyes. "You have acknowledged children by other women. And Eurydike is in her eighth month now. Isn't that so?"

"That is so." The grey eyes were fastened on his face. Appeal in them might have softened him. He had been at trouble enough to train this man for kingship; if he himself fell in the coming war, what other heir could there be? Again he studied the face before him, so unconceding, and so unlike his own. Attalos, a Macedonian of a stock already old when the royal line was still in Argos, had told him country tales about the bacchic revels, customs brought in from Thrace, which the women kept secret. In the orgy, they themselves did not remember what they had done; what came of it they blamed on the god, in a human form or a snake's; but somewhere a mortal man was laughing. That is a foreign face, thought Philip; then remembered it, flushed and brilliant, coming down from the black horse into his arms. Divided in himself and angry at it, he thought, He is here to be reprimanded; how dare he try to corner me? Let him take what he is given and be thankful, when I choose to give. What more does he deserve?

"Well, then," he said, "if I have given you competitors for the kingdom, so much the better for you. Show your quality, earn your inheritance yourself."

Alexander gazed at him with a piercing, an almost painful concentration. "Yes," he said. "Then that is what I must do."

"Very well," Philip reached for his papers, dismissively.

"Sir. Whom are you sending to Asia, in command on the advance force?"

Philip looked up. "Parmenion and Attalos," he said curtly. "If I don't send you where I cannot keep an eye on you, you have yourself to thank. And your mother. That is all. You have leave to go."

In their fort on the Lynx Hills the three Lynkestids, the sons of Airopos, stood on their brown stone ramparts. It was an open place, safe from eavesdroppers. They had left their guest downstairs, having heard what he had to say, but given no answer yet. Around them stretched a great sky of white towering clouds, fringed with mountains. It was late spring; on the bare peaks above the forests, only the deepest gullies showed veins of snow.

"Say what you like, both of you," said the eldest, Alexandros, "but I don't trust it. What if this comes from the old fox himself, to test us? Or to trap us, have you thought of that?"

"Why should he?" asked the second brother, Heromenes. "And why now?"

"Where are your wits? He is taking his army into Asia, and you ask why now."

"Well," said the youngest, Arrabaios, "that's enough for him surely, without stirring up the west? No, if it had been that, it would have come two years ago, when he was planning to march south."

"As *he* says"—Heromenes jerked his head towards the stairway —"now's the time. Once Philip's set out, he will have his hostage for us." He looked at Alexandros, whose feudal duty it was to lead their tribal levies in the King's war.

He stared back resentfully; already before this, he had been thinking that once his back was turned, the others would ride out on some mad foray that would cost him his head. "I tell you I don't trust it. We don't know this man."

"Still," argued Heromenes, "we do know those who've vouched for him."

"Maybe. But those he claims to speak for—*they've* put their name to nothing."

"The Athenian has," said Arrabaios. "If you two have forgotten how to read your Greek, you can take my word for it."

"*His* name!" said Alexandros, snorting like a horse. "What was it worth to the Thebans? He puts me in mind of my wife's little dog, who starts the big ones fighting, and does nothing himself but yap."

Heromenes, who had extravagant tastes as such things went on the border, said, "He's sent a sweetener."

"Birdlime. We must send it back. You should learn to judge a horse, then you'd not owe the copers. Don't you value our heads at more than a bag of Persian darics? The real price, the worth of the risk, that's not his to give."

"That we could take for ourselves," said Heromenes resentfully, "with Philip out of the way. What ails you, man; are you head of the clan, or our big sister? We're offered our fathers' kingdom back, and all you can do is cluck like some wet-nurse when the child starts walking."

"She keeps it from breaking its head. Who says we could do it? An Athenian who ran like a goat at the smell of blood. Darius; a usurper barely settled on his throne, who has enough on his hands without a war. Do you think they care for us? And more, do you think *they* know whom we'd have to deal with, in Philip's room? Of course not; they think he's a spoiled little prince given credit for other men's victories. The Athenian's forever saying it in speeches. But we know. *We've* seen the lad at work. Sixteen he was then, with a head on him like thirty; and that's three years gone. It's not a month since I was at Pella; and I tell you, disgrace or not, put him in the field and the men will follow him anywhere. That you can take from me. Can we fight the royal army? You know the answer. So, is he in the business, as this man says, or not? That's the only question. These Athenians, they'd sell their mothers to the stews if the price was right. Everything hangs on the lad, and we've no proof."

Heromenes tweaked a bit of broom from its roots between the stones, and switched it moodily. Alexandros frowned at the eastern hills.

"Two things I don't like," he went on. "First, he has bosom friends in exile, some no further than Epiros. We could have met in the mountains and no one the wiser; we'd all know then where we were. Why send this go-between, a man I've never seen about him, why trust the man with his head? And the other thing I mislike is that he promises too much. You've met him. Think."

"We should think first," said Arrabaios, "whether he's one who could do it. Not all men could. I think he could. And he's at a pass when he might."

"And if he's a bastard as they say," urged Heromenes, "then it's a dangerous business, but not blood-cursed. I think he could and would."

"I still say it doesn't smell of him," said Alexandros. Absently he scratched a louse out of his head, and rubbed it between thumb and finger. "Now, if it were his dam . . ."

"Dam or whelp, you can be sure they're in it together," Heromenes said.

"We don't know that. What we do know is, the new wife's with child again. And they say Philip's giving his daughter as a sop to the Epirote King, so that he'll stomach the witch being packed off. So, think which of them can't afford to wait. Alexander can. Philip's seed tends to girls, as everyone knows. Even if Eurydike throws a boy, let the King say what he likes while he lives, but if he dies, the Macedonians won't accept an heir under fighting age; *he* should know that. But Olympias, now, that's another matter. *She* can't wait. Scratch into this deep enough, and I'll stake my best horse you'll find her hand in it."

"If I thought it came from *her*," said Arrabaios, "then I'd think twice."

"This lad's only nineteen," said Heromenes. "If Philip dies now, with no other son besides the lackwit, then *you*"—he stabbed his finger at Alexandros—"are next in line. Couldn't you see that's what the fellow down there was trying to tell you?"

"O Herakles!" said Alexandros, snorting again. "Who are you to talk of lackwits? Nineteen, and you saw him at sixteen. Since then, he has led the left at Cheironeia. Go to Assembly, will you, and tell them he's a child too young for war, they must vote for a grown man. Do you think I would live to get there and count my votes? You had better stop dreaming, and look at the man you have to deal with."

"I am looking," said Arrabaios. "That's why I said he has it in him to do this business. Bastard or not."

"You say he can afford to wait." Heromenes' blue eyes in his wine-reddened face stared with contempt at Alexandros, whose place he envied. "Some men can't wait for power."

"I only say, ask yourself who gains most. Olympias gains everything, because this match will lose her everything, if the King outlives it. Demosthenes gains the blood of the man he hates worse than death, if he hates anything worse; the Athenians gain a civil war in Macedon, if we play our part, with the kingship in doubt, or passed to a boy they make light of, the more so since he's in disfavor. Darius, whose gold you want to keep even if it hangs you, gains even more, since Philip's arming for war against him now. Out of them all, not one would care a dog's turd, once the thing's done, if

[345]

we're all three crucified in a row. Yet you put your bet on Alexander. No wonder you can't win at a cockfight."

They mulled it over a little longer. In the end, they agreed to refuse the go-between and return the gold. But Heromenes had debts, and a younger son's portion; he agreed unwillingly; and it was he who set the guest on his way to the eastern pass.

The scent of raw warm blood mixed with the cool scents of a dewy morning, of pine-resin and wild thyme and some little upland lily. Tall dogs as heavy as men gnawed contentedly at deer bones; now and then strong teeth would split one with a crack, to reach the marrow. The dead stag's sad empty face lolled on the grass. Over an aromatic fire, two of the hunters were grilling steaks for breakfast; the rest had gone looking for a stream. Two servants rubbed down the horses.

On a rock-ledge cropping out from small-flowered turf, Hephaistion sprawled beside Alexander in the early sun, seen on the skyline by the rest, but far out of hearing. So, in Homer, Achilles and Patroklos had drawn apart from their dear comrades to share their thoughts. But it had been Patroklos' ghost who recalled it, when they shared their grief; so Alexander thought the lines bad luck, and never quoted them. He had been talking of other things.

"It was like a dark labyrinth," he said, "with a monster waiting. Now it is daylight."

"You should have talked before." Hephaistion drew his reddened hand over a patch of wet moss, to wash off the blood.

"It would only have burdened you. As it was, you knew, and it did."

"Yes. So why not have talked it out?"

"It would have been cowardice, then. A man must deal with his own daimon. When I look back on my life, I remember it always there, waiting at every crossroads, where I knew that I would meet it. From the time when I was a child. Even the wish, never acted, the wish alone, was a terrible thing to carry. Sometimes I would dream of the Eumenides, as they are in Aischylos; they would touch my neck with their long cold black claws, saying, 'One day you will be ours forever.' For it drew me on, by the very horror of it; some men say that standing on a cliff, they feel that the void is drawing them. It seemed my destiny."

"I have known this a long time. I am your destiny too; did you forget?"

"Oh, we have spoken of it often, without words, and that was better. Things are fixed by words, as fire fixes clay. So I went on; sometimes I thought I could be free of it, then I would doubt again. All that is over, now it's been revealed to me what my true birth is. Once I knew he was no kin to me, I began to think what should be done. And from that moment, my thought was clear. Why do it? To what end? Why now? From what necessity?"

"I tried to say all this."

"I know; but my ear was closed. It was more than the man himself oppressing me. It was the gods' 'You may not' stifling my soul's 'I must.' And the thought of his blood in me, like a sickness. Now I'm free of it, I hate him less. Well, the god delivered me. If I meant to do it, no time could be worse than now, at this ebb-tide of my fortune, with the tide ready to turn. He won't leave me Regent here, when he goes to Asia; I'm in disgrace, and besides I doubt he'd dare. He's bound to take me to the war. Once I'm in the field, I hope I can show him something, and the Macedonians too. They were glad enough of me at Cheironeia. If he lives, he'll change to me when I've won some battles for him. And if he falls, I'm the man who will be there, with the army round me. That above all."

His eye was caught by a small blue flower in a rock-crevice. Delicately he raised its head, named it, and added the use of its decoction for coughs.

"Of course," he said, "I shall kill Attalos as soon as I can do it. It will be best in Asia."

Hephaistion nodded; he himself, at nineteen, had long lost count of men he had already killed. "Yes, he's your mortal enemy; you'll have to get rid of *him*. The girl's nothing then, the King will find another as soon as he's on campaign."

"I told Mother that, but . . . Well, she must think as she chooses, I mean to act in my own time. She's a wronged woman, it's natural she should want revenge; though of course that's what has set the King on getting her out of the kingdom before he leaves, and it's done *me* harm enough . . . She'll intrigue to the last, she can't help

[347]

it, it's become her life. There's some business now, she keeps hinting she wants to drag me into; but I forbade her even to tell me." Arrested by this new tone, Hephaistion stole a sidelong glance. "I have to think and plan, I can't be thrown out from day to day by these fits and starts. She must understand it."

"It eases her mind, I suppose," said Hephaistion, whose own was eased. (So she made her conjuration, and the wrong spirit answered; I should like to know her thoughts.) "Well, the wedding can't but be a day of honor for her; her daughter and her brother. Whatever the King may feel, or mean to do, he'll have to give her her dignities then, for the bridegroom's sake. So he must give you yours."

"Oh, yes. But it's to be his own day mainly. Memory and history both surpassed. Aigai's teeming already with craftsmen; and the invitations have gone out so far afield, I only wonder he hasn't sent to the Hyperboreans. Never mind, it's something to be lived through, before we cross to Asia. Then it will seem like *that.*" He pointed to the plain below, and the flocks tiny with distance.

"Yes, it will be nothing then. You've already founded a city; but there you'll find yourself a kingdom. I know as if a god had told me."

Alexander smiled at him; sat up, and with hands clasped round knees looked towards the next range of mountains. Wherever he was, he could never keep his eyes long from the skyline. "Do you remember, in Herodotos, where the Ionians sent Aristagoras to the Spartans, begging them to come and free the Greek cities of Asia? They cried off, when they heard Susa was three months' march from the sea. Farm-dogs, not hunting-dogs . . . That's enough, now. Down." A year-old deerhound, which had just tracked him there by scent after getting loose from the huntsman, ceased its caresses and lay obediently, pressing its nose against him. He had had it in Illyria as a pup, and had spent his spare hours in training it; its name was Peritas.

"Aristagoras," he said, "brought them a map on bronze, of the whole world with the Encircling Ocean, and showed them the Persian empire. *Truly the task is not hard; for the barbarians are people unfit for war, while you are the best and the bravest fighting men on earth.* (Perhaps it was true in those days.) *This is how they fight: they use bows and arrows and a short spear, they take the field in trousers, and cover their heads with turbans* (not if they can afford a helmet); *that shows how easy they are to conquer. I tell you, too, that the people of those regions have more wealth than all the rest of the world together.* (Now that *is* true.) *Gold, silver and bronze; embroidered garments; asses, mules and slaves; you can own it all, if you choose.* He goes over the nations with his map, till he gets to Kissia by the River Choaspes. *And on its banks the city of Susa, where the Great King holds court, and where the treasuries are, in which his wealth is stored. Once you are lords of the city, you may challenge Zeus himself to surpass your riches.* He reminded the Spartans how they were always at war around their borders, over bits of poor land, fighting men who owned nothing worth a battle. Do you need to do that, he said to them, when you might be lords of Asia? They kept him waiting three days, then said it was too far from the sea."

A horn blew from the cook-fire, to say breakfast was ready. Alexander gazed at the mountains. However hungry he was, he never hurried to food.

"Only Susa. They didn't let him even begin to talk about Persepolis."

Anywhere along Armorers' Street at Piraeus, the port of Athens, it was hard to make oneself heard above a shout. The shops were open in front, to let out the heat of the forges and show the work. These were not the cheap off-the-peg factories with their hordes of slaves; here the best craftsmen made to measure, from clay molds of the naked client. Half a morning might go to a fitting, and to choosing from pattern books the inlaid design. Only a few of the shops made armor meant for war; the most fashionable catered for knights who wanted to be noticed in the Panathenaic procession. They would bring all their friends along, if they could stand the noise; comings and goings were little noticed. In the rooms above the shops, the din was hardly muted; but men could just hear each other speak, if they kept close together; and it was well known that armorers grew hard of hearing, which lessened the fear of eavesdroppers.

In one of these rooms, a conference was going on. It was a meeting of agents. None of the principals could have been seen with any of the others, even had it been possible for all of them to attend. Three men of the four were leaning over an olive-wood table on their folded arms. The feet of their wine cups rattled to the pounding of the hammers that shook the floor; the wine shivered, sometimes a drop leaped out.

The three who were talking had reached the last stages of a long wrangle about money. One was from Chios; his olive pallor and blue-black beard derived from the long Persian occupation. One was an Illyrian, from close to the Lynkestid border. The third, the host, was an Athenian; he wore his hair tied over his brow in a topknot, and his face was discreetly painted.

The fourth man sat back in his chair, his hands on the pinewood arms, waiting for them to have done; his face seeming to say that to tolerate such things was part of his commission. His fair hair and beard had a tinge of red; he was from north Euboia, which had long had commerce with Macedon.

On the table was a wax diptych tablet, and a stylos, the sharp end to write, the flat end to erase what had been written, in the presence of all four parties, before they left the room. The Athenian tapped it impatiently on the table, then on his teeth.

The Chian said, "It is not as if these gifts were to be the end of Darius' friendship. As I say, Heromenes can always count on a place at court."

"He is seeking," said the Illyrian, "to rise in Macedon, not to prepare for exile. I thought that was understood."

"Certainly. A generous earnest has been agreed on." The Chian looked at the Athenian, who nodded, drooping his lids. "The bulk sum to follow a revolt in Lynkestis as arranged. I am not satisfied that his brother, the chief, has agreed to this. I must stand out for payment by result."

"Reasonable," said the Athenian, taking the stylos from his mouth. He had a slight lisp. "Now do let us take all that as settled, and come back to the man who matters most. My principal wants an undertaking that he will act on the day agreed—no other."

This brought the Euboian leaning across the table, like the rest. "You said that before, and I answered that there's no sense in it. He is always about Philip's person. He has entry to the bedchamber. He might have far better chances, both to do it and to get away. This is asking too much of him."

"My instructions are," said the Athenian, tapping the stylos on the table, "that it shall be that day, or we will not offer him asylum."

The Euboian thumped the already rattling table, making the Athenian shut his eyes protestingly. "Why, tell me? Why?"

"Yes, why?" said the Illyrian. "Heromenes doesn't ask for it. The news could reach him any time."

The man from Chios raised his dark brows. "Any day will do for *my* master. If Philip does not cross to Asia, it is enough. Why this insistence on the day?"

The Athenian lifted the stylos by both ends, rested his chin on it, and smiled confidingly.

"First, because on that day every possible claimant to the throne, and every faction, will be there at Aigai for the rites. Not one can escape suspicion; they will accuse each other, and very likely fight for the succession; this will be of use to us. Secondly . . . I think my principal deserves some small indulgence. It will crown his life-work, as anyone aware of his life can see. He finds it fitting that the tyrant of Hellas be brought down, not some dark night as he stumbles drunk to bed, but at the climax of his hubris; in this I agree, let me say." He turned to the Euboian. "And, your man's wrongs being what they are, I should suppose it would please him too."

"Yes," said the Euboian slowly. "No doubt. But it may not be possible."

"It will be possible. The order of the ceremonies has just come into our hands." He detailed them, till he reached a certain event, when he looked up meaningly.

"Your ears are good," said the Euboian, raising his brows.

"This time you may rely on them."

"I daresay. But our man would be lucky to come off well out of that. As I say, he could get better chances."

"None so distinguished. Fame sweetens vengeance . . . Well, well, since we are speaking of fame, I will let you into a little secret. My principal wants to be first with the news in Athens, even before the news arrives. Between ourselves, he plans to have had a vision.

[351]

Later, when Macedon has sunk back to its tribal barbarism—" He caught the Euboian's angry eye, and said hastily, "That is, has passed to a King who is prepared to stay at home—then he can proclaim to a grateful Greece his share in the liberation. Meantime, when one remembers his long battle against tyranny, can one grudge him this small reward?"

"What risk is *he* taking?" shouted the Illyrian suddenly. Though the hammers below were noisy, it startled the others into angry gestures, which he ignored. "Here's a man risking death to avenge his honor. And only Demosthenes must choose the time, so that he can prophesy in the Agora."

The three diplomats exchanged looks of scandal and disgust. Who but a backwoodsman of Lynkestis would have sent this rude clansman to such a conference? There was no knowing what he might say next, so they broke up the meeting. All that mattered had been determined.

Each left the building separately, with a little time between. The last left were the Chian and the Euboian. The Chian said, "Can you be sure your man will do his part?"

"Oh yes," said the Euboian. "We know how to manage that."

"You were there? You yourself heard it?"

The spring night blew chilly in the hills of Macedon. The torches smoked with the window-draft, the embers of the sacred hearth faded and flickered on their old blackened stone drum. It was late. As the shadows deepened above, the stone walls seemed to lean inward, craning to hear.

The guests had departed, all but one; the slaves had been sent to bed. The host and his son had drawn three couches close round one wine table; the others, shoved aside in haste, gave the room a disordered look.

"Do you tell me," said Pausanias again, "that you were there?" His head and shoulders were thrust forward; he had to grasp the edge of the couch to keep his balance. His eyes were bloodshot with wine; but what he had just heard had sobered him. His host's son met his gaze; a youngish man with expressive blue eyes, and a mean mouth under his short black beard.

"The wine tripped my tongue," he answered. "I'll say no more."

"I ask pardon for him," said his father, Deinias. "What possessed you, Heirax? I tried to catch your eye."

Pausanias turned like a speared boar. "*You* knew of it too?"

"I was not present," said the host, "but people talk. I am sorry it should be here in my house that it reached your ears. Even between themselves in secret, you would think both the King and Attalos would be ashamed to boast of such a thing; much more in company. But you know, none better, what they're like when they've had a skinful."

Pausanias' nails dug at the wood, so that the blood receded. "He took his oath before me, eight years ago, never to let it be spoken of in his presence. It was that persuaded me to forgo vengeance. He knew it, I told him so."

"Then he was not forsworn," said Heirax with a sour smile. "He didn't let it be said, he said it. He thanked Attalos for the good service. When Attalos would have answered, he clapped a hand across his mouth, and they both laughed at that. Now I understand it."

"He swore to me by the stream of Acheron," said Pausanias, almost whispering, "that he had no foreknowledge of it."

Deinias shook his head. "Heirax, I take back my rebuke. When so many know, it is better Pausanias hears of it first from friends."

"He said to me"—Pausanias' voice was thickening—"'In a few years, when you are seen to be held in honor, they will doubt the tale; then they will forget it.'"

"So much for oaths," said Deinias, "when men feel themselves secure."

"Attalos is secure," said Heirax easily. "Safe with his troops in Asia."

Pausanias stared past them into the dulling red core upon the hearth. Speaking, it seemed, to that, he said, "Does he think it is too late?"

"If you like," said Kleopatra to her brother, "you may see my dress."

He followed to her room, where it hung on a T-shaped stand, fine saffron-dyed linen embroidered with jeweled flowers. She was to blame for nothing; soon they would seldom meet again; he gave her waist a pat. In spite of all, the coming pomps began to charm her; shoots of pleasure broke through, like green on a burnt hillside; she began to feel she would be a queen.

"Look, Alexander." She lifted from its cushion the bridal wreath, wheat-ears and olive sprays worked from fine gold, and walked towards the mirror.

"No! Don't try it on. That's very unlucky. But you will look beautiful." She had shed most of her puppy-fat, and showed promise of some distinction.

"I hope we shall soon go up to Aigai. I want to see the decorations; when the crowds arrive, one can't go about. Have you heard, Alexander, about the great procession to the theater, to dedicate the Games? They're to be offered to all the twelve Olympians, and the images are to be carried—"

"Not twelve," said Alexander drily. "Thirteen. Twelve Olympians, and divine Philip. But he's modest, his image is going last . . . Listen; what's that noise?"

They ran to the window. A party had dismounted from its mules, and was grouping formally, to approach the Palace. The men were crowned with bay, and the leader carried a branch of it.

Sliding down from the sill, Alexander said eagerly, "I must go. Those are the heralds from Delphi, with the oracle about the war." He kissed her briskly, and turned to the doorway. In it, just entering, was his mother.

Kleopatra saw her glance pass by, and the old bitterness stirred once more. Alexander, who received the glance, knew it of old. It called him to a secret.

"I can't stay now, Mother. The heralds are here from Delphi." Seeing her mouth open, he added quickly, "I've a right to be there. We don't want that forgotten."

"Yes, you had better go." She held out her hands to him, and, as he kissed her, began to whisper. He drew back saying, "Not now, I shall be late," and loosened her hands. She said after him, "But we must talk today."

He went without sign of hearing it. She felt Kleopatra's watching eyes, and answered them with some small business of the wedding;

[354]

there had been many such moments, over many years. Kleopatra thought of them, but held her peace. Long before Alexander could be a king, she thought, if he ever was one, she would be a queen.

In the Perseus Room, the chief diviners, the priests of Apollo and of Zeus, Antipatros, and everyone whom rank or office entitled to be there, had assembled to hear the oracle delivered. The heralds from Delphi stood before the dais. Alexander, who had run the first part of the way, made a slow entrance and stood at the right of the throne, arriving just before the King. Nowadays he had to manage such things for himself.

There was a pause of whispering expectation. This was a royal embassy. Not for the swarming petitioners about marriages and land purchases and sea journeys and offspring, who could be dealt with by drawing lots, but for this single question, the grey-haired Pythia had gone into the smoky cave below the temple, mounted the tripod beside the Navel Stone swathed in its magic nets, chewed her bitter laurel, breathed the vapor from the rock-cleft, and uttered her god-crazed mutterings before the shrewd-eyed priest who would interpret them in verse. Old fateful legends drifted like mist from mind to mind. Those of more stolid temper awaited some stock response, advice to sacrifice to the proper gods, or to dedicate a shrine.

The King limped in, was saluted, and sat down, his stiff leg pushed forward. Now he could exercise less, he had begun to put on weight; there was new solid flesh on his square frame, and Alexander, standing behind, saw that his neck had thickened.

There were the ritual exchanges. The chief herald unrolled his scroll.

"Pythian Apollo, to Philip son of Amyntas, King of the Macedonians, answers thus: *Wreathed is the bull for the altar, the end fulfilled. And the slayer too is ready.*"

The company pronounced the well-omened phrases prescribed for such occasions. Philip nodded to Antipatros, who nodded back with relief. Parmenion and Attalos were having trouble on the coast of Asia, but now the main force would set out with good

Mary Renault

augury. There was a satisfied hum. A favorable answer had been expected; the god had much to thank King Philip for. But it was only to greatly honored ones, the courtiers murmured, that Two-Tongued Apollo spoke with so clear a voice.

"I have put myself in his way," Pausanias said. "But I have had no sign from him. Courteous, yes; but then he always was. From a child he knew the story. I used to see it in his eyes. But he gives no sign. Why not, if all this is true?"

Deinias shrugged and smiled. He had feared this moment. Had Pausanias been prepared to throw his life away, he could have done it eight years before. A man in love with vengeance wanted to outlive his enemy, and taste the sweet on his tongue. This Deinias had known, and it was prepared for.

"Surely that does not surprise you? Such things have a way of being seen, and remembered later. You may rest assured that you will be watched over like a friend; subject of course to a good appearance. Look. I have brought you something which will set your mind at rest." He opened his hand.

Pausanias, peering, said, "One ring is much like another."

"Look well at this one. Tonight, at supper, you will be able to look again."

"Yes," Pausanias said. "With that I would be satisfied."

"Why," Hephaistion exclaimed, "you're wearing your lion ring. Where was it? We looked everywhere."

"Simon found it in my clothes chest. I must have run my hand through the clothes, and dragged it off."

"I looked there myself."

"I suppose it lodged in a fold."

"You don't think he stole it, and then took fright?"

"Simon? He'd have more sense, everyone knows it's mine. It's a lucky day, it seems."

He meant that Eurydike had just been delivered of her child; it was another girl.

[356]

"May God fulfill the good omen," Hephaistion said.

They went down to supper. Alexander paused to greet Pausanias by the entry. From so grim-faced a man, it was always a small triumph to win a smile.

It was the dark before dawn. The old theater at Aigai glowed with cressets and flambeaux. Small torches flitted like fireflies, as stewards guided guests to their places on the cushioned benches. The light breeze from the mountain forests picked up the smells of burning pine-resin and packed humanity.

Down in the round orchestra were set in a circle the twelve altars of the Olympians. Fires glowed on them, sweetened with incense, lighting up the robes of their heirophants, and the strong bodies of the sacrificers with their shining cleavers. From the fields beyond came the lowing and bleating of the victims, restless at the stir and torchlight, wreathed already in their garlands. Above the rest rose the bellow of King Zeus' white bull with his gilded horns.

On the stage, its ornate setting still dim with dusk, the King's throne was set, flanked with state chairs for the royal kin: his new son-in-law, his son, and the high chiefs of Macedon.

In the upper tiers were the athletes, the charioteers, the singers and musicians who would compete in the Games when the coming rite had hallowed them. With these, and the multitude of the King's invited guests, the small theater was packed full. The soldiers and peasants, the tribesmen ridden in from the hills to see the show, trampled and stirred on the dusky hillside around the scooped shell of the theater, or thronged the processional way. Voices rose and fell and shifted, like waves on a shingle beach. The pine trees, standing black in the eastward glimmer, creaked under their load of boys.

The old rough road to the theater had been leveled and widened for the great procession. Laid by the mountain dews, the dust smelled sweet in the sharp daybreak air. Soldiers detailed to clear the route came with torches; the jostling was good-humored, shover and shoved being often fellow tribesmen. The torches were extinguished in the lift of a cloudless clear summer dawn.

As pink touched the peaks beyond the Aigai ledge, the splendors of the parade way glimmered into view; the tall scarlet masts with their gilt finials of lion or eagle, the long streaming banners; the festoons of flowers and ribboned ivy; the triumphal arch carved and painted with the Exploits of Herakles, and topped with a Victory holding out her gilded bays. On either side of her stood two live golden-haired boys robed as Muses, with trumpets in their hands.

In the castle forecourt on the ancient stone acropolis, Philip stood in a purple cloak clasped with gold, crowned with a golden laurel-wreath. His head was turned into the light early breeze. Birdsong, the tweeting and twangling of instruments tuning up, voices of spectators and of marshals giving orders, came to him backed by the bass roar of the Aigai falls. His gaze traversed the plain that stretched east to Pella and the dawn-mirroring sea. His pasture lay lush and green before him; his rivals' horns were broken. His wide nostrils snuffed the rich friendly air.

Behind him, in a scarlet tunic and jeweled sword belt, Alexander stood beside the bridegroom. His bright hair, freshly washed and combed, was crowned with a garland of summer flowers. Half the states of Greece had sent the King wrought-gold wreaths as gifts of honor; but none had been passed to him.

Round the forecourt were ranged the men of the Royal Body-guard, ready to form the escort. Pausanias, their commander, was pacing about before the lines. Those in his path would dress ranks anxiously, or fidget with their equipment; then stand easier, aware that he had not looked at them.

On the north rampart, among her women, was the bride, just risen from her marriage bed. She had had no pleasure in it; but she had been ready for worse. He had been decent, not very drunk, much aware of her youth and maidenhood, and not really old. She no longer feared him. Craning over the rough stone parapet, she saw the long snake of the procession forming along the walls. Beside her, her mother stared down into the courtyard; her lips were moving, a faint murmur of breath came out. Kleopatra did not try to hear the words. She felt the sorcery, like heat from a covered fire. But it was time to set out for the theater, their litters were ready. Soon she would be on her wedding journey; such things would no longer matter. Even if Olympias came to Epiros, Alexandros would know how to deal with it. It was something after all, to have a husband.

The Muses' trumpets blew. Under the Victory arch, to shouts of

FIRE FROM HEAVEN

wonder, the Twelve Gods passed in progress to their altars. Each float was drawn by matched horses, caparisoned in red and gold. The wooden images were carved god-size, seven feet tall, and had been tinted by the Athenian master who colored for Apelles.

King Zeus enthroned, with staff and eagle, had been copied in little from the giant Zeus at Olympia, his throne gilded, his robe stiff with gems and bullion. Apollo was robed as a musician, with a gold lyre. Poseidon rode in a sea-horse chariot. Demeter sat crowned with gold corn, between mystai holding torches. Queen Hera had her peacocks; wits remarked that King Zeus' consort came rather far down the line. Virgin Artemis, bow at shoulder, held a kneeling stag by the horns. Dionysos rode nude on a spotted panther. Athene had her shield and helmet, but not her Attic owl. Hephaistos wielded his hammer; Ares, his foot on a prone foe, glared under his crested helmet; Hermes laced a winged sandal. Clad in a narrow drift of veil, a little Eros beside her, Aphrodite sat in a flowered chair. It was observed, in undertones, that she had a look of Eurydike; she was still in the lying-in room; she would not appear today.

The last float of the twelve received its fanfare. The thirteenth float came on.

King Philip's image had an eagle-headed throne with couchant leopards for arms. His feet rested on a winged bull with a Persian tiara and the face of a man. The artist had trimmed down his figure, left out his scars, and put back his age ten years. Allowing for this, he was very lifelike; one almost expected movement from the black painted eyes.

There were cheers; but like a cold current in warm seas, there could be felt a flaw of silence. One old countryman murmured to another, "He ought to have been made smaller." They looked askance at the line of jolting gods ahead, and made ancient averting signs.

The chiefs of Macedon followed, Alexandros of Lynkestis and the rest. It was seen that even those from the back hills wore good loom-woven wool with border-work, and a gold brooch. Old folk recalled days of sheepskin cloaks, when bronze pins were riches; their tongues clucked between doubt and wonder.

To the beat of deep-toned pipes playing a Dorian march, came the van of the Royal Guard, Pausanias leading. The men swaggered in their parade armor, smiling at friends in the crowd; a feast-day did not demand the sternness of maneuvers. But Pausanias looked straight on, at the tall doorway of the theater.

There was a blare of archaic horns, and cries of "May the King live!"

Philip paced on a white horse, in his purple cloak and gold crown. Half a length behind, at either side, rode his son-in-law and his son.

The peasants made good-luck phallic signs at the bridegroom, and wished him offspring. But by the arch, a troop of young men, who had been waiting with filled lungs, yelled all together, "Alexander!"

He turned his head smiling, and looked at them with love. Long after, when they were generals and satraps, they would boast of it to silence envy.

The rear of the bodyguard came after; then, finishing the procession, the victims for the sacrifice, one for each god, led by the bull with a garland around his dewlaps, and gold foil on his horns.

The sun floated up from its nets of light; everything glittered; the sea, the dewy grass, crystal cobwebs on yellow broom; the jewels, the gilding, the cool gleam of the burnished bronze.

The gods had entered the theater. Through the tall gateway of the parodos, the cars drove round the orchestra one by one; the guests applauded; the resplendent images were lifted off, and put on bases near their altars. The thirteenth deity, who claimed no shrine but owned the precinct, was set down in the middle.

Outside in the road, the King made a sign. Pausanias barked an order. The van of the Royal Guard wheeled smartly left and right, and fell back on the rear guard, behind the King.

The theater was some hundred yards away. The chiefs, looking back, saw the Guard retire. The King, it seemed, had entrusted himself to them for this last lap of his progress. Pleased by the compliment, they opened their ranks for him.

Noticed only by his own men, who thought it none of their business, Pausanias strode on towards the parodos.

Philip saw the chiefs waiting. He walked his horse up to them, from the standing ranks of the Guard, and leaned down smiling. "Go on in, my friends. I shall come after."

They began moving; but one elderly laird stood planted by his bridle, and said with Macedonian forthrightness, "No guard, King? In all this crowd?"

Philip leaned down and clapped his shoulder. He had been hoping someone would say it. "My people are guard enough. Let all these foreigners see it. Thanks for your kindness, Areus; but go on in."

As the chiefs went forward, he slowed his horse, falling back between the bridegroom and Alexander. From the crowd each side came a buzz of friendly voices. Ahead was the theater, packed with friends. His broad mouth smiled; he had looked forward to this moment of public proof. An elected King, whom these southerners had dared call tyrant; let them see for themselves if he needed the tyrant's square of spearmen. Let them tell Demosthenes, he thought.

He reined up and beckoned. Two servants came up to the younger men, and stood ready to hold their horses. "You now, my sons."

Alexander, who had been watching the chiefs go in, looked sharply round. "Are we not to go with you?"

"No," Philip said crisply. "Weren't you told? I go in alone."

The bridegroom looked away, to hide his embarrassment. Were they going to bicker over precedence now, before everyone? The last of the chiefs was going through out of sight. He could not walk over by himself.

Sitting upright on Oxhead's scarlet saddlecloth, Alexander looked along the stretch of empty road, empty in sunlight; wide, trampled, wheel-rutted, hoof-marked; ringing with emptiness. At its end, in the triangle of deep shadow thrown by the parodos, was a gleam of armor, a line of red cloak. If Pausanias was there, he must have his orders?

Oxhead pricked up his ears. His eye, bright as onyx, looked sideways; Alexander touched his neck with a finger; he stood like bronze. The bridegroom fidgeted. Why would the youth not move? There were times when one could understand the rumors. It was something about the eyes. There had been a day at Dodona; a bitter wind, a fall of snow lying, he wore a sheepskin cloak . . .

"Get down then," said Philip impatiently. "Your brother-in-law is waiting."

Alexander glanced again at the dark gateway. He pressed with his knee, bringing Oxhead nearer, and looked with deep concentration into Philip's face.

"It is too far," he said quietly. "It's better if I go with you."

Philip raised his brows under his gold garland. It was clear enough now what the lad was after. Well, he had not earned it yet; let him not push for it. "That is my business. I will be judge of what is best."

The deep-shadowed eyes reached for his. He felt invaded. From any subject, it was an affront to stare at the King.

"It is too far," said the high clear voice, inexpressive, steady. "Let me go in with you, and I will pledge my life for yours . . . I swear it to you by Herakles."

Faint, curious murmurs began to be heard among the bystanders, aware of something unplanned. Philip, though growing angry, was careful of his face. Keeping down his voice, he said sharply, "That is enough. We are not going to the theater to act in tragedy. When I need you I will tell you so. Obey my orders."

Alexander's eyes ceased their quest. His presence left them; they were as empty as clear grey glass. "Very well, sir," he said. He dismounted; Alexandros followed with relief.

Pausanias in the tall gateway saluted as they came. Alexander returned it in passing, while he spoke to Alexandros. They ascended the short ramp to the stage, acknowledged the acclamations, and took their seats.

Outside, Philip touched his rein. With a stately gait, his well-trained charger went forward, undisturbed by noise. The people knew what the King was doing, admired it, and took care he heard. His anger passed; he had something better to think of. If the boy had chosen some more fitting time . . .

He rode on, acknowledging the cheers. He would sooner have walked, but his limp robbed it of dignity. Already, through the twenty-foot-high parodos, he could glimpse the orchestra with its ring of gods. The music had struck up for him.

From the stone gateway a soldier stepped forward, to help him down and take his horse. It was Pausanias. In honor of the day, he must have posted himself to this page's service. How long ago . . . It was a signal of reconcilement. At last he was ready to forget. A charming gesture. In the old days, he had had a gift for such acts of grace.

Philip slid stiffly down, smiled, and began to speak. Pausanias' left hand took his arm in a tightening grip. Their looks met. Pausanias brought out his right hand from his cloak, so swiftly that Philip never saw the dagger, except in Pausanias' eyes.

The guard up the road saw the King fall, and Pausanias stoop over him. His lame foot must have stumbled, the men thought, and Pausanias been clumsy. Suddenly Pausanias straightened up, and began to run.

He had been eight years in the Guard, and for five of them commanded it. A farmer among the crowd was the first to call out, "He's killed the King!" As if given leave to credit their senses, with confused shouts the soldiers rushed towards the theater.

An officer reached the body, stared at it, pointed wildly, and yelled, "After him!" A stream of men poured round the corner, behind the backstage buildings. The King's well-trained charger stood stolidly by the parodos. No one had thought fast enough to dare the outrage of mounting it.

A piece of land behind the theater, sacred to Dionysos its guardian god, had been farmed by the priests with vines. The thick black old stocks were dappled with young shoots and bright green leaves. On the earth glinted Pausanias' helmet, flung away as he ran; his red cloak draped a vine-prop. He raced over the rough clods towards the old stone wall and its open gateway. Beyond it, a mounted man with a spare horse was waiting.

Pausanias was in hard training, and not yet thirty. But in the hunt were youths not yet twenty, who had learned mountain warfare with Alexander; they had trained still harder. Three or four drew out in front. The gap began to narrow.

It was narrowing too slowly, however. The gate was not far ahead. The man with the horses had turned their heads, ready, towards the open road.

Suddenly, as if an invisible spear had struck him, Pausanias hurtled forward. An arched knotted root had caught his toe. He fell flat; then rose on hands and knees, tugging free his booted foot. But the young men were on him.

He twisted over, looking from one to another, searching. No luck. But he had faced this chance from the first. He had cleansed his honor. He dragged at his sword; someone set a foot on his arm, another trod on his corselet. He had had no time to feel the pride of it, he thought as all the iron hacked down. No time.

The man with the horses, after one glance, had unhitched the spare one, lashed his own mount, and raced away. But the stunned pause was over. Hooves drummed on the road beyond the vines. The riders spurred after him through the gates, knowing the value of the prize.

In the vineyard, the press had caught up with the leading hunters. An officer looked down at the body bleeding, like some ancient sacrifice, into the roots of the vine-stock. "You've finished him. You young fools! Now he can't be questioned."

"I never thought of it," said Leonnatos, the drunkenness of the blood-chase leaving him. "I was afraid he'd still get away."

"I only thought," said Perdikkas, "of what he'd done." He wiped his sword on the dead man's kilt.

As they walked away, Aratos said to the others, "Well, it's best. You know the story. If he'd talked, it could only disgrace the King."

"What King?" said Leonnatos. "The King is dead."

Hephaistion's seat was halfway up the theater, near the center steps.

The friends who had waited to cheer Alexander had run round, and scrambled in by an upper gate. These were peasants' seats as a rule; but Companions of the Prince were small fry in today's assembly. He had missed the grand entrance of the gods. His father was seated lower down; his mother would be among the women, in the far-end block. The two Queens were already there, in the front row. He could see Kleopatra looking about at the sights, like the other girls; Olympias, it seemed, thought that beneath her. She was staring out fixedly, straight before her, towards the parodos on the other side.

It was out of Hephaistion's sight-line; but he was well placed for the stage with its three thrones. It was magnificent; the back and wings had columns with carved capitals, supporting embroidered curtains. The music came from behind them, crowded out from the orchestra by so many gods.

He waited for Alexander, to give him another cheer; if they

started it well, everyone would take it up. He would be better for that.

Here he came now, with the Epirote King. The cheer spread well through the theater. Never mind the names being the same; he would know from the sound.

He knew, and smiled. Yes, it had done him good. This was a small theater; Hephaistion had seen, when he came in, that he was not himself. In one of his dreams, a bad one, and glad to wake. What can one expect today? I'll see him after, if I can get near him before the Games. Everything will be simpler, when we cross to Asia.

Down in the orchestra, King Philip's effigy sat in its gilded throne, on a base swagged with laurel. The throne waiting on the stage was just the same. Cheers sounded from the road; the hidden music grew louder.

It reached a climactic flourish. There was a hiatus, the sense of a dropped cue. Suddenly, from the women's block where the tiers curved to face the parodos, came a shrill scream.

Alexander's head went round. His face, from which the strangeness had been passing before, altered. He jumped from his throne and went swiftly downstage where he could see out past the wings. He was running down the ramps and through the orchestra, between priests, altars and gods, before the shouting began outside. His garland fell from his flying hair.

While the audience stirred and chattered, Hephaistion leaped down the steps to the halfway gallery, and began to race along it. The friends followed promptly; they had been trained not to waste time. Around the gallery, the young men with their speed and purpose were a spectacle in themselves, suspending panic till they had passed by. They reached the end steps that led down towards the parodos. These were choked already, with bewildered foreign guests from the lower tiers. Hephaistion shoved through with the ruthlessness of battle, elbowing, shouldering, butting. A fat man fell, tripping others; the stairs were jammed; the tiers were a confusion of people scrambling up or down. In the still center of chaos, forsaken by their heirophants, the wooden gods in their circle turned all their eyes on the wooden King.

Unmoving as they, straight-backed on her carved chair of honor,

[365]

ignoring her daughter clutching her arm and crying out to her, Queen Olympias sat staring out towards the parodos.

Hephaistion felt a red rage for anyone in his way. Not caring how he did it, his companions all left behind, he fought his way through to his goal.

Philip lay on his back, the hilt of the dagger standing out between his ribs. It was Celtic work, with an elaborate plaited pattern of inlaid silver. His white chiton was almost unstained; the blade sealed the wound. Alexander was bent above him, feeling for his heart. The King's blind eye was half-closed, the other turned up at the living eyes above him. His face was set in a stare of shock, and an astonished bitterness.

Alexander touched the lid of the open eye. It gave limply with his fingers. "Father," he said. "Father, Father."

He put his hand to the clammy brow. The gold crown slipped off, and fell with a brittle clink on the pavement. For a moment his face fixed, as if carved in marble.

The body stirred. The mouth parted, as if to speak. Alexander started forward; he raised the head between his hands, and leaned towards it. But only air came from the corpse, loosened by some spasm of lung or belly; a belch, with a little froth of blood.

Alexander drew back. Suddenly his face and his body changed. He said, as sharply as a battle order, "The King is dead." He got to his feet and looked about him.

Someone called out, "They caught him, Alexander, they cut him down." The broad entry of the parodos was seen to be full of chiefs, unarmed for the feast, confusedly trying to form a protective wall.

"Alexander, we are here." It was Alexandros of Lynkestis, pushing himself into prominence. He had found himself a panoply already. It fitted; it was his own. Alexander's head seemed to point, in silence, as sharply as a hunting-dog's. "Let us escort you to the citadel, Alexander; who can tell where the traitors are?"

Yes, who? thought Hephaistion; that man knows something. What was his armor ready for? Alexander was looking about the crowd; for the other brothers, Hephaistion thought. He was used to reading Alexander's thoughts in the back of his head.

"What is this?"

The press parted. Antipatros, having forced his way through a turmoil of scared guests, had reached Macedonians who at once made way for him. He had long been appointed sole Regent of Macedon, with effect from the royal army's leaving. Tall, garlanded, robed with restrained splendor, clad in authority, he looked about him. "Where is the King?"

Alexander answered, "Here."

He held Antipatros' eyes a moment, then stepped back to show the body.

Antipatros bent, and rose. "He is dead," he said unbelievingly. "Dead." He passed his hand over his brow. It touched his festal wreath; with a gesture of dazed convention, he dropped it on the ground. "Who—"

"Pausanias killed him."

"Pausanias? After so long?" He stopped abruptly, discomposed by what he had said.

"Was he taken alive?" said Alexandros of Lynkestis, just too quickly.

Alexander delayed the answer, to watch his face. Then, "I want the gates of the city closed, and the walls manned. No one to leave till I give the order." He scanned the crowd. "Alketas, your division. Post them now."

The egg is hatched, thought Antipatros, and I was right. "Alexander, you must be in danger here. Will you come up to the castle?"

"In good time. What are those men about?"

Outside, the second-in-command of the Royal Guard was trying to get them in hand, with the help of what junior officers he could find. But the soldiers had lost their heads entirely, and were listening to some of their number who cried out that they would all be accused of conspiracy in the murder. They turned with curses on the young men who had killed Pausanias; it would look as if they had needed to stop his mouth. The officers were trying vainly to shout them down.

Alexander stepped from the sharp blue shadow of the parodos into the cool brilliant early light. The sun had scarcely climbed since he had walked into the theater. He vaulted up on the low wall by the gateway. The noise changed, and died down.

"Alexander!" said Antipatros sharply. "Take care! Don't expose yourself."

Mary Renault

"Guard—by the right—form phalanx!"

The scuffling mass grew quiet, like a scared horse calmed by its rider.

"I honor your grief. But don't grieve like women. You did your duty; I know what your orders were. I myself heard them. Meleagros, an escort for the King's body. Bring him to the castle. The small audience room." Seeing the man look about for some makeshift litter, he said, "There is a bier behind the stage, with the things for tragedy."

He stooped over the body, pulled out a fold from the cloak crumpled under it, and covered the face with its bitter eye. The men of the escort closed round their charge, hiding it from sight.

Stepping out before the silent ranks of the Guard, he said, "Fall out, the men who struck down the murderer."

Between pride and dread, they stood forth uncertainly.

"We owe you a debt. Don't fear it will be forgotten. Perdikkas." His face smoothed with relief, the young man came forward. "I left Oxhead in the road outside. Will you see him safe for me? Take a guard of four."

"Yes, Alexander." He went off in a blaze of gratitude.

There was a felt silence; Antipatros was looking oddly under his brows.

"Alexander. The Queen your mother is in the theater. Had *she* not better have a guard?"

Alexander walked past him, and looked in through the parodos. He stood there in perfect stillness. There was a stir about the entry; the soldiers had found the tragic bier, ornately painted and draped with purple. They set it down by Philip's body and heaved him onto it. The cloak fell from the face; the officer pulled down the eyelids and pressed them till they closed.

Alexander, motionless, stared on into the theater. The crowd had gone, thinking it no place to loiter in. The gods remained. In some surge of tumult, Aphrodite had been toppled from her base, and lay awkward and stiff beside it. Flung clear in her fall, young Eros leaned on her fallen throne. King Philip's image sat stockily in its place, its painted eyes fixed on the empty tiers.

Alexander turned away. His color had changed, but his voice was even. "Yes; I see she is still there."

"She must be in distress," said Antipatros. He spoke without expression.

Alexander gazed at him thoughtfully. Presently, as if something had just chanced to catch his eye, he looked aside.

"You are right, Antipatros. She should be in the safest hands. So I shall be grateful if you, yourself, will escort her up to the citadel. Take what men you think sufficient."

Antipatros' mouth opened. Alexander waited, his head tilted slightly, his eyes unwavering. Antipatros said, "If you wish, Alexander," and went upon his errand.

There was a moment's lull. From his place in the crowd, Hephaistion came out a little, signaling no message, only offering his presence, as his omens prompted him. No message was returned; yet between one step and the next, he saw God thanked for him. His own destiny, too, was opening out before him, in unmeasured vistas of sun and smoke. He would not look back wherever it should take him; his heart accepted it with all its freight, the bright and the dark.

The officer of the bearer party gave an order. King Philip on his gilded bier jogged round the corner. From the sacred vineyard, borne on a hurdle and covered with his torn cloak, his blood dripping through the plaited withies, some troopers brought Pausanias. He too would have to be shown before the people. Alexander said, "Prepare a cross."

The noises had died to a restless hum, mingled with the roar of the Aigai falls. Lifting above it his strong unearthly cry, a golden eagle swooped over. In its talons was a lashing snake, snatched from the rocks. Each head lunged for the other, seeking in vain the mortal stroke. Alexander, his ear caught by the sound, gazed up intently, to see the outcome of the fight. But, still in combat, the two antagonists spired up into the cloudless sky, above the peaks of the mountains; became a speck in the dazzle, and were lost to sight.

"All is done here," he said, and gave orders to march up to the citadel.

As they reached the ramparts which overlooked the Pella plain, the new summer sun stretched out its glittering pathway across the eastern sea.

AUTHOR'S NOTE

ALL RECORDS of Alexander by his own contemporaries have perished. We depend on histories compiled three or four centuries later from this lost material, which sometimes give references, sometimes not. Arrian's main source was the Ptolemy of this story, but Arrian's work opens only at Alexander's accession. Curtius' early chapters have disappeared; Diodoros, who covers the right time and tells us much of Philip, says little of Alexander before his reign begins. For these first two decades, nearly two-thirds of his life, the only extant source is Plutarch, with a few retrospective allusions in the other histories. Plutarch does not cite Ptolemy for this section of the Life, though he would have been a first-hand witness; so he probably did not cover it.

Plutarch's account has here been set against its historical background. I have used, with due skepticism, the speeches of Demosthenes and Aischines. Some anecdotes of Philip and Alexander have been taken from Plutarch's *Sayings of Kings and Commanders;* a few from Athenaeus.

I have inferred the age at which Alexander entertained the Persian envoys from their recorded surprise that his questions were not

[370]

childish. On the character of Leonidas, and his searching the boy's boxes for his mother's home comforts, Plutarch quotes Alexander himself verbatim. Of the other teachers, who are described as numerous, only Lysimachos (Phoinix) is mentioned by name. Plutarch seems not to think much of him. Alexander's estimate appeared later. During the great siege of Tyre, he went for a long hill-walk; Lysimachos, boasting that he was as good as Achilles' Phoinix and no older, insisted on going too. "When Lysimachos grew faint and weary, though evening was coming on and the enemy were near at hand, Alexander refused to leave him; and encouraging and helping him along with a few companions, unexpectedly found himself cut off from the main body and obliged to spend the night in a wild spot in darkness and extreme cold." Single-handed, he raided an enemy watch-fire to snatch a burning brand; the enemy, thinking his troops were at hand, retreated; and Lysimachos had a fire to sleep by. Leonidas, left behind in Macedon, got only a load of expensive incense, with an ironic gift-tag saying that from now on he need not be stingy towards the gods.

Philip's telling Alexander he should be ashamed to sing so well —presumably in public, since it was recorded—is from Plutarch, who says the boy never played again. The tribal skirmish after is invented; we do not know where or when Alexander first tasted war. It can only be back-dated from his regency. At sixteen, he was trusted by the first general in Greece with a command of vital strategic importance, in the full expectation that experienced troops would follow him. By then they must have known him well.

The encounter with Demosthenes at Pella is all invention. It is true however that the orator, who as last speaker had had some hours in which to compose himself, broke down after a few stumbling sentences, and though encouraged by Philip was unable to go on. With eight witnesses to his story, Aischines can here be trusted; whether he was to blame—they were already old enemies—cannot be known. Demosthenes never liked to speak extempore, but no reason appears for his needing to. He came back with a virulent dislike of Alexander, remarkable towards so young a boy, and seems to have sneered at Aischines for sycophancy to him.

The taming of Boukephalos is given by Plutarch in such detail that one is tempted to guess the source may have been a favorite after-dinner story of Alexander's. My only addition is to suppose the horse had lately been ill-treated. By Arrian's dating it was already twelve years old; it is not conceivable that a mount with a long record of vice would be offered to the King. Greek war-horses were elaborately trained, and this must have been done already. But I cannot credit the astronomical asking price of thirteen talents. Chargers were too expendable (though Alexander cherished Boukephalos to an age of thirty). Philip may well have paid this huge sum for his victorious Olympic racer, and the stories become conflated.

Aristotle's years of fame in Athens began only after Philip's death; those of his works which have been preserved are of later date. We do not know what, exactly, he taught Alexander, but Plutarch speaks of his lifelong interest in natural science (while in Asia he kept Aristotle supplied with specimens) and in medicine. I have assumed Aristotle's views on ethics to be already formed. Among lost works of his was a book of letters to Hephaistion, whose special status he must, it seems, have recognized.

Alexander's rescue of his father from the mutineers is from Curtius, who says Alexander complained bitterly that Philip never admitted to the debt, though he had had to take refuge in shamming dead.

Diodoros, and other writers, describe Philip's victory komos after the battle of Cheironeia; but none of the accounts mentions Alexander's presence.

The sexual mores of Alexander have been much discussed, his detractors tending to claim he was homosexual, his admirers to rebut it with indignation. Neither side has much considered how far Alexander himself would have thought it a dishonor. In a society which accepted bisexuality as a norm, his three state marriages qualified him for normality. His general restraint was much noticed; but, for contemporaries, his most striking peculiarity was his refusal to exploit defenseless victims like captive women and slave-boys, a practice then universal.

His emotional commitment to Hephaistion is among the most certain facts of his life. He displayed an open pride in it. At Troy, in the presence of his army, they honored together the tombs of Achilles and Patroklos. Though Homer does not say the heroes were more than friends, it was widely believed in Alexander's day; had he thought the imputation disgraceful, he would not so have courted it. After his victory at Issus, when the captive women of Darius' family were bewailing their lord for dead, Alexander went to their tent to reassure them, taking Hephaistion along. According to Curtius, they walked in together, dressed much alike; Hephaistion was taller and by Persian standards more impressive; the Queen Mother prostrated herself before him. Warned of her error by the frantic signals of her attendants, she turned in distressed confusion to the real King, who said to her, "But you weren't wrong, Mother; he too is Alexander."

It is clear they behaved with seemliness in public (though high-ranking officials resented Hephaistion's being seen to read, without rebuke, Olympias' letters over Alexander's shoulder). No physical relationship is proved, and those whom the thought disturbs are free to reject it. It is a recorded saying of Alexander's that sex and sleep put him in mind of his mortality.

Alexander survived his friend by about three months, for two of which he was traveling with the body from Ecbatana to Babylon, the intended capital of his empire. The wild extravagance of the funeral rites, the vast grandiose pyre, the request to Zeus Ammon's oracle to grant the dead man the divine status already conferred on Alexander himself (Ammon allowed Hephaistion to be a hero), suggest that at this time Alexander was barely in command of his reason. Not long after, he contracted fever, but sat up all night at a party. Though he pushed on with his campaign plans as long as he could stand, indeed much longer, he is not recorded to have had a doctor. (He had hanged Hephaistion's, for neglect.) His stubborn mistreatment of his own condition seems self-destructive, whether consciously or not.

His experience at the Aigai Dionysia is invented, but expresses, I think, a psychological truth. Olympias committed many murders; her eventual execution was entrusted by Kassandros to the relatives of her victims. She killed Eurydike and her infant the moment Alexander's back was turned after Philip's death. Her complicity in the latter has been much suspected, but never proved. The prophetic "vision" of Demosthenes is historical.

The general reader who wants to follow Alexander's career as King will find it in Plutarch's *Lives* (Volume II in the Everyman Edition), or in Arrian's *History* (Penguin Classics). Both are available in English interleaved with Greek, in the Loeb Classical Library.

Proper Names

ALEXANDER'S real name was, of course, Alexandros; it was so common in north Greece that three other bearers of it appear within this tale alone. Because of this, and because of two-thousand-year-long associations, I have given him the traditional Latinized form.

I have kept traditional forms too for some other very familiar names: Philip for Philippos, Ptolemy for Ptolemaios, Aristotle for Aristoteles; and for a number of place names. The word Bucephalus, however, comes trailing such clouds of nineteenth-century cliché that I have preferred to translate it. In the story of Alexander, no system of nomenclature is likely to please everyone; so, with apology, I have pleased myself.

I have used the name of Eurydike for Philip's bride, though it was a royal honorific bestowed by him, rather than her given name of Kleopatra, to avoid confusion with Alexander's sister.